NECESSITY'S CHILD

NECESSITY'S CHILD

A New
Liaden Universe®
Novel

SHARON LEE &
STEVE MILLER

A Baen Books Original

Baen Publishing Enterprises
P.O. Box 1403
Riverdale, NY 10471
www.baen.com

ISBN: 978-1-4516-3895-0

Cover art by David Mattingly

First Baen printing, February 2013

Distributed by Simon & Schuster
1230 Avenue of the Americas
New York, NY 10020

10 9 8 7 6 5 4 3 2 1

Pages by Joy Freeman (www.pagesbyjoy.com)
Printed in the United States of America

NECESSITY'S CHILD

CHAPTER ONE

· ·

INSIDE THE DUCT, IT WAS HOT AND WET—NOTHING NEW THERE, thought Kezzi, shifting her weight carefully. The metal snapped in complaint, and she made herself be still.

The space felt smaller than it had last time. Pulka would scoff if she said so, and ask if her shoulders yet touched the walls. They didn't, but she had several times bumped her head as she'd crawled to the leaking seam, and scraped her elbows against the metal while she was applying the sealant.

Pulka said it was only her weak heart that made her clumsy. He would tousle her hair as if she were Very Small, and tell her to ask the *luthia* for a prayer and a potion.

After the last repair, when Pulka had laughed at her, Kezzi had done just that. The *luthia*, Grandmother Silain, made her sit at the fire, and poured tea from her kettle for them both. She asked many questions about the ducts, their purpose, and their importance to the *kompani*; sipping, listening with witch's ears while Kezzi explained that the ducts were the path that the boiling water took along the bottom of the floor above their heads, that at once warmed the soil of the garden, and the *kompani*'s living space.

When she had finished, the *luthia* poured more tea into Kezzi's cup, and bade her drink; that a strong head was not a weak heart.

Now, waiting on hands and knees in the damp heat, the little light in her work hat flickering like a flame in a draft, she tried

1

to breathe slow and calm, like Silain had taught her. It was not a sin, that she disliked the ducts; she did not have to like them. All that was required of her was that she do her given-work well.

It was said of the *kompani* by the elders of the *kompani* that what Bedel hands built rarely needed repair.

The ducts, and the steam plant—those had not been built by Bedel, but they had been *rebuilt* by those capable hands, and Kezzi's trips inside were not frequent.

Still, she thought, taking another breath, and thinking, *not* of water so hot it would boil the skin from her bones in an eyeblink, but of Malda, waiting for her at the access point, sitting exactly where she had told him, quivering from pointed nose to skinny tail. She had promised him a run in the upper level, when this work for her elder was done.

What was Pulka doing? Kezzi wondered irritably. Had he fallen asleep?

As if he had heard her thought, Pulka spoke, his voice loud through the metal skin.

"Tolerances check. You may return to us, little sister."

This was the worst part. She had long since grown too big to turn around in this small space, which meant she had to crawl backward to the nearest access point. As slow as it was to crawl in, it was twice as slow and slower to back out.

At last, though, she made it. A breeze cooled her sweaty cheeks, and she bit her lip, forcing herself to keep an even pace. If she went too fast, she risked another seam parting, which would mean she would have to go back inside...

Strong hands grabbed her around the waist, pulled her free of the last inches of the duct. Pulka swung her around high over his head, like she was a baby, then set her gently on her feet.

"Well done, little sister. I am grateful for your assistance, and now I give you leave to go." Pulka pulled the work hat from her head, and gave her a swat on the rump. "By all means, do go! And take your blessed servant with you."

He meant Malda, who sat as she had pictured him, quivering with joy at her return, his pointed snout wrinkled in a smile. Pulka, Kezzi thought, didn't much like Malda, but, then, Malda didn't much like Pulka.

She pulled off her gloves and hung them on the loop of her belt.

"Malda," she said, snapping her fingers. "Come."

The little dog leapt up and ran to her, made one tight, wriggling turn around her ankles, and looked up into her face expectantly, as if he was afraid she'd forgotten her promise.

As if she could. Kezzi took a deep breath of cooler air, and another, hearing the clatters and clanks Pulka made, as he sealed up the hatch. As soon as that was done, he would go to the wheel and turn it, flooding the place she had just been with scalding water.

Kezzi swallowed, and turned hastily toward the ramp, snapping her fingers at Malda to follow.

They were hardly three steps into freedom when a bell sounded, high enough to pierce the ear, soft enough that it would not be heard—outside.

Kezzi groaned. She thought, fleetingly, of running on; of pretending that she hadn't heard.

...but she had heard. And even if she hadn't, Pulka had, and he was calling her.

"Little sister, come! The Bedel are rung together!"

They gathered 'round the common fire, all who had been in-*kompani*, and heard the call. Nearest the fire sat Alosha, the headman, and Silain, the *luthia*. At Silain's right hand was Torv, whose given-work took him often among those outside, to repair what had not been built by Bedel hands, to watch, and to listen.

Kezzi slipped into her place between Vylet and Droi, and gathered Malda onto her lap, hoping that Torv would speak quickly, so that she and Malda could get their run, before dreamwork took her.

The bell rang again, and all the talk and chatter and laughter among the *kompani* quietened.

Alosha the headman rose and looked around at them all, gathered in the half-circle before the fire. Such was the strength of his soul, that Kezzi felt his gaze touch her face, and move on, until he had seen them all.

"Torv of our *kompani* has news from the City Above," he said then. "Listen well, Bedel. After, we will talk."

Kezzi wilted where she sat. Talk. Talk could go on for *hours*. Malda would have no run today.

And neither would she.

The headman stepped back from the fire and sat on his rug.

Torv rose to his lanky, considerable height, and looked out over them as the headman had done, though his soul was not so strong that Kezzi felt him *see* her.

"I come," he said, "just now from the City Above, where there is unrest among the *gadje*—Those Others."

Kezzi dropped her chin onto the top of Malda's head and sighed loudly enough to win Vylet's frown. Unrest in the City Above was a common thing. Why had the headman gathered them to talk about a fact of life?

"Some *kompani* of Those Others have entered into dispute," Torv continued. "They break each the tools of the other, and dismantle those things built and valued by the rival *kompani*."

Again, Kezzi sighed, though this time not so loudly that Vylet heard. Who *cared* if *gadje* disputed with each other, or broke each other's workings? So far as Kezzi knew, *gadje* existed to break things. Had they not broken even Malda, leaving him for her to bring back to the *kompani* so that he might be repaired by Silain, the most potent pair of hands among the Bedel?

"There is more," Torv said, as if someone among them had voiced what Kezzi thought. "A blood feud has been opened against the Folk of the Tree. An attempt was made on the life of the headwoman. An answer is expected—is, I will say, brothers and sisters, *feared*. The *gadje* are in a time of turmoil, and nothing is safe from them." He took a breath, and looked to the headman, who moved his hand in assent.

"Yes. Having seen what I have seen, and heard what I have heard, I advise the *kompani*, most strongly, to remove for a time from the City Above, in order that we not be caught by or made victim of the *gadje*'s madness." He held his arms out as if he would embrace them all.

"Brothers and sisters, ask what you will. I will answer as best I might."

CHAPTER TWO

· ·

THE STRIKE TO CLAN KORVAL'S HEART HAD BEEN TURNED ASIDE, the unlucky blade captured and given over to the assassin judge, Natesa. Between her arts and those of the clan witches, it would not be long before every careful secret of necessity shared with Otts Clark would be in Korval's possession.

And Korval would not hesitate; nor would it waste breath shouting warnings to those who wished them ill. Throughout history, Korval had acted quickly and decisively to threats made against even the least of its members. A strike against the *delmae*—Korval Herself—that would not go unanswered.

So it was that the word went out, from cell leader to cell leader, from first in line to least. A single word, but sufficient.

Run.

Field Agent Rys Lin pen'Chala was not so far down the chain that the word was long in reaching in his ear. Nor was he so ill-informed that the order surprised.

There were not so very many agents of the Department of the Interior on Surebleak; indeed, following Korval's attack upon the Department's Liaden headquarters, there were not so very many agents—at all.

That attack, against the very homeworld, had not been without cost. Korval's allies upon the Council of Clans might have prevented them from being called outlaw, but they had not been able to prevent Korval's banishment.

A Liaden clan no more, Korval entered into a contract of employment with the Bosses of Surebleak, and relocated to that cold and backward world. And here they sat, free of their net of allies and servants, vulnerable to attack.

Though the Department was likewise vulnerable, the Commander had seen opportunity, and deployed agents whose purpose was to undo all of Korval's works, to unbalance their plans, and to strike a mortal blow.

The failure of that blow to fall with precision...

Run.

Agent pen'Chala was not a fool. Certainly, Surebleak Spaceport was a free-for-all, overcrowded with those seeking opportunity, and chaotic at every level. How easy for a single man to lose himself in that unrelenting chaos, to find a ship, and slip away.

The exercise became more difficult when there were a dozen such seeking anonymity and quiet passage. Add into that equation Korval on the hunt, and prudence dictated a less literal understanding of the orders received.

Ships were Korval's chiefest concern; spaceports their second home. Only a fool would try to outpace them on such terrain, while they were alert and searching.

Let others race to the spaceport, to win past Korval, or to be taken up for questioning and worse. Agent pen'Chala preferred to increase his odds of survival.

Run might under certain conditions be understood to mean *hide*.

Hide until Korval's face was turned toward some other problem. Until they had caught whomever they did—and they would catch some. *Hide* until it was... less risky to venture onto port and seek out a ship, to buy passage or sign as crew.

Agent pen'Chala knew how to hide. Indeed, he was an adept, proved by circumstance.

Decision taken, he turned his face from the spaceport, and instead moved further into the city, striking for the abandoned warehouse belt.

He would hide. And, as before, he would survive.

CHAPTER THREE

· ·

"WHEN WILL YOU RETURN TO US?"

Grandaunt Kareen would have approved his form just there, Syl Vor thought. He had framed the question in proper style—anticipating the joyful return of favored kin. If he had not minded his lessons, he might have said, "How long will you be away?"—and that would have been cruel, to burden his cousin with his dismay, when she had duty before her.

He didn't wish to be cruel to Padi—he liked Padi—and so he took care with his words. His eyes did sting, a little, but he blinked hard, and took a deep breath. He wasn't a baby. And, besides, if he cried, Padi would be distressed, and it was his duty to send her to hers with no shadow on her heart.

He had learned a great deal about duty from Grandaunt Kareen. They all had.

"Well," Padi said now, in answer to his question. "It's an adjusted route that we're testing. Father said to plan on half a Standard, but to pack for a whole."

Padi's father was Uncle Shan—Master Trader yos'Galan. Padi would of course be the clan's master trader when she was older, so she had a great deal to learn. And, Syl Vor had heard her say to Quin that she was behind in her lessons—as they all were—because of Plan B.

Plan B was over now, and they—Padi and Quin and Syl Vor and the twins; Grandfather and Grandaunt—had been brought from the sanctuary at Runig's Rock. They had all come...well, not to their very *own* home, Trealla Fantrol, where the yos'Galans had lived forever. Trealla Fantrol was gone. Uncle Shan had explained it—that the clan could only bring one house and of course they had to bring the Tree, so it was Jelaza Kazone that had come to Surebleak, and sheltered all the clan.

Just like olden times, said Uncle Shan.

So, now they were safe back with kin at Jelaza Kazone, and it was right and proper that they take up their usual training and the duties that Plan B had interrupted.

Quin had only a few days ago been fetched down to Blair Road, and his father's city house. Quin was to learn to be a Boss, that's what Syl Vor had heard Grandfather Luken say. Bosses were in a "leadership capacity peculiar to the culture of this new homeworld"—that much Syl Vor knew. He hadn't been able to get anything more useful than that out of his tutor. Yet.

"You'll be quite the expert on Surebleak by the time I come back," Padi said, reaching into her pocket and pulling out a piece of string. "I'll depend on you to bring me up to line."

She wove the string casually between her fingers, until her hand was encompassed by what appeared to be an edifice of space and twine. Smiling, she held it out to him.

Syl Vor hesitated, wondering if he should take offense, while the string and its pattern was held temptingly before him. No, he decided, Padi was only doing *her* duty, as his elder. The string game was pilot-play; it taught...well, he wasn't exactly sure what it taught, but he *was* sure that he knew less about it than Padi did, and if he wished, when he was older, to be a pilot of Korval—which he very much did—then he had better learn everything she knew.

He therefore studied the pattern carefully before slipping his fingers along two joint sections, and pulling the whole structure from her hands onto his.

The pattern was changed in the transfer, as it should be. Syl Vor looked at it anxiously, but so far as he could see it was true, without tangles, knots or twists.

Padi grinned and leaned forward in her turn, pinching a high point and a low—which was a surprise. If it had been Syl Vor's turn to twist the pattern, he would have chosen...

"There!" Padi said with satisfaction. "*Now* what will you do?"

Syl Vor blinked at the newly complex weaving of string and wondered the same thing. Frowning, he studied it for a long moment, seeing nothing but a dense tapestry of line and space, complete in itself, and resistant to manipulation.

Suddenly, the pattern seemed to come into sharper focus and Syl Vor saw a pair of junction points—one deep toward center; the other only one space from the pattern's border. Boldly, he pinched each, lifted . . . pulled—and watched in dismay as the dense weaving unraveled into a limp double loop sagging around his fingers.

Syl Vor bit his lip, expecting Padi's ready laughter, but—

"Forgive me, Cousin," she said, sounding formal and grown-up. He looked up at her in surprise. "I twisted the thread during my transfer, and so gave you a faulty beginning."

"It was awfully complex," he said, to make her feel better.

She smiled and reached out to unwind the sloppy loops from his fingers.

"It was, wasn't it?" she said, coiling the string and putting it back in her pocket. "Let that be a lesson to us both, then: Too much complexity ruins the game."

Later, after he'd gone down with Padi to the little parlor, where tall Uncle Shan was waiting, and had from each of them a kiss . . .

After he'd watched their car go down the drive, between the browning lawns, and walked slowly back to the nursery, to meet his math tutor . . .

After he'd had his dinner with Mrs. pel'Esla, and after Cousin Anthora had come to the nursery to visit—not him, of course, but the twins, though she kindly stopped for a game of skittles . . .

After he'd washed behind his ears, said his own good-nights to Shindi and Mik; and slid into bed, remembering to thank Mrs. pel'Esla for her service this day . . .

And after he'd lain awake for a little while, listening to the soft noises that Mrs. pel'Esla made as she put things to rights in the common room; wishing that he was in the dormitory he had shared with his cousins at Runig's Rock, which Grandaunt would doubtless tell him was a great piece of nonsense . . .

After he had not cried—or only a little—because he was all alone—which of course he couldn't be, safe in-House and under Tree, surrounded by kin—he slid into a doze, remembering how it had been, at the Rock.

They'd had lessons, of course—Grandfather Luken and Grandaunt Kareen had been very strict about lessons. Just because they were in hiding from Korval's enemies, Grandaunt had said often, was no reason to descend into savagery.

They'd had math; history, planetary and galactic; languages, the High Tongue, Trade, Terran, and hand-talk; systems-and-repair; dance; *melant'i* drills; weapon lore and practice.

His favorites had been weapon lore and dance, though he wasn't nearly as proficient as Quin and Padi. Grandfather had said he did well in keeping up with the others, who were, after all, so much older, and more advanced in their studies.

That made him feel good.

Practice was hardest. They had to pretend, which should have been easy, but the things they pretended—that Korval's enemies had found them, there in the fastness of the Rock, and that they had to run away, to the ship that Quin and Padi would pilot. There was the order of retreat—Quin leading, because he was First Board, then Syl Vor, carrying the twins in their special basket, and Padi covering them both. That was right: the pilot, who kept the ship safe; then the passengers, who were under the pilot's care; then copilot, guarding pilot and ship.

There was nothing scary about pretending that—*every*body knew the order of ship precedence.

The scary part though—behind them would come Grandfather and Grandaunt, delaying the enemy in any way they could, so that the pilots and Syl Vor with the babies had time to gain the ship.

They pretended that Grandfather...fell, and they...they pretended to leave him, the pilots sealing the hatch behind Grandaunt Kareen. They pretended that Grandaunt was lost. They pretended that neither elder gained the hatch by the time the pilots' count was done, and the greatest good for ship and folk came down to Quin's sole choice...

One of the twins—Mik, by the little catch in the voice—was beginning a complaint. Syl Vor stirred, hoping he hadn't pulled the webbing too tight, and then the sound, unmistakable, of the hatch sealing tight—

Caught in the web of memory, Syl Vor choked, crying out, "Wait!" and that woke him to his own bed, where he lay, heart roaring in his ears, and his cheeks wet with tears.

He concentrated like Padi had taught him—concentrated on

breathing slow and deep. It was hard, but he kept at it until he was limp beneath the blankets, and told himself that it was pretend—that it had *always* been pretend; that Grandaunt and Grandfather were safe, just as he was, and the babies his charges; and Quin, and Padi...

No longer deafened by his own heartbeat, Syl Vor heard a small sound, and knew that part of his dreaming had been real.

Quietly, he slipped out of bed and ghosted across the dark common room, to the little alcove where the twins slept. Syl Vor peered 'round the corner. A night-dim on the corner table gave the room a faint, pearly glow. Mrs. pel'Esla, usually to hand, was at this moment absent. Doubtless, she had not gone far, and would return quickly to comfort Mik—that was no longer his job. No less a personage than his mother had said that he might put the order of Runig's Rock behind him; that such arrangements were not required within the clanhouse. Still, it was not so easy to do as to say. They had been his to keep safe; his to decide for, if it came to such measures. They were his cousins; he was elder to them—surely *that* still held, even in-House?

Mik complained again, fretfully louder. If he kept up like that, he would wake Shindi, and then everyone would know. A tale-teller's voice, had Shindi. At least, so Grandfather said.

Syl Vor slipped closer to the little bed, and peered over the low rail. Mik was asleep, but muttering, likely caught in some dream of his own. Carefully, Syl Vor stroked the soft cheek, murmuring, like he used to do at the Rock, when they were pretending and it was his job to keep them quiet.

Mik's eyelashes fluttered, his small body tensing toward wake-fulness.

"Mik, sweet one, sleep, brave child," Syl Vor whispered, which were the words he had learned from Grandfather. He moved his hand to smoothe the rumpled dark hair.

Mik sighed, his body relaxing back to sleep.

Syl Vor continued to murmur, his hand against his cousin's cheek, only a little longer, to be certain—and then looked up, hearing a step in the larger room outside.

In a moment, Mrs. pel'Esla arrived, murmuring crossly, "... like to know how that cat—" She cut her complaint off at the sight of Syl Vor leaning over the crib, and sighed.

"Are you wakeful, child?"

"I heard Mik fretting," he said, which was true, even as it sidestepped her question. "I was worried, in case he should wake Shindi."

"And woe to us all, in that case," Mrs. pel'Esla said. She stepped to the crib and looked in.

"You have a good touch with your cousins," she said. "They honor you."

Syl Vor felt warmed. "I did my best to take care of them."

"That you did—and they remember it," the nurse said. "Now, though, you must care for yourself. Can you find your bed in the dark? Would you like some hot milk to help you sleep?"

"It's not so dark," Syl Vor told her, and, "No, thank you."

"Then I shall again bid you good-night, young Syl Vor," Mrs. pel'Esla said. "I will look in on you after I settle this young rogue, in case you change your mind, about the milk."

"Thank you," Syl Vor said, and ran his finger down Mik's cheek one more time before he left the alcove and went back to his empty room.

. . . which was not so empty, after all.

There, curled among the blankets, was a rangy orange cat with white feet. She looked up when Syl Vor entered—and squinted her eyes in a cat smile.

Syl Vor pressed his hand against his mouth to keep from laughing.

"Eztina, you know Mrs. pel'Esla doesn't like you here at night."

The cat yawned, and Syl Vor bit his lip, concentrating very hard on not laughing as he climbed into bed and scooched under those blankets not held down by cat.

He curled around on his side and closed his eyes, Eztina tucked into the curve of his belly, and he flicked a corner of the coverlet over her. The cat began to purr, and Syl Vor rode that pleasant sound into a deep and dreamless sleep.

CHAPTER FOUR

· ·

IT COULD NOT BE EXPECTED THAT THE BEDEL WOULD LONG SUB-mit to meekness—so said Silain the *luthia* to Alosha the headman.

The headman sighed to hear it, and fingered his pipe from his belt, and his smoke-pouch from his vest pocket.

"In truth, we were made to wander, and wander, that we will."

Kezzi, sitting with Malda at some little distance from the *luthia*'s hearth recognized the line from one of the Truing Songs. The next line rose unbidden to her mind, and she hastily pushed it aside. She was supposed to be listening, not remembering!

"Has wandering brought sorrow," Silain asked, "or joy?"

"Neither, as I parse it," Alosha said, filling his pipe and tamping the leaf down with his thumb. "Whatever dispute exists between the Folk of the Tree and those who oppose them has flowed past us. The new order imposed upon the streets by the *kompani* of Bosses likewise flows past the Bedel, barely dampening our boots."

He snapped a firestick with the hand not occupied with his pipe, held the flame to the bowl and drew. Kezzi smelled bark and cherry as the smoke wafted past, and smiled.

"We have been twice fortunate," the headman continued, when the pipe was going to his satisfaction. "Will we be three times unfortunate?"

Kezzi held her breath, and put her hand flat on Malda's side as she leaned forward to hear better. Any question of the *kompani*'s fortune was serious—and doubly so when it came from the headman, who held their future in his hands.

Silence from the *luthia* while she considered this weighty question. Alosha smoked his pipe, and kept his own silence.

Kezzi had counted to nine, taking and exhaling a deep breath between each number, when at last Silain spoke.

"First, we must be certain of our position," she said. "Good fortune may approach the Bedel at this time because the *kompani* has already hosted her fair sister. Can you, headman, recall any recent unlucky events?"

"*Luthia*, I cannot. Song and dream bring me no more than waking memory. We have long been fortunate; the last great distress upon us was the collapse of the second retreat tunnel. Thus, I bring the matter to you, whose memory is longer, whose eyes are sharper, than my own."

That last part—that was a Proper Asking, and in truth, the *luthia* had the longest memory of any in the *kompani*. Her eyes were sharp enough, for her age, but that was great—she had been a child, had Silain, when the *kompani* commenced its *chafurma*.

Kezzi gasped, snatching again at her wandering thoughts—*focus*!

"...I will dream on this. Since the Bedel wander, as is our heritage and our right, it may be well for the headman to convene an Affirmation."

Kezzi bit her lip. An Affirmation was three days of singing, tale-telling, eating, and dance. A time, said the *luthia*, for the Bedel to recall what it meant to be of the *kompani*, and to forget the ways and worries of the *gadje*—Those Others—among whom they lived, but were apart.

"I will think upon it," the headman said, taking his pipe from his mouth and blowing a circle of smoke. He rose with that, and gave the *luthia* her proper salute. "*Luthia*, I thank you for the gift of your wisdom," he said, and went away across the common area, toward his own place.

Kezzi sat back and sighed out the breath she hadn't known she'd been holding.

"Little sister," the *luthia* said from the hearthside. "Come and share tea with me."

· · · ✳ · · ·

There was music in the hallway.

Syl Vor stopped with his hand on the bannister, listening.

He had just come in from the garden, and it was time to go

upstairs and do his prep work for tomorrow's lessons. But the music... it *pulled* him somehow, down two stairs, to the hall, and down the hall, to the library door.

Which was closed.

Syl Vor took a breath, the music tugging at him. The door was closed; he hadn't been invited in. He had work to do upstairs, he was already late, and—

The music crashed, soared; the door opened to his touch, and he was inside the library.

Uncle Val Con was standing at the desk, his shoulder to the door, his hands working the keys of the omnichora, and the music...

Impossibly, the music soared higher, sounding... angry, and joy-filled, and sad, all at once. It pulled at his chest, and he was sure that if he opened his mouth, his heart would fly out and up, tangled in the music, taken by the turbulent air, and never be found, or seen again.

Uncle Val Con leaned into the 'chora, and the music *screamed*. Syl Vor jammed his fist against his mouth, and then—

It was like the music spun, and caught a downdraft, circling down, back down to Uncle Val Con, through his fingers, softer now, and simpler, only sad, but so very sad... and then it was quiet, and Syl Vor realized that he was crying.

He swallowed and tried to think of the calming exercises he had learned on the Rock, but all he could hear was the music. He was cold, and his chest hurt. He bent forward a little to ease the pain.

"Syl Vor!"

Strong arms drew him close, and his cheek was against Uncle Val Con's shoulder and he was trying not to cry, straining all his muscles trying to stop, but all that did was make him hiccup— and cry harder.

"Softly, softly. Cry if you must, sweeting. There's no shame."

Syl Vor felt a slow stroking down his back, over and over, like he would stroke a cat. Slowly, he warmed, and eventually he realized that his chest didn't hurt anymore.

He sniffled, and raised his head to look into his uncle's face.

"Forgive me," he managed, his voice husky.

"For what wrong?" Uncle Val Con asked, and his voice sounded strained, too, like he'd been screaming with the music. "Surely there is nothing to forgive if kin weep together."

And it was true, Syl Vor saw. Uncle Val Con's face was wet, his eyelashes were sticky with tears.

"But why?"

Uncle Val Con sighed, and shifted his position, crossing his legs and drawing Syl Vor onto his lap.

"Let us agree for the moment that I lost something...very precious, that I ought to have guarded more nearly."

"But," Syl Vor said, remembering what Mrs. pel'Esla said when *he* lost something, "you can find it again."

"No." Uncle Val Con used the tips of his fingers to brush the damp from Syl Vor's face. "No, child, I can't."

He looked so stern that Syl Vor didn't like to ask any more questions. He had been quite little when Uncle Val Con stepped away from clan and kin to take up duty as a Scout, but he remembered him as laughing and lighthearted. Now that he was returned, and *properly delm*, as Grandaunt said, he seemed not to laugh so much.

"I do ask your forgiveness," his uncle murmured. "I had not intended the music to distress you."

"I had just come in from the garden," Syl Vor said reasonably. "You couldn't have known I was in the hall. And it was rude, to open the door when it was closed."

He felt a slight jerk; heard a light snort, as if Uncle Val Con had tried not to laugh.

"Well, then," he said, "we are both beyond shame, and need say nothing more."

"Except..." Syl Vor began—and stopped, uncertain if that meant *nothing more at all*.

"Except?"

"What *was* that music, if you please?"

"Ah. *That* music was taught to me by your Grandmother Anne. It is called *Swan Lake*."

"What is a swan?"

"A large and elegant waterbird. Your grandmother said that swans were sometimes mistaken for dancers all dressed in white, so graceful are they on the water. That, she said, was what inspired the story."

"Story?"

"Ah, are you interested?"

"Yes!" Uncle Val Con's stories had always been interesting.

"Hold. You are wanted in the nursery, are you not?"

Syl Vor sighed, seeing the story flutter beyond his reach.

"Yes, sir."

"In that case, you must allow me to escort you, and make your excuses to Mrs. pel'Esla. I will tell you the story as we walk. Do we have a bargain?"

"Yes!" Syl Vor said again.

They rose, Syl Vor first. Uncle Val Con held down his hand, and Syl Vor took it as they left the room.

"Now it happens that the *delm* had decided it was time for a son of the House to enter into his first contract of marriage..."

· · · ❉ · · ·

"You did well, little sister," the *luthia* said, after the first cup of tea and Kezzi's recitation of the conversation with the headman were both finished.

"Your pardon, Grandmother," Kezzi answered politely. "I was twice distracted."

"So you were," the *luthia* said, as if she hadn't noticed until Kezzi spoke of it. "I will give you a small dream, which will teach how to avoid unbidden memories; and another, to reinforce the art of listening for later."

"For now..." She put her cup aside, and held out both hands.

Hesitantly, Kezzi surrendered her cup. In the usual way of things, they would now drink more tea, and the *luthia* would invite her to tell this tale or that, that she had learned from another of the *kompani*.

"You must excuse me, little sister," the *luthia* said with a smile. "I have said that I will dream upon this matter of the *kompani*'s fortune. This I will now do. I ask that you walk past Jin's hearth on your way across the common, and say that I crave her assistance."

"Yes, Grandmother," Kezzi said, rising and bowing, with the tips of her fingers tucked into the sleeves of her sweater.

"That is well. The dreams, I will send this evening. Come to me again in two days, and bring with you a branch of limin blooms."

"Yes, Grandmother," Kezzi said again. She snapped her fingers for Malda and went off to give Jin the *luthia*'s summons.

CHAPTER FIVE

. . . .

"YOU'RE UP EARLY," NOVA YOS'GALAN SAID TO HER COUSIN PAT Rin yos'Phelium, ignoring the fact that she was, also, up before Surebleak's uncertain sun.

"One likes to take the air while it is still crisp," Pat Rin told her loftily, one eyebrow raised.

Had they been on Liad, and she a forward-coming acquaintance met before Day Port, that mode—and that eyebrow—would have succeeded in destroying all pretension. Indeed, it would have suddenly seemed not merely the most natural thing imaginable, that Lord Pat Rin would take the predawn air, but produced a certainty that everyone of proper breeding did so, as well.

Nova, no pretender, but Pat Rin's fond friend and cousin, merely shook her head.

"There is frost on your coat," she said. "Take it off, do."

She looked to the young man hovering in the doorway, and spoke in Terran. "Gavit, please take Boss Conrad's coat to the kitchen to warm—and ask Beck to send a new pot of tea, please."

"Thank you," Pat Rin said, moving effortlessly into Terran.

He shrugged his coat off and handed it to Gavit, who received it with the small, crisp bow that her staff had settled upon as the generally correct mode, and murmured, "Yes, ma'am, Boss. Comin' right up."

He left the room, closing the door softly behind him.

"Come and sit, Cousin," Nova said, dropping back into the

Low Tongue. Theirs was a multilingual House, as befit a family of traders and spacefarers, and Nova spoke Terran well. Still, it was... a pleasure to speak Liaden, and especially to speak familiarly, to kin.

Obedient, Pat Rin sat in the chair next to her desk, sighing, even as he nodded his head toward the radiant wall unit, which was glowing gently orange.

"It is, according to my household, very nearly spring."

"I have received similar information," Nova replied. "I take leave to doubt it."

"Certainly, the hope of spring must be seductive," Pat Rin said. "However, as one who has previously enjoyed the balmy pleasures of that season, I fear I must encourage you in doubt."

"Perhaps we will become acclimated, in time," Nova said.

"Perhaps we will," Pat Rin replied politely. "Or perhaps Weather Tech Brunner will speedily finish his studies, and find an optimum orbit for the mirrors and weather satellites."

Should Mr. Brunner finish his studies after breakfast, and launch the first satellite before dinner, it would be several years before Surebleak would begin appreciably to warm—Nova had seen the summary reports. And even then, Surebleak would never achieve Liad's inoffensive perpetual springtime.

She had seen those reports, too.

There was, however, no sense dwelling on cold news. At least so long as there were radiant heaters.

"You were going to tell me," she said to her cousin, "why you are about so early in the day. Surely now that you are lifemated, you have no need to keep wastrel's hours."

"Now that I am Boss of Bosses, I keep hours that would put a wastrel to the blush," Pat Rin retorted. He shook his head. "No, as it happens, Mr. McFarland had wished to consult with Mr. Golden regarding an expansion of patrol coverage, and to gain his opinion of the child-on-the-street policy."

Cheever McFarland was Pat Rin's head of security, a tough, able man of wit and a certain rough charm. In her household, his counterpart was Michael Golden, whom Mr. McFarland had speedily taken as his advisor in matters of greater street security and implementation of new policy—what one might call "law." Unlike Mr. McFarland, Michael Golden had grown up on Surebleak—indeed, on this very turf, which had come lately under the protection of Boss Conrad—and his insights were, as she had found for herself, invaluable.

"And of course," she said, giving Pat Rin High Mode, "you are a slave to Mr. McFarland's schedule."

He smiled, which he did less easily than her brothers. Val Con of late stood within bowing range of solemn; one had the sense of his listening twice to every utterance, which was, she had persuaded herself, the *delm's* weight. Pat Rin had been serious from a boy. It had been the first bond between them.

"Mr. McFarland of course rules me utterly," he said now. "But, as it happened, there is a matter that I wished to bring to you. Regarding—"

The quick sound of knuckles against plastic interrupted him. A moment later, the door opened to admit Gavit, bearing a tray. He paused just inside the room to look at her, his head tipped slightly.

"On the conference table, thank you, Gavit," she said.

"Yes, ma'am, Boss." He disposed of the tray neatly, and turned again to address Pat Rin. "Beck says, Mr. Conrad, if you'd care to sit down to breakfast, there's griddle cakes and hot apple toppin'."

"Please tell Beck that I am honored," Pat Rin said gravely. "However, I am wanted elsewhere very shortly, and while Mr. McFarland may stay, I—may not."

Gavit nodded. "Heard Cheever tell Mike he was short-stoppin'. I'll give Beck the news."

"Thank you," Pat Rin said.

Gavit bowed and left them, pulling the door to.

Nova rose and Pat Rin with her. She poured a single cup, which was proper, raised it for the sip...and paused when Pat Rin put a second cup forward to be filled.

She met serious brown eyes.

"I recall that it was you who counseled me to learn Surebleak custom and observe it stringently."

"So I did. However, I find it unlikely that Beck would have invited me to stay for griddle cakes if she had poisoned the tea."

"It does seem inefficient," Nova agreed and filled his cup.

"You are aware," Pat Rin said, after they had both returned to the desk and had a grateful sip of tea, "that Korval has taken up several persons in relation to what we now understand to have been a deliberate attempt on the life of the *delmae*."

Eight persons that would be, Nova thought, placing her teacup carefully amid her papers. Nine, if one counted the hapless Otts Clark, who hadn't even tried to use the deadly weapon he had been given, but instead attempted to capture Val Con's lifemate. Questioning had revealed Mr. Clark's reluctance to kill—not the battle-honed mercenary soldier whom his politics informed him was creating a hostile economic environment for Surebleak natives—but the unborn heir.

"I know that Natesa and Anthora are collaborating on . . . questioning," she said.

Pat Rin nodded. "That they are, and a tricksy business it is, holding to the *Delm's* Word while attempting to extract information vital to the clan's protection."

The *Delm's* Word. Nova sighed.

"Does it seem to you that Val Con is being rather tender of those who have proven themselves over and again to be Korval's true enemy?"

Pat Rin glanced at her, dark brows drawn above velvet brown eyes.

"The *delm* is after larger game than those we have gathered into hand," he pointed out.

"Oh, agreed! But the eight are not themselves blameless. They, as much as those they serve, wish Korval's destruction—we have it from their own lips. Otts Clark—"

Otts Clark had no defenses against Anthora's arts, which the eight agents of the so-called Department of the Interior had in abundance. He had willingly given the name of the man who had instructed him, and given him the toxin-tipped pin . . .

. . . and then wept in honest horror and sorrow when the Scout team came back to tell him that they had found the man . . . dead.

"Val Con," Pat Rin murmured, interrupting these thoughts.

She glanced at him, questioning, and found him staring abstract-edly into the depths of his teacup.

"Val Con?" she prompted when it seemed that he was in danger of becoming lost in his thoughts.

He glanced up. "Your pardon, Cousin. It is merely that I had heard from Shan that Val Con had been . . . subverted by this same Department of the Interior. The description of the damage done was quite horrific, and I without Healer's eyes, to truly know what had been done."

"I had heard the same," Nova said quietly, "and yet he won free, while these others—"

"Val Con won free because he had resources," Pat Rin interrupted. "So Shan theorizes—and I agree. Val Con had Miri at his back, he had his music, his brothers of the Clutch—and he was raised under Tree, whatever that does to any of us! These others—they have no such resources nor any kind of aid. And it may be..." He looked to her, earnest and, as she read it, not a little distressed. "It may be that Val Con is the only one who is fit to judge their condition and in what manner they must be contained.

"They admit of no clan, and in any case to return them to kin would seem a disastrous course. Certainly, they cannot advocate...rationally for themselves. Having fallen captive to their great enemy, Anthora reads that none expects the department they serve will seek to free them, and they find pride in being expendable. Each had a geas upon them, to die as quickly as they might upon capture—"

"Which geas Anthora had been able to...circumvent," Nova murmured.

"Indeed—and so we come to my tale." Pat Rin drew a breath, and recruited himself with a deep draught of tea.

"Anthora and Natesa had devised a scheme which they believed would allow them to heed the *Delm's* Word while being more productive of information. There was one among the eight who seemed to...revel less in her lack of worth. One, indeed, whom the conditioning seemed to *push* rather than...consume.

"Anthora said to Natesa that she saw a—let us call it a fault line. She believed that she might separate the conditioning from the conditioned, and thus unlock a rational mind from which Natesa might then gain answers."

He looked down into his empty cup.

Nova drank what was left of her tea, and considered. That her sister Anthora could do precisely what was described, she had no doubt; Anthora was one of the three most powerful *dramliz* in the known galaxy. And once Anthora had produced the correct conditions, there was no doubt at all that Pat Rin's lifemate, Juntavas Judge Natesa the Assassin, would be able to extract much of value to the clan.

All the while leaving the one under questioning intact and alive.

Which was the *Delm's* Word.

She put her cup down and nodded. "So," she prompted, "the attempt was made."

He shivered slightly, though they were quite snug where they sat, by the heater's benevolent orange glow.

"Indeed," he said slowly. "The attempt was made. It was, one might say, a success. Natesa found herself speaking to a woman who was at first somewhat puzzled, and who grew more agitated as the questions proceeded. It was as if, Natesa told me, the personality had become detached from the deeds, and she was for a time able to describe those deeds as if she had observed some other person perform them.

"As the questions continued, however, the woman—Elid yos'Casin, she admitted no clan in either state. As the questions continued, she began to understand that she had performed the deeds she was describing, and she grew more and more disordered.

"Anthora sensed a crisis, and withdrew her influence, thinking that the previous personality balance would readjust itself—"

He stopped and swallowed.

"She killed herself?" Nova asked softly.

"She died, let us say," Pat Rin answered. "Natesa..." Another swallow. "Natesa allows me to know that it was a bad death. As bad as any she has witnessed."

Now, *there* was a statement that must give pause, coming as it did from one who had earned her gun-name.

"So now there are seven," Nova said softly, "and Otts Clark."

"Who must be confined for his own protection. The *delm* was not pleased—the less so, when Natesa provided coordinates, and a name, which Elid yos'Casin had offered. At the moment, all eight are remanded to the care of the Scouts, and there are Healers on watch at all hours, in the event that any of those remaining should seek to embrace their geas."

"These are Korval's enemy," Nova said. "They will not stop until we—or they—are no more."

"It would seem so. Though the Healers may eventually perfect a therapy..."

Surebleak would be the garden spot of the Daiellen Sector before the Healers could perfect such a therapy, Nova thought, and she shivered, there in the warm room.

"How do we dare this?" she asked suddenly. "Any of this? How do we dare to come out from Jelaza Kazone and walk the streets. How do we dare to bring our children into danger?"

"Was our enemy more reticent, on the homeworld?" Pat Rin asked—and she started, having not realized that she had spoken aloud. "And now we are on guard, are we not? Our children are informed of their danger, and they are neither incompetent nor fools. Nor are we, I hope, fools. And as much as I may not guess its ultimate intent, I do not believe that the Tree is a fool. As for the rest—why, Cousin, do you forget yourself?"

She looked up at the smile in his voice, saw the outstretched hand and placed hers into his.

"We dare because we must," Pat Rin said.

"And who else," Nova added, capping the line, "will dare for us?"

· · · ❄ · · ·

Directly after breakfast, before the first lessons of the day, that was when Syl Vor chose to dance. It wasn't as much fun, without the others practicing, too, but there was the shadow-spar, after all, which was much the same as the unit at the Rock.

Syl Vor did his warm-ups, and took his stance, allowing the shadow-spar to pick one of the stored routines at random. Grandfather had said that they had to take care not to do the dances always in the same order, or to only dance preferred routines, lest they grow stale and slow and less able to protect themselves and others.

This morning the shadow-spar offered one of the speed dances. Syl Vor smiled and flowed into the pattern, quick-stepping, leaping, jabbing. At the end, he was breathing fast, his clothes sticky with sweat. The shadow-spar prompted him to cool down, and he turned from the unit to begin a series of stretches...

...and blinked at the elder gentleman leaning against the wall, his sharp-featured face bearing an expression of distant interest.

Syl Vor folded into a bow—honor to elder kin. "Granduncle Daav."

"Nephew," the gentleman said, in his deep voice. "Pray continue."

Continue. Syl Vor took a breath, centered himself and began his cool-down set.

Granduncle Daav was Grandaunt Kareen's brother, Uncle Val Con's father, who had been absent from clan and kin and Tree for all of Syl Vor's lifetime—and more. He had been, until only recently, the stuff of stories.

However so, he had been in-House when Syl Vor and Padi and Quin arrived from the Rock, and had immediately made himself known to them. Grandaunt would say that had been improper—that junior ought to go to elder—but in truth they were all three relieved to have the duty taken from them. Nor did Granduncle Daav stop upon an introduction. He had several times joined them for their midmorning tea and cookies, and on two occasions had asked Syl Vor to walk the inner garden with him. This he had found pleasantly instructive, Granduncle Daav naming out the names of the flowers, and speaking of the days when the garden had been his to keep.

Syl Vor was of the tentative opinion that he might quite like Granduncle Daav, when he came to know him better. Though that might take some time, since Granduncle, with the rest of the elders of the House, was so very busy with the clan's business.

Stretches done, Syl Vor turned, half expecting to find that he was once again alone in the practice room.

But, no—there stood Granduncle yet, tall and lean, his dark hair stitched with grey, his black eyes even sharper than Grandaunt Kareen's.

"May I serve you, Granduncle?"

"Now, there's a gentle offer. But, no, child, in this instance I believe it is I who may serve you."

Had he botched his routine? Syl Vor wondered. The shadow-spar was supposed to stop the pattern and correct him if he—

"Peace, Syl Vor—you dance admirably. It is only—" Granduncle Daav straightened and came forward, silent as Uncle Val Con—but there. Uncle Val Con was a Scout, and so, too, had his father been. And Scouts never made any sound that they did not intend to make.

"It is only…" Granduncle repeated, touching the shadow-spar's screen and scrolling through the routine Syl Vor had just danced. "Yes. These are all avoids and kills—no feints, no bridgework, no—" He glanced over his shoulder, with a swift, sharp smile. "You will forgive an old man his bias—no finesse."

"Quin had said the same," Syl Vor admitted. "He and Padi were forward of me, and had learnt how to dance properly. But Grandfather and Grandaunt said that, if it came—if our enemies found us, and it was come down to myself between the twins and harm, I had best know my kills, because to run away, carrying two, even with a floater..."

"You would be conspicuous, and the babes would slow you." Granduncle Daav nodded gravely, which Grandaunt would scold him for, were she present. "Your elders were wise in their choice; I honor them—and you. However, the bridgework adds an elegance, and sometimes dancing a feint may reveal another approach to survival. I would suggest, now that you are under Tree, in-House, and with numerous kin between yourself and the enemies of the clan, that a study of the dance entire may serve you well."

Syl Vor chewed his lip, remembering Padi and Quin practicing together, and owned that Granduncle had a point.

"If you wish, I will program the shadow-spar so that it will guide you in the complete dance."

"Yes," Syl Vor said, startled by the loudness of his voice, so that for an instant he forgot to also say, "if you please, Granduncle."

"It will be my very great pleasure. And now, my child, I fear that you are late for your tutor. Go, quickly, and say that I detained you."

"Yes!" Syl Vor said again. Hastily, he bowed, received Granduncle's nod in return—and ran.

CHAPTER SIX

. . . .

"GOOD DREAMING TO YOU, *LUTHIA*," KEZZI SAID POLITELY.

She bent and put the limin branch with its white flowers and shiny green leaves on the edge of the rug.

"Good dreaming to you, young sister. Please pour tea for us."

This Kezzi hurried to do, filling two mugs and setting the kettle back in its place by the hearth.

She gave Silain her mug, and knelt at the corner of the rug with her own mug in hand, Malda lying quiet and good at her side.

"Tell me," the *luthia* said, after she had her first sip and sighed in satisfaction; "did you dream the dreams I sent to you?"

"Yes, *luthia*," Kezzi said. In fact, she had twice-dreamed, which Vylet had doubted would do either harm or good.

"Like asking a flutterbee to dream a rock." *That* had been Vylet's wisdom.

Silain drank more tea, and Kezzi did.

"How sweet the limin smells," the *luthia* said.

Sweet it was—sweeter than when she had taken the branch. Kezzi glanced at it, lying on the rug at Silain's knee. The blossoms had opened wider, maybe in appreciation of the hearth's warmth.

She drank her tea to the dregs, sighed and looked to Silain.

"More tea, Grandmother?"

"Not now. Now, I would like you to do a thing for me."

"Yes," Kezzi said, preparing to stand. The *luthia* often asked her to fetch this and that from others of the *kompani*, or from the garden—like the limin branch.

"This thing you can do without leaving the hearth," Silain said. She patted the rug beside her. "Put another brick in, and come sit by me, here."

Another brick? Kezzi thought. It was already warm enough that Silain had put off her shawl. Maybe there was a tonic to boil, or a spell to set. She hadn't heard that any of the *kompani* was in need of either, but it was said that the *luthia*'s ears were so keen that she could hear songs inside of silence.

Kezzi set the brick and waited three breaths, until the edges began to glow dull red. Then, she went to sit at Silain's side.

"Now, if you please, little sister, I would like you to look ahead for me."

Kezzi blinked, and looked up into the *luthia*'s face.

"Look ahead?" she asked. "I..."

"You don't know what I mean? Did you dream the dreams I sent you?"

"Yes, I dreamed both—" But, Kezzi thought suddenly, had there been three? Droi sometimes hid things, or took them away with her. But surely not even Droi would—

"Be peaceful, child." Silain brushed her hot cheek with cool fingertips. "Tell me what you dreamed."

"I dreamed that I breathed, and I breathed so deep that I breathed myself out of my head, and all there was left inside my head was a big silence. And I dreamed that I was given three stories, one after the other. The stories fell into my head, into the silence, and the silence formed the shape of each.

"Then I dreamed that I breathed myself back into my head, and there were the stories, sealed in silence. I touched the first one and it filled up my mouth so I had to say it out, or choke."

She took a deep breath of hot, limin-scented air.

"You have dreamed well and fully, my sister," the *luthia* murmured. "What I ask you to do is to breathe as you dreamed, until your head fills up with silence. Close your eyes."

Obediently, Kezzi closed her eyes. She concentrated, found the dream-rhythm and breathed until she could not feel her body, and her thoughts blurred, and faded, and her head was filled with nothing, silence. Silence and the strong odor of limin.

"Open your eyes!"

She opened her eyes to utter darkness.

"Tell me what you see."

See? She could see nothing here, save threads of red and orange, and . . .

A paper printed with words, blurry and indistinct, and across the paper . . .

"A pen . . . thick and black . . . green . . . red . . . blue . . . black."

It filled her whole sight, a thing of wonder; she ached to possess it, her fingers itching.

". . . mine . . ."

Her vision wavered, the pen blurring—and vanishing into orange-shot blackness.

The darkness produced a voice.

"Well done. Close your eyes, little sister. Take a breath, and come back to me."

. . . ☀ . . .

Duty had called Uncle Val Con and Nelirikk Explorer off-world in the last hours of the night—Syl Vor heard Mr. pel'Kana saying so to Mrs. ana'Tak when he went by the kitchen. He hadn't meant to sneak, but it was only reasonable, he told himself, that he would stand quietly out of the way until the servants had finished their business and took note of him.

Mr. pel'Kana said that Scouts had come after the House had retired, asking for *Delm* Korval. The demand having been made in that *melant'i*, Mr. pel'Kana had of course to pass the message, despite the hour.

So, the message was relayed, and Uncle Val Con had come himself to stand Korval and receive the Scouts, leaving the *delmae* to her rest, which the gods knew she—and that was when Mrs. ana'Tak had seen him, and asked if he'd come for his morning apple.

Syl Vor admitted this, and the fruit was bestowed. There was no help for it then but that he leave the kitchen. And neither Mr. pel'Kana or Mrs. ana'Tak said one word more.

Some time later, apple eaten and lessons done, he went in search of company, or, if not company, then . . . occupation.

Everybody had something useful to do, except for him.

Aunt Miri was busy with Aunt Priscilla; Uncle Ren Zel was busy with Mr. Brunner, the weather tech; Granduncle Daav had gone out early to visit Boss Sherton; Aunt Anthora was doing *something*; and Grandaunt Kareen was going into town to meet with the Civics Committee. Even Eztina was busy, stalking leaves in the inner garden.

Mrs. pel'Esla had recommended that he work ahead of his tutor, but he had already finished all the modules at his current level and lacked the key code necessary to access the next. She had then recommended that he find a book or play a match game, but the books in the nursery library were boring, and the counterchance program had performed a disallowed move that put him unjustly in peril, and besides that, it was bright and sunny outside.

After having studied upon that fact for an entire half hour, Syl Vor put on his sweater, jacket, hat and gloves, then let himself out by the west patio and was soon walking briskly across the crunchy brown grass.

If he had exited Trealla Fantrol by the west patio, he would have gone across the lawn to the edge of the trees, then down a path which eventually found and followed the stream. A little way on, there was a place where the rocks were close enough together that a boy who was steady on his feet could use them as a bridge across the stream. On the other side was a meadow, and another path, not so well marked, that ended at the fence, though Syl Vor hardly ever went all that way by himself.

He didn't mean to go far today—only a walk, on their own land, to see something different from the inside garden.

Before long, he had taken off his gloves and his hat and shoved them into the pockets of his jacket, which he had unsealed. The day was cooler than a similarly bright day would be at ho— on Liad, but the combination of the sun, a lack of breeze and a rather spanking pace soon warmed him. Indeed, he was considering removing the jacket, too, when he came to the crack in the world.

The sight of the irregular joining of the land that had come to Surebleak with Jelaza Kazone, and the land that had been here all along, gave Syl Vor pause. This was the border with their nearest neighbor, Mr. Shaper. One had been cautioned that Mr. Shaper was sometimes irritable and unwelcoming of visitors. One had been told not to cross over the boundary unless explicitly invited, and never to tease or in any way harm Mr. Shaper's cats.

That last had hardly been necessary, Syl Vor thought, irritable at the memory. He approached the boundary with a certain amount of curiosity. Unlike the browning grasses he walked on, each step waking a crunch, the grass on the far side of the boundary was green—short and sharp-looking, but green.

Native grass, Syl Vor thought, which had adapted. He had learned about adaptation and useful mutations and cross-breeding. Perhaps the grass from home would breed with the Surebleak grass and so learn how to survive in this changed climate.

He was at the boundary now, the toes of his boots just barely not over the edge of Korval land. Granduncle Daav had told him that, when first the house and land had been grounded within the old quarry that it now occupied, the gap between Mr. Shaper's land and their own had been as wide as Syl Vor was tall, and quite, quite deep. It had been Mr. Shaper who had suggested that dirt be imported from Boss Sherton's land, on another side of Korval's holding, and the crack filled in.

That had been done, but the level of fill was lower than the land Syl Vor stood on.

"Startin' to settle, is she?"

The voice was right in his ear. Syl Vor jerked, face warming with embarrassment at revealing himself inattentive. He looked up into brown eyes and a thin, chapped face. A Scout, he thought, embarrassment ebbing. No one had told him that Mr. Shaper—for surely this must be Mr. Shaper—was a Scout.

"You'd best tell your granda to call in some more dirt." The Scout-who-was-probably-Mr.-Shaper gave him a hard look. "That's your granda, ain't it? Boss Conrad's uncle?"

Syl Vor chewed his lip. His Terran was good—he'd studied hard, understanding that, if they were forced by enemies to leave the Rock, then it would be among Terrans that the lesser danger would be found. This inquiry into lineage—it was what a civilized person wished, to be able to correctly place persons within their clan. Grandaunt Kareen had made them study clans and lineage for just that reason. But...Cousin Pat Rin—Boss Conrad—that was to say, *Uncle Daav* was, by Line, Syl Vor's *cousin.* Only he was so very old—Grandaunt's brother!—that it seemed rude to use the same mode as one would with Padi, or Quin. Or even Uncle Val Con, who had at least been fostered to yos'Galan, and was of course accounted a son of the Line...

And all *that* was rather too much to explain in Terran to

this stranger with his hard, bright eyes, so Syl Vor only nodded, not without a thought for Grandaunt and the lineage charts. At least, he thought, a nod was surely proper and acceptable *here*, in converse with one who was Terran.

Proper or not, it answered. The man gave a sharp nod of his own in return.

"I'm Yulie Shaper," he said in his abrupt, rough way. "You come down to check the edge?"

"No..." Syl Vor paused, but this was a much simpler truth. "I came because everyone has work, but not me."

Mr. Shaper made a hard sound—the audible equivalent of his nod.

"Got nothin' in hand, is it? Well, you can help me, if you wanna. I got plenty work."

This sounded unexpectedly promising. Syl Vor looked beyond the man, to the wagon full of...trays?...parked next to a plot of turned land.

"I will be pleased to help you work," he said carefully, "if I can be of use." He paused, eying the cart once more, then looked back to the man. "What are you doing?"

"Settin' the spring seedlings," Mr. Shaper said. "An' I better get to it. Hop on over if you wanna work, and I'll show you what to do." He turned away, toward the plot and the wagon.

Syl Vor leapt over the crack in the world and ran after him.

Setting spring seedlings was riveting work. Syl Vor handled the tender leaflets and the threadlike roots with care as he escorted each beginning plant to the hole he had prepared for it, pressing the dirt down firmly, so it stood upright. It was also warm work, and pretty soon he had taken off his jacket and hung it on the low branch of a tree, next to Mr. Shaper's overshirt.

Mr. Shaper was a quiet man, but observant. When Syl Vor had, in his ignorance, made a hole too deep and too wide, Mr. Shaper leaned over and showed him the proper way to go on. He occasionally broke silence to explain what a particular tray of seedlings *was*, the manner in which they would grow, and what sort of "eating" they would eventually provide.

It was all so engrossing that Syl Vor quite lost track of anything but the task in hand, until Mr. Shaper broke his silence once more.

"Here comes somethin' big—you miss your dinner, boy?"

Syl Vor looked up at that, fuzzy-headed, like he'd been woken up out of a sound sleep, raising his head and looking beyond Mr. Shaper, and beyond the crack in the land, where a very large man indeed was walking briskly across Korval's browning grass.

He scrambled to his feet, suddenly very aware that he had told no one of his intended direction when he left the house.

"I have to go," he said, short as Mr. Shaper himself.

"Sure you do—no use arguin' with a mountain. Get, then."

Syl Vor was already in motion, snatching his jacket from the branch and running. He leapt the boundary, landing just as Diglon Rifle arrived.

"Apprentice, you are missed," the big man said sternly in Trade. Diglon was studying, but his spoken Liaden wasn't very good yet. He understood quite a lot, though, and his mastery of the dance was something Syl Vor hoped he might someday approach.

Syl Vor gulped. "I forgot the time," he said.

"Recall it now," Diglon advised, "and come with me."

He turned, not waiting to see Syl Vor darting after, until they were both brought up by a shout.

"Hey!"

They turned. Yulie Shaper stood at the boundary, a seedling in one hand, the other held chest high, fingers open.

"Landholder?" Diglon said politely, in slow, but perfectly intelligible, Terran. "You want to speak?"

Mr. Shaper gave his sharp, hard nod. "Tell the Boss up there to the house that the boy was a big help to me today. With my work. He wants to help again, I got a barn needs paintin'."

"I will inform the . . . Boss, Landholder Shaper. Now, this young one must be returned to his place."

"Boy needs his dinner," Mr. Shaper agreed, and turned back to the garden plot.

By the time they reached the house, Syl Vor all but running to keep up with Diglon, he had come to an understanding of his errors.

First, it was a breach of proper behavior to have left the house without telling Jeeves.

Second, he had been away for quite a number of hours, though it had hardly seemed so long, when he had been working.

Third, he was quite dirty—the knees of his pants were damp and black with soil, the cuff of his sweater was smeared with grime, his hands caked brown. There was mud under his fingernails. He wasn't certain, lacking a mirror, but he felt that there might even be dirt on his face. Mrs. pel'Esla was not, he thought, going to be pleased to have him back in this condition. She would ask him if he were not old enough to take care of his clothes, and she would ask him if he did not know enough to sign out of the house before he went rambling, and she would ask him—Syl Vor gasped as he followed Diglon, not to one of the numerous side doors, but to the formal front door, as if he were a visitor.

A *stranger*.

Mrs. pel'Esla—certainly, she would be annoyed, but she would not—would she?

If she had called *Grandaunt* to take charge of his scolding, he might miss his dinner in truth—and tomorrow's breakfast, as well. He had been most careless—of security and of kin—that was true. Perhaps if he owned his faults at once, it would not be so *very* bad. Some chapters of the Code to read, perhaps, and a few days' close attendance upon Grandaunt—that would be bearable, and no more than he had traded for.

Diglon put his hand on the front door, which was immediately opened by Jeeves, orange headball flickering in the pattern that meant he was distressed.

"Rifle, you have accomplished your mission with dispatch," he said as Diglon stepped into the foyer, Syl Vor hard behind him.

"Master Syl Vor," Jeeves said sadly.

"Jeeves—" he began, but the butler pivoted a half turn and again addressed Diglon.

"You are expected. Please proceed."

The big man went down the hall, walking firm and centered. Syl Vor kept pace with an effort, his dirty boots making gritty, skittish sounds against the floor.

The door to the library stood open, Diglon entered, pivoted so that he stood with his back against the door, and said, expressionlessly, "Syl Vor yos'Galan."

There was nothing to do but step into the room, and so he did, expecting to see Grandaunt in the chair nearest the window, but no—the lowering sun struck hair that was red, not pepper-and-salt.

Syl Vor's stomach plummeted to his feet, anchoring him to the spot.

Mrs. pel'Esla hadn't gone with half measures.

Mrs. pel'Esla had invoked *the delm*.

"Thank you," she said, her voice cool in the High Tongue. "You may leave us."

"Captain," Diglon acknowledged. Syl Vor heard a rustle of fabric behind him, and the snap of the latch catching.

The delm, Syl Vor thought. He had breached security, endangered the House entire. He could not imagine what she would do to him, but he did not doubt that it was deserved.

"Come here, Syl Vor," the voice said, warmer now, in the Low Tongue.

He swallowed. The *delm* would not speak to him in the Low Tongue. Grandaunt had explained very carefully that the *delm* was not *of* the clan, but the clan embodied. It was difficult to understand; he was not certain that he understood it perfectly, even yet. But on one point, he was clear—

The *delm* would not speak to him in the Low Tongue—that was for kin, and for agemates. That being so, it was not the *delm*, but Aunt Miri whom he faced.

He was not completely sure, but that he would have preferred Grandaunt Kareen.

Taking a deep breath, he went forward to stand before the chair by the window.

Aunt Miri closed her book, and slowly looked him up and down. If Syl Vor had not already taken the full measure of his own misdeeds, he might have suspected her of smiling.

"What have you been doing, child?" she asked. "Wrestling in the mud?"

"No, Aunt. That is—I have been helping Mr. Shaper set the spring seedlings."

Slim eyebrows rose over grey eyes.

"Indeed? How do you find Mr. Shaper this day?"

"Very well," Syl Vor answered, and took some thought. "He spoke very little, but taught much. He said . . ." He hesitated, not wanting to overwhelm her patience.

She inclined her head, which meant that he should go on.

"He said to tell—Granduncle Daav that the soil was settling at the boundary, and that he should—he should call in more."

Aunt Miri nodded. "We'll put that on the to-do list," she said, in Terran.

"Yes, ma'am," Syl Vor said. He took a breath and bowed his head. "I am ashamed, Aunt. I endangered the House. Please forgive me."

She sat silent so long that Syl Vor began to fear that forgiveness was, after all, out of the question. Perhaps he should have knelt. Had it been the *delm* in truth, he would have knelt, if only because he suspected that his knees would not have supported him. Should he kneel now? Or would that—

"We seem to have survived the breach," his aunt said at last. "Stand up straight and listen to me." She waited until he had raised his head, and a moment longer, looking closely into his face.

"I understand that you were at liberty and felt that a walk would be beneficial," she continued. "We all have such times. However. You will in future sign out with Jeeves, or directly into the house base. It is not damage to the House we fear so much as damage to yourself. Had you fallen and broken a leg, and all of us unaware—that could have been very dangerous for you. Life threatening. So, it is not *only* for the protection of the House, but for protection of a valued child of the House. Do you understand?"

Syl Vor bowed. "Aunt, I do."

"Good. Tell me more of Mr. Shaper. Did you leave him in good spirits?"

He nodded—caught himself and bit his lip.

"I believe so, yes, ma'am. As we were leaving, he called to us, and said that—that he had a barn that wanted painting, if I wished to work with him again."

Aunt Miri laughed. "Barn, is it? Well, we will see. In the meantime..." She stood and held out her hand. Syl Vor hesitantly placed his dirty one in hers.

"I am glad that your day was enjoyable and instructive. We don't wish to clip your wings, but to provide a net, should it be needed. Now, you must go upstairs and make your peace with Mrs. pel'Esla, who feels that she fell short of her duty. Also"—she extended her other hand and ran her fingers down his cheek, grinning openly—"I think a bath is in order."

CHAPTER SEVEN

· ·

THE COMM UNIT ON THE EDGE OF HER DESK GAVE TONGUE, bringing Nova, blinking, out of an intense study of the plans for the first phase of the warehouse district recovery. So much unused space, under roof aboveground, as well as levels below grade, where it was warmer, for Surebleak values of warm, that might be utilized for—

The comm sounded again. She shook herself, and glanced at the screen. Her brows rose as she looked to the clock—and snapped the speaker on.

"Mother?" Syl Vor's voice was strained.

"Yes, my child," she said soothingly. "Are you well?"

A small hesitation, which instantly placed her on guard. Syl Vor was not an untruthful boy, but he was becoming adept at the fine art of phrasing.

"I am well, yes," he said now, politely. "And yourself? I hope I am not disturbing your work."

Cousin Kareen's influence there. Nova carefully did not sigh. One must know the forms, after all, and to sigh after the artless conversational style of only a year ago was to serve no one. It was the order of things, that straightforward children became facile adults.

"I find myself in the bloom of health, thank you," she told her son. "As it happens I was working, and must therefore claim you for my rescue, for I believe I have been working far too long this day." That style was a little forward of his current ability, she thought—but see what he made of it.

"I am pleased to be of service," he answered, which was perfectly apt, though delivered rather more seriously than was strictly in mode.

"We are well-aligned then," she said, matching his seriousness. "Now, you must tell me how I may serve you."

That hesitation again. Nova closed her eyes; the better to listen on all levels.

"Is Quin well?" Syl Vor asked, wistfully.

"He was perfectly well when last I saw him," she said. "He has piloting lessons every afternoon with a Scout, which reconciles him, a little, to the learning of Boss Conrad's business."

"I don't think he wants to be Boss," Syl Vor said.

"Nor did your cousin Pat Rin. Indeed, I believe that the Rule of Succession must be the same for Bosses as for *delms*."

"Who wants it least will do it best," Syl Vor quoted.

"Exactly."

"Padi has gone with Uncle Shan, on the *Passage*," her son said, after a moment.

"Padi is overdue to take up her training. Only consider! You will be in her place in a very few years. How do you think you will like that?"

Flying on a tangent he might be, but Syl Vor was not to be diverted by so simple a ploy as that.

"Granduncle Daav was kind enough to reprogram the shadow-spar so that I might learn the bridges. I practice every day. Sometimes I practice twice a day. Uncle Shan had recommended I study counterchance, but I fear the unit in the nursery is defective. I've done all my lessons ahead. Tomorrow, I will ask my tutor to unlock the next two levels."

This litany of industriousness was of course gratifying—one wished for one's offspring to be diligent. It came to her then that Syl Vor had perhaps not veered so very sharply on tangent, after all.

"Do I hear a request for a change in schedule?" she asked.

A sigh, perfectly audible. "If you please, Mother. I had asked Mrs. ana'Tak if I could help her cook, but she only gave me an apple and told me to get along outside. I—perhaps I might assist the gardener? I...think I should like to know more about gardening. I am—I am willing to work, ma'am."

Indeed, he was willing to work. A concerned parent might even say—rather too willing. Nova frowned. The burden of Plan B had altered them all, but it seemed that the conditions of refuge in Runig's Rock had exerted strange pressures on Syl Vor. She had hoped that a return to normalcy—but, there. Nothing about Korval's current situation approached normalcy. Even the nursery must know that.

"Mother?" His voice was uncertain, as if he feared that he had made a misstep.

"Forgive me, my son; I was thinking. I wonder—might this discussion of your schedule wait until we are face to face? Some planning is done better, thus, and I would rather that we give ourselves the best opportunity to plan well."

"Y-yes," he said, audibly disappointed.

"That is what we shall do, then," she said, with another glance at the clock. "And now, young sir, it is time for you to seek your bed. *Chiat'a bei kruzon.*"

"Yes," he said again. "Sleep sweetly, Mother."

Nova flipped the comm off, and sat back in her chair, abruptly aware of a presence in the doorway—Michael Golden, tea tray in hand.

"Forgive me," she said. "I did not hear you."

"No problem," he answered, coming forward and depositing the tray on the corner of her desk. It had become their custom, to take tea and some small snack together at the end of the day, comparing notes before each sought their rest.

Nova poured as he settled himself into the desk-side chair.

"That was the boy calling? Everything going aces for him, up under Tree?"

Nova picked up her cup and sighed.

"I fear that he is feeling . . . somewhat isolated. He has no age-mates, and had lately been accustomed to the companionship of his elder cousins, who are now called to duty. His hours hang on his hands, and he asks after other occupation."

"Nobody to play with—that's tough," Michael Golden said, with an air of knowing something about the topic on which he discoursed. "Kids've gotta play."

This was true. Children ought to play. Especially serious children ought to play. She had herself been a serious child, though she had shared the nursery with Shan and Val Con, neither of whom had been serious in the least. It had not seemed so at the time, but in hindsight she had been well served by her brothers' shatterbrained companionship. She shook her head, as her mother had used to do, a gesture of not knowing, rather than denial.

"At ho— on Liad, Syl Vor had been accustomed to spending time with the children of yo'Lanna, a—an old friend of our family. The *delm* willing, he would by now have been fostered into the house of an ally with near-aged children," she said. "I had considered that, perhaps we might—But, no. It is ineligible." She sighed again.

Michael Golden sipped his tea. She did the same.

"Word's come in that the school site's been left alone six nights in a row," he said eventually.

Nova raised her eyebrows. "That...is almost wonderful, Mr. Golden. To what do you attribute this sudden lack of popularity?"

"Well, now, there's the thing. I can't pin it on any particular something. Could be the folks behind it just got worn out. Could be they're gathering themselves together for a big surprise, and they don't wanna risk being caught at the small stuff."

"Could it be that those who have been taken up in the sweep were the decision-makers, and those they leave behind are without orders?"

Michael Golden frowned, his nose wrinkling slightly with the intensity of his thought. Nova, who by this time knew his ways, warmed his cup, and hers...and waited.

"*Could* be," he said at last, "but I can't say that's for sure the case. 'Less you got something from the Road Boss?"

She shook her head. "Merely speculation."

He picked up his cup with an appreciative nod to her. "Thanks. I don't say it wouldn't be convenient if that was the case, but I'm thinking we'd better not count on convenience."

"I agree. What do you suggest?"

"Seems to me we got enough watchers on-site, now, and as reliable as we can make 'em. What we wanna be sure of is that nobody gets paid to go temporarily blind, if you understand me. McFarland says he can set us up with long-distance surveillance, and a couple pairs o'Scouts to mind the screens. I think we'd best take him up on that."

Nova nodded.

"Please proceed," she said. "Quickly, in case this big surprise you argue for so persuasively is near to fruition."

"I'll get it set up tomorrow. McFarland'll give me everything I need. Wanted to clear it with you first." He raised his cup. "Figure it's only smart, to open up extra eyes, but I'd rather that notion of yours was right, Boss. Long run, it'd save us all some trouble."

· · · ✵ · · ·

It was a fine, warm day on the top of the world when Kezzi pushed open her own door to let herself and Malda out.

Before opening the hatch, she had used the mirror tube to look up and down the street. It had been empty, which the street usually was. That didn't mean that there was no use in looking, though. Once, she had seen Rafin stalking toward the *kompani*'s fifth door, his toolbelt clanking and a scowl on his face. Rafin's temper wasn't good at the best of times, and she didn't want to meet *that* frown on the street, or have her ears cuffed, and be dragged back below because she was only a Small, and not permitted to be out alone.

That was the Rule: Smalls were not to go to the top of the world or the City Above, except with an elder.

The Bedel said, "Rules are for weak heads."

Also, Kezzi thought, closing the hatch behind her and snapping her fingers for Malda to follow, she was *not* a Small. That there were no others Smaller, did not mean that *she* remained Small forever.

Because the day was so fine, she and Malda walked out of the quiet streets and down where Those Others—the *gadje*—moved about, busy and important. Far too busy and important to notice a girl and her little black-and-tan dog.

And that was well.

That was very well, indeed.

"Here, now, you little thief, come back here!"

The shopkeeper who yelled it was a red-faced man with freckles and a dirty apron. His legs were long and there was no possibility that she could outrun him.

Kezzi, therefore, fell to her knees, clutched Malda to her and began to loudly lament.

"No! No! He's my dog! You can't have him!"

The shopkeeper came to a halt, a look of confusion on his foolish *gadje* face.

"What the—" he began, as another man came forward. Kezzi saw him out of the corner of her eye—a brown man with big shoulders, and a gun belted on his hip.

"Hey, now, neighbor, leave the kid's dog alone, right?"

"Dog?" The red-faced man blinked and turned. "*Dog?*" he repeated. "I'm not after her damn dog—ain't even enough of it to make a decent stew! She stole a—"

"Easy," the brown man interrupted, putting a hand on the other man's shoulder. "Go on inside and make sure the neighbors don't walk off with the store."

"But she—"

"Yeah, yeah. I'll come in in a few and make it right with you. Just want to have a word or two with the younger here, first. I don't show up, you call in one of the patrol and tell 'em to write down that Golden stiffed you. Got that name?"

"Golden," the red-faced man repeated. "Dorrie Golden's grandson?"

"That's me."

The red-faced man shook his head. "You ain't gonna stiff me," he said, and walked away without saying anything else.

During this exchange, Kezzi had kept up her end of things, clutching Malda—to whom the part of patient victim was nothing new—and weeping desperately into his fur.

"Okay." The man named Golden hunkered down next to her. "He's gone. Nobody's gonna take your dog."

Sniffling, Kezzi raised her head. "Nobody?" she asked, suspiciously.

"Let's just say they'll have to get through me, first," Golden said, brown eyes smiling.

"What's your name?" he asked.

"Anna."

"Pleased to meetcha, Anna," he said politely. "I'm Mike Golden. What's your dog's name?"

"Rascal," she answered promptly.

"Glad to meet Rascal, too. Now, c'mon, stand up." He did, and held his hand down to her.

Kezzi knew better than to let one of Those Others get a hand on her. She came to her feet fast, and went three steps back, not quite beyond Mike Golden's reach, which was long. He didn't look too fast, though, with his short legs, his big shoulders, and heavy bones. Kezzi thought she could outrun him.

"Where's your ma?" the man asked her.

Kezzi pointed vaguely northward. "Home."

Mike Golden nodded. "That bein' the case, and it comin' on to evenin', how about I walk you and Rascal home?"

Kezzi shook her head. "I know the way," she said, and added, for the smile in his eyes. "Good-bye, Mike Golden."

She snapped her fingers for Malda, spun and took off at the top of her speed, dodging between the *gadje* who crowded the sidewalk.

She ran as fast as she could, head down, expecting to hear the man's voice raised behind her, shouting out for somebody to *catch that girl!*

But that didn't happen. Kezzi ran, Malda at her heel, and there was no outcry, and no one moved to stop them.

CHAPTER EIGHT

. . . .

IT WAS A MERRY GROUP AROUND JIN'S HEARTH—KEZZI, ISART, and Droi, who had all contributed food—Silain, of course, and also Memit, Kar, and Gahn, who brought fiddle, sistreen and drum and earned their suppers with song.

Isart's contribution had been a piece of salt meat, which Jin had slivered and fried with the flapjacks she'd made from the flour Kezzi had contributed.

Kezzi thought the meat too strong, and fed hers to Malda. Droi saw, and slipped her another flapjack, dredged in the dusty sugar that she had brought back from the City Above.

Tea had been poured and the musicians were picking up their instruments again, when there came a pounding of feet across the common, and here was Vylet, gasping for the *luthia* to come to her own hearth at once!

Silain looked up from her tea, her silver hair moving along her shoulders like rain.

"What desperate need is this?"

"Udari found a dead *gadje* by the eight door," gasped Vylet, "and brought him inside."

"If the *gadje* is dead, he is beyond us all," said Silain, unmoving.

Kezzi, though, put down her mug, remembering the brown man with the smiling eyes, there Above, who had not called out to Those Others his brothers to catch her. Had he followed her after all on his short, bandy legs? The streets Above were dangerous; sometimes even the Bedel were caught—

"Your pardon, *luthia*," Vylet gasped. "The *gadje* has a number of breaths left in him. Udari thinks—five."

Udari had only a little of the farsight. But, if he said that five breaths remained to the *gadje*, absent the *luthia*'s blessing, then likely he was right.

Silain rose speedily, and Kezzi, too, without being asked.

"I will come," said Jin. "If you wish."

"Yes," said the *luthia*, and so it was the three of them came to where the *gadje* lay, while Vylet ran for the headman.

It was not Mike Golden, rumpled and sticky with blood, on a blanket at the *luthia*'s hearth. At first glance, Kezzi thought the *gadje* a boy, then Jin sponged the blood from his face and she saw that, however small, this was a man grown.

A man grown, but surely dying, his fires low and all but colorless. Even Kezzi could see that much.

"He is broken in many places," the *luthia* breathed, fingering the *gadje*'s dying glow. "Inside more than out."

"Perhaps it is best to smooth the road," Jin said, "and give that which is left to the furnace."

To smooth the road to the World Unseen—that was the *luthia*'s most potent blessing. Surely, in such a case as this, it was the only good thing that could be done. Kezzi blinked and altered her breathing to that special rhythm she had so recently dreamed, bringing what she had learned about such matters to the top of her mind.

Kneeling on the far side of the *luthia*'s fire, Udari watched with his great dark eyes, but said nothing.

"Wait..." the *luthia* murmured, her fingers stroking the cooling fires. They paused at the center of the battered forehead, described a sign.

For an instant, Kezzi saw it—an orb divided against itself, as if the *gadje*'s soul had been sundered, half from half.

The *luthia* breathed in, and sat back on her heels.

"We will do what may be done," she said, meeting Udari's eyes across the fire. "Kezzi, bring my bag."

· · · ✺ · · ·

The new street policy put into play by the Consolidated Bosses of Surebleak said that, if the hospital field unit came up with somebody hurt in ways that seemed to be consistent with violence, they were to call the Street Patrol. The Patrol was to relay the call to the office of the appropriate Boss, where whoever was on comm would pass it to the 'hand on watch, who would either note it, or act on it.

It was, Mike Golden admitted, more likely that such calls would be noted than acted on, given everything else that was prolly going on at the exact same minute. Boss Nova wasn't one to let any snow drift around *her*. Or her 'hands. And, the Consolidated Bosses—or, say, at least Boss Conrad—weren't no dummies. There was a safety net built into the system. The Patrol *had* to send one of theirs 'round to the hospital to have a look an' a chat. If the Patroller found something interesting, then another call would get made to the Boss.

That second call always got an answer from the Boss's household— a high level answer, too, ever since the big thinkers decided to make their lives smooth and easy by retiring the Road Boss's wife. His pregnant wife.

Yeah, Mike thought, some people were too stupid to come in outta the snow.

All that being so, he was in the kitchen, grabbing a cup of coffee and a cookie by way of soothing his hurt feelings, when Ali come in with the message.

"Three repeaters at clinic," she said. "One cut bad, one smashed nose, one broke finger."

Mike shrugged and took a bite of his cookie.

"Come in from the warehouse side," she added.

Oh, had they?

He gave Ali a nod, that being the best he could do with a mouthful of cookie, and she took herself back to the comm.

Him, he sipped his hot coffee with respect and had a minute's quiet thought.

It happened the Bosses were thinking to expand into the company warehouses, which'd been standing empty, absent the odd metal-miner, since the Company'd gone off and left their hired help to fend for themselves while the Company mined timonium in some other, less chilly locale.

Given the realities of Surebleak, you'da thought the warehouses would've been taken down to a few splinters of steel by this time, but—funny thing. They weren't. Peculiar things went on up in the warehouses; folks disappeared, or fell down so hard their brains got shook and they didn't remember quite where they'd got turned around. Didn't take much of that before the warehouses came to be avoided.

And that'd been okay, under the old ways of doin' things.

Under the new way, though...

Mike sighed.

If there was something with teeth living in the warehouses, best to know it before the Bosses sent in the work crews.

'Nother thing, too, while he was thinkin'.

The girl with the dog—Anna, if he was to believe her, which he didn't particularly—she'd pointed off north when he'd asked her where home was.

But she'd run away *east*.

Toward the warehouse district.

Mike finished his coffee and stood there in the corner of the kitchen, staring hard at nothing much.

Three bad acts coming in all banged up from outta the warehouses? One little girl an' her little dog weren't gonna be responsible for that.

Were they?

Only one way to find out, like his grandma used to say. And who knew? The repeaters might've noticed something useful.

Mike rinsed his cup and put it into the sink to be washed.

Then he went to tell Ali to call the clinic and let 'em know he was on his way over.

The Patroller was a short, slight woman with snow-blue eyes who talked off-world Terran with an accent like Boss Nova's. One of the Scouts of which they suddenly had a surplus, he figured, and gave her a nod. "Mike Golden, Boss Nova's office."

"Isphet bar'Obin," she answered. "Blair Road Patrol." She showed him the card signed by Tommy Tilden, Blair's Boss Patroller, and he nodded.

"You talk to these yoyos yet?"

"I thought it best to wait," she said, "as the Boss has an interest."

The Boss only had what he'd left her on the house noteboard, but that wasn't something Patroller bar'Obin needed to know.

"Let's see what they know, then," he said, and led the way down the short hall to the patch-up room.

There were three streeters in the big room, each at their own station; each being tended by a med tech. There were three clinic security posted at points around the occupied stations, guns and annoyance showing.

The streeters were sadly familiar: Hank Regis, with his right hand in a splint; Mort Almonte, with his nose at a funny angle; and Danny Ringrose, swearing and sweating while the tech took stitches up a long, deep cut in his arm. By rights, there should've been two more, but maybe Parfil and Dwight had gotten lucky.

Mike sighed and headed for Hank, not because he was the brightest—that'd be Danny—or the most talkative—that was Mort—but because he was the one most able to be informative at this particular point in time.

"Hey, Goldie. How's the tame streeter?"

"Healthier than you are, seems like," Mike returned, stopping a few steps short of the gurney where Hank sat, legs swinging. Mike crossed his arms over his chest.

"Yeah, well, sometimes there's accidents," Hank said. "Got any smoke, Goldie?"

"Sorry."

Hank shrugged. "Never was much use."

Mike felt Patroller bar'Obin shift at his side, but she didn't say anything, which made her brighter than Hank. On the other hand, who wasn't?

"So, what happened to your hand?"

"Broke the thumb. Damnedest thing—sure been a lesson to me."

Right.

"How'd you happen to break it?"

"Banged it against something harder than it was. Want I should show you?"

"That's okay." He jerked his head toward Mort. "How 'bout your pard, there?"

Hank snickered. "Ran into a pot."

Mort turned his head carefully and gave the three of them a glare, but didn't say anything.

"A pot?" Mike asked.

"S'right, a pot. Did a sight o'damage, that pot, but we got it settled at the end."

"Shut up, Hank." That was Danny, his voice stretched and angry.

Mike moved over to his station, leaving Hank to the Patroller, and peered over the med tech's shoulder.

"That's a nasty slice," he commented.

"Cut m'self shaving," Danny snarled. "What's up with you, Goldie?"

"Just payin' a social call. Heard you come in from the warehouses. Bosses are gonna be renovatin' there, real soon. If there's teeth—or pots—that need flushin' out first, it'd be good to know." He thought for a second, then added, "Reward for information."

The tech did something that made Danny hiss and swear, arm jerking against the webbing that held it taut.

"Stop that!" the tech snapped. "You stay still or I'll knock you out!"

"I'll stay still," Danny said through clenched teeth. "Get on with it, woman."

"Think I'm darning a sock?" she said, bending to her task again.

"So," Mike insisted, drawing Danny's attention back to him, "what's up there to look out for, Danny?"

The other man bared his teeth. "Nothing, now. We took care of 'im for ya, Goldie. Mean little sumbitch. Still breathin' when we left him, but I'm betting that didn't last long."

The tech must've hit Danny with some happy juice when he wasn't looking, Mike thought. He took a hard look at the streeter's face—white and sweaty. Might be shock—or might be fury. Whichever, maybe he'd say more.

"Where?" he asked.

"Up ta north side, two blocks in," Danny said through gritted teeth. "What's my reward, Goldie?"

"Have to see the body first," he said, tucking his hands carefully into his pockets. There was law, now. And the law said he couldn't just break Danny's neck for being a bad act and all-around nuisance. He said he'd killed somebody, but there wasn't no murder until there was a body. Mike took a breath.

"I'll get back to you," he told Danny and stepped away, gesturing to the security.

"Yessir."

"Can you keep these guys close?"

The security shrugged. "Danny ain't goin' nowhere, is my bet. Gin already hit him with a calm-down dose and she'll hit him with another one 'fore she gets done, not to say some antibiotics. That's a bad cut, like you said. She lets him outta here, it'll go septic for sure. Woman hates to see her work wasted."

Mike nodded. "Patrol can take Mort and Hank."

"I'll call 'em and set it up."

"Thanks," Mike said. "They have anything with 'em when they come in?"

"Took some things outta pockets, but I'm guessing the good stuff, if there was any, went with Dwight and Parfil."

Mike nodded. "Me and Patroller bar'Obin will wanna look at what's there."

"Sure."

Like the man'd said, there wasn't much—some coins, a snap knife with a grippy handle, a box of strike-anywheres.

Patroller bar'Obin used her chin to point at the knife.

"That is off-world," she said.

Mike nodded to show he'd heard her, though it didn't help all that much. Lately, anybody with enough money, or a light touch, could have an outworld knife.

"Do you have orders for the Patrol, Michael Golden of Boss Nova's office?"

He sighed and looked at her, seeing only a kind of smooth politeness.

"Yeah. See if you can get a line on the knife. And ask Chief Tilden to send a couple Patrollers up into the warehouses—north side, first—to see if they can find a pot—or a body."

· · · ✳ · · ·

The *gadje* breathed yet, far more than the five Udari had called. That he would continue to breathe through the night, or that he would mend—those were questions even the *luthia* could not answer.

"We will do what may be done," the *luthia* said, her bag repacked and her face pale with strain from her labors. Kezzi brought her a cup of tea, there by the hearth. Inside, Jin sat with the *gadje*, holding his undamaged hand between both of hers, so he would know, even in the depths of his coma, that he was not alone.

"Will he live?" Kezzi asked again, sitting on her heels next to the fire. For many hours, she had bound and held and snipped and washed as directed by the *luthia*. The *gadje*—he had been like a doll, smashed under a heavy, heedless boot. His right hand—the tiny bones broken like so many twigs—his ribs, his face, and things broken inside, too, so that the *luthia* had called for the Deep Healer—the first time Kezzi had ever seen this device used.

"He may live or he may not," Silain said, giving the question the only answer she would. "We have done what we are given to do. We have shown the universe that we do not willingly let him go."

A shadow moved at the edge of the fire.

"And why," asked Alosha the headman, "do we not relinquish him, O *luthia*? What do the Bedel owe this *gadje* that we will return him to life, and trust him not to betray us?"

The *luthia* looked to Kezzi. "Bring tea for the headman, small sister. And take some for yourself."

Alosha sighed, and sat at the *luthia*'s right hand, legs crossed and face weary.

"Udari's actions at the first seem sensible. A dying *gadje* at our very door! Such a thing must be removed, and quickly. The furnace was near, and certain. Child," he said, accepting the mug from Kezzi's hand.

"But does Udari of the Bedel make an end to the sad *gadje*'s pain, and afterward feed the furnace? He does not. Instead, he brings the *gadje* to Silain, our *luthia*." Alosha paused, sipped, and allowed another sigh to be heard.

"Well! Udari has a soft nature; he is devout. And we are taught that the *luthia*'s blessing is required to smooth the way to the World Unseen."

Kezzi poured the dregs of the kettle into her mug and squatted by the fire, listening.

"But does the *luthia* then release the *gadje*'s spirit into the next world? She does not. Rather, she undertakes a healing, for no reason that I can understand. *Luthia*, teach me. I ask it."

There was a small silence while Silain sipped her tea.

"There are those things which are given to the headman's authority and understanding," she said at last. "And those things which are given to the understanding and the authority of the *luthia*."

"So we are taught, and so we believe," Alosha acknowledged.

"So we are taught, and so we believe, *and so the universe is ordered*," the *luthia* said, which was the fuller answer.

She shook her hair back and looked across the fire to the headman. Kezzi could see that she smiled.

"Sleep well and dream richly, Alosha, headman of the Bedel. The universe is ordered, and all is as well as may be."

CHAPTER NINE

. . . .

"GOOD MORNING, GRANDAUNT."

Syl Vor waited just inside the door to the morning room for Grandaunt Kareen to acknowledge him. He had taken particular care with himself this morning, brushing his hair until it lay flat, and choosing for his costume a white shirt, an embroidered vest, and soft dark pants. Of course, he was too young to have formal calling clothes, but he thought he had done rather well, given the resources available to him.

Grandaunt looked up from her book, one eyebrow lifting as she surveyed him. Syl Vor raised his chin and met her eye boldly. Grandaunt did not approve of meeching manners.

"Good morning, Child Syl Vor," she said. "I hope I see you well this early in the day?"

"Indeed, I am very well," he answered, which correct response she herself had taught him. "May I hope that you are the same?"

"I enjoy my usual robust health, thank you." She closed the book and tucked it between her hip and the arm of the chair. "May I deduce from your attire that you have on purpose sought me out?"

"Yes, ma'am," he said. "I have—if you please, Grandaunt—a question of protocol."

"A *pressing* question of protocol, I apprehend. Very well, child; you have my attention. Stand forth and ask."

Thus encouraged, he came an additional six steps into the room and bowed as one grateful for a kindness.

55

"I have been reviewing the forms," he said, which was perfectly true. "And I find that I—that my understanding founders on a matter of timing." He paused, in case she wished to comment on his preface, or perhaps to praise his diligence.

Grandaunt merely moved a hand, inviting him to continue.

"I wonder, ma'am, what is the proper waiting period, when one party has said to another that a face-to-face meeting is required?"

Grandaunt Kareen considered him blandly. Syl Vor folded his hands and composed himself to wait.

"That is a question which cannot be answered before the sub-questions it spawns are properly retired." She raised her hand, thumb extended. "Are both parties on-world?"

"Yes, ma'am, they are."

Her index finger joined the thumb. "Have both parties agreed to the necessity of this meeting?"

"Yes."

Middle finger. "Is there any necessity of clan or survival which prevents one party from attending?"

This was where he had stumbled in his own analysis. Surely, if there was some danger in the city that prevented his mother from arriving home, the House would have heard—and acted. And yet, he was only just learning *melant'i* and form. There well could be some adult circumstance which was hidden from his understanding.

"I am waiting, Child Syl Vor."

He bowed.

"Forgive me, Grandaunt. There is no impediment *that I am aware of.*"

"Ah, this is the crux, is it?" Grandaunt smiled her sharp, slender smile. "If such an impediment exists, it is the duty of the impeded party to communicate this. The Code assumes that we will be observant and thoughtful, Child Syl Vor. It does not assume prescience."

Syl Vor sighed, only a very tiny sigh, but Grandaunt of course heard. Astonishingly, she did not scold him for an unbecoming display, but merely asked, "What does your analysis tell you now?"

"Three days," he said. "Unless word has been sent."

"That is correct." Grandaunt tipped her head. "Is there anything else, Child Syl Vor?"

"No. I thank you, Grandaunt; there was only that."

"Then I will regretfully bid you good morning."

He bowed, younger to elder. "Good morning, Grandaunt. Thank you."

"You are welcome. Please do me the kindness of closing the door behind you."

· · · ✳ · · ·

The *garda* had come up the street, and past three of their doors, including the door where Udari had found the dying *gadje*. Pulka, who watched the cameras one shift out of three, said that they had come to the very place where the *gadje* had lain, and placed a sniffer there on the 'crete. Had the headman's cleansing of the area been less thorough—but Alosha was never careless, and so the devices of the *garda* were confounded.

The Bedel had, for several days after, remained in *kompani*, and only Torv went to the City Above, as the eyes and ears of the Bedel. He brought back that the *garda* searched for a dead man they did not, themselves, fully believe in. They were therefore undismayed to find no trace of him. There was no lamentation in the taverns, nor notices on the message poles, as sometimes there was, asking for news of the *gadje, their gadje*. It would seem from this that he was a man alone—which was not, as Kezzi knew—a strange thing, in the City Above, though it seemed strange, indeed, to the Bedel, who were as the petals on a single flower.

Their *gadje*, since coming among them, had kept to his coma. Silain said that he healed, and it did seem to Kezzi that his fires burned a little brighter. He had many breaths now, between him and the World Unseen, like markers in a game of chance. Still, Jin said that he was frail, and that he must wake soon, for the well-being of his heart and his mind.

To that, Silain the *luthia* said again that he healed, and that he would wake when he could bear it.

Kezzi took her turn sitting at the *gadje*'s side, watching the lines that fed water and virtue directly into his veins. Now that it was less swollen, she could see that his face was comely. His hair, brushed free of blood by Jin's patient hand, was as black as her own, though it curled like a baby's, all over his head. Sometimes, it seemed that dreams took him; he would mutter, his muscles jerk, and the dark lashes flicker along his cheeks.

He never opened his eyes, though.

Kezzi wondered what would happen, when at last he did.

· · · ✳ · · ·

Syl Vor checked his bag once more. He had a positioner, in case he should become lost, and a portcomm; extra gloves; his hat; a sweater; a cereal bar; and a bottle of water. On top, where he could find it easily, was a tin of his mother's favorite tea, because one did not go on an afternoon call without bearing a gift—he had checked the forms, to be certain.

He was a little concerned, that the gift would be found insufficient, since he had simply taken it out of the pantry—*which*, he reminded himself firmly, was *not* stealing from kin, because the tea was for the use of the House.

In his pockets he had money, identification, and his folding knife. His gun was clipped to his belt, hidden beneath his jacket. Biting his lip, he tried to think if there was any other vital thing that he should have with him for this visit, until the chime of the hall clock recalled him to the passage of time.

Quickly, he sealed his jacket, put on his gloves and hat, slung the bag over his shoulder and headed for the door. The taxi would be here soon.

It would perhaps have been more seemly to have asked kin to drive him, but, once again, everyone was busy with this, or that, or another very important task, and he was reasonably certain that he had quite enough local money to pay for the taxi to and from.

He had recorded his absence and his destination in the house base, as he had promised Aunt Miri that he would do, so no one need worry that he had been lost.

He had just gained the main entrance hall when he heard the sound of rapid steps behind him.

"Syl Vor!" came the greeting, light-voiced and pleasant. "Where to in such a haste, Nephew?"

The voice belonged to Uncle Ren Zel, Aunt Anthora's lifemate. Syl Vor liked Uncle Ren Zel; he was quiet and kind and sometimes came 'round to ask Syl Vor if he would indulge him with a game of catch. Because he liked Uncle Ren Zel, Syl Vor paused, and turned—though he would have been obliged to do so in any case, he told himself sternly. He smiled, and waited, which was hard, because *surely* the taxi had arrived by now!

"Good afternoon, Uncle," he said. "I am going to town."

"Are you indeed?" Ren Zel said, with a smile. "Shall I drive you?"

"Thank you," he said politely. "I had seen on the schedule that you were with Weather Tech Brunner and did not wish to disturb you. I have called a taxi."

"Mr. Brunner can spare me for an hour, at need. But I wonder where you are bound, in the city?"

"I am going to see my mother," Syl Vor said. "I am quite well prepared. I have my gun, and my little knife, and extra warm clothes, and fare both ways."

"I would call that well prepared, indeed. Does Nova expect you?"

"I'm certain that she must." Syl Vor looked at the door. "If you please, Uncle—the taxi."

"The taxi has been canceled," Aunt Anthora said, stepping out of the service hall. "Jeeves heard your call and alerted us." She gave Uncle Ren Zel a smile. "Good afternoon, love."

"Good afternoon," he answered, taking her hand. "I see that he does need to go to town," he murmured.

"Do you? Then go he shall."

Uncle Ren Zel laughed his soft, pretty laugh. "As simple as that? But, you know, I have no notion *why*."

"I have to see my mother," Syl Vor said sternly, "on a matter of importance to us both."

Aunt Anthora looked down at him, her face perfectly serious, though there were smile-crinkles at the sides of her silver eyes.

"There you are," she said. "What could be more compelling?"

"If you have a moment for Tech Brunner, I will drive Syl Vor," said Uncle Ren Zel.

"To Nova?" asked Aunt Anthora. "Given the mood in which she is likely to receive you? No, better that I go, I think, and you to return to our weatherman." She leaned over and kissed him on the mouth. "I will be very careful," she murmured, "and pay close attention to everything."

Uncle Ren Zel laughed again, and turned to Syl Vor.

"It is decided, then, you see, Nephew? Your aunt will drive you to the city and wait upon your return. Please give your mother my wish that I may see her again—soon."

"I will," said Syl Vor, while Aunt Anthora danced over to the console and pressed the button, asking that Jeeves send a car around, because she and Syl Vor were driving into the city.

· · · ❋ · · ·

The air was cool, here on the mountain, among the vines; his breath frosted against the dangling shoots. Time, now, to cut the old wood back, to make room for the fruits of the coming season.

He had his clippers in one hand, the other feeling among the tendrils for the hard bark. That hand ached, but, then, he had been at work since the first ray of daylight had threaded the gap between the twin hills.

It was quiet on the mountain. He had come out, shears in hand, early and alone, to the row that had been his to tend. One more time, before he was set a new duty. The season was too early for insects—those would come with the heat—and the few birds that graced the sky were predators, on the hunt for mouse and vole.

That's what he thought they were, the shadow of a predator's wings flickering over the vines—so common a thing that he never bothered to raise his head.

Fwump!

The sound brought him 'round in the instant before the blast rocked the mountain, and a burst of wind and debris slammed him back into the trellis. He fell, rolled, scrambled to his feet—and stood staring down the mountain, at the billow of greasy smoke from the crater where his clanhouse had been.

· · · ❊ · · ·

The *gadje* screamed, muscles spasming. He jerked again, with intent—trying to sit up, endangering himself and the lines into his veins. Kezzi snatched his shoulders and bore down.

"Peace!" she gasped. "*Gadje*, be still!"

He screamed again, shrill and hopeless, twisting in her grasp. Small as he was, he was bigger than her, though made weak by his wounds, and whatever terrible thing held him in his dream. Kezzi was able to put his shoulders against the bed and hold him there. He sobbed now, moving his head from side to side.

"Peace, *peace, gadje*," she said again. "You will break yourself!"

"Let him sit up, small sister, if he wishes." Silain the *luthia* slid next to the bed, slipping her arm beneath the *gadje*'s shoulders. Kezzi leaned back, slowly releasing him, but he made no move to twist away. He lay in Silain's arms, chest heaving with his sobs.

"Peace, peace, small one," the *luthia* murmured in the language they spoke in the City Above, and as if the *gadje* were Smaller, even, than Kezzi. "It is well. Only open your eyes, foolish boy, and see that it's true."

Her words seemed to calm him, so that he rested, his face wet, shivering now, as if his terror had burned out his poor reserves of energy. Then, his chest lifted. He gave a great, shuddering sigh.

And the *gadje* opened his eyes.

They were as black as his hair—as black as Bedel eyes. His gaze was wide and soft, as if he stared into the World Not-Yet.

He turned his head slightly, so that he might look upon Silain's face.

"That is well," she said, even as his breath caught again.

His shattered hand twitched, but the board it was strapped to was too heavy for him to lift.

"*Thawlana?*" he whispered, which was not a word that Kezzi knew.

Silain smiled and answered gently in what might be the same strange tongue. She lifted her free hand and stroked the tumbled curls from his forehead.

The *gadje* closed his eyes, relaxing so completely that Kezzi cried out, thinking that he had left them for the World Unseen.

"Peace," the *luthia* told her. "He only sleeps again. Fetch another blanket, small sister—he shivers. When that is done, you and Malda may go for a run. I will watch here."

Kezzi rose, fetched the blanket and tucked it 'round the *gadje*. On the edge of snapping her fingers for Malda, however, she hesitated.

"*Luthia?*"

"Yes, my sister?"

"What passed between you?"

"Ah." Silain smiled and extended a hand again to stroke the *gadje*'s hair. "He recognized me as *grandmother—thawlana*, that is, in one of the *gadje* tongues."

It was true, Kezzi thought, that the *luthia* was the grandmother of the Bedel, who kept the stories and the dreams and who cared for them all. Even a *gadje* must know that much.

"To him I said that I was indeed the grandmother, and that he might leave his safety in my hands."

And thus assured, Kezzi thought, the *gadje* slept easy. As would anyone.

"Thank you," she said. "Is this tongue a thing that I might dream?"

The *luthia* moved her hand, not quite a full denial. "Not yet, I think, little sister. It is a large dream, and must wait until you have dreamed others, to hold it in place."

She had, Kezzi admitted, thought that might be so. Though she spoke the language of the Bedel and the *gadje* tongue—she had spoken both from her first words, learning from Vylet and Droi. To dream a language—that she had not done, and well she could believe that it was a big dream.

"Would you like a cup of tea before Malda and I go?" she asked.

"That is a kindly thought, little sister. I believe I am well enough for this time. Go, now—you have not run in days!"

That was true enough.

Kezzi snapped her fingers for Malda and ran off across the common.

CHAPTER TEN

· ·

THE DOORBELL RANG WHILE NOVA WAS WITH BOSS SCHROEDER.

She had been with Boss Shroeder for some time, and heartily wished him at the devil, though of course it would never do to let him know that. Tedious as he was, they—which was to say, Surebleak *and* Korval—needed his willing support of both the consolidated school and the increased levels of patrol on the streets.

His complaint today was the consolidated school. One gathered that he had visited Penn Kalhoon, the second ranking Boss on the Council, at breakfast, on the subject of the patrols. Nova supposed she should be grateful for small favors; at least she had enjoyed a pleasantly solitary breakfast.

The security arrangements, in particular, were the object of Boss Schroeder's concern today. The Big Boss, he said, with, unfortunately, perfect justice, hadn't had much luck keeping the building from getting holes in it. How did he intend to protect the children from eight different territories?

There was of course the plan that had always been in place, that the school accept a security perimeter, in order to discourage those who saw opportunity in the gathering of children from those eight different territories. Within the school, it would fall to the teachers to plant the seeds of collegiality. Happily, they were well supplied with teachers in the form of the ubiquitous Scouts, who were also well suited to protecting those placed under their care.

Nova said these things to Boss Shroeder, who found it amusing to be kittenish, though he had previously signed a contract guaranteeing support of the school, and the security perimeter—and also to send those on his street who were in need or want of a basic education to the school.

"Well, I guess you got it all thought out, then. I'll be wanting a look at that perimeter an' those 'rangemints of yours."

At last! Nova thought. The point was hers.

She inclined her head gravely.

"Of course. We welcome such inspections from all the Bosses, and hope that you will not hold shy of giving us advice, or pointing out any inadequacy in the arrangements. It is the goal to provide a place of safety where all may learn together."

He took a breath and her heart sank. Had he found another objection?

But no. He merely sighed, and put his hands on the arms of the chair, pushing himself unceremoniously to his feet.

"Right, then. You keep me posted. An' remember! You ain't getting one kid from my turf in that place 'til I'm satisfied with the security."

"I understand completely," she said, rising and holding out her hand.

He stared down at it for a moment, as if perhaps considering the consequences of refusing to shake her hand. Nova experienced a flash of empathy. She would herself prefer that they exchange cordial bows and have done, but to shake hands was Surebleak's custom.

Custom won, as it so often did. Schroeder gripped her hand tightly, jerked it up and down, and turned away.

Nova touched the button on her desk, then stepped 'round it, wondering if she should attempt to gain the Boss's side, or if it would be seen as something other than a courtesy.

She hesitated, and the door opened to admit Veeno, who took charge of showing the Boss out.

At last, she sighed, and allowed her shoulders to sag while she reviewed the mental exercise known as Pilot's Peace, which returned emotional balance and relaxed one who had been sorely tried.

Refreshed, she continued across the room to the table, and pressed the back of her hand against the teapot—cold, of course. She sighed and went back to her desk.

Scarcely was she seated than the door opened again, admitting Veeno, looking, Nova thought, rather more amused than one might expect of a woman who had just escorted Boss Shroeder to the door.

"Couple here to see you, Boss," she said.

Nova eyed her sternly. Yes, definitely amused. How delightful that one's staff was happy in their work.

"Has the couple a name or two between them, I wonder? Did they state their business?"

Veeno actually grinned.

"I was told to say 'the demands of kin must be honored.'"

Nova closed her eyes, briefly. Such a message held the tang of Kareen yos'Phelium, whose manners were high, even on Liad. On Surebleak...

...and yet, it was true, whether on Liad, Surebleak or on *Dutiful Passage*, Jumping between the stars—the demands of kin *must* be honored. That one statement was the very basis of clan. If they lost that, they would lose Korval—which was to say that they would lose themselves.

She waved a hand wearily.

"Please, show the couple in, Ms. Veeno. And ask the kitchen to send a fresh pot of tea."

"Yes, ma'am." Veeno stepped over to the table, picked up the tray bearing teapot and cups and swooped out of the room.

Nova closed her eyes again, deliberately emptied her mind, and drew three deep, calming breaths.

She heard the latch work, opened her eyes and stood, turning toward the door with her face properly composed, determined to meet her kinswoman cordially.

"Good-day, Sister! I hope I find you well?"

Only the exercise of the very sternest control kept Nova's jaw from dropping. Of all possible authors of that stiff reminder of duty, she had never supposed that it might be—

"Anthora!"

Her sister smiled sweetly. "Exactly—*Anthora*. And I am very pleased to see you after so long a separation." She tipped her head, silver eyes unwontedly serious. "You ought to come home for a day or two, Nova. You're tired."

"Is that an official diagnosis, *dramliza*?" That was said too sharply, and only proved Anthora's point for her.

"At the moment," her sister said, allowing her lack of return heat to say all, "it is merely sisterly concern."

Nova sighed and waved toward the table.

"Sit, do. Veeno is bringing—stay."

Anthora froze in mid-step—a foolishness Nova did not dignify with either a smile or a frown.

"Veeno had said that a *couple* had stopped to see me. Is your lifemate with you? By all means, bid him enter—I engage not to eat him."

"Alas, as much as he wished to come himself, Ren Zel was occupied with Mr. Brunner and the weather satellites." Anthora completed her step and continued to the desk.

"We are all of us busy, Sister," she said, slipping into the seat lately occupied by Boss Shroeder.

"Busy." Nova shook her head. "One might say, *busy*." Indeed, they were *all* of them exhausted in the face of Surebleak's many necessities. Her office owed its existence to the rise of tasks facing Pat Rin and his staff. Overflow control.

"At some point the tide must turn," she said, taking her chair. "The committees and the patrols and the offices of this and that will begin to take up their functions—"

"—freeing the Bosses to be busy, but not so busy that they forget the care of clan and kin."

"Which brings us full circle. What does kin demand of me?"

"I will allow Syl Vor the honor of explaining that himself—in a moment. First—and I speak now as *dramliza*, as aunt, and as sister—Syl Vor is not, let us say, a *little boy*."

Nova inclined her head. "Runig's Rock has taken a toll—that, yes, I had seen. I had thought, perhaps, a fostering, but I cannot find it eligible, Sister! Korval has always been risky to know. To be an ally of the Dragon in these times is to be in active danger."

"That is so. And, yet, he desires—I will say, he *needs* others of his own temper about him. The loss of his cousins to their duty— that was a blow. He takes refuge in proper behavior, which is... exemplary, of course..."

"But a child," Nova said, echoing Michael Golden, "needs to play."

"Just so. Now, I will tell you one more thing, and then I will exchange places with my nephew in the parlor. Ren Zel has said that Syl Vor *must* come to town."

This had weight, considering how far and how strange was Ren Zel's sight. Nova sighed.

"Was it given to him to know *why*?"

Anthora laughed. "When was any gift of the *dramliz* as convenient as that? Allow it to be a measure of his certainty, that he had volunteered to bring Syl Vor to you himself."

Nova blinked, then chuckled. "Poor man. You must tell me what I may do to make him less chary of me."

"I think that familiarity will do the deed," Anthora said placidly. "Only give him a dozen years. Or two."

· · · ✺ · · ·

"Hot tea for the Boss an' her visitor," Veeno said to Beck, putting the tray down on the side counter. "An' a glass of juice with some sweet thing if you got it."

Mike Golden, who was putting his lunch bowl in the sink to be washed, looked 'round, interested.

"That's another tray?"

Veeno gave him a nod. "Little kid in the waitin' room. Looks like a cookie'd cheer 'im up."

Really? That wasn't bidness like normal. Streeters kept their kids away from the Bosses, and with good reason. Other Bosses did the same, for even better reasons.

"Who's with the Boss?" he asked Veeno.

"Anthora yos'Galan. On the Undertree List."

Boss's sister, that was. Mike nodded. "Who's the kid?"

Veeno shrugged. "Didn't say. Figured he rode on her ticket."

He nodded. "Set up another glass on the cookie tray, willya, Beck? I'll take it along to the kid. Keep 'im company."

Beck nodded and looked over her shoulder to Veeno.

"You'd best get back on door. Gavit'll take the tray in when the pot's ready." She slid some seed cookies onto a tray with a beaker of redjuice and a couple plastic cups. "Here go, Mike. Ain't got no proper sweet for the boy."

"A plate of your seed cookies? I'd call that a proper sweet!" he said bracingly.

Beck laughed and slapped him on the arm. "You ain't no little boy, neither. Get outta my kitchen, now!"

"I'm gone," he said—and was.

· · · ✺ · · ·

Syl Vor had chosen a chair with a good view of the doorway and the hall beyond without being directly in the line of sight of someone walking down the hall. The chair he chose was too tall for him, but so were all the chairs.

He had put his pack on the floor next to him, first retrieving the tea tin. It was warm in the little parlor, and he thought about taking his jacket off, but he didn't know the house rules regarding guns. He didn't want to offend his mother's staff, but he found that he didn't care for the idea of being unarmed, either. As a compromise, he unsealed his jacket, making sure that the gun was accessible without necessarily being visible.

That done, he composed himself to wait, tea tin on his knee.

Aunt Anthora had gone ahead to his mother; she had asked him particularly if she might do so, and of course he had said yes. It was a reasonable request, and anyway, he was a child and she outranked him.

Someone passed in the hallway, shadow preceding her—the stern woman who had opened the door to them, shown them to this room, and taken Aunt Anthora to Mother. She was carrying a tea tray, and she did not look into his parlor.

This seemed a rather quiet house, Syl Vor thought—at least, it seemed so *now*. The dozen chairs in this waiting parlor might sometimes be full of people wanting to see his mother, who was *Boss Nova*, and who had agreed to solve for those of Surebleak who had no *delm* to solve for them.

He wasn't *exactly* sure how it had fallen to those of Korval to solve for—well, for all the world. His tutor, unforthcoming as she usually was on matters of Surebleak, had been adamant upon this point—*no one* native to Surebleak belonged to a clan or had anyone but themselves to solve for them, or remind them of the forms, or—or to guard their sleep so that enemies did not fall on them unaware.

That, in Syl Vor's opinion, was a very bad state of affairs and right it had been of Cousin Pat Rin—for it was Cousin Pat Rin who had brought this work to the clan—to take Surebleak in hand.

Except . . . Cousin Pat Rin had perhaps not *quite* understood how much solving was needed. Maybe, Syl Vor thought, a few of the Surebleak people could be taught to solve, too, and then his mother would not be too busy to come home.

Another shadow moved in the hall, accompanied by firm steps. Not his mother nor Aunt Anthora, nor the lady who had opened to them.

Syl Vor sat up straighter in his chair and slid his gun hand down his thigh.

The steps slowed, the shadow wavered and vanished behind a dark-haired man carrying a tray. He gave Syl Vor a smile and a nod.

"Afternoon. Ms. Veeno thought you might like a snack an' some company."

Syl Vor relaxed, for here was no threat, but merely the courtesy of the house.

"Thank you," he said, in his careful Terran. "A glass of juice would be most welcome." He scooched forward in the chair until he could slide off the edge and onto his feet. The edge of his jacket caught on the wood and dragged open. He snatched it closed with a quick look, but the man was busy with the tray.

He put the tea tin on the chair seat and approached the table.

"I am Syl Vor yos'Galan," he said, courteous and proper, as Terran custom did not consider clan affiliation to be part of one's name.

The man looked up, brown eyes bright. "Silver, is it?" he said interestedly. "Now there's a pairing you don't get every day. I'm Golden myself. Mike Golden."

Syl Vor blinked, the Terran words for a moment swirling out of sense—and then he blinked again, rehearing what the man had said, seeing the hint of a smile at the edge of the big mouth.

"Was that a joke?" he asked sternly.

The smile got wider. "Quicker'n your ma, there," he said. "Yep, it was; I'm a sucker for a joke, myself."

"It was not a very *good* joke," Syl Vor told him. "My name is not *silver*. Silver is a trade metal."

"Well, so's gold, last I knew about it. Now, something else you'll want to know is I'm your ma's 'hand, which means I got her back—an' yours, too. So favor me by puttin' the safety on that pistol."

Oh. Mike Golden had quick eyes.

"The safety is on," Syl Vor told him. "I wanted the gun close."

"Can't fault a man for wantin' his protection to hand. Your ma, she don't like for there to be disorder in the house, and we try to keep it like she wants. Mostly, we keep it *zackly* like she wants, no worries. Sometimes things slip, though, so it's good to be prepared." He picked up the beaker of redjuice.

"You know about town hospitality?" he asked.

Syl Vor frowned. "No . . . ?"

Mike Golden nodded. "Here's how we do it. I'm gonna pour both glasses from this same jug here, see? An' then I'm gonna drink first, to show there's nothing wrong with the juice. Then I'll have a bite outta one of Beck's special cookies. After that's finished with, an' assuming I don't fall down, then you can go ahead and drink, and have as many cookies as you want. Got that?"

Syl Vor considered the form, chewing his lip. It was not dissimilar, he thought, to one of the Visiting Rules Grandaunt had taught him from the Code.

"Is this the rule for all houses," he asked, "or this house only?"

Mike Golden smiled as if he had been particularly clever. "Sharp as a tack," he said. "That's the rule for all Surebleak houses, Silver. If somebody wants you to drink, and they ain't doing the same, or if they bring you a glass already full from somewhere else—don't you touch it, and get outta there as fast as you can."

Yes, *very* like that particular Visiting Rule. Syl Vor inclined his head. "I understand. Thank you, Mr. Golden."

"Mike—you call me Mike. Now, here."

He poured juice into a glass, raised it and took a long draught. Then he picked up a cookie and bit into it with evident enjoyment. Syl Vor waited for the count of twelve. Mike Golden did not fall down.

"Now, you," he said, and filled the second glass with redjuice.

Syl Vor drank with satisfaction.

"That is good," he said. "Boss Sherton sends to us redjuice at House." He frowned at his error, and looked up into the man's face. "Your pardon. I mean to say that Boss Sherton *sends the House* redjuice."

"That's okay," Mike Golden said. "I gotcher meaning."

"Yes, but I must speak properly."

"My grandma Dorrie used to say the same thing to me, then give me a swat upside the head so I'd remember it." Mike Golden bit into his cookie and gave Syl Vor a sideways look. "Maybe you got a grandma yourself?"

"I have a grandaunt," Syl Vor said. "Her method is . . . similar."

Mike Golden laughed. "I bet it is. So, if you don't mind my askin', what brings you to town?"

The cookies were very good. Syl Vor chose a second one.

"I must talk to my mother about...having work. Except for the twins—and they are *babies*!—I am the only one who has no work. I thought, there is so much, here in the town, that my mother and—that my mother comes home very seldom. If I could help her, then she could come home more often, and I would be...of use."

Mike Golden blinked.

"Of use—well, sure. We all wanna be of use. An' y'know—I got a thought. Let me lay it out for you and you see what you think..."

CHAPTER ELEVEN

KEZZI AND MALDA RACED UP THE RAMP TO THE GREEN GARDEN, the little dog yapping with excitement when she reached into her pocket and pulled out his ball. Laughing, she threw it toward the service apron, not into the garden. The last time Memit had caught them playing in the garden, she had boxed Kezzi's ears, and spoken so sternly to Malda that he had crouched at her feet with his ears wilted and his nose between his front paws. Worse, Memit had then claimed Kezzi for a week of extra work, weeding, trimming back, and digging.

Normally, Kezzi liked taking her work-turn in the garden. That week, though, Memit had a Teaching to deliver, and she went at it with such a will that Kezzi's back ached for days after the work was done, and her fingers were so stiff she could barely hold the deck, much less spread a fan. Then Vylet had been angry with her, and Kezzi had gone to visit the *luthia*, who gave her a liniment, and asked what she had learned.

"I learned not to throw Malda's ball in the garden when Memit is watching," she had answered bitterly.

The *luthia* had laughed and said, "Well, that is one thing! Dream on it, little sister, and come to me on the morning after the next one. We will drink tea together."

That had been how she had become Silain's student, so there was some good out of Memit's spite.

And Kezzi took care not to throw Malda's ball in the garden, ever again.

She made the top of the ramp, and here was Malda trotting proudly toward her, head high and stubby tail wagging, the blue ball in his mouth.

"Bold Malda!" Kezzi cried. "Swift Malda! Bring it, now, and make a gift."

The little dog pranced up to her, bowed, and placed the ball between Kezzi's feet.

"Well done," she said, rubbing his ears. She picked up the ball, and he leapt high into the air, ran three steps out, spun in a tight circle, and rose onto his hind legs with a yip that urged her to *throw*.

Throw she did, and ran after she had thrown, so that by the time they had raced the length of the service apron three times, she and Malda were panting alike.

"One more," she said, "then we must find Vylet."

She picked up the ball and threw with more strength than she had intended. The ball bounced once and disappeared into the mouth of a service tunnel, Malda in hot pursuit.

"Malda!" Kezzi pelted after, stopping at the edge of the tunnel and peering into the blackness beyond. *That* was strange—twice strange. Not only were the tunnels usually closed with flexwire, but they were lit by the glow strips running down the middle of the floor and ceiling. The strips in this tunnel were as black as the walls.

"Malda!" she called again, reaching into her pocket. She heard a scrabbling sound, like a dog's claws on the stone flooring.

Her fingers found the cool cylinder of the flash; she pulled it out and pressed the stud, waking a beam of light.

It was only a small light against a large darkness. Still, it preceded Kezzi by three steps, so she went carefully forward.

The scrabbling came again.

Kezzi stopped and snapped her fingers. "Malda! Come!"

The answer to this was a yip, and a silence long enough for Kezzi to walk nine more steps into the tunnel. She bit her lip. To leave Malda in the tunnel—that she could not do. There were rats in the tunnels, and other strange creatures, who would find one small dog just good enough for dinner.

Thinking of those other creatures, she was afraid—and that she mustn't be. To bring Malda back to her, she had to sound strong and stern, like she was a dog so big Malda would think of nothing but doing exactly what that big dog wanted him to do. Also, she needed to be so big and so strong that those other creatures would think very hard about showing themselves.

Kezzi took a deep breath, held it—and heard the scrabbling again, louder and faster this time, moving not down the tunnel—

But up.

She swung to the side, keeping the light focused on the tunnel floor. The noise grew louder, and suddenly through the little splinter of light raced a low grey animal pursued by a black-and-tan dog not much larger.

Claws scraping the stone, they ran past, toward the light at the end of the tunnel. Kezzi thrust the flash into her pocket and ran after.

The rat skidded to a halt, as if the light of the open garden hurt its eyes. Malda never paused, but rushed forward, grabbed the rat by the back of the neck, snapped it left, snapped it right—and dropped it, limp and unmoving, to the floor.

Kezzi swallowed, and went forward, pulling her knife out of her belt. She held it ready, just in case—but Malda's kill had been true.

She took a breath then, and forced herself to smile.

"Good Malda!" she said. "Brave hunter!" She snapped her fingers and Malda left his prize to come forward and have his ears rubbed.

"Good dog, brave dog. Truly, you are of the Bedel! Come, now, follow!"

She moved off at a trot across the service apron. Malda hesitated, looking back at the dead rat. Kezzi snapped her fingers again—and the little dog ran after her.

There was a speaker in the wall of the garden, just beyond the fruiting trees. From it, Kezzi could call the gate-watch. A rat in the tunnel so near to the garden, that was bad. She was sad, for a moment, remembering that Malda's ball was lost to the tunnel, then shrugged. She would go out into the City Above tomorrow, and get another one.

· · · ❖ · · ·

Syl Vor bowed to his mother's honor, and straightened, holding the tea tin tight in both hands. He dared a glance at her face from beneath his lashes, so he saw that she was not frowning. That was, he told himself, well.

She was not smiling, either, but his mother did not smile nearly so often as Aunt Anthora or Uncle Shan. And never so easily as Grandfather Luken. It was a prize, his mother's smile. A treasure, and not given lightly.

"My son," she said now. "I am pleased to see you."

Pleased. He relaxed somewhat.

"Did you not," she asked, "*expect* me to be pleased?"

Syl Vor met her eyes. "I had thought—surprised, ma'am."

"Ah." Her mouth softened—not quite a smile, but definitely not a frown. "I believe the point is yours. I am also surprised." She moved a hand, showing him the table, and the teapot. "Please, make yourself at ease."

"Thank you," he said, bowed again—too rapidly, because he had forgotten!

Straightening, he held the tea tin out across both palms.

"I bring a gift of your favored leaf," he said, careful of his mode. "I hope that it pleases."

Her mouth tightened—again, not a frown—and she stepped forward to receive the tin, and to spend a moment regarding its label.

"The gift pleases," she said then. "It is kind of you to recall. Now, my child—sit."

He'd left his pack with Aunt Anthora and Mike Golden in the waiting parlor, but he still wore his jacket. His mother did not seem to notice this, and he sat down at the table feeling both nervous and relieved.

His mother sat in the chair opposite him, placing the tea tin carefully to her right. Syl Vor sighed. Where Aunt Anthora was round and dark, his mother was slim and pale. She had been counted a beauty, so Padi had told him, back ho— on Liad, and added that he looked exactly like her.

That was a piece of Padi's foolery, and it had made him laugh.

"Before we begin, my child, you must allow me to beg your pardon. When I had suggested that we speak face to face, I had not intended to—put you aside, or to belittle your concerns in any way."

"I had thought you were busy in the town," Syl Vor said, "which is why I came to you." He hesitated. "Mike Golden said that you've been running as fast as you can, just to stay in one place."

"An apt man with a phrase, is Mr. Golden. Indeed, it has been precisely so."

"His jokes aren't very good."

His mother raised her eyebrows. "Of that, I fear I am no judge. And I am again remiss. May I pour you a cup of tea, Syl Vorson? Will you have cake? A sandwich, perhaps?"

"I had redjuice and cookies with Mike Golden just now," he said, then added hastily, as he recalled his manners, "A cup of tea would be welcome."

His mother poured, and they both sipped, to show, as Grandaunt had taught him, goodwill. Syl Vor put his cup down, and his mother lowered hers.

"Now," she said, "how may I serve you?"

"It is I who can perhaps serve you," he said. "I would like to go to school, here in the city."

His mother's mouth dropped open. He had never seen that happen before, and what it might portend, he could not say. Hastily, in case he had overstepped in a way that Mike Golden had not predicted, Syl Vor added—"Or I might help Mr. Shaper paint his barn."

"Mr. Shaper..." His mother closed her eyes for the count of six, and opened them to gaze at him sternly.

"Mr. Shaper does not always...enjoy company," she said. "I hope that he has not come to regret us as neighbors."

Syl Vor thought about that.

"I think...not?" he said carefully. "He seems to sincerely regard Granduncle Daav. When I met him, he proposed that I help him plant the spring seedlings, and—and declared to Diglon that I had been of use. It was he who said that I might come again, and that the barn wanted paint."

"I see..." His mother sighed. "Let us place Mr. Shaper's barn to one side for the moment. This other proposition—that you attend school here in town. Do your tutors bore you, my son?"

Syl Vor shook his head—bit his lip and slanted a glance to his mother, who was merely watching him as one awaiting an answer to a question.

"If I am bored, Mother, it would be wrong of me to blame my teachers." He paused. This had to be treated with care. He did not wish to cost either of his tutors their positions, though he thought that Ms. ker'Eklis would not be sorry to leave Surebleak.

"I had not thought of the school—I did not know there was a school here, until Mike Golden told me about it. He said that some of the Bosses are...concerned for the safety of their heirs. If I attended, he said, then it would make your work easier, because—"

He stopped, because his mother had risen and gone over to her desk, where she pressed what must have been a key on a comm unit.

"Mr. Golden?" Her voice was perfectly level.

"Yes, ma'am?"

"I wonder if you might join me and my son in my office."

"Is there a problem, ma'am?"

"Why no, Mr. Golden—why would you think there was a problem? Merely, I wish that you will explain the process of your thought."

There was a small sound that might, Syl Vor thought, have been a chuckle, then came Mike Golden's voice once more.

"I'll be right in, ma'am."

· · · ※ · · ·

"If the *gadje* is in a hurry," Vylet said, the cards twinkling between her dark fingers like stars, "then offer the one-draw. Like this." The deck vanished into one palm and appeared again in a wide fan between both hands.

"One card, to know what the rest of the day will bring?" she asked the pretend *gadje* they practiced upon. When she spoke to the *gadje*, her voice was husky and low, not at all like her normal voice. That was part of the *fleez*—the voice, the cards, the hat or scarf half over the face, like *so*, to make it harder to judge an age; the way to stand—shoulders round, head cocked to a side, like an old, wise bird.

"Pull one—just one—the card that speaks to you," Vylet continued, pushing the fan toward the pretended *gadje*. "Draw it, show it. I will tell you what it means."

The pretend *gadje* drew a card, as instructed. Vylet let her eyes widen, and dropped her voice, so that the *gadje* would need to draw close, to hear.

"You draw the double moons!" Vylet whispered huskily, and then, in her normal voice, asked, "What do the two moons mean, Kezzi?"

"Good dinner and a dry place to sleep," Kezzi recited impatiently, and sighed. "Why do we care what the cards *mean*," she asked, "when it is only for the *gadje*?"

Vylet stood up straight and closed the deck with a *snap*.

"It matters because it is the *art*," she said sternly. "The art must be true."

"Even the art we make for the *gadje*?" Kezzi asked.

"Art must always be true," Droi said from her place by the lamp, where she was mending a torn finger on her glove. She looked up and gave Vylet the particular stare that meant she should listen, too.

"Our smallest sister asks well. We lie to the *gadje* in every-thing else, why say the true meaning of the cards they draw? It is wasted—the memorizing, and the art. Isn't it?"

She looked from one to the other. Vylet made no answer, but Kezzi crossed the room and knelt a little behind Droi, so as not to block her light.

"I know the cards don't see," she said, carefully, because Droi was what the Bedel call *vey*—not blind, as the *gadje* were blind; not sighted as the *luthia*—or even Udari. Droi—Droi saw *some*-thing, and sometimes the things she saw made her angry. She had shared a promise with Vanzin, until she saw *some*thing in the shadows, which had made her draw her knife to cut him.

"The cards don't see," Vylet agreed, dropping to her knees a prudent distance from Droi's needle. "There is no power in the cards. The cards are therefore not for the Bedel, who have no need."

This was all True Saying, and Droi rocked as she stitched, in agreement.

"Chief among those things that the Bedel do not need," she said, "is to be *caught*. The *gadje* do not like to be tricked. Tell me this, little sister: Suppose you had the reading of the cards in the City Above tomorrow. One came and took the single—the twin moons, as Vylet's *gadje* did just now. And you say to them, 'Oh, the double moons! You must watch behind, and count what money you are given three times!'"

"I suppose this," Kezzi said. "And then?"

"And then, two days later, or three, a *gadje* draws the one card, and shows the twin moons. This time, you cry out, 'You are two times fortunate! Today you will eat well and have a dry place to sleep!'"

"I suppose this also," said Kezzi.

"Hah. And then the *gadje* says to you, 'But two days ago, when I drew this same card, you foretold a day of danger!'"

"And then," said Vylet, "the *gadje* grabs you, or dashes the cards down—"

"Or beats you and cuts off your hair, as happened to Riva, who never could keep her cards straight."

Kezzi's stomach clenched. "I don't know this story."

"It happened long ago," Vylet said.

"She died of shame," Droi said, "before any of us was born."

An old tale, then; Kezzi would ask Silain for the whole of it.

"So you see, little sister." Droi looked over her shoulder and caught Kezzi's eye, her own darkly glittering. "We memorize the cards and their meanings for our own protection from the *gadje*, the same as we learn three different routes to each of our doors, and how to throw a knife."

"I understand," Kezzi said, making a promise to herself that she would never be careless with her cards. "Thank you, elder sister."

"The question was well asked," Droi said, and quoted, "Who is old enough to ask, is old enough to know."

· · · ✴ · · ·

Michael Golden arrived, trailing Anthora.

"I think it an excellent notion," that lady announced, not entirely to Nova's surprise. "If Syl Vor likes it." She slanted a mischievous glance in that young gentleman's direction. "Of course, you will still need to have your tutors, so that you do not fall behind, Nephew."

That was rather more sense than Nova was used to having from her youngest sister—truly, her lifemating had steadied her marvelously.

Syl Vor nodded in his solemn way—too solemn for a boy of his years—and looked over to Michael Golden, the rogue.

"I wonder what I would be set to learn, at the school," he said. "If I am only to be a-an *example*, then that might make trouble, instead of ease."

Nova stared. What in the name of the gods had Kareen been teaching the children under her care at Runig's Rock?

"That's a good analysis," Michael Golden said, as serious as she had ever heard him. "Being as there's not anybody on exactly the same level at the school, everybody winds up pitching in to help everybody else. So, one thing you would prolly do is help others who might be older'n you, but ain't so good at, say, reading. 'Nother thing is local history and such, which you might not've had any of. Street geography. 'Rithmetic. Cookin'. There's some. Ms. Taylor was telling me t'other day that she was starting up a Recent Events class, to follow the new rules and committees and such that the Council of Bosses makes. Make sense to you?"

"Yes." Syl Vor was more animated now, leaning forward. "I can be of use."

"Right you are, an' in more ways than one."

"And security?" Nova asked. "Mr. Golden, can staff accommodate an extra prime?"

"Got no reason to doubt it," he said, turning to her. "I'll talk to 'em, and if there's any concern, I'll take care of it. Only thing I would need from you, Silver, is—"

"One moment," Nova interrupted. "Mr. Golden, my son's name—"

"It's his joke," that same son said, astonishingly. "It isn't very good, but I don't mind it."

Well. She inclined her head. "Certainly, you may decide what names are acceptable to you," she said. "Continue, Mr. Golden."

"Yes, ma'am. What I need from you, Silver, in order to make this work, and without puttin' too much strain on your ma, or on staff, or on me, is a promise that you'll be no more trouble than you absolutely gotta be. What's that you call it—necessary?"

"Necessity," Anthora murmured, and glanced to Nova. "I approve of Mr. Golden," she said.

"Perhaps you should tell him so," Nova answered cordially, and had the satisfaction of seeing that gentleman's cheeks darken somewhat.

"I promise to be very little trouble," Syl Vor said, which as promises went was, Nova admitted, very handsome, though it lacked context.

"I would say, 'as Korval recognizes trouble,' my son, else you will lead Mr. Golden to believe something far other than you—or I—may guarantee."

"I'll take that," said her henchman. "Details to be worked out as they come up. In the meantime, ma'am, I'd recommend the back left for Silver's room—'s'got that little extra jig where he can set up a desk and work with his tutors."

Nova considered that. The room in question had what she thought of as a quarter-room extra—the result of bad design, or an artifact of a previous owner's attempt at renovation. Whichever, it would do very well for a classroom.

She nodded. "There does, however, remain one more thing to be done before Syl Vor moves out of the nursery and takes up employment as Mr. Golden's agent in place."

There was a small silence, even Anthora sitting with head cocked, as if she had no faintest idea of what Nova could be speaking.

"The *delm*," Syl Vor said, then. "We need to ask Korval's permission."

"Just so." Nova rose and looked to her sister. "Let me get my coat," she said, "and we can drive...home...together."

CHAPTER TWELVE

. . . .

"WELL, NOW, RIVA. THAT'S A TALE, SO IT IS." SILAIN HELD OUT her mug and Kezzi filled it with tea before filling her own.

"By the starry garters of the night . . . Riva." Silain looked into the depths of her mug, like the tea was a window and beyond it she watched the story unfold.

In fact, Kezzi thought, talking out a thing that had been dreamed *did* feel like someone else was using your voice, your breath, while you sat near the fire, mug in hand, and listened with the rest of those gathered. The stories *she* had dreamed were small stories, and the retelling was enough to separate her from her everyday self. The *luthia* knew stories unimaginably old, though the oldest were rarely told. Kezzi thought that telling such a tale might well consume all of a *luthia*'s energy, so that at the end, she would be nothing but a powdery husk—like a moth that had prayed too close to the light.

"Riva," murmured Silain. "Now, *there* was a woman of the Bedel. Her hair as black as the black places between the stars; her eyelids heavy with lashes so thick that all you would see of her eyes, had you been there to look, would be the reflection of your own face. She had a sweet voice, too, that was often raised in song, and had the carriage of a queen."

Kezzi wondered what a *queen* was, but she did not ask the *luthia*. It wasn't done, to interrupt a story once it had been begun. Even a familiar and often-heard story still had the power to teach.

"O! She was a beauty, our Riva. You may ask, How beautiful

was she? And I would answer, 'She was so beautiful that her sisters of the Bedel loved her as dearly as her brothers.'

"It was this love that made her brothers and sisters wish to protect her. And that is both the danger of love—and Riva's doom."

Silain leaned toward Kezzi, her voice dropping slightly. "You see, our Riva, as beautiful and as kind as the wandering is long; with her sweet voice raised up in song—our Riva..."

She raised her mug and looked wisely at Kezzi over the rim.

"Our Riva was not clever."

Kezzi choked slightly on her tea. Not clever? But—

"It could be," Silain said, after a moment, "that I state the case badly. What I mean to say is—Riva's mind did not function as it ought. There was a fault in her memory, and another, in her understanding. It is said that the Bedel can fix anything, and that the *luthia* can fix the Bedel. But Riva—there was no fixing Riva.

"And yet—she was beautiful, she was kind, her nature was winsome; she tried so hard, and was so sad when she failed... It was one of her sisters who erred first. What harm could it do, she thought, to merely allow the wrong answer to pass? So, she did not correct Riva when she muddled a small cooking tale, and the food was still edible, and Riva's smile more than made up for the odd taste.

"Others followed. Her sisters who were to teach her card lore. Her brothers who were to teach her knifeplay. They watched her closely and kept her near. Riva never went into the marketplace by herself; she did not take so much as a single fruit from a high-piled table. She did sing, and when she sang, she danced. So beautiful was she that even the *gadje* loved her, and threw money, which was well. Otherwise, she could not have kept a place in the *kompani*, and none could bear to turn her out."

Silain paused and drank deeply of her tea.

"She ought to have been married to a wise man, and granted him many children, but the *kompani* stood at *chafurma*, and the numbers were fixed. Had matters fallen otherwise, she surely would have gone happy to a husband when the *kompani* was taken up again. As it was... well.

"She began to meet a man from the town—a *gadje*, yes, I will say it. They would sit under striped awnings and drink coffee together. The man gave her presents—jewelry and electronics. Coins and rare fabrics. All of these things Riva brought back to the *kompani*, for she knew her duty.

"One thing, she took away, at the man's request.

"A deck of cards."

Silain held out her mug and Kezzi hurried to refill it, spilling a few drops. Her own mug was barely touched; she poured a little tea into it, to warm what was there.

"A deck of cards," Silain repeated. "He asked if she could read them—she said that she could, for that is what she believed. Sitting there under the striped awning, sipping coffee, he asked her to find from the cards the number of the horse that would win the afternoon race.

"Laughing, she fanned the deck, invited him to take one, which he did, and showed her the headman card. 'Seven,' she said. 'The horse who will win wears the number seven.'

"The man went away and put money on that horse. It won, just as Riva said that it would.

"This happened once, twice, three times more, and the man saw his fortune glowing golden before him. He borrowed a large sum of money from another *gadje*, promising that it would be trebled by the end of the day. Then, he went to Riva and asked her for the winning number.

"She fanned the cards; he drew—the headman card.

"'Twelve,' said Riva. 'The winning horse.'"

The *gadje* might have hesitated, having a memory that was not faulty. But, he reasoned, the other horses had won.

"He went to the races, and placed all that money on the nose of the horse who wore the number twelve.

"And that horse, believe me or do not—that horse lost more thoroughly than ever a horse has lost a race, before or since. This left the *gadje* in a very bad place, because he could not repay the money he had borrowed. He went back to the little table beneath the striped awning, and he snatched the cards from Riva's belt, smearing them faceup among the coffee cups.

"'This card!' he cried. 'What number?'

"'Six,' said Riva, who did not remember what she had said even that morning.

"'You told me twelve!' the *gadje* cried, 'and before that, seven!'

"'Did I?' asked Riva, laughing. 'Well, and so I might have.'

"That is when the *gadje*'s anger broke, and he slapped her. She cried out, for she had been used to soft treatment. He slapped her again, and she pulled her knife—her knife that she did not know how to use. The *gadje* saw that his life was in danger, and pummeled her—and no one else sitting under that awning moved to stop him. He took her knife away and cut her hair off, then he kicked her. He might have killed her then, but one of her brothers was passing that place and leapt the little fence and knocked the *gadje* down. Then he brought Riva back to the *kompani*."

Silain sipped tea, and looked to Kezzi, her eyes bright with tears. "Where she died, despite all the *luthia* knew how to do."

· · · ☀ · · ·

"You're looking well, Nova," Aunt Miri said to Mother. "Surebleak agrees with you, just like it does all of us."

That was a joke, Syl Vor thought, but his mother didn't smile. Instead she inclined her head, as if acknowledging the truth of what had been said.

Aunt Miri looked to him. "Good-day, Syl Vor. Had you a pleasant excursion into town?"

"Yes, thank you, Aunt," Syl Vor said politely.

"It pleases me to hear you say so. Do you find that Surebleak suits you, as well?"

Syl Vor blinked and looked searchingly at Aunt Miri's eyes and face. Apparently, she did seriously want to know.

"I have scarcely seen anything of Surebleak," he said slowly, so that he not be seeming to find fault. This was his aunt's home-world, after all. "What I have seen today makes me think that I would...like to see more."

She grinned. "I think that might be what I've heard termed a careful boldness. Should you like to be a trader?"

Syl Vor blinked. What sort of a question—but wait. His tutors sometimes did the same—asked a question at odds with the lesson, to see how quickly he could change thoughts. So, then.

"I expect that I *will be* a trader," he said, "unless Uncle Shan finds me buffleheaded."

Aunt Miri laughed. "I will inch out onto a limb and predict that Uncle Shan will not find you buffleheaded."

"Though he may," Mother said sternly, "find a want of manner."

"Nothing wrong with his manners," Aunt Miri said in her Terran that sounded—yes! Like Mike Golden's Terran! "The question, now—that might've been just a touch impertinent." She nodded to Syl Vor. "Good answer."

That pleased him, but it made his mother impatient.

"We are here," she said, "to speak with Korval."

Aunt Miri considered her.

"Right," she said, still in Terran. "You are. Well, then, I guess I better toe the line. Just a sec while I get it set up."

She closed her eyes, took a deep breath and seemed somehow to *grow taller* where she sat. When she opened her eyes, she seemed to be looking *down* at Mother. Syl Vor felt a flutter in his stomach, and swallowed hard.

Aunt Miri—except she wasn't Aunt Miri now—now she was *Delm Korval*—held up her hand, where the Ring glittered on her thumb.

"Korval Sees," she said, in the High Tongue in the mode of *delm* to clanmember—"Nova yos'Galan and Syl Vor yos'Galan. Who will speak first?"

"Korval," Mother said, as clanmember to *delm*, "I will speak first, and also for my heir, who is a minor child, and untutored in the forms."

"Korval will make allowance for one who yet learns. Speak, Nova yos'Galan."

Mother rose and bowed, graceful and composed.

"Korval, I bring before the *delm's* consideration a single solution which answers two problems.

"The first problem is one of Surebleak, and the Office of the Boss. In short, the subordinate Bosses and the people of the streets mistrust the municipal school, seeing it as a venue in which their children will be at high risk. This perception has been made more poignant by the recent incidents of sabotage against the school building, which has put construction back." She paused.

The *delm* inclined her head, lamplight striking copper glints from her hair.

"And the second problem?"

"Briefly, Korval, the clan's child Syl Vor yos'Galan finds himself ofttimes with idle hands. He has lately been accustomed to a stringent routine of study and exercise, and to the company of his elder cousins. To me, to his aunt my sister Anthora, and to several of my household he has expressed a desire to be *of use*."

She paused again, but the *delm* said nothing.

"The proposed solution now placed before the *delm* is that Syl Vor yos'Galan remove to my household in the city, to be enrolled in the local school now, and the consolidated school when it is completed and ready to receive students."

"Korval has heard Nova yos'Galan," the *delm* said. "Stand forward, Syl Vor yos'Galan."

Obediently, he stood, though he felt himself shivering with shock. To address the *delm*? His mother had said—

"A few questions only, Child Syl Vor," the *delm* said. "You may without offense or error speak as a child of the House to an elder."

"Yes, Aunt—Yes." His voice was shivering, too, and that, Syl Vor thought, would never do. Padi would laugh to hear him; and Quin would ask, "are you are *quite* all right, Syl Vor?"

He took a careful breath, imagining the air deep and heavy, spreading out inside him, anchoring his feet to the floor, stiffening his soft knees, straightening his back. Another breath, and he met the *delm's* cool grey eyes. He lifted his chin, for surely Korval must dislike meeching manners quite as much as Grand-aunt Kareen did.

"Are you afraid, Child Syl Vor?" asked the *delm*.

"I am not afraid, ma'am," he answered firmly, which was... mostly true.

"Excellent. You have nothing to fear from your *delm*. When you speak to the *delm*, you speak to Korval Entire—which is nothing more frightening than speaking with your kin. Or with yourself."

Syl Vor bowed as one grateful for instruction, since the *delm* had paused and he could think of nothing to say.

"I wonder," the *delm* said then, "this solution—is it of your crafting?"

"No, ma'am. Mike Golden suggested it—as a way that I might be of use. We were having cookies and..." He paused, conscious that he was perhaps chattering.

"Pardon me, ma'am. Do you know Mike Golden?"

"We met briefly," the *delm* said, catching his gaze with hers. "What do you think of him?"

That was something of a stumper. Fortunately, one was allowed to take a moment to compose one's thoughts upon receipt of such a question. His first inclination, to say that he very much liked Mike Golden, was of course ineligible. The *delm* wished to know what he *thought*, not what he felt.

"I think Mike Golden is... an honest man," he said, chewing his lip and staring hard at the rug. "I think that he wants to help my mother, Boss Nova. I think that he wants the school to succeed. I think he wants *Surebleak* to succeed. I think he knows his solution is dangerous, a little. But not too dangerous to attempt." He looked up and met the *delm's* eyes.

"That is what I think of Mike Golden," he told her, and she inclined her head, indicating that she had heard.

"Mike Golden thinks like a *delm*. Child Syl Vor."

"Ma'am?"

"What do *you* think of this solving of Mr. Golden's?"

"I think it very neat."

"Ah. And the danger?"

Syl Vor blinked. "I have been accustomed, when we were at the Rock, to think that we might at any time be in terrible danger. If I join in this solving..." Horrifyingly, his eyes filled with tears, and his voice wobbled. He cleared his throat.

"If I join this solving," he said, as firmly as he could, "it will be only myself that I must guard."

There was a small silence before the *delm* spoke once more.

"Korval has heard," she said, nearly as quiet as Uncle Ren Zel. "Please sit, Child Syl Vor. Nova yos'Galan."

Mother came out of her chair even as he found his.

"Korval?"

"The *delm* accepts Michael Golden's solving on behalf of the clan's precious child Syl Vor. You will oversee the necessary arrangements."

Mother bowed.

"Korval, I shall."

"Yes." The *delm*—no, it was Aunt Miri now—rose.

"Now," she said in brisk Terran. "I hope you two are hungry, because Mrs. ana'Tak has it in her head to serve up a big dinner in honor of Lady Nova being to House. You'll both sleep here tonight, under Tree." She grinned at Syl Vor. "Tomorrow's soon enough to start being of use."

· · · ✵ · · ·

The scent of tea tickled his nose, teasing him into wakefulness. Not the flower-and-spice blend that was the common drink of the House, but the acrid, slightly burnt smell of the brew he had learnt to drink aboard *Momma Liberty*. If Jasin had brought tea, he was either late, or it was their off-shift, and she meant him to be of use to her. He tried to remember the schedule, but found that he did not recall the ship-day, nor what had been his shift just passed, or—

Of a sudden, his heart was pounding; he felt damp with panic, and wrenched his eyes open.

But this was not the cabin he shared with Jasin! Almost he could believe himself in a tent up on the mountain, new-waked by a cousin to take his turn at the smudge pots used to chase the late frost, and save the budding grapes. If he turned his head—yes! There was a fire, and a figure silhouetted beside it, head draped against the chill perhaps with a shawl, noble nose and decided chin plainly visible. The figure raised what must surely be a mug, held for warmth between both hands, and sipped.

"*Thawlana*," he breathed, though he *knew*—gods, did he not!— that it could not be.

The shawled head turned toward him.

"I will stand so for you, Child of the Other, if that is your true desire."

The words were Liaden, though the mode was uncertain—proof, had he needed such, that the silhouette was not his grandmother. She had been precise in matters of diction, despite a preference for the familiar modes over those more formal.

"Forgive me," he said, wishing to speak aloud, and horrified to hear his voice no more than a grating whisper. "I meant no offense."

"Nor was I offended. Would you like tea, child?"

Wake up, Rys, or I'll dump this tea over your head!

He moved his head, as if he might shake Jasin's voice from memory.

"Tea," he said to the one by the fire, "would be most welcome."

He held his mug in his off-hand, since his prime was strapped to a board. The old woman, shawl cast back now to reveal hair long and silvered, had helped him sit, and propped his back with pillows. That done, she settled beside him, and sipped, waiting until he had done the same.

"My name is Silain," she said. "You may address me thus, or as *luthia*, which is my function."

"My name is Rys..."

"Rys." Silain-*luthia* inclined her head. "Do you speak Terran?"

"I do," he said in that language. He sipped again, the primitive brew imparting a comfort beyond mere warmth. "Thank you for the tea, and"—he glanced at the splinted hand—"for your care."

"Tea is a simple comfort, of which there are too few in life. My care—is rough-and-ready. Your hand will require arts beyond mine, if it is to heal into usefulness, and I fear your left leg will never fully hold your weight. The ribs are already nearly knitted, and the internal bleeding is staunched." She sipped her tea, and for lack of any answer to this litany of disaster and faint hope, he did the same.

"You have enemies, in the city?" she asked.

Enemies?

Again, his heart slammed into overaction, and he moaned in sudden fear—Of course, he had enemies! Dire enemies who would stop at nothing to destroy him, and yet—

Surely, had he such enemies, he would know them, their faces, their clans? His fear produced nothing, other than a tremor that spilt his tea, and the memory of mighty wings...

"The Dragon," he whispered, tears starting. He closed his eyes, but they only ran faster. "Gods, the Dragon will destroy me. You must not—"

Terror overcame him, and he cowered against the pillow, sobbing in earnest now, so lost to shame that he did not resist when Silain-*luthia* gathered him to her, but only hid his face gratefully against her neck.

CHAPTER THIRTEEN

WHEN THEY HAD BEEN SHELTERING INSIDE THE ROCK, GRANDAUNT Kareen had insisted that they eat formally once a day.

"There is no reason to descend into barbarism, because we are in exile," she had said, and Padi had rolled her eyes, and Quin had looked very carefully at nothing, and Grandfather Luken had murmured, "Quite right."

For himself, Syl Vor thought that barbarism sounded very unpleasant, though he didn't understand, quite, how knowing when to use his tongs rather than his spoon would prevent a descent into anywhere.

Tonight, though, he had been glad of Grandaunt's insistence, and gladder still that he had what Ms. ker'Eklis said was a "retentive memory." He had, he thought, acquitted himself well at table, seated as an equal with his elders, between Mother and Aunt Anthora.

When Prime meal was done, Mother had excused them, and they had gone together to the nursery to decide with Mrs. pel'Esla what he should have with him in the city.

As they would be leaving again for Mother's house early on the morrow, most of what was chosen would follow later. Syl Vor packed enough clothes for three days into his backpack, then sat on the bed with Eztina across his knees, waiting for his mother.

When they had left Trealla Fantrol, everything had been so strange—fleeing, as they had to believe, only a single step ahead of Korval's enemies, that he hardly had time to understand that he was leaving all of his things, and every familiarity behind. And at the Rock, everything had been . . . different, and there had been so much to learn that he hadn't really *missed* his bed, or his favorite red pillow. When they were brought back under Tree, and he found those things in the nursery waiting for him, he had felt . . . as if they had been kindly left for his comfort by a cousin who no longer had need of them.

"We do not leave this night, Syl Vor-son," his mother said from the entrance to his small room. "You have time to wash your face, and to nap for an hour."

He looked up at her and smiled. "Is Mike Golden teaching you jokes?" he asked.

Her eyebrows twitched, then her own pale smile appeared.

"In truth, I think that was rather based on your Uncle Shan. Mr. Golden's jokes largely yet elude me. Perhaps you will do me the kindness, when we are settled in the city, to hint me into the proper mode."

"I will do my best," he said seriously. "But you must know that Padi calls me Sober Syl Vor."

His mother sighed and came over to sit next to him on the bed. Eztina raised her head and yawned, which was rude, but cats, Syl Vor noticed, were never scolded for being rude.

Mother extended her hand and stroked Eztina between the ears.

"My brothers treated me similarly," she said, her eyes on Eztina, who had begun to purr. "There is a value in humor, and it is the natural wish of kin, that we share in what delights them."

"Yes," he said. His mother laughed softly.

"I find myself exhausted by the exigencies of the day, and I daresay you are the same. Shall we meet in the small parlor for breakfast, and plan our removal?"

"Yes, ma'am." He hesitated, looking down at Eztina, feeling her deep purr more than hearing it. "Mother?"

"Yes, my child?"

"May Eztina come with us? Down into the city?"

She frowned, and he braced himself for "no." Then the frown faded.

"I will consult with Jeeves," she said, "before I seek my bed this evening. We will discuss it over breakfast."

Syl Vor smiled. "Thank you, Mother."

"You are welcome. Now!"

She rose. Hastily, he shifted Eztina off his knee and onto the bed so that he could rise also.

His mother cupped his face and looked down into his eyes.

"I had almost forgotten to say how very well you did at Prime meal this evening, and in your discussion earlier, with the *delm*. You delight, Syl Vor-son; I value you."

He blinked against tears, and swallowed hard.

"Thank you, Mother," he said, his voice foolishly shaking.

She bent and kissed his forehead, then released him with a stroke along the top of his head, as if he were Eztina.

"Now, sir—it is time and past for you to seek your bed. *Chiat'a bei kruzon*, my son."

"*Chiat'a bei kruzon*, Mother."

· · · ☀ · · ·

Kezzi sat by Silain's hearth, watching the *gadje* sleep. It *was* sleep, and not coma; his face was cool to the touch, and his heartbeat strong and steady.

Also, the *gadje* had a name now, given in truth to the *luthia*, and thus he became something more than a hurt soul in need of the *luthia*'s blessing.

Now, he was *Rys*, weighted with all that the name recalled. It would seem, from what Silain had said to Kezzi, so that she might reassure him, if he woke, that the name recalled fear, and sadness. *Death*, Silain said, moving her hand as if she were turning over a fortune card, *and betrayal*.

It gave one to wonder then, Kezzi thought, sitting by the bed with Malda's head on her knee, what the *luthia*'s purpose had been, to withhold passage into the World Unseen, where there was no fear or pain.

But that question, Silain would not answer.

The side of her face tingled, almost as if Alosha had looked on her, but the headman was not near.

Kezzi raised her head and met the—met the eyes of Rys, who lay under the *luthia*'s care.

"There are no dragons," she said in the language of the *gadje*, which was what Silain had told her to say, should he wake. "We do not allow them here."

He smiled, slowly, as if the assurance amused rather than soothed.

"That is well," he said, his voice gritty and weak.

"Yes," she agreed, and touched her shoulder with the tips of her fingers.

"I am Kezzi," she said—and that, too, the *luthia* had commanded, that it was her true-name she should give him. She looked down and placed her hand on the sleeping dog's head. "This is Malda."

"I am pleased to meet you, Kezzi—and Malda. I am Rys."

"I am pleased to meet you, Rys," Kezzi replied, which was polite, since it was what he had said himself, though it was not what one of the Bedel would say. It might, though, she thought, be *true* in that precise way that the Bedel kept truth within the *kompani*. Kezzi frowned. That thought wanted dreaming upon. It was the order of the universe, that there were the Bedel in their *kompanis*, and then Those Others, the *gadje*, who were not of the Bedel. Could a man be at the same time not of the Bedel, but of the *kompani*?

"Is that a frown, Kezzi?" Rys asked weakly. "Does my conversation dismay you?"

She looked to him, and saw a smile, faint, but willing, as if he were in truth one of her elder brothers, in a teasing mood.

"I have thought a thought," she told him, as she would one of those brothers, for how else might she make answer to one who had her true-name—and Malda's, too? "And it shakes what I know in my heart."

"Ah," he said seriously. "I have myself had such thoughts, on occasion."

She considered him and before she had properly considered, posed him a question. "Do you listen to your heart or your thought?"

He looked startled, black eyes widening inside the mask of bruises, and then frowned, himself.

"I think that it is a case," he said slowly, "of bringing one's heart and one's thoughts into—into balance." He winced then, as if his own words had nipped him. "Silain is your grandmother, is she not?" he asked.

"Silain is *the* grandmother," Kezzi corrected.

"Yes. You are better to ask her such questions, Kezzi, than a man..." His voice drifted into nothing, and Kezzi leaned closer, in order to observe his eyes, and placed her hand over his wrist, her fingers finding the heart-point.

He turned his head toward her and smiled wanly.

"You are a gentle nurse."

His pupils were not dilated, and his pulse was steady. She sat back, recalling the other thing Silain had told her.

"You may sit up and drink some tea. There is bread, and cheese, and fruit—winter apples—if you want to make a meal. Silain said that you must take charge of yourself, now that you are awake, and not depend on others to feed you."

There was a small silence before the *ga*—before Rys again showed his wan smile.

"Silain is correct, as you are—to remind me. Tea would be very welcome, and also"—he took a breath—"some bread."

Kezzi nodded and pushed Malda's head off of her knee.

"I will put the leaves to brew," she said, "then help you to sit up."

· · · ·❖· · · ·

Syl Vor woke up so completely that he thought for a moment that he hadn't been asleep at all. He must have been, though—for Eztina curled bonelessly under his chin, making the little half-snore, half-purr sound she only made when she was deeply asleep.

He kept himself very still, so as not to disturb her, while he tried to figure out what had waked him.

His door was ajar; his room faintly lit by the night-dims in the larger nursery. Had one of the twins called? He listened, but if it *had* been Shindi or Mik, they had settled again. Sometimes, Mrs. pel'Esla was about in the night; he'd woken more than once to the comforting sounds of her making a pot of tea, or the rhythmic rock of her chair, the spill from her reading lamp making his room a little brighter.

But if Mrs. pel'Esla was up this night, she was being very quiet indeed.

And he—he was *awake*, tingling with energy. There was no possibility of going back to sleep. Perhaps, he thought, he should go down to the gym and contend with the shadow-spar for a round or two. Or—no!

He would go for a walk in the inner garden. In fact, he must do so, and at once! If he was to remove to the city in the morning, he must say his proper good-bye to the Tree.

No sooner had he thought the thought than he was moving, easing out from beneath Eztina's weight and leaving her curled among the disordered blankets, still sound asleep.

Syl Vor opened his chest, found his warmest sweater by touch and pulled it on, pushing his feet into slippers. His house robe hung on its hook by the door; he had it on and slipped out.

Quiet and still, the nursery. He crossed the big room, keeping to the rugs and avoiding the creaky boards, hesitating at the door. If he put his hand against the plate, the door would wake Mrs. pel'Esla, and possibly the twins, so he simply punched in the override code and stepped into the hall.

The hall outside was shadowed, but the night-dims were more than bright enough for his dark-accustomed eyes. He went down the back stairs, through the short service corridor, and was confronted once more by a door.

It was very likely, he thought, that the door would tell Jeeves it had been opened, and the AI would come to look for him, or, worse, wake Mother. Unfortunately, and unlike the nursery door, he did not know the override for this one.

Or did he?

There was something like a tickle at the back of his head. He stepped closer, and raised his hand to the code pad. His fingers moved in a quick pattern that his mind didn't quite attend to, and the door swung open before him, admitting a chill breath of breeze rich with the scents of leaf and soil.

Syl Vor smiled and stepped out into the garden.

He hadn't known that the Tree glowed in the dark, bathing its place at the center of the garden in green light as soft as mist. Syl Vor went across the short grass, being careful not to catch his slippers on any of the root humps, and so arrived at the great trunk.

With a sigh, he leaned against it, arms spread, as if his small reach could encompass it in a hug, and put his cheek against the warm bark.

"Hello, Tree," he murmured. "I am going into the city to school and to be of use to Mother, and to Mike Golden, and to Cousin Pat Rin. I will come to visit—I promise!—but not so often as I have done."

A soft warmth filled him, and he relaxed closer against the trunk, comforted by the Tree's approval.

He might have fallen asleep for just a moment, leaning there all warm and safe, because he came awake all of a sudden, just as he had in the nursery. But this time, he knew what had waked him.

Syl Vor yos'Galan Clan Korval.

Someone had spoken his name, though not precisely aloud, the not-sounds tickling the inside of his head.

He straightened away from the Tree, smiling, and heard a rustle in the leaves above him.

Startled, he looked up, and then down, at the seed pod that had landed in the grass at his feet.

It was his, he knew it, just as he knew to pick it up and hold it in his palm until it opened for him, revealing the kernels. They smelled so good that he was suddenly very hungry, though he had made a good meal at Prime.

He swallowed, and remembered that his Mother had told him that one should always thank the Tree for its gifts.

"Thank you," he said, and made a little bow—child to elder—before he succumbed to his hunger and ate the kernels.

As soon as they were finished, he was full, and satisfied, and beginning to be a little chilly, despite his sweater and his robe.

He bowed to the Tree again, and said, "Good-night," before returning to the garden door, and passing through the sleeping house, to the nursery again, and his bed.

· · · ❄ · · ·

Rys had fallen asleep with Malda's head on his knee.

Kezzi looked at the two of them, feeling a nip of jealousy. Why should Malda favor a *gadje* with his care?

And yet . . . she sat down in her place by the bed.

Why should he not? There was a bond between them, after all. Both had been beaten and broken by *gadje* in the City Above; both had been given into Bedel hands. Surely, Malda would dream with a brother in misfortune, if only to assure him that all would be well.

Kezzi smiled, and leaned forward, first to touch Rys' forehead, which was warm, but not alarmingly so, and a little damp; and then to stroke Malda's head.

The man did not wake, but the dog opened his eyes, and his stubby tail thumped on the blanket, once, and then twice.

CHAPTER FOURTEEN

. . . .

"NO," SYL VOR SAID, GLARING AT THE BRACELET SITTING BESIDE his teacup. As bracelets went, it was inoffensive enough, with nothing in the way of jewels, bells, or ribbons. Merely, it was a bright brass cuff that fastened with a hook and chain, innocent of any adornment, without even the Tree-and-Dragon etched into its shiny surface.

"I beg your pardon, Syl Vor-son?" His mother's cool voice carried a sharp edge of surprise.

That recollected him to his manners, and he hurriedly transferred his gaze from the bracelet to her face.

"What I meant to say, ma'am," he said more moderately, "is that such a thing will mark me out. It is not in the usual mode, for persons of my age."

His mother frowned, but her reply was also moderate.

"We spoke of this. You agreed to accept a tracking device, so that the house may be assured of your whereabouts and your safety during those hours you are apart from us."

Well, and so he had done. But that had been before he had seen the device. He had envisioned something small enough to be slipped into a pocket, or, at most, a pin, like the clan-sign clipped to the collar of the shirt he wore under his sweater. This bracelet—it was not what any of his agemates had worn, back ho— on Liad. Children wore their clan-sign; jewelry was for those who had been tutored in the proper modes of adornment.

But, there, they were on Surebleak, he reminded himself. Perhaps the mode was different here.

"Will the other students, in the school," he said to his mother, "wear similar?" If it was the mode, then it was. Grandaunt might not approve, but he would at least not stand out as odd.

His mother's frown was more marked. "Perhaps some will; perhaps some will not. You, however, will wear this, Son Syl Vor, or you will return to the clanhouse this morning."

Syl Vor looked down, biting his lip. He had angered her, which had not been his intent, but—

"Problem, ma'am?" came Mike Golden's voice from just behind his chair.

"My son was merely objecting to the necessity of the device, Mr. Golden," Mother said, as tart in Terran as she had been in the Low Tongue.

"Oh, well." Mike Golden stepped 'round the table so that he made the apex of the triangle. He gave Syl Vor a friendly nod.

"Don't like the bracelet, Silver?"

"No, Mike," he answered, and added, politely, "if you please."

"Nothing to please," the man said, and Syl Vor felt his heart lift. He had an ally, he thought; his mother listened to Mike Golden. Perhaps he could avoid the bracelet after all.

"No need for the tracer." Mike Golden was speaking to his mother, and Syl Vor's heart lifted higher.

His mother's eyes narrowed. "Is there not?" she asked icily.

Mike Golden spread his broad hands, showing them empty, and shrugged.

"If the boy wants to play Boss, I'll just get Larnce from his breakfast and tell him he's not just doin' escort, but he'll be goin' to school."

Syl Vor's spirits plummeted. He accepted that someone of the household would walk with him to the school's entrance. The safety of Surebleak's streets, as his mother had said, were such that she herself did not venture forth, except in company with Mike Golden or other of her gun-sworn. Certainly, his lessons at Runig's Rock had shown him the virtue of backup, if such could be arranged.

Walking to school with Larnce, then, was one matter, and acceptable. But to have Larnce with him all the day, standing at his back while he did his lessons, glaring at the other students, and showing his gun plainly on his belt?

"No!" he said, rather more loudly than he had intended. He looked down, face hot.

"Two *nos* in the course of one meal is rather too many," his mother noted. "Especially for so short a meal as breakfast. Pray strive to limit your use of the negative until at least tomorrow lunchtime, my son."

He swallowed, and raised his head to meet Mike Golden's brown eyes.

"I esteem Larnce," he said slowly, feeling his way in Terran. Esteem was perhaps not *precisely* accurate, since he knew little of the man beyond his face and the fact that he was on Boss Nova's staff. It did, however, seem the polite thing to say.

"So you won't mind him standin' your 'hand." Mike Golden nodded and turned, as if heading at once to the kitchen to roust Larnce to duty.

"No!" Syl Vor said, and bit his lip, not daring to look to his mother. Mike Golden turned back, face quizzical.

"What's on your mind, Silver? Say it out plain, so we can all hear it."

"Yes." He took a hard breath. "I will wear the bracelet."

School was nothing at all like guesting with Maelin and Wal Ter at Glavda Empri, and sharing their tutors and lessons. For the first thing, he had known Wal Ter and Maelin always; their House was closely aligned with Korval, and their Line with yos'Galan. Maelin's grandfather had been cargo master for Syl Vor's own grandfather Er Thom, on *Dutiful Passage*; and for Uncle Shan, too.

Here at school, there were no familiar faces or House ties. Here, the teacher, Ms. Taylor, had him stand up with her at the front of the room, facing twenty-three seated strangers, whom he guessed to range in age from slightly younger than he to a boy who was surely old enough to have been 'prenticed.

Ms. Taylor put her hand on his shoulder, as if they were kin, and had him say out his name and his street. Then, she asked those seated to say their names and streets. Recognizing this as his first test, Syl Vor committed each face-name-street combination to memory.

After the introduction was complete, he was let to sit in an empty chair next to a boy with red hair cut so short it stood up on his head like bristles, and who stared at him with a frown before turning his face, deliberately, away.

Syl Vor bit his lip and faced forward, wondering how he might have offended. But, there, maybe this boy—Rudy Daniel, he recalled, from Gough Street—maybe this boy's Boss had a policy against those from Blair Road, or maybe his Boss didn't agree that there should be a Road Boss. And it was, was it not, exactly the sort of thing Mike Golden had said his going to school would help fix? Though not all at once.

A projection picture coalesced on the wall directly before them, fuzzy at first, then suddenly sharp. Syl Vor frowned, then smiled at the map—a flat map, in fact, of the whole city, from the port to the end of the road.

"All right, everybody!" Ms. Taylor called. "Time to do routes. Tansy, what's the quickest way from school to Al's Hardware?"

From the first row, a small girl with her hair in braids stood up, took the pointer from Ms. Taylor's hand and aimed at the map. A red dot appeared on the position of the school.

"Here's us," Tansy said, her voice high and breathless. "The quickest way to Al's is go out the back door, down Brehm Alley to Rendan, take a right and down three doors." The pointer wobbled unhelpfully, but Syl Vor's eye followed the lines of the map, finding the alley, the intersection, the turn. "Doors" as a direction puzzled him for a moment, until Ms. Taylor took the pointer back.

"Very good, Tansy. Thank you." She retraced the route more smoothly and Syl Vor was able to see that Al's Hardware Store was the third shop from the corner of Rendan Road. Each shop would of course have a door onto the street, therefore—"three doors."

"Anders!" called Ms. Taylor. "Get me to Patrol, quick!"

Anders was the tallest person in the room. Anders Jeff, Syl Vor told himself in reminder, from Moravia.

"Out the front, cross the street, left to the corner."

The red dot traced the route.

"Good! Vanette!"

And so it went, until they had each provided a route to a landmark nearby. Syl Vor was asked to pilot them to Boss Conrad's house, which he thought too easy for the last question in the game.

Except it wasn't the last question.

Ms. Taylor looked out over them with her hands on her hips and a grin on her face.

"Warm, now?" she asked.

"We're warm, all right!" all the class but Syl Vor shouted.

"Let's do round two!" she shouted back, and threw the pointer across the room to Desi Beale, who caught it with a laugh and jumped to her feet.

Round two was *not* easy. Ms. Taylor would call out the name of a place or an intersection somewhere on the map, and the student with the pointer would have to find the straightest route. The rules allowed the pointer holder to name one advisor, which meant that Rudy from Gough Street called on Anders of Moravia for aid, and Tansy of Alvarado Square asked Jack Vance of Hamilton Street for assistance.

Syl Vor was fair bouncing on the edge of his chair, committing the routes to memory, and the location of restaurants, groceries, and patrol stations across the city. So engrossed was he that the pointer nearly grazed his head before he realized that his name had been called.

He ducked, snatched, and jumped to his feet.

"I need to get to Boss Wentworth's turf," Ms. Taylor told him. "Shortest route."

He blinked up at the map, at a loss; not even knowing who he might call on among his classmates. Boss Wentworth's turf? He fingered the pointer, pushed the bracelet up under the sleeve of his sweater, and yet the map gave him no—

"Wentworth's Jopha," said a boy who looked as if he ought to be 'prenticed. Peter Day, Syl Vor remembered. He got up slowly, as if standing pained him, and gave Syl Vor a nod. "Jopha," he repeated.

Syl Vor looked back to the map, stomach tightening as he didn't at first—there! Jopha Road ran on a long diagonal from their location. And the shortest route?

His eye measured, and he brought the pointer up.

"The shortest route to Boss Wentworth's turf takes us out the back door, to Brehm Alley, following until it ends at Taplow Street. A left turn onto the street and up the hill to—"

"Don' wanna go that way," Peter Day interrupted.

Syl Vor blinked, frowned at the map, reran the possible routes— and turned to his self-appointed assistant.

"It is the shortest?" he said.

"Well, yeah, it is, by steps. But it ain't by time."

Oh. A blocked road, then, which the map wouldn't show, but which someone local to the area would be aware of. Syl Vor nodded.

"If the way is not passable, then—"

"Ain't nothing the matter with the *way*!" Rudy Daniel shouted. "Don't listen to that dope."

"Rudy!" Ms. Taylor said sharply. "No name-calls. Make it right with Pete."

Rudy took a deep breath, held it and let it all come out in a hissing rush which sounded rude to Syl Vor. Then he rose and went to Peter, holding his hand out.

"Sorry, Pete."

The elder boy nodded, and put his hand in Rudy's. They moved their linked hands up, then down, and loosed their grips, each going one step back.

"Now!" said Ms. Taylor. "Pete—tell Syl Vor why you advise him not to go that way."

"Yes'm." Pete turned around and looked down at Syl Vor. His eyes were different colors—one blue and one brown, both sleepy-looking.

"Your way's right through the middle of the old store-buildin's," Pete said, as if that explained everything.

Syl Vor nodded and, when Pete said nothing else, repeated. "But, it is the shortest route?"

"Looks that way, but ain't so," Pete said.

Syl Vor thought he could understand why Rudy had lost patience. He took a breath, thought, and asked the best question he could think of.

"What bars the way?"

Pete smiled and nodded once, as if he had been particularly clever.

"Ghosts," he said. "There's ghosts up there in them old buildin's. Best to go around."

After routes was history, and after history was lunch. That was vegetable soup and bread and milk, which they ate in the room next to the classroom, where there was a table, chairs, and a serving stand.

Ms. Taylor stood at the serving stand, ladling soup into their bowls as they filed past. They carried their bowls to the table, and sat, hands folded in their laps, until everyone was in place and Ms. Taylor had sipped from her spoon, and nodded once.

It was oddly spiced, the soup—not bland, like the tinned supplies they'd eaten from in Runig's Rock; and not sour or sweet, like Mrs. ana'Tak's soups. Syl Vor ate his, doggedly, as he had used to eat the tinned soup, before it had become something that was ordinary and even, in its very blandness, comforting. The bread was good, chewy and brown—but the milk was the most unpleasant that he could recall drinking, speaking as one who did not favor that beverage.

While they ate, Ms. Taylor asked each of them in turn a question. For Tansy, it was the health of a younger sister, which was reported to be, "Much better, ma'am, and my ma thanks you for asking."

Syl Vor listened as he spooned soup, and drank milk in small, loathsome sips. Anders worked after school at Bentler's Brewery, as "scrubs," which Syl Vor gathered had to do with cleaning the equipment; Delia was walking a beat with a Patrol team . . .

"Syl Vor, how do you like Surebleak?"

Hastily, he swallowed the last of his milk, and took a breath.

"I've hardly seen much of Surebleak yet, ma'am," he said, remembering that Grandfather had told him in polite conversation to be as truthful as was gentle, and as gentle as was wise. "But what I have seen, I find interesting."

"*Interesting*," Rudy Daniel said in a low hard voice, from the next chair. "Boss's brat."

"Rudy? Did you have a question for Syl Vor?"

The other boy's face turned a dull red.

"No, ma'am," he said.

"Well, then," said Ms. Taylor. "Have you decided whether you'll try out for the All Street Stickball Team?"

If possible, Rudy's face got redder.

"No, ma'am. I-I think I won't be signing up for that."

"That's too bad," Ms. Taylor said. "I think you'd be an asset to the team."

Rudy swallowed and stared down into his soup bowl. A moment passed, then Ms. Taylor asked Vanette how her mother was recovering from the flu.

After lunch, they returned to the schoolroom for arithmetic, which was boring; then calisthenics; then prep groups for reading.

Syl Vor's partner was Peter Day, who just shook his big head at the book, and leaned back in his chair.

"Naw, I ain't no hand at letters, the way they always move around like they do. You just read it at me and I'll say it back when it's my turn."

Syl Vor frowned at the page—just a plain paper book with the words printed in big Terran letters.

"These letters don't move."

"Not for you, they don't. For me, they don't set still. Got something wrong with my eyes. Just read it out, like I said. Nothin' the matter with my memory."

There didn't seem to be anything to do, but what he was told. Syl Vor put the book on the desk, so Peter could look at the words, too, if he wished, pushed the bracelet up out of the way, and read out their two assigned pages about a girl named Hannah, who had gotten separated from her elder brother on the wrong side of the toll booths.

Peter leaned back in his chair, eyes closed, not watching the page at all, nodding his head slightly.

After reading—or, in Peter's case, reciting—was dismissal.

"For tomorrow," said Ms. Taylor, "everyone bring a news report from the Council of Bosses. Walk alert! Taxi's waiting for Moravia and Townsin!"

Anders and Vanette dashed toward the front door, while the rest of the class headed toward the back, coats open, and heads bare. Standing by his seat, Syl Vor sealed his jacket and pulled on his hat and gloves. If it had gotten so warm that he might do without either, he could always take them off.

"How did you like your first day of school, Syl Vor?" Ms. Taylor asked him.

He looked up into her face, but found no immediate words that were either gentle or wise.

The teacher smiled.

"Speechless, eh?"

That was Padi's sort of joke, and Syl Vor returned Ms. Taylor's smile.

"In truth, I am not certain what I think. It has been . . . different from what I . . ." He took a breath, and decided on a flat truth, as the others were far too complex. "To go to school is not something that I have done before."

"Gotcha." She nodded. "But, you know, that's the case for all the other kids here, too. School's a pretty new concept. And a school that's not on your turf? With kids from all over? That's just radical." She smiled again. "We're learning, though. All together."

She touched his sleeve.

"I'm glad you decided to give school a try. You come on back tomorrow, okay? It'll be less different."

"I plan to come every day," he assured her.

Her smile grew broader, and she patted his sleeve, walking with him toward the back door.

"That's the spirit! You go on home now. I'm looking forward to seeing you tomorrow." She opened the door.

"Thank you," he said, and stepped out into the alley.

The door closed behind him, and Syl Vor spun, suddenly remembering that Larnce had brought him to the front door this morning, and would be waiting there for him.

Face hot, he thought about going back inside. Ms. Taylor would think he was a foolish student, who couldn't even remember his arrangements for going home. That *did* figure into his calculations.

And also that, really, there was no problem. All he had to do was go 'round to the front. Brehm Alley to Rendan, go right at the corner, then up six doors. That was his route.

Nothing could be simpler.

Decision taken, he turned right, toward Rendan Road.

A hand hit his shoulder, hard enough to send him staggering. Before he could catch his balance, another blow landed, and he fell.

Something heavy pinned him facedown to the alley floor before he could roll, and a strong hand grabbed his arm, pulled it back at a painful angle, and tore the bright brass cuff from his wrist.

"Interesting, ain't it?" asked a voice, and the weight was gone, amid the heavy sound of running.

Syl Vor rolled to his knees, took a couple of deep breaths. His arm hurt, and his back did, and so did his shoulder, but he didn't think anything hurt bad enough to be broken. He got to his feet and thought about running after Peter Day. Then he thought that perhaps that would be one of those "stupid notions" that Mike Golden had particularly asked him not to act upon.

He scrubbed at the grit on the front of his coat, and gulped, the alley blurring out of sense as his eyes filled with tears.

He gulped again and squeezed his eyes shut.

When he was pretty certain that he wasn't going to really cry, he resumed his walk down the alley to the corner, on the alert now.

He wouldn't be surprised again.

CHAPTER FIFTEEN

FROM HIS COT TO THE FIRE WAS SCARCELY A DOZEN STEPS, WHICH Rys accomplished, leaning heavily on the child's shoulder with his good hand, balanced on his right leg, the ruined left dragging painfully behind.

By the time the fireside was accomplished and he had half fallen onto the rug there, he was damp with sweat and shivering with reaction. The child gave him a thoughtful look and went away, returning almost immediately with the blanket from his cot, which she silently draped over his shoulders.

"My thanks," he said, hearing his voice shake. "It is a kindness."

"No thanks," she answered, sounding sharp.

He bowed his head. "I meant no offense."

Kezzi shook her mass of black hair back from her face. "There's tea. Would you like some?"

"Tea would be welcome," he said courteously, and watched as she poured from a blackened kettle.

When the mug was in his good hand, he took a sip, then rested hand and mug against his thigh.

"Is it permitted that I sit alone for a time?" he asked. "I wish to ... order my thoughts."

The child's eyes widened, and she came to her feet with such alacrity that he feared he had again given offense. When she spoke, however, her voice was soft, even reverent.

"Of course it is permitted. If you have everything that is

needful, Malda and I will go. I will stop at Jin's hearth and tell the *luthia* that you are praying."

Praying? Rys thought. Yet, if it gained him a hour of solitude...

"I have everything that is needful," he assured her, and gave her a smile.

She inclined from the waist, hands tucked into the sleeves of her sweater, an oddly solemn gesture, then straightened and turned away, snapping fingers for the dog, which yipped once, and ran after her.

Rys watched them race toward the clustering hearths that bloomed dark red at some distance from the one he sat beside, until he lost their silhouettes amongst the larger shadows.

He closed his eyes, and listened.

A small breeze kissed his cheek, wanton in the darkness, scented with smoke, and hot bread, and dust. From overhead came a quiet, steady rumble, which he realized that he had been hearing constantly since his first waking here. It was neither a large sound, nor alarming—rather, it comforted, as the steady hum of life support might comfort a seasoned spacer.

He considered that thought—but no, most certainly he was not on a ship. Had not the grandmother asked after his enemies, when first he'd waked? And had she not supposed that those enemies were located in the City Above?

He was, therefore, situated on a planet, beneath a city, assuming that Silain-*luthia* was more practical than alliterative. If he might bring himself to recall which planet, or yet, what city...

But that was the heart of the thing, was it not? He could not recall.

His stomach clenched, and he swallowed bile. Carefully, he opened his eyes, raised the mug and sipped tea. From the direction of the grouped fires came a series of high sharp notes, supported by a low thrumming. Music, he supposed.

The tea calmed his stomach; the music calmed his thoughts.

Perhaps, he thought, he might fly another course with more profit. What *did* he recall?

That was scarcely less distressing. He recalled... he recalled tending the smudge pots with his elder cousins through a frigid, long night. He recalled weeping with relief the next morning, when his father said that the vines were no longer in danger. He recalled his pride at being given his own set of shears, and a row to tend.

He recalled his grandmother straightening his collar and abjuring him to be clever for Master Pilot pin'Epel. And he recalled the feeling of bewilderment upon learning that he had somehow qualified for pilot training, and that the season just commenced would be his last among the vines.

He recalled—the sight graven into his bones—the shadow of the wings flickering across the long rows of grapes, hugging the contour of the hill, staying secret and hidden until...

He was sweating. Putting the cup carefully on the rug next to his knee, he used a corner of the blanket, clumsily one-handed, to dry his brow.

So, then, he asked himself patiently. What else could he recall?

The cave—oh, very clearly, he recalled the cave and the long hiding, after which the rescue, and the crowded transport to the nearest refuge—a Terran station.

He recalled sitting in the trade bar, a nothing staring at nothing—clanless, kinless, and lacking a future. And he recalled a thump and a scrape as the chair across from him was taken. He looked up into a pair of mist-blue eyes.

"I'm Jasin Bell, mate on *Momma Liberty*. We got crew work, if you're lookin'."

Work—that had gotten through. Even a man without kin needed work.

"You lookin'?" Jasin Bell had snapped, and that roused him a little. Roused him enough.

"I am looking," he answered in his careful, textbook Terran. And then, because his grandmother had not raised him to be a fool, "I will see the contract, if you please."

Rys took a hard breath and deliberately drank the rest of his now-tepid tea, putting the empty mug beside his knee. His muscles were quivering as if he'd been doing the hand-stacking on a dock where the gravity was high.

Jasin...His recollections of Jasin were vivid. But just...there was something, about Jasin—no! *Beyond* Jasin! His thoughts were abruptly in turmoil, scattered like grape spiders from the impact of a man's boot. He snatched after them, and gasped, tears starting. Clumsily, he drew up his good leg and leaned his forehead against his knee, weeping with terror and confusion and loss; glad that there was no one to see.

* * *

Perhaps he drowsed, weak as he was and worn out with trying to remember. Indeed, he *must* have drowsed, and dreamt that he was on-comm with Jasin, demanding to know in what mad port she had abandoned him, broken and desperate as he—

"Well met, Brother," a soft voice uttered.

Brother? thought Rys, the dream making him sticky and slow. He had no living brothers, and none that would address him so—least of all Jasin's brother.

"I overheard my small sister say to the *luthia* that you prayed, Brother. I do not want to intrude, but I thought you might wish not to be alone, when you are done."

Rys raised his head, looking across the fire at the shadow that addressed him.

"Good e'en," he said, both cautious and courteous. "Brother."

It might have been that his caller sighed. Certainly, it seemed so.

"May I sit with you?" he asked. "I have a pipe, if you will share smoke with me."

No, decidedly it was not Jasin's brother, who had never once offered him a kindness. Rys blinked, trying to focus his thoughts.

"It is a joy," he said, even more careful, "to share with a brother."

"Glad I am to hear you say so," the other said and stepped 'round the fire. He dropped, crosslegged, onto the rug at Rys' right hand, and gazed at it for a moment, useless and strapped to its board, before raising his head and meeting Rys' gaze.

"I am," he said quietly, "Udari. It was I who found you, and brought you to the *luthia* for healing. I hope you will forgive me."

"Surely, you have saved my life," Rys protested, and added, "Brother."

"Surely, I did," Udari agreed. "But perhaps it would have been better, had I walked 'round the corner, smoked a pipe, and granted you time to pass the gate. It would not have been many breaths more of pain, and you would have risen whole and filled with light in the World Beyond, full able to tend those things that a man should and must.

"As we have it now, the *luthia* says that hand will not grip again, and the leg will never bear you. A man in his prime—as we are, Brother—might argue that those losses are bitter."

"They are," Rys said slowly. "But I hold the hope that . . . some assistance may arrive." He meant Jasin, come to find him, and the autodoc unit in *Momma Liberty*'s sick bay.

Udari nodded, slow and solemn, and reached into the neck of his sweater. He withdrew a drawstring bag, and a small glass pipe that caught the glow from the dying fire and gave it back with a heart of red.

"There is something in what you say," Udari said, as he filled the pipe's bowl with a pinch of stuff from the pouch and tamped it with his thumb. "It might be that help will arrive. I will dream on it."

He pulled the strings of the bag tight and replaced it within his sweater, then extended his hand and plucked an ember from the edge of the fire.

Rys sat up straight with a wordless gasp—but Udari was perfectly composed, holding the ember to the stuff in the pipe's bowl whilst drawing on the stem.

Fragrant smoke came from the bowl—reminding Rys of sweetsuckle blooming amid the still leafless vines, bloomed and dead within two sunrises, crumbling by the fourth, giving itself to nurture the soil.

"Ah . . ." Udari sighed, and offered him the pipe, stem first.

"Go carefully," he advised as Rys took the thing, his clumsiness betraying his unfamiliarity. "The smoke is hot, so draw slow and steady. I will put something more on the hearth."

So saying, he rose, leaving Rys alone on the rug, puffing cautiously on the pipe. The smoke was hot, and the perfume caught at the back of his throat. He coughed once, and puffed again, gratified to see the bowl glow orange.

"Here." Udari was back, dropping lightly to his knees, and placing something Rys didn't quite see on the fire. Flame licked up, showing a long face dominated by a bold nose and a pair of liquid dark eyes. He sat back with easy grace, legs once again crossed, and took the pipe from Rys' hand.

"Enough smoke makes a man wise," he murmured, drawing until the bowl glowed scarlet. He raised his head, eyes closed, seeming not to breathe—then sighed out a cloud of scented smoke with a smile.

"Too much makes a man foolish."

That, Rys thought, sounded familiar. He sighed softly.

"No more for me, then, Brother. I am already fool enough."

"Say you so? But I have tasted wisdom's draught. Show me your foolishness, Brother, and I will tease sense from it."

Rys looked at him, this ragged stranger, who was in truth neither brother nor comrade...who had saved his life, and who had come on purpose to bear him company when he was alone and frightened.

"I cannot remember," he said, speaking frankly. "I have lost who I am, and the path I walked, that led to this place."

Pipe in hand, Udari nodded solemnly.

"Your soul has gone a-wandering, which souls are apt to do, when we are weak, or when we are undecided. You must grow strong, and be decisive. At that time, you will no longer be lost, and will recall all that you are and have been."

There was certainly nothing to argue about in that, Rys thought. And then he thought that the little smoke he had ingested had indeed made him foolish. He felt as if he floated, pain-free and undistressed, some few inches above the top of his own head, and was looking down into Udari's face.

"How fare you, Brother?" that one asked.

"Very well indeed," Rys answered. "I thank you, Brother, for your care."

"There is no thanks given, between brothers," Udari said, mildly. "It is our way. A moment and I will help you to bed, if you think that you might sleep now."

"I think that I might," Rys said.

Udari reached to the fire and carefully knocked the last of the stuff from the pipe's bowl before slipping it away inside his sweater.

He rose then, and bent.

"Hold my arm," he said, "and I will raise you."

This he did, effortlessly, and Rys was once more balanced on his good leg, Udari's arm tight around his waist.

"Now, we walk. Lean on me, Brother."

There was no choice, but Rys didn't say so. He only floated above his own head and watched as the tall man half-carried the small one the few steps from the fire to the cot, laid him down, and covered him over with a blanket.

"Sleep," he heard the tall man say. "Grow strong."

Rys, floating, yawned, and felt sleep weigh on him, bearing him down gently, back into his broken body, where he sighed once, deeply, and knew nothing more.

CHAPTER SIXTEEN

HE HAD COST LARNCE HIS POST, WHICH WAS BAD ENOUGH, IF that was the worst of it, but he feared—he very much feared—that Mike Golden would lose his, too, before this day was done.

His mother was *that* angry.

He had tried—after Ms. Veeno had come and solemnly escorted Larnce to the front door—he had *tried* to explain that the fault was his, but that only made his mother angrier. She had snatched his shoulders and shaken him and then hugged him against her, pressing his face into her shoulder, which would have been pleasant, except that his cheek hurt from having rubbed against the alley, and he had twitched a little. His mother had thrust him back, still holding onto his shoulders, and stared at him hard, violet eyes glittering, before raising her voice to demand the immediate attendance of Pounce, the house's medic.

Pounce took him, not to his room, but to the kitchen, the warmest room in the house. Beck brought a basin of water to the table, and some towels, and an aid box, and Pounce carefully cleaned Syl Vor's face, and put ointment on his raw cheek, then helped him take off his sweater and his shirt so that ribs and back could be inspected.

"Starting to see some bruise, here," Pounce murmured, touching the place between his shoulders where Peter had struck him. "Anything else hurt? Arms? Knees? Hips?"

"No," Syl Vor told him.

Pounce nodded seriously and had him stand up and hold his arms out, then raise them, make fists and shake his fingers out, bend over to touch his toes, twist from his waist, bend his knees into a crouch, then straighten again to stand first on one foot and then the other.

"Lookin' good," Pounce said finally. "Shoulder might stiff up overnight. I got some warmin' oil that'll loosen it again." He grinned and shook his hair out of his eyes. "No missin' school for you."

That of course was his other fear, that his mother would send him back to Jelaza Kazone and never allow him in town, or down to the port, or *any*where, ever again. She could have already called for the car, and he would be back in the nursery this evening.

His eyes stung and he sniffed, just a little, as he tucked in his shirt and pulled the sweater over his head.

Pounce folded his kit and went away, leaving Syl Vor standing by the table, uncertain of what he ought to do. Perhaps, if he spoke to his mother again—she might not be so very angry...

"You have yourself a setdown now," Beck said from the counter. "There's your mug o'tea comin' over there in half a shake, an' a couple slices new bread with jam to wash it down with."

"Thank you," Syl Vor said to the cook's broad back. "But I am not very hungry."

"Sure ya aren't," Beck said and turned around, mug and plate in hand. They landed on the table soft as snow, and big hands pulled out the chair. "Just take a setdown, if ya don't want yer tea. Makes sense to stay close; yer momma's gonna want you soon."

"Yes," Syl Vor agreed. "I—she is very angry."

"Can't blame 'er for that," Beck said, turning back to the work counter. "None too happy, my ownself, you want the truth on it. Just 'cuz we-all took our licks when we was curb-high don't mean we wanna see our youngers get the same."

Syl Vor frowned.

"*You* got knocked down, Beck?"

"Hell, yeah, I got knocked down, 'til I learnt better. That took some time." A quick glance and a grin over one shoulder. "Not a fast learner. You, now—yer right quick."

"Did Larnce get knocked down?"

Beck pursed her lips. "Prolly so, just thinkin' 'bout the usual way it goes. He din't never say, specific."

"And Mike Golden—did he get knocked down?"

Beck's eyebrows went up, both together, and she turned right around and put her hip against the work counter, arms crossed over her chest.

"You wanna hear somethin'? Mike got knocked down more'n all the rest of us together. I know on account we come up on the same street, see? And it wasn't that he couldna knocked heads, but his granny, she wasn't havin' *none* of it. 'Head 'n' heart,' was what she usta say. 'Head 'n' heart wins over fist an' fear.'"

Beck nodded. "She was right, I'll grant it. What she didn't say was—you get more bruises, her way."

Syl Vor leaned forward, watching Beck's face, red-cheeked and plump.

"But it does work," he said, meaning it for a question.

Beck nodded. "Sure, it works. Takes time, like I said." She shifted, unfolded her arms and half-turned. "You have a sip o'that tea, why not? Don' wanna go into your momma dry."

That made sense, Syl Vor thought. If, in fact, the car was on its way from the House, then the next chance—the *last chance* he would have to try to explain—would be in the front hallway, not in her office with tea laid to hand.

He sipped from his mug, sighed for the warmth and the comforting taste, and had another sip. After that, he thought he might have just a bite of bread and jam, so that Beck wouldn't think that her service was without value.

By the time Ms. Veeno came into the kitchen to say that his mother wanted to see him in her office, he had finished both pieces of bread and was drinking the dregs of his tea.

Mike Golden was standing in front of Mother's desk, hands folded behind his back. Syl Vor's heart leapt—and then fell into the pit of his stomach as he saw how serious Mike's broad brown face was. Mother—he shot a glance at her where she sat tall and stern behind her desk, her face coolly expressionless, and his heart slid from his stomach to his boots.

Mother had not improved in temper. Indeed, it seemed that she was in *worse* temper than she had been when she had taken Larnce's duty from him.

Mother, Syl Vor very much feared, had called him in so that he could witness Mike Golden being cast from the House, which he would not abide. Not for *his* error!

"My son, please stand forward," Mother said, in a voice that for all its coolness meant *now*.

He did, trying to walk firmly, but not too quickly, nor too

slowly, and trying, also, to catch Mike Golden's eye. That gentleman, however, was focused entirely on Mother; Syl Vor might have already been in the nursery at Jelaza Kazone for all the attention he was spared.

Stomach clenched, he stopped in line with the corner of his mother's desk, so that he could see her and Mike, too. He took a breath and raised his head to meet her eyes. She inclined her head.

"Thank you," she said, and extended a hand to pluck up something that gleamed bright brass in the room's lights.

His bracelet.

Syl Vor swallowed and looked to Mike Golden.

"Is Peter—" he began . . .

"Sold it," Mike interrupted, giving him a serious look. "Took it right down to Vin's Pawn Shop. Didn't even bother to get off Boss Conrad's turf."

"An overconfident young man," his mother added.

Mike shrugged. "Hard to tell if that's not-smart or too-smart," he said.

"Not-smart," Syl Vor said decisively. "He knew I would recognize his voice."

"Now, see, that could still be too-smart," Mike said earnestly. "Boy—Pete, was it? Pete Day?"

Syl Vor nodded.

"Right. Pete could be trying to provoke something. You know who took the bracelet, now what're you gonna do about it, see? He wants to find out what you're made of."

Syl Vor blinked at him. "Blood and bone and microbes," he said, which he had learned very decisively from his tutor. "The same as Peter is."

Mike Golden shook his head.

"Blood and bone and microbes ain't what's bothering Pete Day. What he wants to know is, are you gonna fight, or if knockin' you down once was all it took for him to be boss."

"Boss? He's a boy."

"Boss of you, is what I mean. The one who stands ahead in line is the one who gets to tell the next one down what to do." Mike nodded toward Mother, sitting with the bracelet in her hand, watching him with unreadable violet eyes. "Your ma, there, she stands first in line in this house. I stand second, so she tells me what needs doin', and I pass it down the line to the one who's gonna do it."

Syl Vor looked at his mother. His mother met his gaze, and said nothing.

"Boss's brat," he said, remembering.

She raised an elegant eyebrow.

"Was this also Peter Day?"

"No, that was Rudy." Syl Vor looked to Mike. "What is a *brat*?"

"Well, that's like *kid*, 'cept not so nice. *Boss's brat*—that kinda carries the meaning that you got everything soft 'n' easy and always have it zackly like you want."

Syl Vor stared, and bit his lip against a sudden impulse to laugh. This was not, he was fairly certain, the correct time to laugh.

Mike Golden gave him a nod.

"This Rudy," his mother said. "He was also in the alley?"

Syl Vor shook his head. "No, ma'am. There was only Peter in the alley. Rudy...disliked a thing that I said at lunch."

He took a breath, not wanting to ask, and yet—

"Am I to be sent—back—back under Tree?"

"Is that your choice?"

"No, Mother," he said carefully. "I would prefer to stay in our house here, and to go to school."

"*Our house here*, is it? You grow facile, my son."

He shook his head. "Grandaunt would not allow it. If one can remark the doing, then it was clumsily done, she would say."

His mother's eyebrows lifted. "Would she. Myself, I allow it to be a good effort by one still new to his boards."

"Thank you," Syl Vor said politely, and took a deep breath, before adding, as calmly as he could manage, "I would prefer not to wear the bracelet, when I go to school."

She tipped her head, blond hair tumbling across her shoulders. "I believe that may no longer be an option. Mr. Golden, do I have that correctly?"

"I think so, ma'am. Look, Silver, I know it's the root of the trouble, but the thing is, if you stop wearin' it now, Pete thinks he got away with somethin'. He sees that 'round your wrist tomorrow, an' he'll maybe start thinkin' a mistake was made. That'll get him worried, see? He won't know what else you might do, or if he's gotta watch his back."

This sounded somewhat familiar. Syl Vor chewed his lip, remembering the Rock, and overhearing Grandfather Luken and Grandaunt talking over the moves available to Korval's enemies, and what sort of *melant'i* games they might undertake in order to blacken Korval's honor among those who were not completely informed of facts.

"I understand," he said, and then, more abruptly than he had intended, "Are you staying in-House, Mike Golden?"

The man's brows pulled together briefly, then his face relaxed as he went down on one knee, which put him more or less level with Syl Vor.

"I ain't fired yet," he said. "'Less you think I oughta be."

"No!" Syl Vor said forcefully.

Mike nodded seriously. "I 'preciate that, 'specially since you gotta be pretty corked off at me, insistin' on the bracelet in the first place. You wanna take a swing, you go 'head. I got it comin'."

"You want me to—knock you down?"

"Well, I don't say I *want* it, but I did earn it, and I'm not one to deny a man his rights, or grudge him fair payment."

"I don't want to hit you," Syl Vor said. "I—" He glanced at his mother, who inclined her head as if she could hear his thought. "We are in Balance, Mike Golden."

"That sounds like something I might live to regret," the man said, voice light. He came to his feet, and looked to Mother.

"With your permission, Boss."

"Yes, Mr. Golden," she said. "Thank you."

He bowed, just a stiff little incline from the waist, which wasn't really a proper bow, but Mother accepted it calmly, and Mike Golden left the room, his footsteps firm in the hallway.

Syl Vor sighed and looked at his mother, who was toying with the bracelet, turning it this way and that so that the brass caught the light.

"Your tutor is waiting for you," she said. "Do you feel able to attend your lessons?"

"Yes," he said decisively, and saw the small curve of her smile.

"It pleases me to hear you say so. When you are done, pray do me the favor of returning to me here. We might share a cup of tea before dinner, while you tell me about the rest of your school day."

Syl Vor bowed. "I would like that extremely, ma'am," he said properly.

"Excellent. Go, now, and study well."

CHAPTER SEVENTEEN

THE DAY ABOVE WAS BRIGHT AND STILL. KEZZI, WALKING AT DROI'S elbow down the busy morning street, regretted the shawl her elder sister had draped over her shoulders, though, if the wind blew up, she would be grateful for its added warmth. Annoyances are blessings whose time has not come. That was what Pulka said. And then he would ask, "And when will *your* time come, small sister?"

It was Kezzi's belief that her time would come well before Pulka's, but, there! She wasn't supposed to be thinking about Pulka. She was supposed to be standing in Droi's shadow, absorbing her skill at interpreting the meaning of the cards. Kezzi hoped that skill was all she would absorb from her elder sister. She didn't think she would like to see the things that Droi did, that lived around corners, and under rocks, and in the lightless place of the World That Might Be.

Though the day was fine and the street was busy, they had so far very little fortune, themselves. It was in Kezzi's mind that the street was *too* busy, that its very fullness worked against a single *gadje* stepping out of the bustling crowd to offer a coin, and draw a card to learn what the day would bring.

She was a shadow; it was not her place to suggest, or to do anything, other than watch, and learn. Still, it was on the tip of her tongue to suggest that they find a cup of 'toot and a place to sit in the sunshine for a little time, until the crowds of *gadje* gave over their rushing and took the time to look about them.

Even as she began to speak, however, a *gadje* did step out of the crowd, a small, thin woman who walked as if she were a tall, broad man. Her face was round and soft, her mouth straight and hard, and her eyes were like rat eyes, bright and merciless. Inside the warm shawl, Kezzi shivered, and missed Malda who had been left with Silain, since dogs, said Droi, had no place in lessons.

"Good morning," the *gadje* said, dipping two fingers into her belt. When she drew them out, a coin shone bright between them.

"Will my day be fair or foul?" she asked, extending the coin to Droi while her gaze rested on Kezzi.

Droi whisked the coin away into a hidden pocket, fanned the cards between both hands.

"Draw a card and learn the answer," she crooned, and slid one step to the side, intercepting the *gadje*'s gaze. "Pull one—*only* one—the card that speaks to you. Draw it, show it, and I will tell you what it means."

The *gadje* snorted, extended a hand and without looking plucked a card from among its fellows in the fan.

Carelessly, she flipped it up, showing Droi, and Kezzi, the Lantern.

Droi dipped her head, and contrived to seem to be looking up into the *gadje*'s cruel face.

"Today, you seek," she said, whispering, as if it were a secret, just between herself and the *gadje*.

"Will I find what I seek?" the *gadje* demanded.

Droi smiled, and caught the card back, folding it into the deck with a snap.

"That depends on you, O seeker," she answered, and drew her scarf closer about her face. Two steps she retreated, and Kezzi also, neither of them, it seemed, willing to turn their backs on the *gadje*, who watched them with chilly interest, then abruptly spun and swaggered down the street, in the direction she had come from.

Droi's hand snaked out and fastened around Kezzi's wrist, urging her to a quick walk until they came to the mouth of an alley. They slipped into the dimness, their backs against the wall.

"Seeking," Kezzi whispered. "Us?"

Droi shook her head. "Not by intent," she said, and Kezzi relaxed.

"Though the path to what she does seek may lie through us," Droi added, which made Kezzi's stomach hurt again.

"*Garda*?" she asked.

Droi shrugged.

"When we return, I will speak with Rafin," she said, being one of the few who might, without risking either a blow or a bellow.

"I will speak to the *luthia*," Kezzi said.

"Yes," Droi said, which only meant that she had heard.

They stood in silence for another few breaths, watching the *gadje* bustle by, then Droi stood away from the wall and straightened her shawl and her headscarf.

"Come," she said. "Let us find a cup of coffeetoot and something sweet to give us strength. Then we will walk to the other side of the tollbooths and try our fortunes there."

"Yes," Kezzi agreed, and followed her elder out of the alley and down the street.

They took a table just inside the door at Joan's Bakery. Droi bespoke for them a raisin cake each, and a pot of 'toot to share. She placed the coin the cold *gadje* had given in exchange for her fortune on the edge of the table, and said airily to the one who brought the tray, "That is for you; I will see no change."

Kezzi blinked, but said nothing, recalling just in time her role as Droi's shadow. Well she could understand that a coin received from such a *gadje* might be ill-wished. But the usual remedy for ridding oneself of an ill-wished coin was to have it made into other coins. To send the whole thing away from them, accepting no smallest tie to it—well. It was rare that one of the Bedel paid *gadje* for what they took, much less overpaid.

Still, it was Droi, with Droi's strange sight.

And, Kezzi reminded herself, she had herself been distressed by the cold *gadje*'s air. Perhaps it was wisdom, to accept nothing from that one.

Thinking so, she turned her attention to her cake, finding it sticky enough to warrant two cups of hot 'toot.

When she was done, and Droi was, they rose and left the bakery, leaving cups, dishes, and cutlery behind.

· · · ❄ · · ·

It was not particularly easy to shell peas one-handed, but it could be done and, after some practice, done with a certain amount of dexterity.

Thus, Rys sat at Jin's hearth and shelled peas. Jin studied his progress with narrowed eyes, then gave him an abrupt nod.

"That's well, Rys. Keep on as you are. I'll be back before you're done."

And so he was left alone, with a garden basket at his left hand, an empty bowl into which the shelled peas were given in the crook of his knee, and another basket at his right hand, to receive the shells.

Those, he understood, would go with Memit, a blade-thin woman with big hands, to the composting heap, and thence return virtue to the garden.

He had spoken a few words with Memit regarding composting, a topic of which he had some knowledge. After an initial frown she had warmed to the subject and ended with an apology that duty-work called her elsewhere, and a promise to show him the gardens, some day soon.

So, he sat, alone with his thoughts, and the work, which was... pleasantly dull. His thoughts were similar. Since his smoke with Udari, he had adopted a course of soft thinking, mostly concerned with those persons and matters directly before him. It was his hope that those memories he felt missing would return to him, if he did not press too hard, nor berate himself too sternly.

It was... difficult... to adopt this attitude of gentleness with himself. He wished to reach into his own head and shake loose those recollections and motives—his very history!—which had hidden themselves from his waking self. Most definitely, he wished to ransack his walkabout memories for any shred of a clue of how he might contact *Momma Liberty*. Jasin would not have left him... well, Jasin *might* have left him, given cause enough; he did not suppose himself the equal of the ship in her regard. But she would not have left him without resources. Without contact, or hope of rendezvous.

His fingers fumbled the pod he had been worrying, and it fell, whole, into the bowl at his knee. Rys closed his eyes and concentrated on breathing, slow and deep. His heart hammered in his ears and his brow was damp. This was what came of stepping off the path of gentleness. Such distress served him—not at all. Indeed, he might be driving those things he most wished to recall deeper into hiding.

Another breath, and he opened his eyes. He retrieved the pod he had dropped, cracked the seam and released the peas. The broken pod went into the basket with its comrades.

He shelled another pod; another... and another, moving deliberately, half drowsing now, in his determination not to think at all.

"Well met, Brother," a soft and lately familiar voice spoke near at hand.

Rys raised his head.

"Udari," he said. "Brother. It is good to see you." He blinked, recalling his lesson in the manners of those he found himself among. "I hope it does not give affront, that I say so."

"No affront, but only joy. I return the joy, by saying, it pleases me to see *you*, Brother, and at work for the good of all the *kompani*. Truly, it is more than I thought I might look upon in this world, when I found you at our door."

He came forward, and Rys saw that there was something hanging from his belt—a dagger, perhaps, but before he could be certain, Udari had seated himself on the other side of the basket and reached in, bringing out a handful of pods.

"Let me help you, Brother. When we are done, I ask that you walk with me."

Walk. Rys sighed quietly and broke the current pod down its seam.

"I fear that you will not walk far with me at your side," he said. "But I will gladly go as far as I might, with a brother."

"Perhaps it will be further than you think," Udari said, nimbly shelling peas with his two good hands. "I have dreamed upon you, as I promised I would, and I have found solutions—one simple and one...less so. I have brought the simple with me so that together we may pursue that which is complex."

He tossed the depleted pods across to the compost basket and reached 'round his belt, pulling free the item which hung there and offering it across his palms to Rys.

It was black and shone like enamel in the light of Jin's fire—a stubby rod only a little longer than Udari's two palms were wide.

"Take it—a brother-gift."

Such a gift surely could not be refused. Rys took the rod, and sat holding it in his hand while Udari fetched out another fistful of pods and shelled them.

"What is it?" Rys said at last. "Brother."

"A walking staff."

Rys felt anger, looking at the length of it—anger, sudden and potent. A joke, and in the style of Jasin's brother—very much at his expense, though why Udari had not waited until there was a crowd about—

"There! That is the last!" Udari cast another handful of empty pods into the compost basket and smiled. "It was well you had done so many before I arrived. Now, we are free to pursue other matters."

He rose to his feet and held his hand down.

Rys gave him the black tube, which he tucked back in his belt before extending his hand once more.

Goaded, Rys took the offered support and allowed himself to be pulled upright.

"So, then!" Udari had the short tube from his belt, held it between his two hands, twisted—and pulled.

The rod began to lengthen, to loose bulk, to become something very like . . . a walking staff.

"Take hold, Brother." Udari directed him, and he gripped it 'round the center, the knob nearly to his shoulder.

Udari dropped to one knee, teasing the tube longer, until it touched the ground.

"How does that suit you for length?" he asked, coming to his feet.

"I fear it is too long," Rys said, and Udari laughed.

"No, it is only that your brother has forgotten what he was about. A moment." He reached again to his belt and withdrew a crescent shape, which he kneaded until it became rather less flat, like a pillow with a spike at the end.

Udari took momentary charge of the staff, screwed the pillow to the top and returned it to Rys.

"A crutch," he said, understanding at last.

"I hope it will be of use," Udari answered. "Slip it beneath your arm and let us see how well it matches—a little long yet, I think. A moment; I will adjust."

Adjust he did, and Rys settled his arm into the support of the pillowing crescent.

"Try a few steps," Udari said, coming to his feet.

A few steps was all he needed to understand the balance of it, and the necessary rhythm. His shattered leg still was a burden, but less so.

Rys smiled, began to speak—and recalled himself.

"You wished us to walk together," he said instead, "Brother?"

"So I did," Udari answered, his grin wide and white. "Come this way, if you will, Brother."

. . . ❊ . . .

Silain the *luthia* sat alone at her fire. Malda, whose head had been on her knee, suddenly looked up, then leapt to his feet with a joyous yip, and stood, quivering with joy, on the edge of the rug.

In a moment, Kezzi came into the firelight and bent, making a basket of her arms. Malda leapt into them, barking and licking her hair, while the child laughed, and hugged him.

The *luthia* smiled and poured tea into a mug, uncovered the plate that had been warming at the edge of the fire and placed it on the rug.

Eventually, the child released the dog and came to give greeting to her elder.

"Good night to you, *luthia*."

"Fair return to you, small sister. Sit and tell me the tale of your day. There is tea and food to ease the telling."

Food for the first little time delayed the telling, but the *luthia* was patient. She warmed her own cup, and waited.

Eventually, in starts and stops, and then more smoothly, as the plate was set aside for the dog to clean, came the story of the day, the cold *gadje* and her coin, Droi's actions, and the *fleez* resumed, at a prudent distance.

"And I read the cards for two *gadje*," the child said, holding her mug in two hands, her eyes shining. "Droi said I must take the coin the first gave to me, and hang it 'round my neck, for luck."

"Droi's sight does not mislead her in this," Silain said. "Go, find me a length of good cord and it will be done."

"Yes, Grandmother." The child rose to do as she had been bid, snapping her fingers for the dog to follow.

Silain refilled her mug and the girl's, then sat looking into the fire, thinking of the strange *gadje* and her coin. It was troubling, in a way that felt heavily threatening, though she could not have said particularly why.

Well, then, she would dream on it. Doubtless, the matter would come clear.

· · · ❉ · · ·

Their pace was slow, which was expectable, and must have tried Udari's patience, though he gave no sign of it, merely keeping pace and from time to time pointing out rough patches or holes in the surface they traversed.

For himself, he was discovering the usefulness and limits of his new tool. It was, he found, wondrous firm, which imparted a feeling of purpose. He gave it his weight with gusto and was able to swing his shattered leg somewhat, gaining momentum while keeping it above irregularities and rocks.

"You take to this as a bird to wings," Udari said. "Soon we will see you dancing 'round the common fire."

Rys laughed and shook his hair back from his eyes. Immediately, it tumbled back. Perhaps he might ask Udari for a pair of scissors. But first, a question.

"What is our destination, Brother?"

"We go to the hearthside of a sister, whose aid I will ask on behalf of yourself."

Rys thought about that, swinging along with his crutch settled comfortably under his arm. One step, two steps . . .

"May I not ask on my own behalf?" he asked at last.

Udari pointed down, where a darker shadow snaked along the dark surface. "Mind the crack, Brother," he murmured.

Rys swung his crutch beyond the tricksy bit, and his bad leg, too, counting one step, two steps, three . . .

"You may speak on your own behalf," Udari said slowly, "to the *luthia*, and to the apprentice and assistants of the *luthia*. To me, your brother, you may unburden your heart. To those brothers of your brother who have accepted your acquaintance, you may also speak in your own voice. To our sisters . . ." Udari drew a deep breath. "You must not speak to any of the sisters of your brother unless you have been properly introduced. Whether you will be permitted to speak after—that is for each sister to say."

"I understand," Rys said carefully, which was truth. He was an outsider; there must be some—even most—among this cloistered settlement who disapproved of his presence. And of Udari, for bringing him here.

"I fear," he said then, "that I may have transgressed with Memit. I spoke to her of compost—a topic of mutual interest."

"Did she answer?" Udari asked.

"After a pause. She had a few moments only, before duty called her. But she promised to show me the garden she oversees."

Udari laughed. "My brother Rys can charm a stone! If Memit had taken offense, your ears would be ringing yet!"

He smiled, warmed by Udari's pleasure, and by the fact that he had not after all made an error with Memit.

"Here now," his brother said, waving a hand toward a hearth a few dozen steps distant. "We arrive. We will see a modest Rys now, with eyes lowered and lips together. A soft voice and few words in answer, only if you are spoken to. Droi is no Memit, which you will recall."

"Yes, Brother," Rys said softly, and followed Udari to the hearth of Droi, swinging a little less robustly on his crutch.

His task was to stand tall on his crutch while Udari's sister Droi—a buxom young woman with untidy hair and untamed eyes—while Droi measured shattered leg and whole in all dimensions and directions, three times for each, to be certain they were correct.

Neither she nor Udari wrote these careful measurements down—certainly, he did not, lacking pen, pad, and the use of his primary hand. He supposed that Udari memorized what was needful, and he did the same, though to what use he had no idea.

"There's the last," Droi said, straightening so suddenly and so nearly that only quick action kept his nose from being caught between her proud breasts.

He said nothing, which had been his role; Droi had done as Udari had bid, but as if the one being measured were nothing more than a particularly uninteresting block of wood.

Now, then.

Now...

She stared directly into his eyes, hers showing green in the dark depths.

"You see them, don't you?" she whispered, her breath hot against his cheek and smelling faintly of mint. "You see them, inside the darkness. They're waiting for us, eh? Aren't they? Waiting to eat us, and spit out our souls."

He drew a careful breath, suddenly hearing the whisper of wings against the quiet air—and inside of that heartbeat between hearing and panic came Udari, a smile on his face and his hands raised, palm out, as if warding madness away.

"A bolt of crimson it will be, and as much purple ribbon as a man can carry! I will bring these things from the City Above and place them by your hearth, sweet Droi."

Rys felt Udari take his arm, and brought his crutch to the ready, more than eager to go.

"He sees," Droi said, placing herself directly before them. She leaned forward and caught Rys' gaze with her own. "Tell me what you *see, gadje!*"

He shivered, lips parting—and firmly closed them again.

Droi smiled and leaned closer still.

"Rys..." she crooned, her voice soft and treacherous, her breath warming his ear. "Savory morsel. Tell me what you see."

"I hear," he whispered hoarsely. "I hear the wings of a dragon against the wind. Hunting..." He snatched after his wits and pressed his lips together, refusing with all his will to speak further. The trembling—continued, and he was grateful for Udari's bruising grip on his arm, that kept him upright.

Droi leaned back, her smile deepening with what might be satisfaction. "Hunting," she repeated, and licked her lips. Her eyes never left his.

"Sister," Udari said, his voice soft and careful. "We are wanted by our brother Pulka."

"Of course," Droi said, while Rys stared, fascinated at the dance of green flame in her eyes. "Of course. You will come and see me again, Rys Dragonbait."

He swallowed in a tight throat, and she laughed low in hers.

"Say *yes, Droi,*" she instructed.

"Yes, Droi," he repeated obediently, though it seemed that Udari must surely break his arm.

She swung aside, transferring her gaze to Udari.

"Go, now, and give our brother Pulka my greeting."

"Yes," said Udari, and hastened Rys forward. He stumbled, then got the crutch into play and swung along with a will, matching the other man's hasty stride as they left the glowing hearth, and Droi's watching shadow.

CHAPTER EIGHTEEN

SYL VOR PUSHED THE BRACELET UP UNDER THE SLEEVE OF HIS sweater. It had been nine school days since Pete had knocked him down in the alley and taken it away. Nine days since Mike Golden had bought it back from Mr. Vin at the pawnshop.

Nine days in which there were no more attempts—from anyone—to knock him down or to steal from him. He still offended Rudy—only by coming to school, Syl Vor thought. Or maybe Rudy stood on principle with the brats of Bosses.

Whichever it may be, neither Rudy nor Peter was his concern this morning.

This morning, the rotation had teamed him with Desi and Jeff for current and past event.

That was a new thing, the rotation. Every morning now, before the first lesson, Ms. Taylor would have them count off by threes, form three lines and dance, line to line, until the music stopped. Whoever you were standing next to when that happened were the members of your team for the day.

And it might be, Syl Vor thought, that the dance—or the music—was the first lesson of the day. Ms. Taylor made a point of talking about what they were going to hear, who had written it and what instruments were involved.

Lesson or not, the system had thus far worked to his benefit, since he had been teamed with neither Pete nor Rudy since its inception. At some point, of course, they *must* make a team, given the limited numbers of dancers.

133

Or perhaps not.

There had been another student added to the class, a boy named Kaleb, who had been brought in by one of the Street Patrol on the morning of Syl Vor's third day of class. Tansy had attached him, as if he were lost kin found. Of course, the class could not expand infinitely. But, Syl Vor thought, if they continued to add students, perhaps the group would be split in two, with Rudy and Pete in one group, and Syl Vor in the other. That was something, perhaps, to hope for.

Everyone came to school and left school by the front door now. That meant using the hallway through Ms. Audrey's house, which Vanette had said was a scandal. Syl Vor didn't quite know what sort of scandal, and when he had asked her the only answer he'd gotten was a shake of her head.

"Hey, you asleep over there, Syl Vor?" Jeff asked.

"No," he said quickly, and leaned over Desi's shoulder, the better to see the timeline on the shared screen. "When was the first tollbooth put in place?"

· · · ✷ · · ·

Rys tucked his crutch under his arm and swung down to the hearth, where the solitary figure sat on her rug, long silver hair loose on broad shoulders.

She looked up at his approach, black eyes reflecting firelight. Her face bore a long record of years, yet the furrows did not suggest weakness so much as the strength born of travails survived.

He bowed as well as he was able.

"Grandmother."

Silain-*luthia* smiled.

"My child. How do you fare this day?"

"Under your care, I grow more well every morning."

She cocked a sapient eye. "Excepting only those things which do not heal."

Rys bowed his head.

"It was not in my mind to complain," he said softly, and with complete truth. "You have saved my life—yourself, and the child, and my brother Udari—and if there are those hurts which do not heal, then at least I grow strong enough to bear them."

This was somewhat optimistic. His physical health improved—certainly that. Between pipes, and long discussions that seemed to his untutored ears tangential, Udari and Pulka were designing a brace for his bad leg, based on Droi's careful measurements. Soon, perhaps, he might walk again, and after a fashion, with only the very least bit of assistance from the crutch.

However much he looked forward to that event, yet he could not but worry that the gap in his memory—the very understanding of who he was and how he had come to be broken and bleeding his life out on the Bedel's doorstep—remained. Clearly he had enemies, and until he knew them, he was vulnerable. Worse, his ignorance endangered, perhaps, those very persons to whom he owed his life.

"I wonder," he said now to Silain-*luthia*, before she could question him more closely, "if there is any task that awaits me this day."

"I know of nothing such," she said calmly. "Do you go again to the men's camp?"

"If there is no duty-work before me," he said firmly, well aware that Pulka would be horrified to hear him say it. Pulka, however, was not in debt to the Bedel, or to Silain. He was *of* the Bedel and, between members of the *kompani,* there could be no debt.

"Again I say that I know of nothing such, though I would ask you to tarry one moment, Rys, for an old woman's question."

"Certainly, Grandmother. Ask and I shall answer to the best of my poor ability."

She smiled slightly, raised her head and met his eyes like a hammer blow.

"Are your wings strong enough to bear you?"

Shock chilled him even to his vocal cords. Udari had coached him, so that he understood this question to be both ritual and contract. Averring strong wings relinquished all rights a young man had to the hearth of his mother. Although he had been urged most strongly to this action by Pulka, who was frankly horrified that a man should be put to such children's work as shelling peas, Rys did not wish to leave Silain's hearth. True enough that these last few days had found him most often in the so-called men's camp, still he returned here, to Silain's hearth, at the end of each long day, as he once had done to his own House...

Something stirred at that. Something from that shrouded place inside his head, where all his recent history hid.

Something...he recognized it as contempt. Self-contempt, that *he*, Rys Lin pen'Chala, should cling to this old and ignorant savage as if she were kin. He was *Liaden*. He was...

He *was*...

Pain shot through his head, sending Silain and her hearth spinning, waking nausea, so that he huddled against his crutch, striving to stay upright, and not to shame himself.

He was...

"Rys!"

A strong arm came 'round his waist, supporting him until the agony ebbed and he dared to open his eyes.

"Will you sit?" Silain asked, and helped him to do so.

He sighed, and sought her face.

"You see there is no strength at all in my wings," he said, breathless. "The mere thought of leaving your care sends me to ground."

Silain did not smile, though the hand that yet rested on his shoulder was kind and warm.

"What pain was that, grandson?"

"It seemed... a memory," he told her slowly. "Slicing the inside of my skull."

Silain sighed, but said, "Healing is not always pain-free."

He looked at her sharply. "This is *healing*, do you think?"

"I think that it may well be," she answered. "It is the order of life that lesser wounds heal first."

Considering the severity of the wounds he bore, that were healed as well as they might be, *that* was sobering indeed.

"Now!" Silain said briskly, releasing him and pulling her shawl closer 'round her shoulders. "I had not meant to mock you, Rys brother of Udari. There is no need to strain your wings; when you are ready, you will fly. You have a son's place at this hearth, for as long as your heart desires."

She tipped her head and considered him.

"Does this ease you?"

"Grandmother," he said truthfully, as relief that Pulka would doubtless decry as unmanly washed through him, "it eases, and gladdens, me."

"Sweet bird. Tell me, are you still afraid of dragons?"

His blood chilled, and he bowed his head, drawing a deep breath, waiting... But there came no half-memory or flash of pain to inform him.

"I am," he said. "The thing makes no sense, and yet... Droi..." He let the sentence go, seeing no way to untangle his fears into orderly sentences.

Silain, however, merely nodded.

"Droi Sees truly, grandson, but the strain of Seeing such things as she does has made her telling of them . . . unreliable. This is not malice, nor a weakness of will. It is no failing of courage, to fear the terrible. Know, for your own protection, that Droi does sometimes strike out. Be gentle, if she strikes at you."

"Yes, Grandmother."

"That is well, then. And now, if my eyes do not lie, here comes your brother."

He glanced over his shoulder, and there in truth came Udari, who stopped at Rys' side and placed a hand upon his shoulder.

"*Luthia.*"

"Udari of the Bedel."

"Brother, do you accompany me today?"

"I do," Rys said, and shifted his crutch, but Udari's hand was there and he took it, allowing himself to be pulled gently upright.

"Care well for your brother," Silain said to Udari.

"*Luthia*, I will. A man is fortunate in such a brother, and I will keep him as the treasure he is."

"Well said, and no less than man or woman expects from Udari. My blessing upon you both. Rys, remember what I have taught you."

"Yes, Grandmother," he said, and again gave the small stiff bow the crutch allowed him. "My thanks," he said, his voice suddenly rough, knowing it was not the custom, and yet, he must speak, or his heart would burst. "Silain. My *thanks.*"

She lifted a hand to trace a sign in the air. He heard Udari draw a sharp breath, felt the other man's fingers tighten where they rested on his shoulder.

"I will return," he said to Silain. "As can and may."

· · · ✳ · · ·

The sky frowned on the City Above, and the great gusts of wind had teeth.

"Rain before midnoon," Kezzi heard one *gadje* say to another as she and Malda walked past the corner where they stood.

"Long's it ain't snow," the second *gadje* answered, basket balanced against her hip.

Kezzi cast a thoughtful glance in the direction of the basket, which was half full of tubers. Roasted, and with a little bit of salt sprinkled over, the tubers tempted Rys' appetite, which was not robust, even now that he was well.

Silain said, because he was so much smaller than a man of the Bedel, Rys required less to sustain himself. Kezzi herself was of the opinion that Rys *would* grow, if not to Pulka's height and breadth, than at least to Udari's, if only he would *eat*.

The *gadje* with the basket passed on, and Kezzi let her go, tubers intact. She would, she promised herself, take some food Rys favored back with her. Just now, though, she had an errand of her own.

Droi had said that it was time for her to begin tracing out the designs and making her own deck of cards. Vylet had agreed, and had given a packet of stiff paper tied with a blue ribbon. It was a rich gift, even to a sister, and it had been given to Vylet herself by her sweetheart, Zand. Kezzi wondered if that meant Vylet had after all put his blanket into the darkness beyond her hearth, as Silain had counseled her. It would, Kezzi thought, be just like Vylet to weep and refuse Silain's counsel, only to quietly accept it a few days later, as if it were her own idea.

Still, Kezzi thought, walking head up among the hurrying *gadje*, she needed colors, and that was her purpose today.

Kezzi turned the corner, Malda at her heels, thinking of having her own deck, and the colors she would—

"Hey, there, Anna, good-morning! And Rascal, too!"

Startled out of the World of What Might Be, she froze, and in that moment felt a hand drop, not ungently, on her shoulder, trapping her.

She took a breath, thought a prayer for wisdom, and looked up into a *gadje*'s broad brown face.

Among the Bedel it was said that all *gadje* looked alike—a joke of the *kompani*. And even were it not a joke, Kezzi thought, she defied anyone to say that this *gadje* looked like *any*one else.

"Mike Golden," she said sternly, striving to produce a frown as fierce of one of Droi's fiercest. "Let me go."

"And have you go peltin' off like you did last time? I might look stupid, but I know enough to come in outta the snow."

Kezzi forced herself to stand patiently beneath the man's hand. Let him think her meek and obedient; she could play at that. And when he moved his hand...

"Where's your ma?" he asked.

She considered him. "At home."

He nodded gravely. "She know you're on the roam?"

"I have an errand."

"Which I'm meant to hear as *yes*," he said cheerfully. "Okay, Anna, let's go."

His hand moved, not to release her, but to grip her shoulder more firmly.

"Go where?"

"School," he said, as if the word meant something.

"I don't—"

"Boss Conrad's orders," Mike Golden interrupted her. "If any of the Patrol—which I am, on account of being Boss Nova's 'hand, see?—if any of the Patrol sees a *youth at risk*, then they're supposed to either take 'em to school, or to jail." He tipped his head. "That *youth at risk*? That's how they talk where Boss Conrad's from. What it means is a kid who's about to commit mischief, like maybe stealin' somethin' out of a shop."

"I have stolen nothing," Kezzi told him with dignity.

"Today, you ain't," Mike Golden said. "Precision counts. Last time we talked, though, you'd nipped a bag o'flour from the grocer—he showed me where you took it from, after you run off. I had to make it good with 'im, 'cause I said I would, so now *you* owe *me*."

That was *gadje* foolishness. The Bedel did not *owe*.

"I did not agree to that bargain."

Her voice was not quite so bold as she would have wished; in fact, it trembled somewhat. *School* might be a strange word, but *jail*? There were tales told about jail. Bedel had *died* in jail—caged, denied *luthia*, headman, and the solace of the *kompani*. Died with only their own prayers to ease them into the World Beyond...

Kezzi swallowed. Malda barked, sharply, once. Perhaps he smelled her fear. The man looked down, and suddenly all her fear was for Malda, who had been used as an object of sport, beaten and broken by *gadje*, and left crying in the street.

"Don't hurt him!" she cried, twisting hard against the man's hand.

She surprised him, but not enough. He shifted his balance, and put his free hand on her other shoulder.

"I'm not going to hurt him," he said roughly. "Anna, look at me."

For a moment, she stared grimly at his chin, then raised her eyes to his.

He nodded seriously. "I'm not gonna hurt your dog. Or you.

What I am gonna do is ask you to come on down to school and give it a try."

"No," she said, frowning.

"How else you gonna make it square between us?" Mike Golden asked, his brown eyes bright with interest.

She opened her mouth to tell him not to be stupid—and then did not speak. For it came to her that she did owe Mike Golden, and the sort of debt that the Bedel *did* acknowledge. The last time they had met, he had let her go; he had not raised the alarm, or set the other *gadje* after her.

"How long," she asked, "is this *school*?"

"Just today, then you go on home and come back tomorrow," he answered, and Kezzi's heart lifted.

One day—less! Only what was left of this day—and maybe not even that, if she was fortunate, or clever.

"There's stories," the man was saying. "Lunch. Lessons, too, but I got word from a friend that even the lessons are interesting."

"I will come to this school," Kezzi said, and smiled up at him as Vylet had taught her. "And Rascal, too."

· · · ✳ · · ·

Events was just over, and Ms. Taylor had them standing to follow a list of commands she called out in the *melant'i* of "Simon." Syl Vor theorized that Simon had been the school's exercise master, called away now to other duties, and leaving Ms. Taylor to fulfill his. He wasn't quite able to settle in his own mind whether the sets of commands were original with the exercise master, or current with Ms. Taylor. Whichever, they were *very* silly. In fact, Tansy and Kaleb laughed outright at the various directions to *raise your left foot and bounce on your right*, or *pat your head and rub your belly*, or—

"Simon says, *turn around as fast as you can!*" Ms. Taylor said sharply.

Syl Vor gasped, hearing an echo of Grandaunt's voice in that sharp command, and turned every bit as quickly as he could— and there was Kaleb, staggering as he spun, shouting laughter.

Syl Vor pulled in his shoulders and twisted.

Kaleb yelled, "Watch it!" and jumped for the space behind Delia's chair, which was where Syl Vor had been going, and he twisted again; Kaleb bumped the chair, knocking it into Syl Vor's knee.

He overbalanced, chairs screeched across the floor, kids yelled, and he fell, barely managing to tuck up so he didn't hurt himself.

Much.

"Don't the Boss teach you not to fall over chairs?" That was Rudy.

"Who'd thought such a little kid could make such a big mess outta Simon Says?" *That* was Peter.

"Kaleb! You okay?" And Tansy.

Syl Vor, curled on the floor, sighed and took stock, which the training tapes, and Grandfather and Grandaunt, and Quin and Padi had *all* told him that he must do, once he had time.

He'd hit his elbow hard when he fell, which was his own fault for not tucking fast enough; and his knee hurt where the chair had banged into it. Beyond that...

"Syl Vor," Ms. Taylor said, softly. He felt her stroke his hair. Horrified, he opened his eyes and saw her knees on the floor in front of him. "You okay, honey?"

He took a breath. "Yes, ma'am," he said, and wriggled into a sitting position, out from under her touch. She wasn't kin. She had no—He swallowed, and looked down, deliberately reviewing the calming exercise. The bracelet had slipped down over his hand. He pushed it back up under the sleeve of his sweater.

"I'm all right," he said, looking firmly into Ms. Taylor's face.

"What happened?" she asked.

"Fell over his own feet," Rudy said.

Ms. Taylor looked over Syl Vor's head, frowning darkly. "I am *speaking* with Syl Vor," she said sharply.

There was a short silence, then Rudy muttered, "Yes, ma'am."

"Syl Vor, what happened?" Ms. Taylor repeated.

Surely, she'd seen what had happened, he thought crankily. And then thought that she might not have, because she had everybody to watch, and during the Simon game she tended to watch Peter and Rudy, Tansy, Kaleb, and Arn.

"I turned as fast as I could," he said carefully, "and s-saw that I might...bump Kaleb, and so I tried..." He bit his lip, unsure of how much he needed to say, and not wanting to seem to place blame on Kaleb.

"You tried to miss him and that put you off-balance," Ms. Taylor finished, and Syl Vor felt relief. She *did* understand, then.

"Can you stand up?" she asked.

"Yes, ma'am," he said, and did so, then stood looking down into her face, which wore a startled expression. She was his elder, so he offered her his hand, politely, heard Rudy laugh, and Peter snicker, and saw Ms. Taylor's lips thin.

She put her hand in his and rose, hardly using his support at all.

"That was very courteous, Syl Vor, thank you."

She looked around, and nodded briskly.

"All right, everyone, put things in order, then back to your seats! Geography next!"

· · · ✳ · · ·

Mike Golden kept a firm grip on her shoulder as they walked toward the *school*. Kezzi kept a sharp eye out for another of the *kompani*, but saw no one she could signal.

"Here we go," the man said, steering her toward three scrubbed stone steps, and a bright red door at the top, with a handsome knocker made out of good Bedel blackwork, in the shape of a goat-footed man playing the short pipes.

Kezzi stumbled, seeing that knocker, for she remembered Pulka laughing at Rafin over his care of work that was destined to adorn the *gadje* house of love, until Rafin had growled at him to shut up, or go away, and in either case leave him in peace.

This, Kezzi thought, was bad, and now that she knew what *school* was, she almost thought that she might prefer jail. But no. There were stories she had dreamed, that told of escape from such houses as this. It could be done. And she had an ally.

Twisting in Mike Golden's hand, she faked a stumble. He went to one knee with her, his grip firm, but that was all right, the only thing she needed to do was drop a single word in Malda's up-perked ear.

"*Ezat.*" Help.

Malda yipped once, spun, and raced off the way they had come.

Mike Golden never faltered.

"You okay?" he asked.

"I'm not hurt," she answered, allowing herself to be brought to her feet. She looked up into his face. "I don't want to go there."

He sighed, his brown *gadje* eyes seeming sad. "We been through this, right? It's school or jail. You chose school. For what it's worth, I think that's the good choice, and I think you're gonna

enjoy yourself. Just gotta go in, is all. Give it a try. Can't hurt."
He tipped his head. "Your dog gonna be okay?"

"He knows the way home," she replied, and he nodded.

"Right, then. Let's go, Anna."

He exerted pressure, and she went. There was no use fighting him, when he could easily carry her, if he decided to do so.

And wherever she was going, Kezzi thought, she preferred to go on her own two feet.

CHAPTER NINETEEN

. . . .

"WHERE DO WE WALK TODAY, BROTHER?" RYS ASKED UDARI.

Some six paces back their path had deviated from the well-known route to Pulka's hearth, and Udari, usually so informative, had said nothing. Perhaps, Rys thought wryly, there was proper work of men to be done, and he had been called to it. He had, after all, only assumed that they were bound for Pulka and another session of tea, and smoke, and half-sketches made in chalk on the hearth-stones. Sketches that were more often than not rubbed out, while more tea was poured, and the pipes refilled.

"Today, we go to the forges, where you will come to know our brother Rafin."

"And has my brother Rafin work to which I might set my hand?"

Udari considered that in silence as they turned onto a ramp that tended, ever so slightly downward. Rys swung along beside, having grown accustomed to Udari's silences, and minding how he set his crutch on the slope.

"It is possible that Rafin will discover tasks for all of us, in time. Just at first, though, Brother—a word in your ear. At first, Rafin may be a bit short in his temper. It's his way. Possibly, he will send us from his hearth. It has happened that he has cast brothers forth. If it should chance to happen today, be of firm heart. Firmness speaks to Rafin, and perseverance, which your brothers have in abundance."

"But," Rys said carefully, "what do we attempt?"

"What do we attempt?" Udari laughed. "The design is complete, so Pulka insists, and who would know better? There is no one in the *kompani* who can match or come near Pulka's designs! What else should he do, then, but bring his dream to the best builder among us?"

So, the talk and the smoke and the countless pots of tea had borne fruit? Yet, where *was* this design?

"Does Pulka meet us," he asked carefully, "with the rendering of the design?"

"We will find Pulka at Rafin's hearth," Udari said composedly, which was a less complete answer than Rys could have wished. However, just then, the ramp took a turn and angled more sharply downward, and he was obliged to pay close attention to his balance, leaving other questions unasked.

"Damned if I will!" A voice rolled down the narrow tunnel, echoing off the walls like the sea.

If it were Rafin moved to such a pronouncement, Rys thought, it would seem that Pulka's design had not found favor.

"Damned if you don't!" Yes, that was Pulka, his voice recognizable even at such a pitch.

Rys planted the tip of his crutch carefully against the tunnel's molded floor, and shifted his weight onto his good leg.

"I hear our brothers at prayer," Udari said from behind. He patted Rys lightly on the shoulder. "There is nothing out of the ordinary here, Brother. Nothing to concern you. Come, let us add our blessings to the occasion."

More shouting rumbled along the walls, the words unintelligible. Perhaps they were spoken in the Bedel language, in which Rys was in nowise fluent. Perhaps it was simply that volume overtook sense. He was not much inclined to go forward into the din. Had he been alone, he would have turned and sought Silain's hearth again, or made the long journey to the garden to offer his hand to Mcmit.

However, he was not alone, and he had come into the habit of trusting Udari, who was never anything but gentle in their dealings, and who had indeed shown him a brother's care.

So it was that he let the crutch take his weight and continued on toward the rumbling racket, with Udari walking a little in advance, shoulders stiff, despite his tone of amused affection.

A light showed ahead, brighter and broader than the spots in the tunnel's ceiling. The shouting had stopped now; the walls were informed with a low hum, like an engine idling. Udari walked on and so, perforce, did Rys—to the end of the tunnel, into a wide, vaulted room. In the room's center, fire roared in a forge twice Udari's height, pipes crisscrossing above it, taking off heat and steam it was certain, though the destination of those elements was not immediately apparent.

"A blessed day to you, Brothers!" Udari said cheerfully, walking toward the two men by the hearth—Pulka, bald and plump, his face red in the heat. The other man was stripped to the waist, showing a well-muscled belly and dark skin slick with sweat.

It was the second man who turned to Udari with what came to Rys' ear as a curse, despite the fact that he did not know the words.

"There's no need of that!" Pulka snapped. "Udari has a brother to care for, whatever you—"

"A *brother*, is it?" The lean, angry man—Rafin, surely—spun fast, one hand snatching Udari's arm and pulling him, unresisting, closer to the dangerous flames.

"What means of man brings a *gadje* to the *kompani* as a brother, Udari of the Bedel?"

"A man of heart, Brother Rafin," Udari answered, his voice calm, and his shoulders tense.

Rys moved forward, deliberately, any noise his crutch might make against the floor hidden in the fire's dull roar.

"*A man of heart* brings a mewling broken kitten of a *gadje* into the *kompani*, calls him brother and seeks repair for wounds too terrible to bear. A man of action—attend me well, Udari of the Bedel!" Rafin yanked the younger man forward, overbalancing him, so that he steadied himself with one hand on Rafin's naked shoulder. Rafin's face, sharp cheekbones, strong brow, and prominent hooked nose, was very nearly cheek to Udari's cheek.

"*A man of action*," Rafin said, his voice low and rough, "would have prevented what pain he might, bestowing a blessing, and holding the *kompani* close." He tightened his grip and Udari's boots gritted on the floor as he sought his balance. "A man of action cannot change what a man of heart has done, but I swear upon—"

"Let my brother Udari go," Rys said, hearing his voice calm and cold against the heated roar of Rafin's forge. "Brother, he is unbalanced and will do better without your aid."

Rafin turned his head; his eyes were a hot blue in his lean, dark face. For a long moment, the room was silent. Even the fire seemed to cease its growl.

Then, Rafin thrust Udari back. The slighter man spun like a dancer, perfectly balanced, keeping a wary eye on Rafin.

Rys eased his weight onto his good leg. Having released Udari, it naturally followed that Rafin would turn his attention, and his enmity, to the man who had demanded it.

He had, Rys reminded himself, dry-mouthed, *wanted* that.

He took a deep breath and felt a certain coolness flow into him. The man before him was tall, his big hands in fists, standing well-balanced on two sturdy legs.

Yet, Rys thought, as the coolness flowed and deepened, he was not himself without resources.

He shifted his grip on the crutch, and surreptitiously flexed his other arm, testing the heft of the splint.

"You!" Rafin snarled. "Do you think that I—I, Rafin!—will build a leg for you? That I will not, little *gadje*. Heed me; *I will not.* Nor will I call you brother, or give you any soft word or gentleness such as my brothers-born might have from me."

"You have, in fact, taken me in dislike," Rys said, from a center so cold it might have been said to be ice.

"Dislike?" Rafin gave a sharp snap of laughter. "You are unnatural, *gadje*, do you know it? You are a dead man, yet you . . . *walk*, let us make it. You have no place in life, and yet you seek a place in the *kompani*."

He had moved, two small, stealthy steps. Rys stood his ground, balance assured, holding himself ready. Without question, Rafin *would* make a move—Udari thought so, too. From the side of his eye, Rys saw Udari dance one step forward, as if he would intervene, only to have his arm caught and held by Pulka, who signed something quick and low with his off-hand.

"What you may have from me, little *gadje*, is what any dangerous vermin may have."

Rafin extended, his arm coming out and down, like a branch falling, and like a branch falling it would break what it struck.

Rys gave his weight to his good leg and threw the crutch up, meeting Rafin's arm with an audible crack. The man spun to the side, wide open, depending on speed, reach, and reputation to win his point. Rys did a quick calculation, and swung the crutch again, clipping Rafin smartly above the ear. Deliberate, that blow—hard enough to give pause—but not hard enough to kill.

Rafin dropped back a step, and raised a hand.

"Hold," he said, rubbing his head with the other hand.

"Hold," he said again, and walked to the right, circling Rys, where he stood braced, his thoughts cold and clear, waiting. If Rafin rushed him from behind, he must drop to his better knee and sweep the crutch to knock the other off his feet, then jam the point of the crutch into the vulnerable throat, for the kill. If he lost the crutch, there was the splint left for a weapon.

"So." Rafin was standing before him again, hard hands behind his back. He glanced aside, to Pulka and to Udari, and used his chin to draw their attention to Rys.

"Behold him, Brothers, as he stands there, one-legged, fending off a wolf of the Bedel with his *crutch*, eh? Eh?" He slapped his hands on his thighs and laughed as noisily as he had cursed.

"I see it!" he said, looking to Udari. "Brother, I see what you saw! Even a man of action might love the tiny cock, fire in his eye and one wing trailing." He slapped his thighs again.

"I will do it!" The ductwork rang with his shout. "By the blood of the Bedel, I *will* do it! Come, Pulka! I would dream what you have dreamed."

The two moved aside, away from the forge, toward an alcove and the table set there.

Rys closed his eyes as the icy surety melted and flowed away, leaving him overheated and shaking, his heart pounding in his ears. He sagged on the crutch—and snapped straight, eyes opening as he sensed a body within reach.

"Brother." Udari extended a gentle hand and touched Rys on the shoulder. "Brother, you played that exactly! You have won Rafin's help."

"But not his brotherhood," Rys said. His stomach was churning. He feared he might shame himself, and—where had those thoughts come from? he asked himself. The detailed series of moves that would end a man's life, framed in a clarity as hard as crystal.

"Rys?" Udari murmured.

He drew a breath. "I believe... that I need to sit down, Brother."

• • • ❖ • • •

The door opened into a small room that smelled sweet and smoky. There was a red rug under Kezzi's boots and a red lamp hanging from a chain.

To her right, she glimpsed a larger room with yellow covers on the chairs; the red rug had yellow flowers woven into it, and there was a branch with yellow cloth flowers tied to it in a bowl on a wooden table. Somewhere in the part of the room she couldn't see, she heard a man's voice, followed by a woman's laugh, and a dry rustle.

Ahead, the red rug ran down the center of a narrow hall, somewhat more brightly lit by wall lamps in white and yellow.

To Kezzi's left was another door, and this now opened. A man stepped through, sock-footed, brown-haired, and rumpled, with a red mark on his pale cheek, sleep heavy in his eyes.

"Who... Oh. Mike. 'Mornin'." The man pulled his shapeless grey sweater closer around him, and yawned.

"'Mornin'," Mike Golden said. "Rough night?"

The other man raised a slender hand to his cheek to rub the red mark.

"Fell asleep on the 'counts book," he said with a shy smile. "Don't tell Ms. Audrey, now."

"Not a word," Mike Golden said. His fingers tightened briefly on her shoulder; he might have glanced down at her—the other man did, and smiled.

"Hey, honey. What's your name?" he asked, his voice pitched slightly higher than it had been for Mike Golden. It was, she realized, the voice a certain kind of *gadje* used when they talked to Malda, and asked if he was a *good fella*.

"Anna," she said, and gave the man the *other* smile Vylet had taught her.

"You're a real cutie," he said, giving her back the exact same smile. "I'm Sheyn. You come find me when you get tired of Mike. I'll take good care of you."

"She's here for school," Mike Golden said from behind her, his voice sounding growlier than usual.

"Oho!" Sheyn winked broadly, like Pulka when he was teasing her. "You'll like Jansy. All the girls do."

"Sheyn." That was Mike Golden again.

"Hey, don't get mad, Mike." Sheyn aimed Vylet's *other* smile over Kezzi's head. "*You* won't flirt with me—how else am I gonna practice?" He raised a hand, showing a soft, white palm. "Never mind. You know where you're going. I gotta get back to the 'counts." He looked at Kezzi and smiled again—not at all like Vylet, but like Udari, sweet and kind. "Study good, Anna."

"All right," she said, gravely, and moved in obedience to the pressure of Mike Golden's fingers—forward, down the narrow hallway.

· · · ✹ · · ·

They'd put the chairs back in order, and settled into them, Syl Vor sitting quietly beside Jeff.

"You really okay?" Jeff asked, speaking indistinctly out of the side of his mouth, while Ms. Taylor fiddled with the desk controllers. "Looked like you banged your knee pretty bad."

"I am okay," Syl Vor assured him, and added, "thank you for your care."

Jeff shrugged. "Whatever. Just—if it swells up, you put snow or ice on it, 'kay?"

"I will," Syl Vor promised.

Up at the front of the room, Ms. Taylor had turned toward the hall; Syl Vor heard the sound of heavy feet on the carpet. He sat up interestedly. Had the patrol brought in another student?

The door opened, and Mike Golden walked into the classroom, his hand firm on the shoulder of a black-haired girl in a dusty green coat that was too big for her.

Ms. Taylor went to Mike's side, and he leaned over to talk to her, his hand still on the girl's shoulder. She looked out over the room from narrowed black eyes, chin up. Syl Vor knew that look. It was what Padi did when she was scared and trying to figure out what to do next.

"Wonderful!" Ms. Taylor said brightly.

She stepped to the girl's side and curled her hand around the dusty green sleeve, holding firmly. Mike put his hands behind his back, and stood with his legs braced, like he expected the floor to move—or the girl to run, Syl Vor thought suddenly, seeing a tiny shift in her balance. Ms. Taylor must have felt the move, because she put her other hand around the girl's arm, too.

"Everyone? Your attention, please! We have a new member of the class."

Behind Syl Vor, a chair creaked, and over to the front right of the room, somebody scuffed their shoes against the floor. Otherwise, their attention was on the front of the room. The black-haired girl glared at them all, lips pressed tight.

"This is what we do, honey. You tell the class your name and turf, and then they'll each tell you theirs, by turn. After introductions are over, you'll take a seat." Ms. Taylor smiled brightly. "You're just in time for geography—my favorite class!"

The black-haired girl turned her head to wordlessly stare at Ms. Taylor.

Mike Golden cleared his throat.

The black-haired girl took a deep breath.

"My name is Anna," she said, giving the *s* an extra hiss. She took another breath. "Anna Brown. Boss Wentworth's turf."

"Wentworth's turf, huh?" Peter said from the back of the room. "How come I never seen ya?"

The chin lowered, black eyes wide now. "Maybe you're blind," Anna said with great disinterest, "or maybe you're stupid."

"Children!" Ms. Taylor's voice was sharp. "Pete, I'll expect you to bring me a complete list of everyone in Boss Wentworth's territory tomorrow morning. Anna, we don't call our classmates stupid. Now! Introductions, starting from the front right please."

One by one, the *gadje* stood up from their chairs, spoke their names and the name of their Boss—pale faces, dark faces, tall, small, boy, girl, eyes as bright as colored glass, high voices like mice. Kezzi didn't bother to listen to what they said, only glared at each in turn. At least Mike Golden had gone away, and if the *gadje* woman would loosen her grip, the door was only three long steps away.

Except there was the man Sheyn between her and the outside door. He would only bring her back here. For all she knew, Mike Golden himself stood guard at the doorway and...

Yet another *gadje* stood up from his place—yellow hair and blue marble eyes, his face neither pale nor dark, but a smooth gold, like Rys' skin, now that the bruises and cuts were gone.

Kezzi glared at the yellow-haired boy and breathed in the pattern that cleared the mind. Trying to run away would only make them watch her the harder, she thought. Better to be like these—or as much like as she could—so that they would grow careless. *Then* she might make an escape.

Or Mike Golden might have said the truth, and at the end of the day she would go out the door and back to the *kompani*...

"Thank you, everyone; that was very nicely done," the *gadje*— the "Ms. Taylor" said, chirping brightly, like a bird. She nodded at one of the smaller boys. "Arn, please show Anna where to hang up her coat."

"Yes, Ms. Taylor," he said, and jumped to his feet, running noisily down the room toward a wall hung with many garments. "C'mon, Anna!" he said, turning and waving at her.

They were all watching her. This was not what one of the Bedel wished for, within a crowd of *gadje*. Kezzi felt a little sick to her stomach, and swallowed, and remembered Malda—brave and clever. She walked—head up, with modest steps that did not crash against the plastic floor—down the room, to the place where the boy Arn stood, pointing to an empty hook.

It was hard—very hard—to hang the coat on that hook, though the pockets were not as full as she had intended. And, she told herself, she had her small knife, some flashers, and a kerchief full of dried apples from their own trees in the pockets of her vest.

"Hurry up," Arn said, jostling her elbow. "We're missing geography." He ran noisily back to his seat. Kezzi turned around and looked up the room, frowning into Ms. Taylor's smile.

"Good," the *gadje* said. "Now, Anna, you can take the seat next to Syl Vor."

Syl Vor? Now, she saw her error. She should have listened to the *gadje*'s names, and remembered them. Had Silain not taught her—*to remember is to know*?

She swallowed, trying to think, to remember, while she looked here and there around the room, and—wait!

There was a chair—a single empty chair among the clustered *gadje*, next to the boy with the yellow hair who reminded her of Rys.

She sat on the edge of that empty chair, tucking her hands into the warm tail of her scarf.

In front of the room, Ms. Taylor raised her eyebrows, and nodded as if to say that Kezzi had done well, which made her feel...pleased. It *had* been well done, she told herself, and a good sign that in this place the *kompani*'s fortune remained intact.

Silain, and Pulka, too, said that the *kompani*'s fortune came from the wit and the heart of the Bedel. She must not be stupid again.

She leaned forward in her chair as Ms. Taylor picked up a small black stick and called out, in a voice that rang the rafters, "All right, everybody! Time to do routes!"

Routes today was a quick review of nearby landmarks, for the new girl, Syl Vor thought. At least she was paying attention now, frowning slightly after the red dot, and nodding to herself when each route was completed. Syl Vor sighed. She had made a good recovery in figuring out which seat she was to take. He had thought he was going to have to give her a hint, which he didn't think she would have liked very much. But, really, she should have listened at introductions, rather than just pretending that none of them were there—or that she was someplace else.

"Warm now?" Ms. Taylor shouted.

In the chair next to him, Anna twitched; she hadn't been expecting that.

She twitched again when Syl Vor joined the class in shouting back, "We're warm all right!"

"Let's do round two!" Ms. Taylor threw the pointer to Vanette, who jumped up and caught it between two hands, then stood bouncing on the balls of her feet, grinning.

"Everett's Market," Ms. Taylor said, which was barely a clue at all.

Syl Vor frowned. Everett's Market was in . . . was in . . .

"Whitman's turf!" Rodale, who hardly ever volunteered, jumped up from his seat in the back. "It's in a big ol' garage thing over out east o'the Hamilton Street."

Vanette spun, stared at him, spun back and raised the pointer. The red dot traced a quick route from their location to Hamilton, hesitated . . .

"East . . ." Rodale almost-whispered, leaning forward. "Look east, see? Next to the booths, just about . . ."

Syl Vor stared at the map, finding the tollbooths, but—a big garage? He leaned forward, his hand gripping the back of the chair in front of him, staring . . .

Vanette squeaked; the red dot jumped, then traced a smooth

path 'round a corner and up two streets, to rest determinedly in the center of a large rectangle.

"Very good!" Ms. Taylor applauded. "What teamwork!"

"But—" Vanette turned to look at Rodale. "How did you *know*? You're Cruther's."

"Ustabe we were Whitman's," Rodale said, looking down at the floor. "M'dad street-hopped when I was a kid, on account the Alleys had work."

"That's a good memory," Vanette said. "Thanks."

"No prob," Rodale muttered, and sat down abruptly, head hanging.

Vanette tossed the pointer back to Ms. Taylor, who looked around the room, a considering frown on her face.

Suddenly, she grinned, and threw the pointer to—Syl Vor tensed, hand rising—

But the throw was to Anna.

She jumped up and sideways, catching the pointer in her off-hand like she was turning an opponent's knife.

"Show me the quickest way to Finder's Junk Heap."

Anna raised the pointer, touched the school briefly, then traced a swift, unhesitating path down the back alley, across several streets into Boss Kalhoon's territory, then a sharp right, down another alley, across a red do-not-cross line, and into the heart of Finder's.

For a moment, no one said anything. Then Rudy jumped to his feet.

"That route don't work!"

Anna turned to stare at him, the pointer held loosely in an attitude Syl Vor knew well.

"It does," she said flatly, and looked him up and down, one side of her mouth lifting slightly in what was *not* a smile. "Unless you're afraid of the fence?"

Rudy's face flushed as red as his hair.

"I ain't afraid a no fence! But that route's not straight!"

"It is straight! Straightest there is!" Anna answered hotly.

"Yes, it is," Ms. Taylor said, so strongly that Anna turned away from Rudy to face her. "It is the straightest route, Anna, thank you. Rudy's right to call a foul, though. The routes we're looking for are those that can be walked, with—with a sack of groceries on your arm. For class, we don't want emergency routes, or your family's special ways. Okay?"

Anna was silent for the time it might take somebody to sigh feelingly.

"Yes," she said, and lifted the pointer again, touching the Junk Heap. "To not climb the fence, you walk this way, around half, then to the road, turn on the right hand, and back to the corner by the rag shop."

Syl Vor blinked, and looked up at her. She spoke as if she had walked the street in question not once but many times.

But Finder's Junk Heap was in Marriot's turf, which was six turfs over from Wentworth's.

"Thank you, Anna," Ms. Taylor said composedly. She held out her hand. "Please throw the pointer to me. Gently. Thank you." She tucked it into her pocket.

"We're running a little behind today, class. Let's get some lunch and see if we can catch up!"

Rafin himself verified Droi's measurements, and with a surprisingly gentle hand. He then returned to the alcove, and Pulka, whereupon the two took up their discussion, enlivened by much waving of the hands, and the occasional loud exclamation.

Rys watched it all from the chair Udari had found for him—a splendid thing of smooth, varnished wood, the seat and back woven leather, the whole comfortably balanced on rockers, that gently accepted the guidance of his good leg.

So it was that he sat, and rocked, drank the tea that Udari brought him, and eventually drowsed, until Rafin's sudden shout brought him wide awake, nerves tingling.

"Enough! We dream as one! Let us now gather what is needed."

Udari, who had been sitting on a rug at Rys' right, sipping tea and observing the comedy, came to his feet at that, and extended a hand, as if to help him up.

Rys grabbed his crutch and came out of the rocking chair, clumsy, even given the strength of his brother's arm.

"We, too, Brothers," Udari said.

Pulka stopped in his headlong rush and blinked at the two of them.

"You, certainly, Brother," he said. "But for Rys to undertake such a journey..."

"Why should the fighting cock not come with us?" Rafin

shouted. "The journey and what we find at the end of it are in his service, eh? Let him come!"

"He will slow us," Pulka protested.

"He! Oh, *he'll* keep up, won't you, my cock?" Rafin slapped his thigh and roared laughter. "Keep up? He'll be there before us!"

He turned and strode away, past the forge. Pulka shrugged, and cast a glance at Udari.

"Come, then," he said brusquely and departed in the noisy wake of Rafin.

"Where are we going?" Rys asked.

"Into the City Above, to Finder's Junk Heap," Udari said, pacing him.

Rys stopped, swallowing hard in a throat gone tight. His face was hot; his hands were cold.

"Brother?" Two paces ahead, Udari turned to look at him.

"The City Above," Rys managed, his voice rasping, and shivered, hearing the sound of air parted by a mighty wing.

"I . . ." *cannot* withered on his tongue. He had observed betimes that he seemed to be a proud man. He had not previously understood that he was a fool.

Despite his not saying the word, Udari seemed to hear it. His face softened and he came back to stand by Rys and place a gentle hand on his shoulder.

"You need have no fear, in the City Above. The ones who beat you have long since gone away. If any should try to make you their sport—why, you will be with your brothers, who do not hesitate to use their knives in a brother's defense."

From somewhere—from nowhere—from the murkiness inside his head, a pattern arose. He attended it in some fashion that felt both entirely natural and wholly alien. His breathing smoothed, his heartbeat slowed.

Fear receded.

"What do we want," he was able to ask sensibly, "at this . . . junk heap?"

Udari was seen to smile, just slightly.

"Metal and fittings and those other things that shared dreaming has revealed." He paused, then added, very gently, "It is as Rafin says, Brother; you should be part of this, as what comes of it will be part of you."

"I agree," Rys said, calmly. Thin though his knowledge of metals seemed to him as he stood here, had he not learned that it was possible he knew something of use, which would rise from the murk when it was needed?

And the dragon? It was as Udari said—he was not alone.

"I thought you would agree, bold heart. There are hats and jackets hung at the gate. Use what you need."

"Yes," said Rys and smiled up into Udari's face. "Thank you, Brother. Let us go."

CHAPTER TWENTY

THE YELLOW-HAIRED BOY WITH THE GLASS-BLUE EYES POSSESSED a remarkable thing. A thing of dreams.

He had...a *pen.*

Not just any pen, but a pen that wrote in four different colors, depending on which button was pushed on the barrel.

The moment she saw it, Kezzi knew that she had to possess it. Indeed, it seemed that it *was* hers, so familiar was it to her eye. Her fingers ached to hold it, and she desired it with her whole being.

The shared meal had taught her that it was very easy to steal from these *gadje*. Perhaps it was because they were young. Or perhaps they were only stupid.

She was patient, bending her head above the paper she shared with the yellow-haired boy, pretending to study the words printed there, and nodding whenever he drew a line—a red line between words that had the same meaning, and a green line between words that had an opposite meaning. Time and again, a heavy bracelet would peer out from under his sleeve, and he would immediately push it back into hiding again. It seemed a rich thing for a boy to have, but nowhere near as enticing as the pen.

In good time, her patience was rewarded. The Ms. Taylor called for their attention on the screen. The boy put his pen down and obediently lifted his head. Kezzi leaned forward, her eyes on the screen while she fingered the pen into her palm, and slipped her hand to her lap—

Fingers closed around her wrist, strong fingers for all they were so thin. She met the *gadje*'s blue eyes.

"That," he said in a fierce whisper, "is *mine*."

"It is mine now," she answered haughtily.

His mouth thinned. "No. It belongs to me."

"Well, *I* need it."

The blue eyes narrowed.

Before she knew what he was about, he had slipped his other hand under hers, twisted the pen out of her grip, released her wrist, and again turned his head toward the screen. The coveted pen was now held firmly in his fist.

Kezzi drew a hard breath and sighed it out noisily.

"Anna?" The Ms. Taylor said from the top of the room. "Would you like to tell the class the difference between *inflate* and *deflate*?"

· · · ※ · · ·

Rys leaned against a toothy boulder of broken 'crete, having been sternly warned away from the fence, which held a charge, so he surmised, except for those few heartbeats after it had been touched by the device Pulka had pulled from his belt.

He had not, after all, slowed them *very* much, though the effort had cost him. He was clammy with sweat, his muscles were aquiver, and his face burning. He very much wished for the quiet rocker in Rafin's shop, and a cup of bitter Bedel tea in his hand.

Yet still, there had accrued some good to his account. Rafin had been seen to smile, and Pulka heard to grunt softly in what was understood to be approval as he crossed the fence in Udari's wake.

And then there was this place, itself.

A treasure trove, this so-called "junk heap," and more neatly filed than his understanding of "heap" encompassed. Not that it would ever be mistaken for a porcelain shop, but there was order, of a kind. Metal was sorted with metal, wood with wood, stone with stone. Within each large category, some attempt had been made at a more detailed catalog: rebar was bunched together, and piping; wires and rope were coiled by weight; tubes and small electronics were piled into half-barrels and roughed-together bins.

Among this bounty, his brothers prowled, on the hunt among

the piles of treasure, for he knew not what. From beyond the yard came the sounds of vehicles passing on the road, and some few footsteps; a laugh, sharp and short. If there was a keeper of this heap, he was engaged elsewhere. Or perhaps Rafin had a draw account.

"Brother?" Here was Udari, coming back to him, bright copper coiled 'round his arm like a warrior's wristlet, and a spool of dull grey wire in his hand.

Rys found a smile and pushed away from his support, willing overworked muscles to bear him, shivering as a breeze slipped chilly fingers down his collar.

"I come," he said. "I only needed a moment to rest."

Udari smiled. "A moment and a day you will have of rest, your brother swears it to you. But first, your eye and your wisdom are needed on the gifts we stand among. Pulka would have the thing done sturdily, which you know means it will weigh more than you and I together. Rafin cares naught; his art is in the crafting."

"And it is, after all," Rys said, giving more of his weight to the stick than he usually cared to do, "for my benefit."

"There you have it."

Udari, seeing him on his feet and stirring, faded back into the mysteries of the heap. Rys continued onward, toward the rusted piles of metal, trying to envision what might be crafted from such rough fare. He was not, alas, a worker in metal, or an artisan of any kind, such as Rafin and Pulka must be. Repairs, yes, and rough carpentry, much like the knocked-together boxes just here, enough to hold cuttings for compost, or a load of sweet soil for mixing among the roots. But—

A flash of blue and silver caught his eye, not stacked with the sharp, dark metals, but *there*, in a box of transparent tubing, beneath a scattering of thin glass bulbs in various colors, a shine of blue, a glint of silver...

"Well, little cock, what have your bright eyes seen?"

Rafin leaned past him, shifted the glass with care, and brought out a rough knot of mingled blue and silver metals, the whole thing slightly larger than Rys' head. He sighed. Two metals had melted and fused, so it seemed to him, and if anything worthwhile could be made from either...

"By the blood of the Bedel," Rafin breathed, "you *have* eyes, do you not, little one? This..." Strong teeth showed in a dark, angular face, as he held the ragged lump up and shook it. "This *will do*, I think. Eh? *Eh*?" The grin became a shout of laughter that rang metal piled about.

The knot of blue and silver vanished into Rafin's bag. He bent again and chose a length of tubing and several of the glass bulbs, which also vanished into the bag.

He then slipped a hand under Rys' elbow and guided him to a relatively smooth block of stone.

"Rest you here; your work is done. Your brothers will garner what supplies we yet lack." A rough pat on his shoulder, as surprising as it was gentle, and Rafin was gone.

Rys settled on the block, sighed—and sat straight up.

Somewhere nearby a dog barked—a familiar high yip that brought him to his feet.

"Malda!" he called, and heard the yip again, closer now.

From across the yard came Pulka's voice, rough in what must have been a curse. "If that girl has followed us on brother-work—"

"No!" That was Udari.

Rys saw him stride to Rafin's side and thrust his gleanings into ready hands.

"The dog is alone. Hold these, Brother. I will bring him in."

· · · ❄ · · ·

The Ms. Taylor had called dismissal. All the young *gadje*, talking and laughing, with Kezzi silent in their midst, filed to the bottom wall, took their coats down and pulled them on.

Kezzi sealed her coat, and followed Desi up the row along the wall to the hallway. Soon! Soon, now, she would be free. She would return to the *kompani*, and she would never leave again—*never*!

Well... for at least a long week. Or two. Bitterly, she regretted not having gotten the colors before Mike Golden had forced her here. Two long weeks might have been well spent, tracing out and coloring her cards.

The pen... that was another regret. Four colors was not very many, but—

A hand closed over her wrist.

Instinctively, she snatched it back, but the hand only tightened. She turned her head and met the firm, glass-blue gaze of the yellow-haired *gadje*.

"Let me go," she snapped.

"Presently," he said coolly, and walked with her down the hall, the other *gadje* noisy around them.

Ahead, she saw the door to the street, open. Sheyn stood in the doorway to the red-and-yellow room, watching. He raised a hand as Kezzi went past.

"Hey, Anna! See you tomorrow!"

She turned her head away, pretending she did not hear.

Through the door they went, she and the yellow-haired *gadje*. At the top of the stairs, she threw her weight against him, meaning to knock him off his feet, but he thrust a hard shoulder into her, which unbalanced both of them, and they stumbled together to the walk...

...where Mike Golden stood, hands tucked into his pockets, his broad face placid and his eyes as sharp as one of Rafin's throwing thorns.

Kezzi took a breath.

"Let me *go*," she hissed at the boy.

"Presently," he said again, and pulled her with him, to Mike Golden's side.

"Evenin', Anna. Silver."

"Good evening, Mike."

"School is finished," Kezzi said. "I want to go home."

Mike Golden eyed her. "Nothin' stoppin' you, is there?"

She threw her captive hand into the air, surprised that the boy allowed it.

Mike Golden pursed his lips.

"Silver. What's up?"

"Anna is coming home with us."

"I am not!"

The boy turned his head and looked directly into her eyes.

"You said you needed my pen."

It didn't quite seem a question, but she nodded. "Yes."

"Then you must be brought to my mother."

"Why?" she asked.

"So that she can see you," he snapped.

"I don't want to!" Kezzi snapped back, and yanked her arm, hard. He didn't let go. She glared at him. He glared at her. Neither looked aside.

Mike Golden shifted where he stood, but said nothing.

"I want to go home," Kezzi said finally, without yelling.

"After my mother sees you," he answered calmly.

Kezzi took a breath.

"I offer a bargain," she said. "I see your mother—" His fingers tightened slightly and she stopped, staring at him.

He shook his head, and said slowly, like he was teaching her a story and she had gotten an anchor line wrong: "After my mother *sees you...*"

"After your mother *sees me*," she repeated precisely, "I go home to my grandmother. Can you make this bargain?"

"Yes," he said, bowing his head slightly. "The bargain is made. On my clan."

"All right! Good!" Mike Golden said, briskly. "Let's go, then. No sense standing around and freezing our noses off." He turned, and the boy did, still holding Kezzi by the wrist.

"Silver, you can let her go. She promised to come with us," the man said, and Kezzi's heart rose. *Gadje* were so stupid!

But the boy shook his head, and looked directly into her eyes.

"You didn't promise not to run away, did you, Anna?"

Her heart fell. She glared at him.

"If you want to drag me down the street, do it!" she snapped, because *gadje* didn't like to seem foolish, and maybe the taunt would work where the bargain had failed.

But the boy just bent his head again, like they'd made another bargain, turned, and marched down the walk. Kezzi, perforce, went with him, temper at high boil.

"Right," said Mike Golden, following a step or two behind. "Let's all go see the Boss, then."

· · · ❋ · · ·

"The dog is always with the child," Rys said. "Surely, she can't be far."

"Our small sister has an understanding with her good friend," Udari said, kneeling beside the trembling Malda, and stroking him firmly. "They have dreamed much together, and her good friend accepts her wishes as his own."

Rys drew a hard breath.

"He would come for help, if she were injured?"

"If she told him, and if his memory were long enough," Pulka said sourly, and sighed. "But, yes. This one would die for our sister, and gladly. She found him broken, and nursed him, tended him like he was a babe, then brought him into the *kompani*, with the *luthia*'s blessing on it."

"Which is near enough my own case that I, too, would gladly exchange her safety for my own," Rys said, his breath coming too quickly. He tried to draw a deep breath, to find that core of crystal calm that had served him so well earlier in the day.

"The fighting cock speaks our hearts for us, Brothers," Rafin said. He jerked a shoulder at Pulka. "We divide what must be done. Thus! We three who know the streets best shall go in quest now, while our sweet dreamer of design takes what we have gathered to the *kompani*, and rouses the citywise to the search. We will come, if we have success, to the third gate east, eh?"

"It is done," Pulka said, and without another word received the various bags, spools, and coils from the other two. These he disposed about himself, then turned and walked briskly back the way they had come into the yard.

Udari looked to Rafin.

"Let you and I search, with our sister's friend. The most tried of us—"

"I would spare him more effort," Rafin said, and looked to Rys. "What say you, little one?"

"I will search," he said, pushing himself upright with the crutch, to demonstrate that he was able.

"I had no doubt," Rafin said, and nodded to Udari. "Loose the dog."

The doorbell roused Nova from her perusal of the latest feasibility study for repurposing the warehouse district. She raised her head, lips curving unconsciously as she heard the voices in the hall. Syl Vor, home from school, giving Ms. Veeno her good-afternoon. The doorwoman answered gravely in kind, which had become her habit. She added, "Hey Mike!" loud enough to be heard down the hall, in case one should have fallen, struck one's head, and collapsed insensate to the rug, and thus been unaware of the arrival of the rest of the household.

Nova bent her head over her file once more, still smiling.

Syl Vor's return home from school had become a marker in her day. There was no more eating at her desk, on those days when she was home. She stopped work and had dinner with her son, as they talked over the events of their very different days. If she was wanted elsewhere on the evening, they would then bid each other good-night. If she was in, they would play a few rounds of Ping-Pong at the table in the basement before he closed his day and she returned to her office for another hour or two of work.

It was, in all, a pleasant routine that was beginning to form, and she found herself... soothed.

First, though, he would detour to the kitchen, where Beck would ply him with cookies, or fruit jam on toast, or some other savory thing. Then, he would go upstairs, to his tutors.

Nova flicked a page over—and raised her head again, smile becoming a frown.

Syl Vor's footsteps had not diverted to the kitchen way, but continued toward her office, escorted by Mike Golden's firm, well-known tread—and by another, lighter, set of footsteps that were entirely unfamiliar.

Had there been another... incident at school? she wondered, and took a hard breath against a flash of anger.

Peace, she told herself. *You will know soon enough. The child does not tarry.*

She straightened in her chair, folded her hands atop the file she had been reading; composing herself not a moment too soon.

Footsteps were joined by shadows, which very quickly became Syl Vor, his brisk pace unchecked, and his hand 'round the wrist of another child—a girl, Nova saw, her hair in need of a stern combing and her face smudged with what might be soot.

She was wearing what Nova had come to think of as Surebleak Ordinary—layers of clothing, which could be adjusted, according to the demands of the weather—and she was certainly not as bulky as the overlarge coat and dangling scarf made her seem.

She was also something out of the common way, even for Surebleak, which had a wide range of forms and faces in its gene pool. A broad face, a bold nose, and black eyes sparkling like the very soul of space. She was, Nova thought, angry.

And so was Syl Vor.

He halted just two paces before her desk, bowed briefly, and raised the girl's hand—a grubby item, to be sure, the square fingers entirely unadorned.

"Mother, this is Anna Brown. I wish to propose her as my sister."

If Nova felt a shock at this pronouncement, and she did, it was of a far lesser degree than that experienced by Anna Brown.

"What?" she cried, and yanked against Syl Vor's grip so strongly that he staggered a step. "Are you *stupid*?"

"Not *stupid* enough to steal the plates and forks off the table in front of everybody!" he shouted back. "Or to—"

"*That* is enough," Nova said sternly. "My son, moderate your voice, and pray release your...guest."

"She'll run away."

"Will you?" Nova asked the girl, who glared at her, chin well up.

"No," she said with scant courtesy.

Syl Vor stared at her. "Why not?"

"Because Mike Golden is in my way, you stupid *stupid* boy!"

Nova glanced over her visitor's head. Michael Golden raised his eyebrows and glanced to the left, where there was nothing to engage his attention. So. A tale hung 'round the girl, and Boss Nova's chief of security was complicit in this present...entertainment.

"That is a very good reason," she said gravely. "I myself would hesitate to try to go through a doorway that was held by Mr. Golden." She glanced to her son, noting the signs of continued high temper.

"I understand that you bring...this young person here so that I may See her. Is this correct, my son?"

"Yes, Mother."

"Excellent. We are on the same path. Let us proceed together a step further. You have taken up the *melant'i* of sponsor. Speak to me of your proposed sister's excellencies. What will we gain? How will she profit?"

Syl Vor bit his lip and glanced at the girl beside him—a glance she met with a hard stare, and an explicit frown.

As if that frown was an answer, Syl Vor nodded, and turned to face the desk squarely. He bowed, child to parent, with exact timing. Straightening, he took a breath, and his temper visibly cooled, as if he accessed the mental exercise known as Pilot's Peace, which was nonsense; he was too young.

No sooner had she thought the thought than Nova suppressed a shiver. Of *course*, he had been taught Pilot's Peace. In so many ways, he was not a little boy.

And in others, he was very, very young.

"Mother, I present to you one who gives her name as Anna

Brown. Mike Golden brought her to school today, so I think she must have been a child-on-the-street. She did not want to be in school, and she was afraid of us—"

"I was *not* afraid!"

"—even though she pretended not to be. She was a little stupid at first, and did not attend to the introductions. Later, when Ms. Taylor told her to sit down by me, she figured out where she was to be, even though she hadn't bothered to learn my name. This shows that she's not truly stupid, and that she can think. It also shows that she knows it is important to take orders.

"At lunch, she stole some spoons, a fork, and a plate. While it is not done, to steal from the school, she was very quick, and I don't think anyone else saw her. I don't think what she did was easy, so that demonstrates someone who can learn complex tasks, and who has...dexterity and a good eye." He paused, as if he debated something with himself, glanced to the girl, and moved his shoulders before continuing.

"I feel that she won't like me to say this, but I think it shows her...her mettle. While at lunch, she first made sure to put three rolls away into her pockets before she ate what was on her plate, even though I think she was hungry. I don't know if she took them for, for others at her home, or against her own later need. In either case, she planned ahead."

He raised his chin a bit and met Nova's eyes firmly.

"We will gain a person who is smart, quick, and strong. She plans for her own necessity, but understands that obeying orders is important."

He paused. Nova inclined her head, inviting him to continue.

"From us, she will gain..." He frowned, and bent his head to stare at the papers on the top of her desk, or perhaps—considering the intensity of his regard—through them.

Nova waited, hands folded, eyes on the girl, who was staring at Syl Vor with her mouth slightly open.

"Time," Syl Vor said suddenly, and looked up. "Time to learn and to plan more fully, when there is no reason to steal."

He stood for a moment, head tipped to one side, as if reviewing what he had said, then took a breath and bowed.

"That is what I know of this person, Mother. I think that we and she will profit in Balance."

There was, in Nova's opinion, some doubt of that. However,

strict Balance was not kept in such cases. How could it be? There was no Balance nor keeping of debts between kin.

She nodded.

"That was very creditably done, Syl Vor-son. You are a formidable sponsor, and I am favorably impressed on behalf of your proposed sister. However, as it falls to me to judge merit fully, I have questions which I would put to her. Do you permit?"

Syl Vor glanced to the girl.

"Just tell the truth," he told her.

She said nothing, and in a moment he bowed.

"Mother, please, ask what you will."

· · · ※ · · ·

Syl Vor's mother was...like a star, Kezzi thought—bright and cold. *Gadje* that she was, she sat as a *luthia*, listening to all things said, and unsaid. And now, there would be questions. How not?

Kezzi felt a flutter in her stomach, which would be her body's response to this woman's power. Not fear. She was *not*, she told herself firmly, afraid.

Just tell the truth, the boy had said.

Well.

"You understand that my son proposes to stand as your brother and to have you come into our house as his equal?"

She hadn't quite understood that, no. It seemed an odd thing, but *gadje* ways were all of them odd.

"I understand so now," she answered, which was both polite and the truth.

The woman bowed her bright head.

"That is good. Now, I must know your name. Your *true* name, if you please."

"Kezzi—"

She bit her lip—too late. She had meant to stare, bewildered, but the truth slipped between her lips, and now her true-name had been spoken, and fallen into *gadje* ears.

Horror shivered through her. What would she say to the *luthia*—her own *luthia*, Grandmother Silain? She had dreamed—there were ways to remove unlucky names and rename a person. But she—she did not want another name! She was—

"Kezzi is such a pretty name," the *gadje luthia* said, in her cool, sweet voice. "Whyever did you trade it for Anna Brown?"

"It was a name for the *gadje!*" she cried, blinking back hot tears. She stared into the woman's blue eyes. "*My* name is not for them to know or to call upon!"

"I understand." The voice cooled the heat of her distress. "We will honor your true-name, whether Syl Vor gains a sister this day or no. Anna Brown you shall be, in all our public dealings."

"In school, too," Syl Vor said. "Don't worry, Kezzi. I have a good memory."

She wished he had *no* memory, and no ears, either! But, she remembered, she was done with school now. Recalling that, it was easy to give him one of the smiles Vylet had taught her, and nod.

"If you come into this house as the sister of my son," the voice continued, "there will be matters of the house of which you will not speak to those who are not of our house. Can you mind your tongue, Kezzi?"

"Yes!"

"I believe you," the woman said gravely. "I thank you for your answers and for your forbearance with our poor manners. We will see you properly refreshed immediately. Syl Vor, pray take Kezzi to the kitchen and place the matter before Beck."

"Yes, Mother." Syl Vor bowed, which he did prettily, Kezzi thought, but if he were the son of a *luthia*, then he would have learned many things—as she had.

He hesitated now, however.

"Mother?"

"Yes, my son?"

"Is Kezzi my sister?"

"That is as yet undecided," his mother said, and included Kezzi in her glance. "While you see our guest refreshed, I shall be thinking. When both of these activities have reached their natural conclusion, we will all of us speak again. I promise a decision by the end of the hour, and beg the gift of your patience, my son."

"Yes, Mother," Syl Vor said again, and turned, raising a hand to beckon Kezzi to follow him.

"This way, Kezzi. Beck will be very glad to see you."

She frowned. "Why?"

"Because I never eat enough. I expect you to do better."

Her stomach rumbled, as she turned to follow him—and turned back, remembering her manners.

Solemnly, she bowed to the woman behind the desk.

"I take leave," she said, "with thanks to you." It wasn't at all what she would have said to a *luthia* who was not also a *gadje*, but it was polite.

A cool smile told her that the *luthia* was pleased.

"It is well. Go now, child, and refresh yourself."

She nodded, and followed Syl Vor down the room. Mike Golden stepped aside to let them through the door. He winked at her as she went past.

She pretended not to see.

CHAPTER TWENTY-ONE

"NO, GO! I WILL FOLLOW." RYS COLLAPSED—HE HOPED IT LOOKED as if he leaned—against the rough wall. "In a moment, I will follow."

Udari had kept pace with the dog, so it was to Rafin these things were said, and sharply.

The other man hesitated and cast a glance over his shoulder at Udari and Malda, who were crossing the Port Road and entering the long shadows thrown by the empty tollbooths.

"Go!" he snapped again. "The child..."

Rafin made his decision with a sharp nod.

"Stay here. We will come back for you."

Then he turned, loping away on two good, long legs, a swift shadow passing through the shadows—and vanished.

Rys closed his eyes, shaking, his shattered leg on fire, his muscles gone to water. He remained upright only because he was caught between the tension of crutch and wall. If either moved, he would fall, and become prey, to those who would beat him...

...hard laughter while they stamped on his hand, and kicked him, time and again, and he screamed at last, unable to rise, to fight, to move, one arm over his head, broken with a kick, and another...

"Well met, Rys Lin pen'Chala."

A woman's voice shattered the...memory. He gasped, eyes snapping open, straightening against the wall so that the crutch might be brought in, if—

The woman standing before him smiled, her attitude gentle and without threat. She extended a hand and gently cupped his cheek, as if it were her right. Her fingers were cold.

"Well met," she said again, in the blessed language of home. "I might have guessed that *you* would elude the Dragon."

. . . ⚬ . . .

"Mr. Golden." Nova fixed her henchman in her eye. "Would you care to explain your part in this tangle?"

"My part?" He came into the room and dropped into the chair beside her desk. "My part's simple enough, ma'am, and just like the boy said. I saw a child-on-the-street and since I'm a duly appointed law enforcement officer, accordin' to the way things are standin' right now, I saw that there was some law to be enforced." He gave her a grin. "Just doin' my duty, ma'am."

Nova sighed. "The tangle I refer to is Kezzi's arrival in this office on Syl Vor's . . . arm. I wonder that you failed to use your considerable address, Mr. Golden, to intervene."

He sighed. "Well, see, I didn't get to use any of that address, and if I'd've tried, ain't neither one of 'em woulda heard me, they were that hot under the hair. What I piece together is that the girl might've taken Silver's pen—there was a bit of byplay about did she *need* it, which she didn't say she did or didn't, precisely. What I figured was that he was bringin' her to have you put the fear o'winter into her, very insistent that she see his ma—your pardon, ma'am—that his ma see her."

Nova resisted the urge to rub her forehead.

"Thank you, Mr. Golden," she said instead. "That is an important distinction."

"Yes'm, the boy seemed to think so, too. Made her say it out in the right order before we got on."

"With my son dragging her by the wrist down a public street, with your apparent approval."

"There again, I'm not exactly sure I caught the undertalk. The girl saw he was serious about havin' his way, is what I got, and she offered as a bargain that after she'd got seen, she'd go home to her gran. Silver agreed, quick and easy, but he still kept hold of her."

"Perhaps because the bargain did not include a promise not to take to her heels the instant he freed her."

"Well, there, see? I'm too trusting."

Nova laughed.

"Very well, Mr. Golden, advise me. How shall we handle this for the child's best safety? I fear I did harm, in pulling her true-name. If she is not to share such information with those beyond her house, then she may be punished—even severely."

Michael Golden frowned. "What's the rule when somebody's kin to two houses?"

Nova blinked. "I beg your pardon?"

"You said yourself that there's some things that happen in this house that ain't the bidness of those outside the house. So, if somebody belongs to two houses, with the same rule..."

"You counsel a preemptive course. It may serve, though custom in such matters varies considerably." She paused, considering. "She was to return home to her grandmother?"

"That's what she said."

"Is that likely to be true?"

It was actually comforting, that Michael Golden paused for a long moment of thought before making a slow reply.

"I think that's straight. The gran only come into it when the bargain was made, and I think that was a solid offer"—he glanced at her sideways—"even if it wasn't all-inclusive. Early in the day, there was a mother in the works, but she was talkin' street."

Which was to say, offering whatever fantasy might serve her. Nova nodded.

"The grandmother, then, is the person Kezzi looks to for comfort and for justice. I will write a note." She opened the desk drawer and removed a sheet of paper—the formal paper, thick and eager for ink, with Korval's Tree-and-Dragon in the top right corner and her name below.

"I will see the children here in ten minutes, Mr. Golden, if you would be so kind as to fetch them."

· · · ✳ · · ·

"Do you...know me?" Rys stared at the woman who smiled upon him with such kindness. She had touched his cheek as if they were kin—but they were *not* kin, that he knew without doubt. She bespoke him in the mode between comrades. Were they shipmates, then? Lovers?

He stared at her.

She was Liaden, yes; her eyes light blue, her stance that of one who had no doubt of her ability to defend herself. Her face... her face was not familiar. Not in any wise familiar.

He pushed himself to recall her, strained until a sullen flare of headache warned him to tax himself no further. So, she belonged, perhaps, to the time that was lost to him. And yet, his heart...

He felt no spark of affection—no thrill of joy. He was, he noted distantly, shivering, but that was surely only the cooling breeze.

"I know you," the woman said, with no alteration in her gentle attitude. "Perhaps the question ought to be—do *you* know *me*?"

"Forgive me," he said carefully. "I... sustained injuries..."

"Indeed, indeed! You need not exhaust yourself in explanations— I had learned... elsewhere of your misfortune. You must allow me to express my delight in beholding you! It had been my very great fear that you had not survived such rough handling."

She touched his face again, her fingers lingering. His shivering increased, and he pressed his back against the wall, wishing with everything in him that the brick might open and swallow him up.

"You are very well situated for now, I think," she murmured. "Though we will surely wish to speak again."

She looked closely into his eyes. "You will come to me, Rys Lin, when I desire it."

It was not a question. He felt the words strike something... something in that hidden place, each syllable waking a flare of agony.

"I..."

Her fingers pressed his lips, silencing him. She bent her head until her cheek rested against his, her breath warm in his ear.

"*Son eber donz Rys Lin pen'Chala.*"

Pain flared in his head; his vision shook with violent light; his stomach heaved, and he closed his eyes...

• • • ✻ • • •

Beck had laid down a plate of cookies *and* a plate of cheese and crackers, with a pot of tea, at the little table in the corner.

"'Less you want milk, there, missy?"

"No," Kezzi answered. "Tea!"

"'Nother one just like the first one," Beck said with a sigh. "Tea all around then—and not a cookie nor a drop for you, girl, until you wash those mitts. Show her where, Silver."

He took her to the wash-up room in the hall behind the kitchen, and washed his hands first, so she could see how everything worked.

When it came her turn, she set to with a will, until her hands were white with lather.

"What is your name?" she asked, abruptly.

"Syl Vor yos'Galan Clan Korval."

She frowned slightly, nose wrinkling as she rinsed her hands clean, and reached for the towel.

"But that's not what *they* call you," she said, "Mike Golden and Beck. They call you Silver."

He sighed. "It was Mike Golden's joke," he explained. "Now the whole household has it."

"Hmph," she said, and hung the towel on its bar. Syl Vor led her back to the kitchen.

They sat across from each other at the little table. Kezzi picked up her cup, sipped—and Syl Vor did the same.

"This is good, the tea," she said.

"I am glad that it finds approval," Syl Vor murmured, remembering Grandaunt Kareen's instruction in how to behave at tea. "Beck's cookies are good, too."

She gave him a hard stare, then took a cookie from the plate and bit into it, noisily. She chewed, swallowed, sipped. And nodded.

"Yes," she agreed, and reached for a cheese cracker.

Syl Vor ate a cookie and drank his tea, watching her. She ate with neat efficiency, very quickly, as she had at lunch. Grandaunt would say that she ate too quickly, and had no conversation.

Having conversation was important so all who attended the meal could be entertained, and the pleasures of the table increased.

As if she'd heard him—or had remembered a similar lesson in manners, Kezzi looked up.

"You need to eat more than a cookie, if you want to, to..."

He tipped his head, watching her cheeks darken. "To what?"

She sighed sharply, but surprisingly answered, snappish as Padi when she was caught out by surprise. "To grow tall, we say."

"I'm not tall yet," he told her. "But I will be. My mother and my uncles are tall, and my cousins, too." Aunt Anthora was slightly less tall, but there was, Syl Vor thought, no sense bringing Aunt Anthora into things just yet.

"Don't let 'im pull your leg, missy," Beck said from the stove. "Ain't a single one of 'em *tall* by Sureableak measure."

"But we are by Liaden measure," Syl Vor pointed out. "I told you."

"You keep on telling me, hon. Meanwhile, a little bit o'cheese ain't gonna hurtcha."

Kezzi used a forefinger to nudge the cheese plate toward him, meaningfully. It seemed that good manners insisted.

Syl Vor took up a cracker with cheese and bit into it. It was good; the cheese sharp and the cracker spicy. He took another bite, which finished both, and sipped his tea.

Behind them, the door to the kitchen opened.

"Hey, Mike," said Beck. "Snack?"

"Gimme a snow-check on that. Silver, your ma wants you and Kezzi."

"Yes." He drank the last of his tea, and stood up. Kezzi did, too, leaving half a cookie on her plate, which, he thought, showed that she held Mother in proper respect.

She took a deep breath, then, and looked around the kitchen.

"The House," Syl Vor said quickly, and she blinked at him.

"What?"

"The House keeps you safe," he expanded. "You don't have to be afraid."

"I'm not *afraid*," she told him.

"Well, good," Mike Golden said, holding the door wide, "'cause I am."

"You," Kezzi told him with dignity, "are very stupid."

"Mike is *not* stupid," Syl Vor said sternly, and stalked through the door.

Kezzi took a deep breath and followed him.

Syl Vor led the way to his mother's desk with Kezzi a step or two behind, which was the proper configuration for sponsor and hopeful supplicant. Whether they had adopted the mode purposefully—that was more difficult to tell.

Nova accepted her son's bow with an inclination of her head, and hoped she wasn't about to do something foolishly dangerous.

"My son, I have considered your request and the merits of your proposed sister. In the interests of clarity, I have one question more, if you will allow?"

He frowned, but made a courteous enough answer. "Yes, ma'am."

"I thank you for your forbearance. It came to me, as I was

turning the matter over in my mind, that you perhaps see this matter of achieving Kezzi as a sister to be . . . a solving. Do you?"

He blinked. She had surprised him, this prodigy of hers.

"I—the *delm* solves," he said, suddenly and entirely a young boy caught unawares and offering up the bedrock of the universe for his answer.

"Just so. The *delm* solves for the clan entire, and for those of the house who ask. But we all and each of us, my son, solve sometimes for ourselves. It is part of the process by which we become ourselves."

Syl Vor bit his lip.

"I think," he said slowly, "that, yes, Mother, it is a solving. I—"

She raised her hand. "Enough. If you wish, we will speak more fully on the matter later. For now, I have promised a speedy decision." She turned her head deliberately and met the girl's eyes, held the contact for a slow count to six, then returned her regard to Syl Vor.

"Your sponsorship is commendable, my son. I accept Kezzi as your sister. On condition."

"Condition?"

That was the girl herself, stepping up to Syl Vor's side, her eyes wide and the pulse in her throat beating a little quickly.

"Not, I think, an onerous condition. Merely a time limit. You are accepted, Kezzi, with fullness and with joy, as Syl Vor's sister."

"But for how long?" That was Syl Vor.

"Three months, local." She picked up the envelope she had prepared from the desktop.

"Kezzi, come here, please, child."

She obeyed, stepping lightly, and Nova remembered to smile into that set face as she extended the envelope.

"I have taken the liberty of writing to your grandmother to explain this small custom of ours. Please take it and place it in her hand immediately you are returned to her." She paused, and added, giving each word weight: "I make this request as your mother."

Kezzi's mouth sagged, then firmed. Excellent. The child did have wits.

She took the envelope in a hand not so grubby as formerly and bowed her slight, quaint bow.

"I will deliver this to my grandmother," she said, and the promise carried the ring of truth.

"Excellent. I will then bid you good-day, Kezzi-daughter, and remand you to the care of your brother and of Mr. Golden. They will see you home. I expect that you will complete whatever home study Ms. Taylor has assigned. On the morrow you will be attentive at school, and strive to learn as well as you may. If your grandmother permits, you will please come home with Syl Vor tomorrow after school."

"Yes," Kezzi said in a low voice, and added, quickly, "Good-day."

"Syl Vor, you and Mr. Golden will come back immediately after you have seen Kezzi safely to her kin. I will inform your tutors that your study hours have been set back an hour. You will attend to them when you return. Dinner will also be set back an hour."

"Yes, Mother."

· · · ✳ · · ·

Kezzi walked down the hall between Mike Golden and Syl Vor yos'Galan Clan Korval. The thought at the top of her head was that she was being let go. And once she was back among the *kompani*, she would never *ever* venture into the City Above again. She would stay below, and work in the gardens with Memit, or in the steam shop with Pulka. She and Malda would run up and down the ramps for exercise, and she would, she would—

"Wait," Syl Vor said. "Kezzi, here."

She blinked out of her thoughts, and stared at the thing in his hand—a pen.

The pen, she remembered suddenly. The very pen that had caused her to give her true-name to *gadje* and be taken into their family—for three months? No. No, she would not. She would return to the *kompani*. She would never—

"*Take* it," Syl Vor snapped, and she looked at him, irritated.

"Why? It is yours, you say, and leave bruises on my wrist in proof."

His cheeks darkened somewhat, but he held the pen out still. "You said you needed it. You're my sister. What's mine is yours. If you need it, take it."

Need it? She never wanted to see it, or him, again. But it seemed plain that the quickest way back to the *kompani* was to take the pen from his hand and slip it away into the pocket that carried his mother's letter to the *luthia*.

"I have it," she said.

"Now that bidness is all caught up," Mike Golden said, forcefully, "let's go. I don't like the idea of making Beck hold the dinner all that long."

She led them toward the shops, thinking that, if Malda had done as she had asked, surely there would be someone along the streets of the City Above, watching for her with sharp Bedel eyes. If Malda had *not* done what she had asked, or if he had been caught...

No. She wouldn't think of that.

And, indeed, she had no need. Scarcely had they come into Commerce Street, and before Mike Golden could ask any inconvenient question, there came a high-pitched bark, and here was Malda himself, streaking down the sidewalk, dodging between *gadje* legs.

Kezzi fell to her knees and opened her arms. From ten steps away, he leapt. She caught him, hugging his wriggling body to her, laughing when he licked her ear.

"Ah, yes, yes! Bold and brave..."

"Sister," a voice interrupted their reunion, soft, but insistent. Well-known. Udari.

She blinked up at him, Malda ecstatically licking her chin.

"Brother?"

"We were worried," Udari told her, his eyes flicking twice—to Mike Golden and to Syl Vor.

Kezzi sniffled, and came to her feet, holding Malda close.

"These are Mike Golden and Syl Vor yos'Galan Clan Korval. They were bringing me to family," she explained. "I have a letter, for grandmother."

Udari's face altered; he looked at Mike Golden with courtesy.

"Your care of my sister is appreciated, Mike Golden. She is safe in my hands, and I will take her even now to our grandmother."

"'Preciate it," Mike Golden said in that particular tone of voice.

She turned to face him. "This is my brother Nathan, Mike Golden. I will go with him."

"Right you are."

"Anna," Syl Vor said, then. She turned, and he reached out to touch her sleeve lightly, and with a wary eye on Malda.

"I'll see you in school, tomorrow," he said. "All right?"

She stared at him, the pen and the letter like stones in her pocket.

She had the measure of his stubbornness now; he would not go until he had an answer. Until he had the answer *he wanted*. That was well, then.

"All right," she said.

"That's set firm, then," Mike Golden said briskly. "C'mon, Silver—we both got work to do before this day is over. 'Night, Anna. Nathan. Good you happened by."

He put his hand on Syl Vor's shoulder, and the two of them walked off.

Kezzi looked to Udari, who nodded.

"Come," he said. "We must find Rafin and Rys, and then deliver you, O daughter of surprises, to the *luthia*."

They turned as one, Udari moving quickly. At the first turn toward the *kompani*'s gate, they met Rafin, who asked her roughly if she were harmed.

"No, I'm well," she told him.

"Must you carry the dog?" he asked then, and she swallowed against the hard lump in her throat.

"I want to."

"Some burdens are no weight," Udari agreed, and looked to Rafin. "Where is our brother Rys?"

"He was at the end of his strength, and bade me leave him, saying he would catch us, when he had rested."

"You left him alone?" Udari's voice was harsh.

"He would have it so," Rafin replied, frowning. "I swore that we would return for him."

"Yes," said Udari, and on that word leapt into a run.

CHAPTER TWENTY-TWO

THE CHILD SAT ON THE HEARTHRUG, HER HEAD BENT, AND SILAIN'S shawl tucked around her. The dog, her faithful friend, was asleep with his head on her knee. It seemed that the child must be asleep, too, worn out from her adventure, but the *luthia* saw the hand resting on the dog's side move in a slow stroke.

Well, then.

Silain sat on the rug next to the child and put her hand on the drooping shoulder.

"What time," she asked softly, "does school begin tomorrow?"

"I don't know," Kezzi answered.

"That will make it difficult to attend."

Kezzi stirred and looked up.

"I'm not going to school," she said. "I'm going to stay here, in *kompani* and never go to the City Above again."

"You are Droi's apprentice," Silain pointed out mildly. "You must go to the City Above, to perfect the art of the cards."

Kezzi bit her lip.

"Of this other thing," Silain persisted, though it struck her to the heart to badger the child when she was so tired. "Did you say to your brother that you would see him tomorrow, at school?"

Kezzi sniffed. "Who tells the truth to a *gadje*?"

"Does a sister lie to a brother?"

"I am *not* his sister!"

"Did you tell me that he gave you the pen, from brother to sister?"

"Yes." Black eyes were wary, now.

"And you received the pen, as the sister of your brother. It is done, and sealed. Tell me what we owe our brothers, and our sisters, and all of the *kompani* of Bedel."

"Truth," Kezzi whispered, "kindness, food, air."

"And what do you owe this boy, your brother?"

Kezzi stared at her, eyes wide and shocked. "*Luthia*..."

"What do you owe your brother, Kezzi of the Bedel?" Silain repeated, implacable.

There was a long silence before the child bowed her head and whispered.

"All that I would have myself."

"So, then." Silain extended a hand and touched the child's knee.

"After all," she said, "it was foretold."

Kezzi blinked at her, and Silain smiled.

"Do you remember, when I asked you to dream for me? In the darkness, you found a most marvelous pen..."

The child's eyes widened. She snatched at her pocket and pulled the pen out, staring, even as her fingers caressed it.

"Four colors," she whispered. "Green...red...blue...black."

She looked up, lips parted.

"But—why?"

Silain shook her head. "Why we are given to glimpse one thing out of all that might be seen, not even the *luthia* know for certain. It does seem that we are allowed to see those things which will...weigh heavy in our lives."

"A pen?" Kezzi asked, her brows drawing together.

"Or a boy," Silain said, serenely. "Time will teach you what and why. Now, of this other thing: You will attend school tomorrow, as you promised your brother. Afterward, you will go with him to pay proper respect to your mother, and to perform any work she asks of you. Also, you will give her my letter, which I will write tonight."

"Yes, Grandmother," Kezzi said, looking again at the pen in her hand.

After a moment, she looked up. "How will I learn when school opens?"

"You will ask your brother Torv if such a thing lies in his knowledge. Go now, and when you come back, we will drink tea together, and talk about tomorrow."

· · · ✳ · · ·

Ms. ker'Eklis had pushed his math lesson—had pushed *him*, allowing shorter and shorter time for consideration of the problems she posed. The last three . . . he had simply answered the first thing that came into his head. When the questions stopped coming, he sat shivering in his chair, as if he had extra adrenaline to work off, while she went through his responses, marking off three with her pen against the screen.

"This, this, and this. For the first two, you will produce the correct answer; I will expect to see all of your work. For the third, which is correct, I will see the work, also."

"Yes, ma'am," he said, his voice shaking.

She gave him a sharp glance. "You will also complete the next module so that we may review it together at our next meeting."

"Yes, ma'am," he said again, slightly stronger this time.

"That is well. Have you any questions regarding today's exercises, or the self-tests?"

"No, ma'am."

"Very good. I will meet you at the usual time on the day after next. I do not expect you to be late."

Syl Vor sat up straight, hearing a scold.

"I hadn't expected to be late today, ma'am," he said, wishing his voice wasn't so shaky. "Necessity . . . intervened."

"So I learned from your mother."

Ms. ker'Eklis rose, and Syl Vor scrambled to his feet to bow respect to the teacher.

"Good-day," she said coolly.

He held his bow until he heard her close the door, and her steps receding down the hall. Then, he straightened, fast and hard, and spun into a tight dance that was all kicks and jabs; knees, elbows, shoulders, hands, feet, spinning and ducking to avoid the walls and the corners and the furniture, and collapsing all at once on his back on the bed, arms and legs wide, panting, his hair sticking damply to his forehead, heart pounding.

In this position, the ceiling was his view.

The ceiling of his sleeping room at ho— at Trealla Fantrol had been painted with flying dragons. He had used to stare at them sometimes and pretend they were playing games—tag, see-you, and Jump-in. Of course, he had been very young, then.

At Jelaza Kazone, the nursery ceilings were painted with stars in strange constellations, ships, and geometric shapes in bright colors. And of course the ceilings, and the walls, and the floors at Runig's Rock had all been grey stone.

Here at his mother's house, there was a garden on the ceiling. There were many flowers, in a confusion of colors, and a number of low bushes with prickly looking dark leaves. Under one such shrubbery was a furry creature with longish ears that Syl Vor thought might be a rabbit. There were birds in another—one each of blue, red, and yellow—and purple berries.

Something hit the bed by his head, making the very softest of thumps. He turned his head slowly, and met Eztina's eyes. There was a little rumple in the fur of her forehead, as if she was worried to find him here on top the blankets, sweaty in the aftermath of his dance, and staring at the ceiling.

"Good afternoon," Syl Vor said softly, and added, because Eztina would of course be interested in such matters, "I have a sister."

Eztina blinked, leaned close and snuffled the sticky hair at Syl Vor's temple.

"That tickles. My sister's name is Kezzi, but that's only for the House. For the street, her name is Anna Brown. She has a dog, and an older brother whom she called Nathan."

Eztina put her nose on his. Hers was cold, and her whiskers tickled.

"Stop that!" He moved his arm, got a hand clumsily under her belly and lifted her to his chest. She stood where he had put her, each foot weighing more than she did.

"She said—Kezzi said—that she would come to school tomorrow. Do you think she will?"

Eztina blinked.

Syl Vor sighed. "Well, I hope she will, too ... but I think she might have not been *quite* truthful. We're ... *gah-gee*—I think that means *outworlder*. It—I—it would be very bad if her honor were ... impinged. Because of me."

He frowned, trying to work out if one's honor could be sullied by breaking faith with an outworlder. Grandaunt said that the Code governed Liadens wherever they went—but Kezzi wasn't Liaden. Grandfather ...

Grandfather said that one ought to act with honor on all occasions, and that *honor called honor*.

Grandfather deferred to Grandaunt's greater knowledge of the Code, but he was, so Padi had said, very nice in his manners, and extremely particular in matters of Balance.

If Kezzi's honor were drawn to—well, not to *his* honor, really; he was only a boy, but to *the clan's* honor, with which he was invested—at least, that was what the Code said. If Kezzi's honor were drawn to Korval's honor, then she had told the truth, and would come to school.

Syl Vor closed his eyes, immensely relieved to have reached a reasonable conclusion.

Of course, Kezzi's grandmother might not allow it, he thought then, his stomach clenching—and then relaxing. Obedience to an elder was honorable, so—

Four points of pressure on his chest increased painfully—and were gone.

"Gnh!" Syl Vor sat up, staring at a cat's high, sinuous tail as she walked into the little alcove that was his study room.

He sighed, and rolled off the bed.

Eztina was right. Ms. ker'Eklis had left him a lot of work to do, and he'd best get to it if he wanted to finish before dinner.

· · · ✵ · · ·

"*Luthia*, a word, if you will."

Silain opened her eyes.

"For the headman, a sentence," she said. "Will you have tea?"

"Tea would make the telling less dry."

She stood to fetch the kettle and the mugs. The child had not yet returned from her errand. Perhaps Torv had not been easy to find.

She poured tea, and brought the mugs to the hearth, handing one to Alosha. He stood politely while she settled herself, waiting for her permission before he dropped cross-legged to the rug.

It was the way of the Bedel to sit quietly over tea for a small time, until the hearts of those gathered beat as one. This had never been Alosha's way; he was one who led with his head, and did not stint his tongue.

Silain therefore sipped her tea, waiting . . . and waiting more, with growing surprise.

Half a mug was drunk, by patient sips, before Alosha the headman cleared his throat and spoke.

"How fares Dmitri?"

Here was another surprise. The headman could himself walk to Dmitri's hearth and inquire of Ves and Luma. There was no need to make inquiry of the *luthia* on so straightforward a matter.

Yet, he had asked, and he was the headman. The *luthia* could but reply.

"He proceeds at a stately pace. Early this day, he and I prayed together. He spoke at length of what, and who, he hoped to meet, when he came into the World Unseen. I think that another three days will see him safely over. He is content, and his death will be a good one."

"His death," Alosha repeated, and leaned toward her, his eyes intent.

"*Luthia*, the Bedel are on *chafurma*; the numbers are fixed."

Ah. Suddenly it made sense, this visit; and this specific inquiry. Alosha thought long, as a headman must.

Silain moved her hand, inviting him to continue.

"The numbers are fixed," he repeated. "When Dmitri crosses into that kinder place, the numbers will be in disarray. There is no coming birth to balance his death. I have counted, I have dreamed, and again have I counted and dreamed. Now I come to the *luthia* to beg her wisdom. If we are not to be fruitful with each other, how then will we survive? If we become fruitful with those in the City Above, how will we remain who we are? And—this troubles me most of all—are we, after this length with no news, to suppose that something ill has befallen those others of us, and that *chafurma* . . . will not, for us, end?"

Long thoughts, indeed.

There was a rustle near the hearth, and the smallest click of claw on stone. The child and her faithful friend had returned. Silain considered sending them to Jin, and then decided not. The child was her apprentice, and strange knowledge was the lot of both the *luthia* and the *luthia*-to-be.

"We went outside," Silain said to Alosha, "and got Rafin."

"We did. But how many others can we get before we are something else?"

Silain waited. After a moment, Alosha sighed gustily, and put the mug down by his knee.

"There is more. The *garda* have expanded their watch. You know this. What you do not know, I think, is that we have closed and sealed two of the nearer gates. The risk of them was too great. If this continues, we will no longer be hidden, *luthia*, we will be trapped."

"Will it continue?" Silain asked. "The *garda* have come before and, after a time, they have gone away again."

"This Boss Conrad. He lights a fire in their bellies. More! Those others who have come on-world—the People of the Tree, and their allies—they are eager for work. And hungry for room. It is said in the City Above that Boss Conrad looks at the buildings above us, and sees housing and hydroponics for his people."

Silain closed her eyes. There was something—the tang of something dream-known, at the back of her tongue. But faint. So very faint.

"*Luthia?*"

Without opening her eyes, she raised a hand, and Alosha the headman composed himself to silence.

The dream...it tasted nearly as old as the story of Riva, and for a moment she thought that it was too far and too fragile to bring forward. If she could but locate some marker, she might find it again, among the dreams she held in keeping for the *kompani*—and suddenly, it was there, in fullness. Not a story-dream, but a piece of history, filed under Bedel cleverness, and strategies for survival among the *gadje*.

"How if," she said to the headman, her voice dreamy and slow. "How if we say to Boss Conrad that we the Bedel have... *established tenancy*, and the buildings are ours."

Silence greeted this; a silence so charged with misgiving that it crackled along the *luthia*'s nerves and awakened blue lightnings in her long sight.

She opened her eyes.

Alosha the headman sat cross-legged on her rug, arrested in the act of filling his pipe.

"You—" he began, swallowed and began again. "The *luthia* would advise us to deal openly with the *gadje* and claim *ownership* of this, our *kompani*'s grounds?"

Frank horror informed the headman's voice, and Alosha was not one who came easily to fear.

"It has been done before," Silain told him calmly. "And we do not say that we own this building—though we might, with no breaking of custom. After all, it is *not true* that we own this space or the warehouses above us." She gave him a sharp glance. "Or is it true?"

"No," Alosha said shortly. He finished packing his pipe, and reached to the hearth for an ember.

"This was done before, you say? By the Bedel?" he asked, after the pipe was going to his satisfaction.

"It was."

"And the outcome?"

"The *gadje* granted to the *kompani* the right to remain where they had set camp. The *garda* was made to know that the Bedel were not vagrants." She raised a finger as another bit of information rose from the old dream.

"The *gadje* populated that space hard by the *kompani*, which the *kompani* had not claimed."

"And so the *kompani* was absorbed by the *gadje*? Or did *chafurma* end in bright joy and happiness?"

Silain frowned; shook her head in frustration.

"I will need to dream again."

Alosha nodded, drew on his pipe and exhaled a fragrant cloud of smoke.

"And the question of the numbers?"

"There, too, I will dream. We know there have been those who have not returned from *chafurma*, but their dreams are lost to us."

Silence while the headman smoked gloomily.

"It may be that it will be solved for us, if we adopt this *established tenancy* and the *gadje* come to live eye to eye with the Bedel. We will cease to be Bedel. Our dreams will be lost, and our children's children will be *gadje*."

"It may be. It may not be," Silain said to him. "I will seek the fullness of this dream. We have time for that. When we have dreamed in fullness, then perhaps we ought to share with the *kompani*, and call for an Affirmation."

Alosha smoked for a time, then abruptly extended a long arm to knock the ashes out of his pipe.

"There is much in what you say, *luthia*." He tucked the pipe away and rose. "I leave you now to your hearth and your dreams."

"Headman. The *kompani* sits in your hand."

"Well I know it, Grandmother."

He bowed, and walked away, down the commons, toward his own hearth.

Not until the headman's shadow had melted into the larger shadows, did Silain the *luthia* raise her head and say, "Come forward, Sister. Bring the teapot and a mug for yourself."

Kezzi dropped to her knees on the rug, poured tea into Silain's mug, and what was left of the pot into hers.

"So, little sister?"

The child looked up, her eyes opaque.

"Torv says that school begins an hour past the winter dawn."

Silain smiled. "That is well done, and well said. Now, sit, and tell me what you heard pass between myself and the headman."

CHAPTER TWENTY-THREE

RYS OPENED HIS EYES, AND IMMEDIATELY REGRETTED DOING SO.

What light there was—and it was not by any means brilliant—assaulted him, waking the dull throb of a headache. His mouth felt furry, and tasted foul; his stomach was queasy and he was not at all certain that it was proof against even the slightest movement.

He closed his eyes again, which settled his stomach somewhat, and tried to force his laggard brain to recall what had occurred, that he should waken in such a state, in...in...

Gingerly, he opened his eyes to the thinnest of slits, surveying his surroundings through his lashes.

He lay on his side on a thin pad; a blanket had been thrown over him, though he was fully dressed, even unto his boots. Before him, not many handspans from the tip of his nose, fabric rippled, like a curtain drawn over an open window. He raised his eyes. The ceiling was swathed in more fabric, and there were two small, round disks set into it. It was these that provided the meager light.

Unless his memory was now also malfunctioning in the short term, he had never seen this place before. Certainly, he did not remember lying down on the mattress, nor pulling the blanket up around himself.

He took a breath, trying to remember, but gently and without urgency.

First, where was he not?

Absolutely, he was not in Silain's hearth-room, which was bright, airy, and open to the common area.

He was—he *knew* he was—back with the Bedel, beneath the city. Well.

Deliberately, he relaxed into that conviction, eyes closing against the silence.

Slowly, as if he were watching bladder lilies rise to the surface of a pond, the events of the last several hours elucidated themselves.

The meeting with Rafin, the expedition to Finder's Junk Heap, the advent of Malda, and the decision to go with those who sought for Kezzi.

He had fallen behind, his handicaps having overset him, and leaned against a wall to recruit himself.

There had been—he had been more exhausted than he had known, and must have fallen into a...doze, for the next thing he recalled was Udari bending close and asking if he was well.

The headache snarled, and he winced.

One deep breath; and another, deliberately thinking of nothing. He shifted on the mattress, and turned onto his back. The blanket was twisted 'round him irritatingly, and he snatched at it with—

With a hand that gleamed liquid brass in the dim lights.

Rys froze. His prime hand had been badly damaged, he told himself very carefully indeed. It was splinted and padded, lest any random bump cause him pain. He could use it for gross tasks, and to keep balance, but on the whole, it was useless, and likely to remain that way for the rest of his life, if he understood Silain correctly, even if he found an autodoc in this place.

And yet, here was no splint, padded out with rags. Here...was a thing of precision and beauty. He brought his hand closer to his eyes, understanding that he wore a glove, a glove to which hundreds—thousands!—of golden scales had been meticulously adhered by some art that was beyond him—the whole being wondrously light, and—

He clenched his fist.

There was a small hum from among the larger scales at the glove's hem. That was all.

He opened his fist and spread his fingers as wide as they would go, rotating the hand at the wrist. The palm and the underside of his fingers were covered with dark, flexible mesh. It had a metallic glitter to it, but was soft against the skin of his opposite palm.

His heart pounding in his ears, he closed his eyes, resting his hands on his chest, where both relaxed with a slight curl to the fingers.

The remainder of yesterday flowed into his consciousness, as easily as if he had never been at a loss.

After he recovered from his swoon, they—being Rafin, Udari, Kezzi, Malda, and himself—had walked slowly back to a gate, where Rafin let them in.

It was not the gate they had passed through on their way to Finder's. Indeed, his knowledge of the Bedel led him to suppose that there were *several* gates, and that the location of all were known only to a few. Once they were inside, their coats and hats hung on hooks for the use of those next to venture outside, Udari had taken the child and her dog to the *luthia*, while he and Rafin had returned to the forge.

There, they had found Pulka, who was sorting the bounty they had gathered at the junk heap. He pulled out the ragged knot of silver and blue, and laughed aloud, tossing the thing to Rafin, who cried, "Eh? *Eh*?"

And tossed it to Rys.

Instinct had thrown up his prime hand, clumsy in its splint. Instead of catching the metal ball, he knocked it aside. It struck the floor and rolled toward the alcove where Rafin had his worktable. Rys started after, and was caught short by Rafin, who grabbed his arm and held his ruined hand high.

"When does the splint come off?"

"Never," Rys told him. "The *luthia* would have it that the bones are ground into uselessness, and no art of hers can mend it."

Rafin pursed his lips. "Is that so? Well!" He released Rys and turned to look at Pulka.

"After such a day as we have had, a man wants a beer! Do you not find it so, Brother?"

Pulka had looked momentarily surprised, but replied readily enough that beer would be most welcome.

Which is how Rys came to have a glass of beer, and another, and possibly a third. *There* his memory did fail him, but given the measure and the weight of the beverage involved, that was perhaps not surprising.

He must, he thought, have passed out from the effects of too much pleasure. His final memory, before waking up in this dark, silent place with two functioning hands, was of his own voice, screaming, very far away.

"He wakes!" Rafin shouted from the workbench. His grin was a wonder of white in a sweaty, soot-soaked face. "What do you think of our beer, eh?"

Rys stopped, setting the tip of his crutch carefully, and looked up into the other man's eyes.

"I think the beer of the Bedel is amazingly restorative," he said, and held out his beautiful hand, palm up, for Rafin to make of what he might.

The grin became a laugh. "The fighting cock would clasp my hand in brotherhood! Almost, you tempt me. But first, you must be the master of yourself. Catch!"

He plucked a metal mug from the edge of the bench and threw it, muscles rippling with his effort.

Rys raised his prime hand, catching it easily—

And crushing it into uselessness in the same moment.

He stared, then looked back to Rafin.

"Have a care with that work glove," the other told him, "and train it well. That is your job today, while your brothers pursue other tasks of interest."

"How?" Rys asked.

Rafin waved vaguely into the open space of the forge.

"Find heavy things, things that break, things that weigh less than yourself. Practice handling them, until you can do so without damage. To anything."

"Yes," Rys said, and asked, "Is there a place where a man might shower?"

Rafin jerked his head to the right. "Over there."

Rys looked about, trying to pinpoint *over there*, without much success. He did see Pulka, back to the pair of them, as he worked at the forge.

"Where is Udari?" he asked then, risking a third question and the end of the other's sunny mood.

Rafin shrugged. "The *luthia* needed a thing done, that only he could do. Leave me now, little one. We each have our tasks this day."

As dismissals went, it was both straightforward and without rancor. Rys bowed, very slightly, and headed in the direction of *over there*.

· · · ☀ · · ·

Kezzi hadn't come to school.

The dance had paired Syl Vor today with Rodale and Kaleb. Right now, they were doing arithmetic—multiplication problems. He'd finished his, and now his task—assigned by Ms. Taylor—was to help his tablemates. Mostly, that meant reminding Kaleb to add the deferred units to the multiplicand, a task that unfortunately left too much time for Syl Vor to think of other, less simple, things.

Why hadn't she come? he asked himself. Had her grandmother forbidden it? That was possible. Maybe her grandmother was one of those who didn't think a cross-turf school was a good idea.

In that case, her grandmother would send a letter to Mother, explaining her concerns. That would be the polite thing to do. If she had written to Mother, then Mother would be able to show her the benefits of school and learning to work together. Veeno said that folks had forgotten that, over the years since the Company had left, and that some folks found remembering a hard road. Mike Golden had said that it wasn't so much forgetting and remembering, but that mostly people were scared of change.

Syl Vor wondered if Kezzi was scared of change. Or—he bit his lip—if she was scared of *him*. Mother hadn't been pleased with the *manner* in which he'd brought Kezzi to her. Even if there hadn't been any other way to be sure she wouldn't run away... it wasn't done, to drag people down the street, and—*force them*...

"You forgot to add in the one," he said to Kaleb.

Rodale looked up from working his own problems. "Again? I'm tellinya, Kaleb, I'm gonna write that out on your forehead, so's you stop forgettin'!"

"No good on m' forehead," Kaleb objected. "Can't see my own forehead."

Rodale frowned, apparently struck by this, then he leaned forward. "I'll write it on your arm, then. And when it wears out, I'll write it again 'til you remember, or 'til your arm falls off!"

Kaleb blinked, clearly disturbed, and put his pencil down. "You're not touching my arm!" he said, loudly enough to be heard by Ms. Taylor, who was up at the front table, working with Tansy and Delia.

"Quiet!" Syl Vor said, keeping his own voice low. "Kaleb, Rodale was only making a joke. Rodale—tell him."

"Ain't a joke!" Kaleb said, not bothering to keep his voice down, his eyes filling with tears. "I saw a guy, his arm had swelt up all black an' all, and m'brother said he was gonna hafta have it off, 'less he wanted to be poisoned."

Rodale blinked, looked at Syl Vor, then back to Kaleb. He leaned forward and slid his hand across the table, palm up, fingers curled.

"Hey. Hey, Kaleb—that's not what I meant. It's just a thing we say at home. S'posed to be funny, like Syl Vor said. I din't know that could happen, like you tole us."

Kaleb sniffled, swallowed, and then nodded. "Happens when a cut goes bad."

"Yeah?" Rodale looked interested, and Syl Vor felt a spark of curiosity, too, beyond his worry about Kezzi.

"Ain't the only thing can do it," Kaleb said, seeing their interest. "My auntie—"

The sound of the door opening drew his attention—and everyone's—to the front of the room.

Kezzi stepped into the room, her eyes narrowing in the face of so many stares. She took a breath, and pushed the door closed, then stood, looking from face to face.

Syl Vor stood up, and her glance leapt to him. He thought she looked relieved.

"Good morning, Anna," Ms. Taylor said, looking up from Tansy and Delia's table. "Please be on time tomorrow. Now, hang up your coat and join us here. We're doing multiplication problems."

"Yes," Kezzi said.

She passed Syl Vor's table on her way to hang up her coat, and threw him a dark, unreadable look. He inclined his head and sat down again. She turned her back and marched back up the room.

"Anna's sweet on you," Rodale said, and nudged him with his elbow. "How 'bout that?"

"She looked mad to me," Kaleb said, which is what Syl Vor thought, too.

He, on the other hand, felt a relief so profound it made his stomach hurt.

"Have you both finished your problems?" he asked, not looking at the front of the room. "We should check each other's work."

· · · ※ · · ·

Pulka and Rafin had reached a point in their shared work which required a great deal of gesticulating, accompanied by raised voices. The noise pounded nastily against the beer headache, and woke an unpleasant roiling in his stomach.

As it appeared that the . . . discussion was going to be lengthy, Rys rose from the place where he had been practicing picking up items of various stages of fragility, holding them, and putting them down. The crutch took his weight, and he swung out of the forge, into the mouth of the tunnel he and Udari had traversed only yesterday.

It was a shorter walk than he had recalled, and the ramps not so steep that they thwarted a determined man.

He found himself determined, as the voices faded behind him—determined to show Silain his beautiful, functional hand, even now swinging lithe and beautiful at his side. She had said that she could not mend the damage done—and he believed her. What he did not know was whether she knew of this . . . *work glove* of Rafin's, and if she did not . . .

The tunnel ended in a wide hall, floored with stone. Some distance ahead, he could see the solemn glow of hearths 'round the common area. He paused then, and took stock.

His head was still sullen, and his stomach uneasy. It was, he thought, possible that Silain had a potion to ease a hangover, though he thought it more likely that she would laugh at him for having drunk more than his means.

He had taken nothing but some water since waking in Rafin's quiet room, not merely because of the uncertainties of his stomach, but because he did not see where Rafin's larder might be. Perhaps he kept no food at the forge, but came in to the common area and ate at the hearth of one with whom he was . . . affiliated.

Rys sighed and moved on, careful of uneven stones.

His length of time among the Bedel had taught him some rather curious things, but what he had not yet been able to discover was the web of their relationships. To the naive eye, it would seem that the Bedel were . . . the Bedel. One clan, undivided. Silain stood grandmother, and Alosha the headman as captain, if not *delm*.

But of the finer webs that exist within a clan, which bound two more tightly than another two? Those, he did not see.

Where, for instance, was Kezzi's true-mother? Or Udari's sister-by-blood? Where, indeed, were the children, beyond Kezzi herself?

Had Rafin a lover? Was there a place within the *kompani*, like the women's section and the men's, where those who were joined by passion shared a hearth?

He sighed. It was difficult to know how long he had been among the Bedel—if there were a timepiece or a calendar among them, Rys had not discovered them. It was certain, however, that he had not been with them long enough to learn all their secrets. No, nor his own, either.

Silain's hearth was the last in the common area. From that direction, he spied a tall figure well-draped with shawl and scarves, a small, four-footed shadow walking subdued at her heel.

Rys frowned. Where was the child?

"Rys!" Silain called out, raising her hand. He raised his own in answer, and increased his pace, arriving very shortly at her side.

"Grandmother, well met."

"I chose to believe it," she answered with a sharp glance from black eyes. "What distresses you, my child?"

"The dog and the child were parted for some hours yesterday. I had thought to find them inseparable today," he said, glancing down at a very sober Malda, indeed. "I hope that my small sister has taken no hurt."

"Not hurt, but gone where her friend cannot follow."

He felt relief. It sometimes happened that the child was sent in company with an elder, pursuing her various studies.

"I am called to Dmitri's side," Silain said, "on duty that will not wait. Walk with me, if you will. Or return to our hearth. You look as if you would welcome a mug of tea and a nap."

He would, he acknowledged, welcome both of those things. But there was still the matter of Rafin's work glove.

"I will walk with you," he said determinedly, and swung along on his crutch as she started out again.

"You say that you're Kezzi's brother?" Silain asked after a moment.

"I say it," he said slowly. "I think it."

He slanted a glance into her face, finding it serene as always, her eyes watching, not him, but the path ahead. "You may doubt me—indeed, you would be wise to do so. A man who has no memory of who he is, though he seems to recall everything that he is not? Can he trust even himself?

"I know that I *had been* a brother, once. My elder sister is dead— and all of my brothers, older and younger. I am—I was accustomed to being one of many—not, perhaps, as the Bedel are, but near enough that the Bedel call to me. Udari names me brother, and I say now that as much as he is, I am. It would pain me to lose him, or the child, or yourself, if I may dare to be so bold."

He paused, walking beside Silain in a charged silence.

"There is a *but*, I think; heard, if not said."

He nodded.

"*But*, I can only feel as the man I am, and speak the truth of one who is a fragment—who knows how small?—of a whole. Should the rest of my memories return, how can I predict what I might say to you then?"

"We can only speak the truth that we know at the time it is known," Silain said. "For myself, I delight in my grandson Rys, though I fear that he will be tested, soon."

"Tested?" Had Silain found some salve that would mend his fractured memory? It seemed unlikely in the extreme, and yet—so did the glove covering his shattered hand.

Reminded, he raised his arm and stretched his gleaming fingers wide.

Silain stopped, full still, between one step and another, staring down upon it as if she had never seen the like before. His hunch had been correct, then. He was relieved. He would not like to think that Silain had lied to him. And now that she knew of the existence of such an item . . .

"How did that come to you, grandson?"

"Rafin gave it, upon hearing that my hand was beyond repair." He felt his mouth twist into a half-smile. "He and Pulka made sure I was well anesthetized."

Silain, perhaps wisely, did not touch the glove.

"I have full motion," he said, clenching his fist, spreading his fingers, turning his wrist. "There is no pain, though there is a training period. I fear that I will be a danger to tea mugs and to the hands of my friends for some little while yet."

"It is," Silain said slowly, "a temporary solution."

He blinked up at her.

"How temporary?"

She laughed at that, and began to walk again, as if the laugh had melted the surprise out of her muscles.

"Practical Rys. It might serve you well for years, grandson. But in the end, the last bone and thread of sinew will fail, and then you will be crippled again. There might also be peripheral damage, to the bones of your wrist, the muscles in your arms." She slid him a look. "You wondered why I didn't offer it to you."

"I did. Now you tell me that Rafin has done me a mischief."

"No. I tell you that it is done, and for a time, at least, done well. Rafin has seen clearly. A young man needs his strength. An old man needs his patience."

She turned aside, toward a hearth brightly lit, the room beyond it closed, and glowing from within. Two shadows sat at the hearth. One rose as Silain approached, and bowed, fingers tucked respectfully into sleeves.

"*Luthia.* Our father races to that fair country like a young man to his first love."

"I will see him," she said, and turned to Rys.

"Go to our hearth, grandson," she said. "If you look in the red box, you'll find a round amber bottle. Five drops into a mug of tea will settle your stomach."

"Thank you," he said, but Silain had already turned toward the closed hearth-room.

· · · ✳ · · ·

At lunch break, Syl Vor looked about for Kezzi, and found her, not in the line of those waiting to receive their hot cheese and noodles from Ms. Taylor's spoon, but at the bureau, where the plates and spoons and cups were set out. As he watched, her hand went from the stack of plates to her scarf. She was stealing, again!

Syl Vor walked over to her.

"It is not done," he said, keeping his voice low, "to steal from the school."

She gave him a look of dislike.

"I heard you say so, yesterday."

"Then why—"

"My grandmother," Kezzi interrupted, "said that we don't need these things and that I should put them back." Another smoky glare. "*That's* why I'm putting them back."

Syl Vor nodded. "Of course, you ought to do as your grandmother asks," he said. He glanced down the room. Almost the whole class had gotten their lunch. They'd better get in line quickly, or Ms. Taylor would notice them.

"Do you need help?" he asked. "The line . . ."

"I'm done," she snapped. "I don't need your help."

"All right," he said mildly. "Let's get lunch."

Together, they walked to the serving station.

"She did like the rolls, though," Kezzi said, as they each picked up a bowl.

Syl Vor stared at her. "*These* rolls?" he asked in disbelief, which was not very respectful of school or Ms. Taylor. Still, he thought stubbornly, Kezzi's grandmother must be very hungry, if she thought the school rolls were good.

"She ought to have Beck's rolls," he said. "Remind me to give you some to take to her."

They sat down in the last two seats at the table, which were side by side. As far as he could tell, Kezzi didn't take anything for her own aside from the meal. Ms. Taylor asked after the health of her grandmother, which was courteous.

"My grandmother is in good health," Kezzi answered. "I hope that your grandmother is the same."

Ms. Taylor looked momentarily startled, then smiled one of her wide, pleased smiles.

"My gran's spry as a fox. She's got all the seedlings set out, and now she's into the spring cleanup. Guess I know what I'll be doing on my off-days."

That brought a chuckle from Vanette, and Jeff said *his* gran had him washing the windows a room at a time when he come home from school.

Ms. Taylor smiled, looking pleased, and asked Rodale if he was working at the port on his off-days, and the table went back to the usual.

Syl Vor sighed to himself. Almost, a conversation had begun. He thought that was what Ms. Taylor was trying to teach them, with her lunchtime questions. He should have found a way to carry the discussion forward, he thought. Grandaunt would have expected him—well, no. Quin and Padi—*they* were expected to have address, and common sense, and reserve, and wit. Grandaunt didn't expect *him* to have address, he was only a child.

"Syl Vor, how's your cat?" Ms. Taylor asked. "What was her name?"

"Eztina," he said. "She's very fine. Beck says that she comes down to have lunch with everyone in the kitchen." It was nice to think that he and Eztina and Mike Golden and Mother, too, on those days when she wasn't out, were all eating lunch at the same time.

"No rats at *your place*, I guess?" Rudy asked, in the same tone he used for *Boss's brat*.

"Rudy..." Ms. Taylor frowned.

Syl Vor leaned a little forward so that he could see the red-haired boy, who was sitting three seats up on his own side.

"No, I told you," he said, borrowing Quin's tone of overpatience, "I have a cat."

Jeff shouted a laugh, and Delia giggled.

"Cats are pretty useful," Rodale said. "We got a couple, to keep the mice outta the larder. M'gran wouldn't be 'thout 'least one."

"My dog also hunts rats," Kezzi said surprisingly. "My grandmother doesn't allow them."

"There, see, Rudy?" Vanette said. "If you got rats at *your* place, you need to get yourself a cat—or a good rattin' dog, like Anna's got."

Rudy didn't answer. He stared down at his plate, his face red.

"You know what my cat does?" Tansy asked from down-table and opposite. "He sits on top the door 'til somebody comes through, then he jumps on their head!"

That occasioned more laughter, and gave Rudy's face time to fade to pink. There would have been more stories about cats, too—Kaleb started one—but Ms. Taylor held up her hands and said that lunch was over and the first one who cleared away their dishes and was back in their place in the classroom got to do the first route.

CHAPTER TWENTY-FOUR

· ·

IT WAS ARN'S TURN TO READ ALOUD. SYL VOR, WHOSE TURN WAS yet to come, followed along in the book that he and Rodale shared. Rodale's head was angled downward, as if he were attentively reading, too, but Syl Vor could hear that his breathing was much too even. Rodale was asleep.

He was wondering how to wake him up so that Ms. Taylor wouldn't notice, when there was the sound of heavy footsteps in the hall, coming toward the schoolroom.

Ms. Taylor held up her hand, but Arn had already stopped reading and was staring at the door. In fact, the whole class was staring at the door, including Rodale, who had woken up very neatly.

The footsteps continued toward them; the door was snatched open and a Patrolman in a bright green vest and a bright green cap strode through, his hand around the upper arm of a boy as tall and as broad in the shoulder as he was. Even though the Patrolman had a firm grip on his arm, it didn't seem like the boy was considering running away. In fact, he matched steps with the Patrolman, and sent a quick, interested look around the room as he was marched up to Ms. Taylor, like he was looking for somebody.

Two rows up and to the left, Peter Day sat up straight, and raised a hand.

The boy with the Patrolman grinned and jerked his head in a quick nod.

"'Nother child onna street for ya, Miz," the patrolman said. "Big enough to be workin' at sumpin', you ask me. Ain't though, and he's under years for bein' idle."

"Thank you, Mr. O'Dell," Ms. Taylor said. "You may let him go; he doesn't look like he's going to run away."

So Ms. Taylor saw it, too, Syl Vor thought, that the new boy wasn't going to run—he *intended* to be here.

The Patrolman grunted, released his hold, and gave the room a general hard stare, as if warning them all not to try anything, looked back to Ms. Taylor, touched the brim of his cap, and marched out, closing the door loudly behind him.

"Careful, there," Rodale muttered. "No need t'crack the frame."

"Now," Ms. Taylor said to the new boy, "this is what we do. You tell us your name and turf, then we'll all introduce ourselves. All right?"

"All right," the boy agreed. He looked directly at Peter, and nodded.

"Hey, Pete."

"Luce," Peter answered. "Good t'see ya."

"Same." He raised his head then, and looked over the heads of the rest of the class. "I'm Luce Jacobs. Boss Wentworth's turf."

"Very good. Now, class? Starting with Vanette."

They introduced themselves, quick and orderly now that they'd had practice. Luce Jacobs stood with his hands tucked into the pockets of his jacket, one side of his mouth turned up, and didn't, Syl Vor thought, pay very much attention.

When it was his turn, though, Luce Jacobs looked directly at him, eyes narrowed, his half-smile turned to a frown. He stared at Syl Vor, even after he'd sat down and Rodale got up to introduce himself.

Syl Vor stared back, not frowning, and finally the older boy looked away.

"Thank you, everyone!" Ms.Taylor said, smiling widely. "That was good." She looked up at their new classmate.

"Luce, you can hang your jacket up in back with the others," she said. "And, since you know Pete..."

Syl Vor had happened to be looking at Peter, who'd been smiling his lazy smile all the time introductions were going on. The smile became a grin, now—and crashed into a frown.

"...you can sit next to Rudy. All right?"

"Yes, ma'am, that's fine," he said, and walked to the back to hang up his coat.

"Arn, why don't you start reading your piece at the top of the paragraph you were on when Luce came in?" Ms. Taylor said, and the class settled back into normality.

· · · ⁂ · · ·

School had been less strange today; the *gadje* faces more readily recognizable. Ms. Taylor had told her that she'd done her multiplications very well, which had again pleased her. Last night, after she had told out her day to Silain, the *luthia* said that there was no shame in being pleased in honest praise. Kezzi thought that Ms. Taylor was honest—she didn't tell everyone they'd done well, and she willingly showed those who had gotten something wrong in their problems where they'd made their mistake.

True, she hadn't seen Kezzi putting the plate and forks back on the bureau, but it wasn't supposed that a *gadje*, no matter how gifted, was quick enough to see a Bedel at work.

Syl Vor, though—*he* had seen her. And scolded her. And offered to help. Which was, Kezzi thought, very like most of her brothers of the Bedel. So maybe it wouldn't be...very hard to deal with him as a brother-in-truth.

The boy who had come in with the *garda*, now; she didn't care for that one at all. He looked like a boy who might kick a small dog with his heavy boots, and laugh when the dog screamed.

"Class dismissed!" Ms. Taylor called. "Everybody remember to come in on time tomorrow!"

Kezzi went to the back and took down her coat. She shrugged it on, turned—and wasn't completely surprised to find Syl Vor beside her, sealing up his jacket and looking at her sideways, from beneath his lashes.

"Hello," she said to him, which sounded grudging in her own ears, but apparently not to Syl Vor.

He looked up with a quick smile.

"Hello. Are you ready to go home?"

Home. Kezzi sighed.

Act as if he is your brother, and he will become your brother-in-truth, the *luthia* had said.

"I'm ready," she said, turning with him toward the door. "I have a letter for your mother."

"For *our* mother," he corrected. "From your grandmother?"

"Yes." She frowned, suddenly struck. "If *your* mother is *my* mother," she said slowly, "is *my* grandmother *your* grandmother?"

He blinked, and was silent as they went down the hallway with the bustle of their classmates.

"I don't know," he said. "We'll look it up in the Code, when we get home."

They had reached the doorway, and suddenly Kezzi was thrust aside into the side of the door, and Syl Vor pushed into the sharp frame.

"Hey, sorry there, *slowbees*. Make room for the *big kids*." That was Luce Jacobs, the new boy. He laughed and pushed through the door, bumping into Delia on the step, and knocking her hat off.

Pete Day was right after him, walking wide, like Rafin when he wished someone would fight with him, and taking up the whole door.

"For sleet's sake, Syl Vor, yer the clumsiest kid I ever met," he snarled as he went past.

Kezzi wasn't exactly sure, but it looked like he slammed his elbow into Syl Vor's shoulder.

Hard.

Syl Vor swung into the doorway, and Kezzi went after him. They reached the steps just in time to see Pete and Luce shove their way through the kids and others on the walk, and head up the street, in the direction opposite from theirs, laughing loudly.

"I don't like that boy," she said.

"Which one?"

"The new one—Luce." She thought for a moment. "Or Pete, either."

"They seem to like each other."

"I don't like that either," Kezzi said.

"Neither do I." Syl Vor jerked his head at a thin, dark-haired man standing on the walk a little away from the staircase and the crowd of their classmates.

"Look, there's Gavit, come to take us home."

CHAPTER TWENTY-FIVE

· ·

RYS WOKE WITH A SNAP, AS IF A TOGGLE HAD BEEN PRESSED, and came up on his elbow, blinking against the hearthlight.

"Far-dreamer, welcome," a familiar—even a beloved—voice said from the opposite side of the hearth. "Glad I am to see you return to us."

He smiled.

"Are dreams so dangerous, then?"

"Some are," Udari said slowly, as if considering the question in all seriousness. "Some, are not. And who can know which is what, until our dreams have engaged our waking minds."

"Well, in that case, I cannot say that I dreamed at all," Rys said, smiling. "It was five drops from the amber bottle at Silain's direction that beguiled me."

"A healing sleep," Udari said wisely. "Rafin used you roughly, I think."

"He may have done," Rys said, raising his hand so that the scales took fire from the hearthlight. "But I call us in Balance."

"I thought that you would." There was a suggestion of a sigh there.

"Do you not?"

"Who am I to judge?" Udari returned. "If my brother finds the bargain fair, then my heart is full of my brother's happiness."

Rys felt tears rise in his eyes, and managed a smile despite them. "You are good to me, Udari."

"And you are good to me," the other replied.

"Now," he said, more briskly, "are you recovered? Do you wait upon the *luthia*'s word, or are you free to come with me?"

"Silain was called to tend Dmitri. She bade me come to our hearth, find the amber bottle and put five drops in my tea."

"So, you have done as you were bade, and kept faith with the *luthia*," Udari said. "I fear we'll be called together soon in celebration of our elder brother. For now, I think we should go to Rafin, Brother, if you're well enough to walk."

Rys smiled, and reached for his crutch.

"Almost," he said, "I am well enough to run."

· · · ⁜ · · ·

Kezzi walked next to Syl Vor, Gavit the *garda* walking behind. It was, she thought, better than being pulled along by her wrist, or pushed along by a hand on her shoulder, but not *very* much better. Did he still think she was going to run away?

She thought about that for a moment, and was forced to admit to herself that he might think so, since he had no way of knowing about the *luthia*'s judgment on the matter, or her instructions regarding Kezzi's brother.

Sighing, she glanced at him, and encountered a pair of worried blue eyes.

"Are you angry?" he asked; his eyebrows drew together in a frown. "Were you hurt, when Peter pushed us?"

"No, and no. It's only that..." She hesitated, but the *luthia*'s judgment had been plain. She owed this boy—this brother—the gift the Bedel gave only among themselves.

Truth.

"I don't like to walk under the eye of a *garda*," she said.

He nodded. "It does seem silly, doesn't it? Our house is quite close, and none of the others have escorts." He looked over his shoulder. "Do you think my mother will let us walk home without an escort, Gavit? Now that there are two of us?"

The *garda* shrugged, his mouth twisting up like he'd taken a bite of a limin.

"Best ta ask Mike, Silver. He knows your ma's mind best, bein' her 'hand like he is."

"Yes, that's very true, thank you." He looked back to Kezzi.

"We'll talk with Mike when we get home—and we have to

remember to set your watch by the house clock, so you'll be on time to school tomorrow."

Time. The *gadje* were all ruled by *time*, which was a far different matter than *timing* and *intervals*. Kezzi sighed.

"I don't have a watch. The Bedel have no need."

"Ms. Taylor said that you must be on time," Syl Vor pointed out, which was...true. "Mother expects us to do well in school, and to conform to the teacher's instructions."

"That means," Gavit the *garda* put in, "Silver'll be gettin' you a watch outta the house supply and makin' sure you wear it."

She turned her head to glare at him, and was surprised to see him give her a wink and smile.

"I don't want a watch," she told Syl Vor.

"How will you be on time, then?"

That was a puzzle, and Kezzi began to feel a little short-breathed, as if walls had sprung up too close beside her.

"The Bedel..." she began again, and stopped, hearing again Silain telling her to do what tasks Syl Vor's mother gave her as well as she could.

"You'll have to teach me to use it, then," she said sulkily.

Syl Vor nodded.

"All right."

· · · ✷ · · ·

"Ah, here he is, and much improved in spirit." Rafin's face was black with soot, his eyes as blue as lightning.

"Where is Pulka?" asked Udari, glancing 'round. "He will want to see his dream with waking eyes."

"He was called to duty," Rafin said, spitting into the forge. "The *garda* have come too near the old western gate and the headman has ordered it sealed."

Udari looked grave.

"That's the third gate closed within two hands."

"It is, and if you say that we're on the edge of closing too many, your voice will join the voices of all our brothers—yes, and our sisters, too!"

For no reason that he could summon to mind, Rys felt his mouth dry. He swallowed, and looked to Udari.

"The...*garda*. What do they seek?"

Udari shrugged.

"What do they seek?" Rafin said. "Rat holes! Torv brings the news from Above—the new Boss doesn't believe in ghosts. He looks at the buildings over our heads and he sees a place for *gadje* to live; a place to grow fruits and vegetables, protected from the cruel weather."

"They seek to be like the Bedel, then," Rys said, since Udari continued in frowning silence.

"No, *that* they do not!" Rafin declared. "They seek to be dry, and warm, and fed."

"All people seek those things," Udari said at last. "It's plain, Brothers; if the *gadje* come here, then the Bedel must go . . . somewhere else."

"Best if the *gadje don't* come here, I say—and others of our brothers with me. There are ways to be certain."

"If Boss Conrad doesn't believe in ghosts, he'll look for men," Udari argued.

Rafin sighed.

"As for that, the *garda* did find something of note, according to Zand, who followed them."

"What was that?" asked Udari.

"The remains of a camp, above the third floor, two buildings east."

"*Above* the third floor?" Rys asked, frowning.

"A subattic, not easy to find, except Zand said that one of the *garda* had played in that building as a boy. There was a pipe from the rain catcher on the rooftop, that was cut and a faucet installed. Wires had been cross-woven to power a small communication system. Some blankets, and a stove—a snug nest. There was no food or sign that the place had been habited recently. The *garda* took away what was there."

"Another brave one, who was not afraid of ghosts," Udari commented drily.

Rafin shrugged. "Or who was more afraid of something else. But, come! We're here for another purpose! The frame is roughed. Now, the fighting cock must come over to the bench and suffer himself to be enclosed, so that I can take fine measurements and consider the best locations for releases and springs. This, we may safely do while Pulka is at duty. It's the finished piece that he'll want to measure against his dream!"

· · · ✹ · · ·

"Boss and Mike gone out callin','" the woman named Veeno told Syl Vor when they came into the house. "They'll be back in time for supper. Boss said you and your sister was to play nice."

Silver nodded, and pulled off his jacket to hang away. The sleeve of his sweater was pulled up, exposing the heavy bracelet. He sighed and pushed the sleeve down.

"Come on," he said, after Kezzi had hung up her coat. "Let's play a game!"

Syl Vor's room at the top of the house was no larger than the hearth-room she shared with Droi and Vylet, and the side-place where a table and computer stood seemed oddly like a hearth. She had, Kezzi owned, expected it to be larger, and more full of...*things.*

She had not expected it to be bright—or at least as bright as the late day sun could make it, glowing through glass windows framed by dark curtains. The *kompani*'s place Beneath was always in twilight, despite the use of dims, and the constant glow from the hearthstones.

In the hearth-room was a bed, covered over with a blue blanket, and in the center of the bed was a furry orange-and-white circle.

"Here she is!"

Syl Vor leaned over the bed to stroke the curved back with the flat of his palm until, slowly, the cat uncurled into a long furry tube, eyes closed and ears twitching.

"Come sleepy one, wake! Here is my sister Kezzi, who I told you about. She is come to meet you!"

The cat opened green eyes, not very wide, and yawned, showing dainty pointed teeth.

"There, that's better," Syl Vor said, and turned his head. "Kezzi, come and make yourself known to Eztina."

She came to his side, and stood looking down at the cat, who had rolled half onto her head, with her paws in the air and her white belly exposed, so much like Malda when he wanted a tummy rub that Kezzi chuckled.

"What you must do," Syl Vor said, "is to extend your first finger toward her nose. Do not *touch* her nose, or bump it—that would be rude. Just hold your finger still and allow her to decide what she will do."

Carefully, Kezzi followed these instructions. The cat blinked green eyes and did nothing.

"It may take a little while," Syl Vor said. "Only be patient."

"She looks like she wants her belly rubbed."

"On no account! She tries to tempt you."

"Tempt me?"

"If you touch her belly, she will instantly wrap herself around your hand and wrist and hold on with all her claws. Which I assure you does not sting a little!"

"But—" Kezzi caught her breath on the question she was about to ask, for Eztina had rolled bonelessly to her feet, deftly avoiding Kezzi's finger, stood gracefully on three feet while she stretched one back foot up behind her.

"Ah," Syl Vor said softly, just as a cool, slightly damp nose met Kezzi's fingertip.

"There, she is polite," he murmured. "You may now lightly rub her behind the ears."

This Kezzi did, nowhere near so robust as if it were Malda's ears she rubbed, for she had no wish to damage this fragile-looking creature, who was, she thought, not at all like the cats who took employ with the Bedel, or their cousins in the City Above.

Kezzi smiled as Eztina bumped her head vigorously against her fingers, then turned half about and sat, lifting a back leg and beginning to groom.

"The cats I know aren't friendly," she commented. "They have their duty-work and don't want anything from us."

He nodded. "But Eztina is a house cat—a pet—and I fear that Padi is right in saying that we spoil her."

"Padi—this is a sister?"

"My cousin," he said. "She's gone with her father—my Uncle Shan—on the *Dutiful Passage*, to learn to be a trader. And that reminds me of the game!"

He crossed the room, pulled open a drawer and took out a pouch.

"Come!" He beckoned her to the table, pulled the tie loose and upended the pouch over the tabletop.

Coins spilled out, ringing like bells, and a stub of pale chalk no longer than her smallest finger.

And—no, Kezzi thought, they weren't coins, at least not any coins that she knew.

"*Aequitas*," Syl Vor said. "Trade tokens. They're used when the trade is for information, instead of things." He glanced up at her, blue eyes wide.

"*Things* are easy to get," he said, seriously, "but information can save lives."

She blinked at him—so serious—then again at the tumble and shine of coins—of *aequitas*—littering the tabletop.

"Choose a color," Syl Vor said, pulling out a chair and coiling onto it, one leg bent under him, and the other foot swinging above the floor. "Take all the coins of that color to your side of the table."

She chose red and quickly sorted them to her side. Syl Vor did the same with the blue coins, then picked up the chalk and drew a line across the middle of the table, dividing her side from his.

"This is how it works," he said. "You ask a question, and I answer. If you learn something from my answer, you pass one of your coins to my side of the table. Then, I ask you a question. If I learn something I pass you one of my coins. If the answer is *very* informative," he said with a grin, "or surprising, two coins may pass."

He swept the unused colors to one side, with the chalk bit.

"There are more rules, but the simple ones should do for today. I haven't played since Padi left us, so I'm out of practice."

"And I," Kezzi said, picking up a coin and weighing it in her hand, "have never played, or heard of this game."

"We play it because we're a trade house," Syl Vor said, and looked at her expectantly.

She stared back at him, frowning.

"Did you know that?" he asked, casting a significant glance down at her coins.

Kezzi stared, and suddenly, like a lesson learned in dream, the rules of the game became vividly clear, and she grinned

"I didn't know that I'd asked the first question," she said, and slid a red coin to his side of the table.

He nodded. "Now, it's my turn. What does *gadje* mean?"

"Those Others," she said. "People who are not Bedel."

A blue coin came across the table to her, and she felt a glow of accomplishment.

Syl Vor folded his arms on the table and the bracelet again peeked from under the sleeve.

"What *is* that?" she demanded.

"What? This?" He lifted his arm; the bracelet gleamed in the light from the window. "It tells Mike Golden where it is."

She gave him a coin for it—and blinked as he unclasped and held it out to her.

"Here."

Kezzi frowned down at the thing in her hand. It was dull bronze in color, but not quite as heavy as she had expected it to be. She pressed on the clasp, approving the solid snap as it closed.

She turned it over, looking for a maker's mark or a pressure point that might open an inner pocket, but the inside was smooth and featureless. Finally, she glanced up to find Syl Vor watching her curiously. She felt her face heat and handed the cuff back to him.

"It's well-made, though fine for a boy," she said austerely.

He grinned.

"At ho— on Liad, I would never have had such a thing," he said, putting it aside, with the unused tokens. "Children don't wear jewelry, except their clan sign." He touched the collar of his shirt.

"What is Liad?"

"The planet we lived on, before the *delm* brought us to Surebleak," he answered promptly.

All right, that was reasonable; many people had come to Surebleak from elsewhere, since the Boss Conrad had arisen. It was even said, she remembered, that Boss Conrad had come from elsewhere. She pushed a coin to him.

"What is Bedel?" asked Syl Vor.

"A *kompani*," she answered, and pointed at his collar before he had taken his finger from his coin.

"What purpose is the clan sign?"

"To let others know what clan one belongs to," he said.

She glared at him and didn't pass a coin.

Syl Vor grinned.

"My clan—now yours—is Korval. Our sign is the Tree-and-Dragon."

The coin had already left her finger, but she stared at him.

"Dragon?" she repeated, remembering Rys' fear, and what Silain had taught her to say to him, immediately he awoke.

There are no dragons here.

"Are you," she asked carefully, "a dragon?"

He laughed.

"Well, I'm not a tree!"

"But...there *are* the People of the Tree," she protested, "who took contract with the Boss Conrad, to build the road!"

"Yes, some people here call us that—the People of the Tree. At ho— on Liad, we were called dragons. Other clans were called by their signs, too. It is...it *is* a Liaden cultural marker."

That last sounded as if it were dream-learned. Kezzi nodded and gave him another coin.

"What is a *kompani*?"

"A *kompani* is—Bedel on *chafurma*."

Syl Vor tipped his head, the blue token gleaming between his fingers.

Kezzi sighed.

"*Chafurma* is the gathering time."

Two coins came across to her side of the table, rolling lazily on their edges. She flattened them with her palm.

"What's a *delm*?"

"The *delm* is the head of the clan, who makes decisions and settles disputes," he said. "The *delm* is the face and the voice of the clan." He wrinkled his nose. "That's what the Code says."

"What—" she began, but he shook his head.

"It's my turn."

"Oh, all right."

"Why were you...afraid to find that I'm a dragon?"

"I was *not* afraid," she said. "I was...surprised. A person I know doesn't like dragons."

He frowned. "Which person?"

Kezzi folded her hands on the table. Rys had been *afraid*. Information might save lives, but it was like some of the medicines in the *luthia*'s box, that could both cure and kill.

"That isn't mine to sell."

Syl Vor's eyebrows rose, he bowed his head—and two coins came across the line to her.

"Why did you make me your sister?"

He sighed.

"Because I didn't want to make another enemy."

She blinked at him, pushed a coin, another, and—thinking of Rys—a third.

Syl Vor stared at them for a long moment, his mouth pressed into a thin line, then looked up at her.

"What is your dog's name?"

"Malda," she answered, and gave him a sharp stare. "But that is *not* for the street. For the street, he is Rascal."

"I understand," he said.

She took a breath, already fingering a coin.

"What," she began—and stopped as a shadow came across the tabletop, and a slim finger slid one blue coin and one red coin into the center of the table.

"Who," Syl Vor's mother said in her cool, calm voice, "would like to come downstairs for dinner?"

CHAPTER TWENTY-SIX

THE "ROUGH" WAS A BLACKENED CAGE OF METAL THAT RAFIN bent 'round his leg with a pair of large pinchers. Recalling that the acquisition of his glove had not been without cost, Rys braced himself to endure, but his leg was scarcely touched. Calipers were brought into play, certainly, and the aforesaid pinchers; a variety of hinges and fasteners were matched against the seam, and set down, some in this pile, others in that. His part was only to stand tall upon his crutch, and to repose himself to stillness.

After this had been going on for some time, Udari, who had been standing to one side as an observer, suddenly straightened and caught Rys' eye.

"I am wanted Above," he said, "on business of the *luthia*. Brothers, I will return."

Bent over the brace, Rafin grunted. Rys smiled.

"Go carefully, Brother," he said.

"Always," replied Udari, and left them.

"Mother?"

Kezzi could have wished her voice had sounded stronger, more certain. *Droi* wouldn't have let the word quaver, or trend upward at the end.

No matter, Syl Vor's mother did not seem to notice, only pausing with her hand on the back of a chair and inclining her head gently.

"Kezzi. How may I serve you, my child?"

"My grandmother asked me to give her letter to you into your hand," she said, repeating Silain's very words.

"Ah, very good. I will receive it with joy. Does she expect an answer to travel with you this evening?"

"She didn't say so," Kezzi answered, reaching under her sweater to the inner pocket where she had placed the letter that morning. "Ma'am."

The paper was rumpled from having been in her safe pocket all day. Kezzi ran it between her fingers, to try to straighten the worst wrinkles out, before offering it.

"Thank you," said Syl Vor's mother gravely. "I will read it after we eat our meal. Please sit next to Syl Vor. You remember Mr. Golden, I know. It's our custom to share a meal in the evening to catch up with each other, after being apart all day."

And here was another *gadje* thing that was very like a Bedel thing. Didn't she stop at Silain's hearth in the morning to share tea and talk over the night just past and the day to come? And in the evening, to share the day's excitement, and plan the night's dreaming?

She slipped into the chair next to Syl Vor, staring at the array of utensils laid on each side of a yellow plate with a design that might have been flowers or birds, or both, painted around the edge.

Bowls were passed up and down the table, from Syl Vor's mother to Mike Golden to Syl Vor and, lastly, to her. This was fortunate, since Syl Vor made sure she knew what was in each bowl as he handed them to her—squash, chicken with sauce, and...

"Mess greens," said Syl Vor, not quite wrinkling his nose. "Beck says."

Kezzi hesitated, looking into the bowl at the tangle of wilted dark leaves. A sharp scent came out of the bowl, not particularly pleasing. Syl Vor, she noticed, had taken less from this bowl than the squash bowl.

"That's vinegar dressin' on the leaves," Mike Golden said, and gave her a smile when she looked at him. "We call it *mess greens*, 'cause it looks a mess, all wilted up that way. Tastes pretty good, to me. 'Course, I grew up with 'em." He brought up a fork twisted with greens. "Silver don't hold the same opinion."

"I would rather have a fresh salad, than everything all wilted," Syl Vor said. "But these leaves are bitter until you cook them."

Kezzi put a small amount of the *mess* on her plate, and set the bowl aside.

"Mike," Syl Vor said, "now that there are two of us coming home from school, it won't be necessary for Gavit to break his day for escort duty."

The man's eyebrows rose, but he only nodded.

"You talk to your ma about this?"

"This is the first I've heard of such a proposal," Syl Vor's mother said. "It is very good of you to concern yourself with Gavit's schedule, my son. However, the necessity of standing your escort does not *take him* from his duty; it *is* his duty."

Syl Vor bit his lip, and looked up to her.

"In fact, ma'am, Kezzi feels that Gavit is...like a Patrolman. She's not accustomed to being escorted."

"I'll vouch for that," Mike Golden said unexpectedly. "The first two times I saw her she was by herself—except for the dog, who I don't discount."

Pleased by this praise of Malda, Kezzi smiled, and tasted the very smallest amount of *mess*. It was, she thought, chewing grimly, *not* very good.

"I think that we must continue with Gavit as escort at least until the new school is opened. Once we see how the patterns have changed, we will revisit the topic. I depend upon you and your sister to remind me."

"Yes, Mother," said Syl Vor, and addressed himself to his plate.

Kezzi followed suit, finding the squash much more to her taste than the leaves, and the chicken very good.

"How did you find school today, daughter?"

She swallowed hastily, and looked up into the cool, beautiful face.

"It was...less strange today than yesterday," she said. "A new boy was brought to class toward the end of the lessons."

"Yes, and Kezzi must have a watch!" Syl Vor interpolated. "Ms. Taylor specifically said that she was not to be late tomorrow."

Kezzi glared at him, but he was looking at Mike Golden.

"Then Kezzi must certainly have an accurate timepiece," his mother agreed gravely. "Mr. Golden, have we a House watch?"

"Sure do. Excuse me a tick and I'll get it now, before it slips my mind."

He rose from the table and was gone through the door into

the kitchen, returning very soon with a small watch on a chain, that he compared to the larger timepiece strapped to his wrist before placing the smaller by Kezzi's place.

After dinner was finished, and Syl Vor's—and *Mother* had poured a final cup of tea for everyone, Mike Golden showed Kezzi how to set various alarms, quizzing her on how long it took to walk to school by the best route, how long to have the waking meal, to wash her face—none of which she could tell him.

"I haven't had a watch," she told him, with what patience she could muster. "The Bedel have no need."

He frowned a little at that—not at her, but at the watch in his hand—then nodded once.

"Gotcha. Here's what, Kezzi. I'm gonna set this for my best guess at a good wake-up time. When it beeps, you'd best get outta bed, dress, eat breakfast. It beeps a second time, that's when you leave the house and head down to school, see? I'll let Ms. Taylor know you might be late tomorrow, but we'll get it all worked out soon."

"What if she's early?" Syl Vor asked. He was leaning over Mike Golden's shoulder, watching the proceedings with interest.

"Then whoever's on door'll let her in, give her a cuppa 'toot, and prolly a donut, too. So that's what we call win-win. Here you go."

He draped the watch over her neck.

Mother looked up from reading the *luthia*'s letter, which had lain by her plate, unopened, during the meal. She smiled her faint, cool smile.

"Well done. And now, my child, it is time for you to return to your grandmother. Please convey to her my very best wishes for her good health, and say that I will do as she has suggested. Gavit and Syl Vor will escort you to the corner of Blair and Dudley, where your brother Nathan will meet you."

"I'll go, too," Mike Golden said, with his big grin. "Nice night; likely a walk'll blow the cobwebs outta my head. 'Less you need me, Boss."

"Not immediately, and even if I did I would be willing to defer whatever business I had until these *cobwebs* were vanquished."

"Back soon, then," he said, and rose, shooing Kezzi and Syl Vor ahead of him.

· · · ✴ · · ·

Silain the *luthia* lay quiet, caught between dream and waking.

Slowly, the dream faded, emotion draining away to leave behind facts, like stones drying just beyond the long reach of the sea.

Silain had never seen a sea in her waking mind, but a long lifetime of dreaming had opened such things to her knowledge.

Such things, too, as the memories, not of those for whom *chafurma* had never ended, but of those who had felt their lack.

And of those who had made the decision not to return for them.

The sum of which, added to the knowledge well-known to both *luthia* and headman—the *why* of this particular *chafurma*, this *kompani* of Bedel, set down, of all possible planets, on this one, this Surebleak...

"Grandmother? Will you have tea?" The voice was soft, each word casting a dark shadow into the waking world.

Silain took a breath, and turned her head to smile into Droi's eyes, and onto her very soul.

"Tea in a moment, daughter. First, let me sit up. You will make me seemly, then give me your arm to the hearth. Tea, then, yes, shared between us. After, you will go to headman, and ask him to attend me."

· · · ❉ · · ·

"Nathan!" Kezzi called out, as she had the evening before, and here in fact was her brother stepping out of the shadows with her dog at his heels.

"Here," she said, kneeling down on the walk and snapping her fingers. "Syl Vor, you ought to meet...Rascal."

He went to her side, and held his hand out as directed, palm up. It was thoroughly and noisily sniffed, then licked vigorously, after which he was directed to rub the sharp ears. Rascal wriggled alarmingly, but Kezzi said it was because he was pleased to have a new friend.

"Now, Sister," Nathan said mildly, and Kezzi rose at once.

"Remember," Syl Vor said, "to be on time for school tomorrow."

"I have the watch," she said, which was no promise, but Syl Vor could hardly blame her for that.

Instead, he smiled and lifted his hand and stood with Gavit and Mike Golden, watching the man and the girl and the dog walk away.

"Well, there," Mike said, and looked over Syl Vor's head to Gavit.

"Tell you what; I got more cobwebs than I reckoned on. Gonna get another couple blocks under my boots, for what good it'll do me. Let the Boss know, right?"

"Sure, Mike," Gavit said.

"May I come with you?" Syl Vor asked.

"Nope," said Mike Golden and walked away into Surebleak's chilly spring dusk.

· · · ✳ · · ·

"I found something of yours in town today." Udari spoke softly, and in the language of the Bedel. "Here."

Kezzi felt something slip into her outside coat pocket. Something blocky, and of a good weight.

"Really?" Kezzi said eagerly. "What is it?"

He laughed. "If you can't guess, you'll need to wait until you see it! Now, tell me—how was your mother today?"

"She seemed well. I only saw her at the meal. Before it, my . . . brother taught me a game of coins and questions." She hesitated, chewing her lip. "It might be a thing for the headman."

"Not for the *luthia*?"

"I don't—" She shook her head in frustration, and paused to bend and pull on Malda's ears. "I don't know," she told Udari.

"Well. Can you teach this game to me? Maybe I can help you know."

"Yes! Will you be able to learn today?"

"Yes."

Kezzi sighed. The Bedel said, *A burden shared is a burden halved*, and it certainly felt as if a weight had been lifted from her shoulders.

"There's another thing," she said, as they walked into the shadow of the warehouses. "Two other things."

"Tell me."

"The boy—Syl Vor, my brother. His . . . *kompani*—clan. They are the People of the Tree."

"I'd guessed this."

"Yes, but—in the place they left, they were called *dragons*."

Silence from Udari for as many as four hands of steps, then a soft sigh.

"I will dream on it. And the third thing?"

She put her hand up to grip the disk hanging 'round her neck.

"I have a watch."

· · · ✦ · · ·

"*Luthia*, you have need of me?"

"We have need of each other, headman. Droi, my daughter, tea for us, please, and then you may take yourself to your own hearth."

"Yes, Grandmother."

Droi bowed, and moved away. Presently, there came the quiet sounds of tea being poured.

"Has the *luthia* dreamed of the numbers?" Alosha asked, before the mugs were even brought to hand.

Silain sighed, but he was the headman, and he had asked her, after all, to dream.

"The numbers are, as the headman has said, fixed, and we have gone beyond the time when we may be fruitful with each other. To breed with the *gadje* means that we will lose ourselves. In all of this, we agree."

She looked up as Droi came toward them, soft-footed, bearing mugs.

The headman received his with a nod and a softly spoken, "Sister."

"Daughter. You watched well for me this day. I release you now to your duty-work."

"Grandmother." Droi bowed, pliant and agreeable as a child, turned and left them, silent and dark against the dimness.

Silain turned back to Alosha.

"I have dreamed the decisions taken, and the loss and pain endured by those in the past who left a *kompani* to founder, and *chafurma* to crumple into disaster. In my dreams, twice the decision was motivated by a ship crisis; three times, it was the condition of the planet chosen for *chafurma* that made a proper ending impossible. I ask if the headman has lately dreamed *this* *kompani*'s purpose."

He looked at her over the rim of his mug, and for a long moment was silent. When he did at last speak, he answered her question obliquely.

"We were set down at a bad time, when the Gilmour Agency, that opened this world, had just withdrawn. During *chafurma*, conditions grew worse, and—yes, I believe you're right, *luthia*!— the ship would not risk itself. Now, it is too busy with all the change the Boss Conrad has brought with him, and the ship could not be secret."

Alosha the headman took a deep breath, and shook his head.

"We, the Bedel of *this kompani* will not see the end of *chafurma*. We will only see ourselves become *gadje*."

"That may be," Silain said sternly, "but equally, it may not be. The youngest of us has been guided by the Sight to a condition which may work to preserve us, and even bring a proper end to *chafurma*. We may need to hazard something of who we are in order to win this, but—"

"But if we are lost, already, what matter? I understand you! Tell me about this hazard, *luthia,* and how we might tempt fortune to favor us."

CHAPTER TWENTY-SEVEN

THE ROOM WAS DARK, WITH ONLY THE LAMP ON THE DESK LIT, and her hair shining with it, head bent over a file.

She looked up on hearing his step, and she—well, she didn't smile, but her face eased, and she took a deep breath.

"Mr. Golden, I had almost given you up. Did you see my daughter safely home?"

"Roundabout I did, letting her brother so-called Nathan take the visible part."

She nodded and moved her hand to show him the chair next to her desk. That done, she pressed a key on the house comm, and asked...Annis it would be, this time of night, to send in the tea tray.

Mike eased into his chair and stretched his legs out in front of him. She had the heater on like it was midwinter; he felt it beating down on his neck.

"And where, one wonders, does Kezzi live?" Nova asked, leaning back in her chair and giving him her whole attention.

"Right where we both thought she did—up inside the warehouses. I can get back to the door they used tonight. After I saw her safe inside, I did a little walkin' around, an' a little standin' around. Saw some cameras hung up clever, saw some steam coming through the seams in the 'crete-walk. Could be somebody saw me; could be not. Didn't really wanna spook 'em."

"I expect that the Patrol may already have done so," she commented, and looked up as the door opened, admitting Annis with the tray.

She set it down soft on the corner of the desk and managed to raise her eyes to meet Nova's, which she couldn't've, three months ago.

"Will you be needing anything else, Boss?"

"No, thank you, Annis; the tea will be sufficient."

"Yes, ma'am. 'Night, Mike."

"'Night, Annis." He gave her a grin, and got a full smile out of her before she turned and left, shutting the door nice and quiet behind her.

"Thanks," he said to Nova, who had filled his usual mug. He picked it up and sipped it, sighing in equal parts satisfied and tired.

"The Patrol," he said, coming back to her point. "Could be they've caused some upset. Was gonna talk to McFarland 'bout that, tomorrow—see what's been found, an' who. Look over the sweep pattern, maybe, see if we can adjust it some."

"A good plan," she agreed. She leaned back in her chair, a cream-and-blue cup balanced on slim fingertips.

They sat for a few minutes in comfortable silence. The radiant heater finished its cycle and Mike sighed.

Nova smiled faintly.

"Kezzi's grandmother writes that she favors this new relationship which has found her granddaughter, and feels that it cannot but benefit both principals. She concurs that we two would do best to meet and speak together, and suggests as neutral territory, Joan's Bakery the day after tomorrow, in the quiet hour." She looked up, her face guileless.

"Now, what do you think the quiet hour might be?"

"After the breakfast crowd's gone an' lunch ain't got started," he answered promptly. "I'll find out the exact o'clock tomorrow." He tipped his head. "You'll be meetin', I take it?"

"If it can be arranged. Soonest begun, soonest done, as my father had been used to say. And as this now appears to have grown larger than Syl Vor's mere acquisition of a sister..."

"Right."

He sighed again and drank off his tea, stretching out an arm to put the mug on the tray. "Tell you what, it's lucky Silver took that notion of his. Gives us an in that don't have anything to do with the Patrol, if they're livin' up there."

"Which did not surprise you," Nova commented.

"Well, no, it didn't. But, see, I come up on these streets right here, and it's always been risky to go near the warehouses. 'S'why I told McFarland we needed to take it slow, send up Patrols to have a look around, see what we oughta know before we start renovatin'."

"Kezzi's brother Nathan . . ."

"So-called," Mike muttered.

She raised her eyebrows.

"Mr. Golden, you must forgive us."

He eyed her. "What for?"

"It seems that we have been instrumental in making you less trusting. Surely, it must sadden one to see innocence lost."

He snorted.

"You got the wrong guy, maybe."

"If you say so, Mr. Golden, then perhaps I do. One would not wish to distress you in any way."

He forbore from snorting again.

"You was sayin' about Kezzi and Nathan?"

"So I was. I happened to wonder if they were very similar to each other in appearance. The child is something out of the way, for Surebleak. Of course, if Nathan, so-called, is her true-brother, then it may be that it is merely what you call a *family resemblance*." She finished her tea and put the cup next to his mug on the tray.

"Well. It may be a topic to introduce with Kezzi's grandmother, should conversation lag."

"Sure. She got a name, the grandma?"

"None that she sees fit to commit to paper." Nova sighed, and rose, looking down upon him with that look that wasn't exactly a smile.

"I suggest that the day has been long enough, and that we could both use some rest," she said. "I leave the arrangements for Joan's Bakery in your hands, as well as the adjustment of Patrol work in the warehouses with Mr. McFarland."

"Right," he said, coming to his feet.

She snapped off the desk light and walked across the room, light-footed and graceful in the dim-lit office. He followed her out into the hall, and watched her safe on her way upstairs before continuing to the back of the house, and his room there.

· · · ✷ · · ·

It was a box of color sticks that Udari had slipped into her pocket as they walked. Kezzi squeaked, and fell to her knees to present it to Malda's curious nose.

He snuffled and sneezed. Kezzi laughed and put the box tenderly away into the pocket of her sweater, before rising, and looking up to meet Udari's eyes.

"It's good that you found these," she told him, seriously.

He smiled and unwound the scarf from about her neck, hanging it with the rest on the hooks by the inner gate.

"The *luthia* told me that she expects dreaming to go long, and that you were to go to Jin. Do that, and bespeak dinner for us, then meet me in the garden. We can eat and learn together."

Kezzi hesitated.

"Memit doesn't want Malda and me to play in the garden."

Udari grinned.

"I'll deal with Memit, Sister; *you* deal with Jin."

She laughed. "Done!"

A turn, a thought, and a turn back to find Udari already walking away.

"Brother!"

He turned, a hand upraised in question.

"After Memit, find us—oh! twigs and pebbles, a double hand of each."

"I will," Udari promised, and was gone.

Kezzi made certain her colors were firmly buttoned into the pocket of her sweater, snapped her fingers for Malda, and set off for Jin's hearth at a run.

· · · ✳ · · ·

She dreamed the amounts and the mixture, for it wouldn't do to make a mistake. Not in this. After she had dreamed, she rose from her nest of blankets, moving quietly.

Vylet's sleeping place was empty; expectable, since it was her turn to pray with Dmitri.

Kezzi's nest . . . Droi heard a shuddering snore and leaned close. Yes. Kezzi was curled into a complicated knot among her blankets, and the dog, foolish in his devotion, had done his best to lie across her. His nose had gotten under a tangle of cloth and produced the muffled snore.

Droi rearranged the blankets to better use over both, then moved to the back of the hearth, as silent as the plentiful shadows.

Carefully, she made the tonic, and knocked it back, swallowing without tasting, as experience had taught her that such draughts were prone to be bitter.

She smiled at that thought, and washed the glass.

Then, she moved to her chest, opened it, and sorted fabrics by touch before undressing and dressing again. She unwound her hair, brushed it out, then pinned it up loosely. The tonic by this time was making its effects known, and Droi smiled as she worked.

In the shadows around her, half-seen things moved; that was as usual, and comforting in its way. Prudence, though, prudence had her leave her knife behind her, when at last she left her hearth, the hem of the bright skirt brushing bare ankles, the coins on her belt chiming with every step.

· · · ☀ · · ·

Udari left the child and the dog at her cousins' hearth, with a promise that he would be ready when she called him to walk out with her on the following morning. From there, he betook himself to the equipment locker, where he withdrew a timer; and went on to the gate he and the child earlier entered. He donned a coat, pulled a dark hat down over his head and let himself out, clicking the timer on.

When he returned, it was to find Pulka just inside the door, frowning and chewing on his mustache.

"Brother," Udari said, pulling off the hat off, and hanging the coat on a hook. He glanced at the timer, and slid it into his pocket.

"Brother," Pulka answered. "Did you meet anyone on the street?"

Udari frowned. This was abrupt even for Pulka.

"No, Brother, I met no one. Why?"

"Come with me."

"Here, then here, and later, here."

Udari watched the playback from the watch-cameras. The shadow was circumspect... and had by the cameras' evidence, completely walked around the buildings under which the Bedel held camp.

"Did he make any attempt to enter, or to force the gates?"

"No," Pulka growled, and shook his head. "Brother, you know that we've already sealed too many gates. If this one comes back..."

Udari reached to the console and triggered another playback. There was something about the shadowy figure that seemed familiar—the walk, the particular bulk, the—

"Hah!"

"What?" demanded Pulka.

"It's Mike Golden, who...who is under the study of the *luthia*."

Pulka's frown became ferocious. "Does she bring him in to us?"

"No, but I think...I don't think that he means us harm, Brother. I will tell the *luthia*—tonight, if she's not already asleep."

"It can wait on the morrow; he's gone now," Pulka said gruffly. "Before you find your own rest—and if it can be told in a moment— how goes Rafin's work?"

"He believes it will be ready tomorrow."

"So soon? I'll be there, tell him. I must see it done."

"He knows it. We will all be there, to witness, and to support our brother."

· · · ※ · · ·

Rafin was banking the forge, and looked 'round with his eyebrows well up.

"Sister?"

"Where's Rys?" she asked. The tonic was well in control now, her nerves were bright with desire, her companion shadows nestling dark around her shoulders.

"Rys, is it?" Rafin came forward, his fingers flexing. "I'm awake."

She shook her head, feeling the pins slip in her hair.

"I come as the soul of the *kompani*."

"Do you?"

That quickly, his fingers were 'round her throat, his grip tight enough to bring her breath short. Droi stared up into his eyes.

"Within the next day, Dmitri will pass into that Other Place," she said calmly. "The numbers will be unbalanced; the *kompani* placed at risk. The headman and the *luthia* between them see the danger. What they do not see is that the tool is to hand, needing only to be grasped—and used."

His gaze dropped to her naked shoulders, and her breasts but half draped in filmy purple.

"Rafin, release me."

He again raised his eyes to meet hers, opened his fingers, and shrugged.

"The *kompani* could do worse. The cock is small, but never have I seen a heart as bold."

"So, we agree, and again I ask—where is Rys?"

He jerked his head toward the small tent, which place was known to her.

"Will you eat him here?"

"Shall I carry him out to the common and call the *kompani* to stand witness?"

He snorted.

"I seek my own bed. Try not to kill him. It would break Udari's heart."

· · · ⁂ · · ·

Momma Liberty was at dock; crew enjoying off-duty until the inspection team requested entry—and them a half-day down on the roster. Incoming had been tense, and Rys had been glad enough to go off-shift, shower, and stretch out on his bunk for a nap. Vern—Jasin's brother—had been more particular in his attentions to himself than usual. The loss at Ondileigh had not made his temper any sweeter, and though he had nothing to do with the trade, still Rys bore the brunt of the trader's displeasure, until Jasin had snapped at him to have done.

It was warm in his bunk. He sighed, and spiraled into sleep...

"Rys." A soft exhalation of breath, warm against his ear.

"Jasin?" he murmured, his mind weighted with sleep.

"Rys..." the voice said again, accompanying a gentle stroke down his cheek. "Open your eyes, Rys, and let me see you."

He struggled to throw off the heaviness. Her fingers were in his hair now, pulling a little where the curls knotted, and he felt the damp tip of a tongue or finger tracing the edge of his ear.

"Jasin...a moment."

He gasped as teeth indented his ear lobe, his eyes snapping open to behold a face at once beguiling and dangerous.

"Droi." He took a breath, remembering now that he was at the forge, in the small tent, and that it had been late when he took his leave of Rafin—

And it was by no means morning now. The forge was silent; the darkness dyed a tricksy grey by the dim light above him.

He was stretched on his back, Droi's knee between his, and one hand on his shoulder, pressing him down onto the cot.

"Rys Dragonwing," she crooned. "Sweet morsel."

Her fingers twisted in his hair and she leaned down, smiling, her eyes glowing cat-green in the slender light.

Rys took a breath, recalling Silain's warning regarding this woman whom even Udari found unsettling.

"Sister," he said, lifting his ungloved hand softly to her shoulder. "My sight is not as long as yours."

She smiled, showing sharp white teeth.

"Then I will see for both."

Her lips were warm and moist; her kiss so cruel that he moaned against her mouth, aroused in the instant, his traitor hips moving. She laughed into his mouth, bit his lips, and kissed him again, more cruelly still, her hand leaving his hair to guide his hand to one full breast, moaning in her turn as his kneading gave her pleasure, and...

"Harder," she ordered, nipping his throat, and he tightened his fingers in a violent caress while she plundered his mouth, and her hand slipped down to where he strained against the confines of his clothing and with a cunning twist freed him to spring against her skirts.

"Now," she murmured, and moved fully over him, skirts spread, hot, naked thighs gripping his, but not engaging, not yet. Instead, she knelt above him and pulled her thin blouse over her head, exposing herself. She looked into his eyes as she cupped her breasts. Slowly, she put one hand down to grip his other wrist. Her eyes widened, breasts lifting with the intake of her breath, as she raised the gloved hand and guided it to her throat.

Horror lent a dark frisson to passion.

"Have a care! That's dangerous," he gasped, and swore he grew harder.

Droi laughed, a low growl in her throat.

"Yes, it's dangerous," she whispered. "I want to feel your fingers around my throat. Those fingers, broken and beautiful. Do it now, Rys."

As if her will commanded them, he saw his sparkling fingers enclose the dusky throat. Eyes half-closed, she licked her lips.

"Harder."

Excitement lanced through him; he gasped, watching as his

deadly fingers tightened, and deliberately raised his ungloved hand and pinched her nipples.

Droi moaned, her eyes fully closed, swaying above him for a timeless interval, and he about to spend, only watching her, until she raised one hand to his gloved wrist and he opened his fingers. Keeping her grip, she used his hand as if it were a paint-brush across her breasts and belly, and it seemed that he felt more through the mesh palm than through his own skin.

"You are the most powerful man who has ever touched me," she crooned. "You might break me with a finger, and yet you tremble, little brother."

Tremble? Yes, he trembled. More—he was panting with desire, and she in like state, both as near conflagration as consummation, and yet still she held them apart.

"There must be another, to fill the gap Dmitri will leave in the *kompani*," she whispered, her eyes holding his. "This child that we make, soon, sweet brother, I promise..." She raised a hand and traced his lips. "This child will preserve the numbers, and keep us safe...for a time. Now..."

Her nails scored his cheek; and this kiss was the cruelest yet, robbing him of both breath and sense. All he knew was need, and the hard drive of desire, upward. She met him, twelve times crueler than her kiss, taking him, and draining him, wringing him until he cried aloud, weeping in mingled exultation and anguish—and at last was done, spent, exhausted, her weight crushing him flat.

CHAPTER TWENTY-EIGHT

THEY WERE NEARING THE STREET ON WHICH THE SCHOOL STOOD—
she and Udari, and Malda, pushed along by the brisk wind. Kezzi
fished her watch out from beneath her coat, and considered it,
frowning.

"How can I know if I'm late or early?" she asked. "Mike Golden
said he had put in his best guess of how long it might take me
to walk from home, but he doesn't know where home is . . ."

"And so guessed generously," Udari interrupted.

She turned her head to glare at him, but he was smiling, so
she smiled, too.

"He said, if I was too early, someone would let me in and give
me 'toot and a donut."

"And your brother, too?"

"If they give you food, they'll make you stay for school."

"I might be interested in school," Udari said thoughtfully. "But
today, I am promised to my brothers."

"Maybe tomorrow, then," Kezzi said, teasing him.

"Maybe so," he answered, calmly, as they turned the corner
into Rendan Road. Barely six paces ahead was a boy in a blue
jacket, his bright hair gleaming in the grumpy sunlight. With
him was a man wearing a gun openly on his belt and a resigned
look on his thin, stubbled face.

"There, what did I say!" the boy cried and ran forward.

"Your new brother is devoted to you," Udari remarked, "as all
of your brothers are."

Kezzi ignored him, all of her indignation for Syl Vor.

"What are you doing here? Didn't you think I'd come to school?"

"No, I was afraid you would be too early and have no one to wait with you," he answered. "Good morning, Nathan and Rascal."

"Good morning, brother of my sister," Udari said courteously. He met Gavit's eye, and nodded agreeably.

Gavit returned the nod, with a lift of his shoulder.

"Least it ain't snowing," he observed.

"I agree. It's a fine morning for a walk."

"*Am* I early?" Kezzi demanded, still curious on this point.

"Yes," Syl Vor said, falling in beside her. "Though not as early as I had feared. And I only let Gavit have a cheese roll for breakfast, while we walked!"

"It was nice o' you to make it for me," Gavit commented, dropping back to walk with Udari. "And you can't beat Beck's rolls, not with a stick." He delivered himself of a sharp glance.

"You got the timing down, so's we don't hafta go through this tomorra morning?"

"I do. Your care of my sister and her brother is appreciated."

"Ain't been a problem so far."

Udari nodded, and raised his voice somewhat.

"It's fortunate that we met, Syl Vor yos'Galan. Our sister tells me that you're a dragon. Is that so?"

Kezzi caught her breath and shot a quick glance at Syl Vor's face. If Udari had just said on the street something which was for the *kompani* only...

And indeed it must seem that it was so. Syl Vor blinked, and threw *her* a look, then turned to face Udari, which meant all four of them had to stop, right there in the middle of the walk.

"It's true that I am a dragon," he said, sounding even more solemn than usual. "I had heard that there was someone who was afraid of dragons. Do you know that person?"

"I might," Udari said, sounding almost like Droi when she was trying to draw out a fortune for more coin. "Say that I do know such a one. What advice would you give?"

"I'm a very *small* dragon," Syl Vor said. "Advice is difficult, without knowing the circumstances, or the person. If this person has done something to harm dragons in general..."

"Then they might have a reason to fear," Udari finished.

Syl Vor wrinkled his nose, his head tilted a little to one side.

"Maybe—or not. Without knowing the circumstances, I would advise that the best thing, for a person who fears dragons—the *very* best thing to do is to speak with my Uncle Val Con, who decides for all dragons. It may be that Balance will need to be made, and that Balance might be—*hard* to make. But . . . my grandfather says that it is better to live in honor than in fear."

"This sounds like something our grandmother would agree with. Am I correct, little sister?"

"Yes," Kezzi said, and pointed. "There is the school, Brother."

"I see it," Udari answered. "What a handsome knocker! Do you go and raise it, Sister, and see if there is any to let you in."

"Bit over half hour early," Gavit commented. "Still, there oughta be somebody on the door."

"Let us find out," said Syl Vor. He grinned as he walked past. "Come on, Kezzi! Don't you want a donut?"

As it happened, her stomach having gone through more than one upset during the last few minutes, Kezzi wasn't sure that she *did* want a donut. She bent down to rub Malda's ears, then ran for the stairs, mounting them two at a time, so that she was standing at Syl Vor's shoulder when Sheyn opened the door, and stood blinking down at them.

"And who are *you* for?" he asked, sounding stern.

"For school," Kezzi said

"If you please, Sheyn," Syl Vor added. "We know we are early, but we had to be certain Anna's watch worked."

"Works a little too good, you ask me," Sheyn said, and looked over their heads, to Udari and Gavit, down on the walk.

"Either one of you here as patrons of the house?"

"'Fraid not," said Gavit and, from Udari, "Not so long as we may leave our young students in your care."

"Oh, sure, they can come in," Sheyn said, stepping back to allow it. "Ain't even the earliest, today."

He closed the door and turned to look at them.

"You two had breakfast?"

Kezzi's breakfast had been more than she usually ate—a flapjack left over from last night's dinner had joined her apple and tea.

"Yes," she told him, and Syl Vor said the same.

"You need anything else to fill in the corners?"

"No," Kezzi said firmly, having listened to her stomach.

"No, thank you," said Syl Vor. "May we go into the classroom?"

"You'd *better* go into the classroom," Sheyn told him. "Can't have you wanderin' all over the house and scarin' the guests, can we?"

"Would we scare the guests?" Syl Vor asked with interest.

"Well, you scare *me*," Sheyn told him. "Now get outta here, and don't break noth— anything, all right? Just...read or something until the rest get in."

"All right," Syl Vor agreed sunnily, and led the way down the hall.

The lights were on, though the room was empty. It was also cold, Kezzi thought, as if the hearth hadn't been properly banked overnight. Beside her, Syl Vor shivered.

"There's a breeze," he said. "I wonder if someone left the back door open."

He crossed the room with purposeful strides, and Kezzi, interested in the existence of this back door, followed him out of the room and down a short hallway.

At the end of the hallway a door *was* open, showing tarmac and shadows beyond.

"*Ain't got it,*" a boy's voice said, sounding breathless. "I'll bring it soon as I can—"

"You was supposed to bring it today," another voice interrupted.

"I told you! I ain't—"

There was a sound, like Droi's palm striking Vylet's cheek, a grunt—and Syl Vor was through the door.

Kezzi stared at the place he had been and did not follow. This was some quarrel between *gadje* and nothing to do with her. If Syl Vor wanted to involve himself, then he could! *He* was *gadje*, but such an argument had nothing to do with *her*, a Bedel.

"Peter—stop," Syl Vor's voice was perfectly calm, and it was—it was *Pete* he was challenging? Pete, who was three times his mass and twice his height? Had he lost his mind?

Somebody laughed—not Pete, because it was Pete who said, "You gonna make me, *Syl Vor*?"

"If I must, but there should be no need. Rudy, come inside with me."

Worse and worse! Rudy was no friend of Syl Vor's; he was—

"No bidness of yours, Boss's brat. Go back inside yourself!"

"Oh, hey, no!" That was the other one—the new one, Luce. "I got a better idea! Let's close the door so me 'n' Pete can have some fun. What say, Pete?"

"I say I want the cash I was promised."

"We needed it for the rent," Rudy said. "I *told* you. I'll pay you, Pete; it's just gonna take a while."

"Already taken too long. I'm tired of waitin'—"

Sounds, as if of boots against gravel, a yell, a muffled thud, a shout—"You stupid kid!"—and Kezzi was through the door, something other than good sense propelling her into the alley and under Luce's arm, taking in the scene before her.

Pete stood shaking his hand, a look on his face that reminded Kezzi of Rafin when he'd drunk too much beer, and needed to knock somebody down. In front of him, his back to Kezzi, was Rudy, his jacket torn. Between him and Pete stood Syl Vor in his blue jacket, yellow *gadje* hair blazing like an Affirmation Fire in the dimness. His legs were slightly apart, his balance distributed in a way that she recognized from her own knife-fighting lessons.

Except that Syl Vor had no knife.

"Get outta here, Syl Vor," Rudy said, his voice shaking and rough. "Ain't your fight."

"No." Syl Vor said. "Peter, stop this and go away."

Luce laughed again.

"Talks tough, don't he?"

"Let's see how good he talks with his teeth knocked out."

Pete swept forward, a fist jumping toward Syl Vor—

Toward the place where Syl Vor *had been*.

He'd ducked, Kezzi thought, and watched as he spun and kicked Pete's knee.

It didn't look like he kicked it hard, but Pete yelled and went down. Syl Vor kept spinning, grabbed Rudy by the arm, and shoved him toward the door.

"Run! Go inside, now!"

Rudy let himself be pushed, but there was Luce between him and the door, his fist coming 'round hard.

Rudy dodged, but not quick enough. Luce grabbed his jacket in both hands, picked him up and slammed him back against the wall. Kezzi heard his head hit, and when Luce let him go, Rudy just slid down the wall to the alley floor. Luce raised a foot, and Syl Vor was between him and the fallen boy, catching the rising boot by the heel and twisting.

Luce yelled and fell, and Syl Vor stood firm where he was.

"Help Rudy!" he shouted, and he couldn't, Kezzi thought with a sinking heart, have meant anyone but her. She darted forward, fingers seeking the pulse in Rudy's throat. He was alive, but he was unconscious. He might've hit his head hard enough to crack the skull, and she was only a *luthia*'s apprentice...

Luce had come up fast, and Pete was on his feet, too. The door was a distant country. There was no way she could get Rudy through it, even if she could carry him. The other two had Syl Vor...not quite boxed, but—

Luce's hand shot out, like he was trying to grab Syl Vor's coat. But Syl Vor was too quick. He spun away—and there was Pete, who snatched his arm.

"You little—"

Kezzi didn't see what happened. That is—she was looking at them—at Pete and Luce and Syl Vor, but she didn't see Syl Vor move.

She heard the bone break, though.

And she heard Pete scream.

The big boy went down, Syl Vor under him, the soft sound of the fall not masking the fighters' harsh breathing.

Luce was up in a yell and a twist, moving toward the combatants, and Syl Vor—Syl Vor had squirmed free, coming to his feet—

"Look out!" yelled Kezzi, and her knife was in her hand. She snapped forward, staying low, just like Udari had taught her, and slashed Luce's leg, right behind his knee

Luce screamed, swung at her, missed—and fell, grabbing his leg and cussing.

Kezzi straightened, and stared at Syl Vor. He had blood on his face and his left arm was hanging limply. The rest of his posture said *fight*, and he stood, eyes sweeping the small battlefield as if daring anyone to try him, the grimace under the blood more determination than pain.

"Are you—" she began, when the alley was filled with a sudden bright light, and there in the door was Ms. Taylor, and Sheyn, and a burly woman in a Patrol vest.

CHAPTER TWENTY-NINE

RYS WOKE ALONE, WITH MORE RELIEF THAN DISAPPOINTMENT.

The forge was empty, the fires banked, and Rafin not at all in evidence, by which Rys took it to be very early. As he had no inclination for more sleep, he crossed to the shower, emerging in short order, curls still damp, and wearing a pair of canvas pants that were only a little too large, a high-necked blue sweater of similar sizing, and a new pair of socks, still bound in paper. Rys smiled as he drew on his boots. Someone—he suspected Udari—had been into town on his behalf. He must find what was permitted to him as a Balance—and his smile faded.

Indeed, what Balance could he make—to Udari, to Silain-*luthia*, Kezzi, Pulka, Rafin—any or all of the Bedel? Together and separately, in greater part and lesser, they had given him his life and were working to return to him as much function as might be possible. The gift of the glove alone... And today—*today*—Rafin said that the brace would be ready. He would be able to throw down his stick, and walk...

His stomach chose this moment to remind him, audibly, that he had been several hours without food. Grabbing his crutch, he levered himself upright, and was very soon on the move to Jin's hearth.

It was there that Udari found him some while later, sitting a little removed and drinking tea from a mug held carefully in his gloved hand.

"Brother, well met!"

Udari dropped cross-legged to the uncovered floor, facing him. His hair was tousled, and he wrapped both hands around his mug like a man who had been chilled.

"Out so early?" Rys asked. "Have you eaten?"

"Oh, I ate while you still slept, before walking with the youngest of our sisters to school."

Rys frowned. "I am behind in the news. I had thought Kezzi determined never again to return to school."

"*She* was. But the *luthia* was of another mind, there being a question of brotherhood involved. The short tale is that our sister has found herself a new brother, and is bound by those ties to attend the *gadje* school."

"This sounds complex. One wonders how the school fares."

Udari grinned, and sipped his tea.

"As of this morning, the building stands. But it is of our sister's brother that I wished to speak, for I've learned a thing that might interest you."

Rys caught his breath. Did this new brother of Kezzi's—was it possible that the child had found someone who *knew* him?

Scarcely had he thought the thought than a bolt of pain sizzled through his head.

Do you have enemies in the City Above?

"I learned yesterday from our sister that her new brother is a dragon. This morning, he told me so in his own voice." He sipped his tea and sighed before bringing his gaze up to meet Rys'. "I believe him, though he is, as he says himself, a very small dragon."

Rys took a careful breath. No new bolt assaulted his head, though his stomach was abruptly uneasy.

"Has he a name," he asked, pressing his ungloved hand flat against the floor; "this very small dragon?"

"Syl Vor yos'Galan," Udari said, soft as if he whispered love words. "Clan Korval."

Pain shuddered through his head, lanced down his spine. "Ah!"

Strong fingers gripped his shoulder. He closed his eyes, panting, forcing himself in the quiet aftermath of the pain—*pushing* himself—to remember.

Clan Korval.

Of course, *Korval*. Tree-and-Dragon. How could he have forgotten something so...

But what reason had *he* to be frightened of Korval? His clan had been off-world, and nothing like High House. There could be no reason, ever, for him to—have met, to have, to have . . .

He swayed; felt the grip tighten on his shoulder.

"Why?" he breathed, scarcely knowing that he spoke aloud.

Why was he afraid of dragons? Had he done something—something *dishonorable?* Was he here on this world because he had taken employ with Korval, incurred their anger—

Pain cracked like lightning inside his head. He gasped, gathered all of his fortitude, and *pushed.*

Jasin. Where was Jasin in this? He would not believe that she had betrayed him—abandoned him. She might, yes, have put him off-ship, if necessary. But she would not have left him without resources, without protection.

The inside of his skull was on fire; he was panting, he was weeping, and he *would know this!* He would—

Jasin. Dragons. How had he come here, to the Bedel's very door? Who had beaten him? Why? What man had he become in the time he could not remember? A man afraid of Korval—there must be a reason!

There was a crack, as if his very skull had split. His vision whited, agony cramped his muscles—and he fainted where he sat.

· · · ❊ · · ·

"Hey, Mike." Tommy Tilden looked up from his screen, and spun his chair around to face front. "Long time."

"Boss keeps me runnin'. If I'd known she was gonna be this much work, I'd've stayed with slackin'."

The chief of Blair Road Patrol laughed.

"You was a real slacker, okay, back in the day. I 'member your gran couldn't figure out what to do with you."

"I was too smart for her," Mike admitted, settling comfortably into the chair across the desk.

"I'm tryin' to imagine this," Tommy said earnestly.

"Lemme know how that works out. Listen, you got a couple cool-heads on Patrol I can borrow tomorra, just midmorning, for maybe hour, hour-and-a-half?"

"This official bidness for Boss Nova?"

"Is. Got a quiet meet set up at Joan's Bakery. Don't expect trouble. I'll be there, o'course, but I don't want us to seem mistrustful. A couple Patrollers outta vest, sittin' by, having a cup an' a donut, not payin' much attention to much—that'd go a long way toward easin' my mind."

Tommy nodded. "Can do. How many's the other side bringing?"

"Dunno. Wouldn't think more'n two—prolly just one, like Boss, to do any heavy liftin' comes by. Like I say, a quiet meet, on neutral ground, no anticipated trouble."

"But it's always good to have somethin' extra in your back pocket, just in case," Tommy said, in complete understanding. He pulled a pad of paper toward him and made a note.

"No problem. I'll have 'em in place a little ahead of your time. Prolly you won't even see 'em."

· · · ⁑ · · ·

Jasin. Jasin, I will...

"Rys. Wake to me, Brother. There is none here to harm you."

He stilled.

"Udari?"

"Open your eyes, Brother, and let me see you."

The words woke a shiver, and a vivid memory of sharp teeth on his ear. He took a hard breath—and opened his eyes, unsurprised to find himself at full stretch, his head on Udari's knee, his brother's kind face bent above him.

"How do you feel?"

Cautiously, he took stock. The inside of his head felt sticky and disorganized, which he knew for the aftermath of the headache. Aside from that...

"Exhausted."

Udari looked grave, and brushed Rys' damp forehead with cool fingers.

"This Jasin," he said. "A sister?"

Wisely, Rys did not shake his head. "A...lover," he said. "First Mate Jasin Bell."

"And her ship?"

"*Momma Liberty.*"

"Where is she now, this first mate and her ship?"

"I don't know."

Udari looked grave, and held up a hand. "How many fingers do you see?"

"One."

"And now?"

"Four."

"And again."

"Two."

"Well, I'm no *luthia*, but I think we haven't done you irreparable harm. Sit up, Brother. I will bring you a new mug of tea."

"I had a mug," Rys said, sitting up with his brother's aid. He looked about—and blinked in horror at the mangled thing that Udari held silently out to him.

"I will find another mug for Jin," he said, levelly.

"Later. Today, we have other business."

Udari rose, and Rys ran his hands through his hair, trying to order his slow, sticky thoughts.

"Here." The mug was pressed into his ungloved hand. He took it gratefully and raised it to his lips.

"Now," said Udari. "This Syl Vor—is he the dragon you fear?"

Rys took a hard breath. "I don't know."

"Is it his mother you fear? Nova, the *luthia* names her."

"I don't know," Rys repeated, wincing as tiny sparks of anguish assaulted his abused head.

"What would be your reason?" Udari pursued, as if Rys had not spoken. "Did you steal from her? Has she made some demand that risked your honor? Your life?"

"I don't *know*," Rys said again, muscles tensing. He made to set the mug down.

"Drink, drink," Udari said, and raised his own mug.

Rys hesitated, but it seemed that Udari truly did mean that he should drink. Again, he raised his mug, and sipped, relaxing as the tea filled his mouth.

"Your lover," Udari murmured. "Why is she not here?"

He closed his eyes. "I don't know."

"Were you cruel to her? Did she tire of you? Did you put her in danger, too, when you despoiled the dragon?"

"*I don't know!*" The shout rocked his head; lightning played inside his eyes; he forgot to breathe, then gasped greedily for air.

"Udari—" He stretched his gloveless hand out, felt it gripped, firm and steady. "Forgive me."

"What have you done?"

"I shouted. You deserve better of me."

"If it comes to that, you deserve better of me." Udari sighed.

"I forget my training. One repair at a time, eh? Yesterday, the hand. Today, the leg. Tomorrow, the soul."

Rys sighed. "Perhaps it's wiser, to let the hidden past hide."

Udari tipped his head, as if considering this.

"No, Brother, I don't think that. How can you go forward, shriveled by fear, divided in soul? A man should know the tale of his deeds; the names of his friends, and his enemies. This... this not knowing is the last of your injuries. I swore, as your brother, to see you made whole again. And that I shall do."

Rys sighed, and drank off what was left of his tea.

· · · ✺ · · ·

"Is Syl Vor badly hurt?" Pat Rin demanded.

"A dislocated shoulder, already put to rights, save some residual tenderness. He would have it that he could return to school today, but as it happens Ms. Taylor gave an early dismissal to the whole class, not just those who were exhausted from early brawling in the alley. I left him and Kezzi studying ship silhouettes." Nova sighed and sipped her tea.

"I come to you because the three principals in the brawl—Peter Day, Luce Jacobs, and Rudy Daniel—all agree under separate questioning that the cause of the altercation was Rudy's failure to pay his insurance in a timely manner."

Pat Rin put his cup down with a sharp click.

"Insurance," he repeated, expressionlessly.

"Yes, I thought you'd be delighted. Also," she sighed, "also, it would seem that there is someone upline from Peter and Luce, to whom they pay insurance. Both are more afraid of that person than they are of me."

Pat Rin nodded absently. "Both look to Boss Wentworth, I think you said?"

"Yes."

"I will be certain to have a personal talk with the Boss after the council meeting this evening. If someone is trying to set up a personal insurance system, that must concern him," Pat Rin said.

"And if Boss Wentworth is seeking to reestablish an insurance system?" asked Nova.

Pat Rin smiled. "Then that, of course, concerns me."

"Very well, then; I leave the matter in your hands."

"You honor me."

She laughed slightly. "I fear I am about to shower even more honor upon you. When I was at the schoolhouse today, I spoke to Ms. Audrey, who tells me that the new furniture has arrived."

Pat Rin considered her earnestly. "One must of course be gratified to hear it, but I wonder what the new furniture has to do with me."

"Precisely what I asked! Audrey tells me that business is good. So good that there has been a remodeling project some weeks in planning, and an expansion of the secondary house at the port."

"That," Pat Rin murmured, "I had known of. I apprehend that the furniture is to adorn the primary house."

"It is. Luken is in some way involved in the whole scheme; I hesitated to inquire too closely there, but the short tale is that Ms. Audrey needs the space now occupied by the school as a staging area—and of course, a place to store the new furniture."

"Of course. And Ms. Audrey's suggestions regarding the school?" Pat Rin asked.

"That the students be moved to the Consolidated School, which had, after all, been the plan all along. She confesses that she hadn't thought her establishment would be required to play host for quite so long, and while she grudges us not a day, she can give us only six more."

"Well, there's something," he replied. "I had feared she wished to close the doors tomorrow. Mr. McFarland has informed me of Mr. Golden's opinion, that the sabotage at the site is at an end. I have just yesterday received a report from the Building Committee which suggests that the building is ready for use. I had hoped for an orderly—but Audrey gives us six days, and the Council of Bosses meets tonight. We will merely need to dance more quickly than we had anticipated. If we move the core schools into the new building on the same day and hour, they will within a two-day have opportunity to bond as a team, and so be ready to assist those who arrive during open enrollment." He frowned, perhaps at his desktop, or his teacup, or at nothing at all. "Yes. I think we may contrive. May I assist you in any other way, Cousin?"

"Well...no," she replied. "Though I may have something else tomorrow."

"After meeting with the grandmother of Syl Vor's sister, I apprehend?"

"My plan is to ascertain their location and their intentions."

"Do that," Pat Rin said cordially. "I will be most interested to be informed of both."

CHAPTER THIRTY

IT WAS A THING OF BEAUTY AND ELEGANCE. INK BLUE WITH A subtle silver stripe, it snapped close 'round his shattered leg, an exoskeleton that transformed ruin into beauty.

"It is...a jewel," Rys murmured. "Rafin, this is art!"

"It is less art than a man's natural leg, but it will do what you ask of it, as your own strove to do. Well, Brother?"

That last was to Pulka, who was on his knees, running his fingers down the woven metal, testing the fastenings and fingering the thin tubes.

"Yes," he murmured. "Dreaming did not lead me astray. The hydraulics?"

"Bench tested well. The fighting cock will now test in place, and we will make what adjustments are necessary. If you are satisfied with the construction, Brother?"

"Past satisfied. It is as Rys says—this is no ordinary fabrication, Brother; your skill surpasses my dream."

"Half of the fabrication is the material," Udari said. "The discovery of that lies with Rys."

"True!" Rafin nodded. "I had hoped for a coil of aersteel or a skein of carbolite. To find a knot of refined bintamium—I tell you nothing but the truth, Brothers, when I say that *I* dared not to dream so large. Here now," he said to Rys, going to one knee and stretching out his arms like a fond father to a toddler, "come to Rafin, little one."

Rys closed his eyes, the better to find his balance. The brace was so light that he scarce felt its weight. He pressed his enclosed heel down, felt gyros engage, and heard a small sound, as emitted from time to time by his glove. Microengines, he thought, smaller than his thumbnail.

"Well, do you intend only to stand and display your beauty to passersby?" demanded Rafin.

Rys smiled. "I was seeking my balance."

"Seek it in flight, my cock! Come to me now so that we might see the function of your jewelry, eh?"

Rys nodded and stepped forward.

Two steps he made before the unexpected spring in his bejeweled leg betrayed him into a stumble, a twist, and a graceless collapse into Rafin's ready arms.

"Too much energy, eh? Here, let us find the weight of you upon the world. Udari, your arm! Steady the small one while he walks the length of the pressure ribbon. Wait!" Rafin had hurried to his bench; there was a storm of short snaps as he brought various functions to life, then a shout.

"Now! Walk now, Rys!"

Walk he did, the spring not so much of a surprise this time, but still, he needed Udari's arm.

"Too much push back," Rafin said. "Also, our fledgling is lighter on his feet than I had judged. Sit him on the bench; I will adjust."

· · · ✳ · · ·

"Why do you learn these?" Kezzi asked, flipping back through the silhouette pack.

"So that when I am a pilot, I will be able to identify the ships around me."

"Doesn't the ship have a program for that?"

"Yes, but sometimes programs go awry," Syl Vor answered, shifting restlessly in his chair. "It's why we learn to do the math and form the equations for navigation, even though there is a navcomp on the ship. At least, *I* haven't gotten to piloting equations yet—but I will!"

"Because you are going to be a pilot."

"Yes."

Kezzi looked up. "You should rest," she said. "Your arm hurts you."

He glared at her, but she knew him well enough already to see that it wasn't his best effort.

"Who said that my arm hurts?"

"Your eyes say it, and the way you press your mouth together," Kezzi told him. "You might as well rest today, you know. Tomorrow, we'll be at school again, and you won't want Pete or Luce to see you tired."

"Well..."

"Just lay on the bed next to Eztina," Kezzi said. "I'll sit and talk to you, if you want."

"How did you know my shoulder was dislocated?" Syl Vor asked, stretching sideways across the bed so he didn't disturb the cat.

"Because I'm apprentice to the *luthia*."

"The *luthia* is the medic?"

Kezzi sniffed. "The *luthia* is *much* more than a medic," she said haughtily. "Anyway, because I am her apprentice, I have dreamed many injuries and how to treat them."

She sat cross-legged on the bed by his knee.

"Syl Vor?"

"Yes."

"I was just thinking—if you had the silhouette of a *particular* ship, that—that had become lost, could you find it?"

He frowned.

"Find it? I suppose—but not from the silhouette. The silhouettes are ID tools—I told you."

He paused, frowning up at the ceiling.

"If the ship were *lost* then you would need to know where it had been and where it was going and whether it had been seen in-between, and—oh, many things! Also," he added, stifling a yawn, "you would need a grown-up pilot."

"But it could be done."

"Well...yes."

"Do you know any *grown-up* pilots?"

He laughed.

"Is that funny?" Kezzi asked, bristling.

"No—yes. Our whole family is pilots. Except Grandaunt."

"I didn't know that."

"Now you do," he said, sounding cranky.

Kezzi sighed and turned the subject, thinking that the pain in his arm and her ignorance were together putting him out of patience.

"Why did you protect Rudy?" she asked. "He doesn't like you."

"No, nor I don't like him," Syl Vor said drowsily. "But it was wrong, two on one." His eyes were more than half closed now.

"Why did you—help Rudy?" he asked.

Kezzi sniffed. "I didn't help Rudy," she said, watching his eyes drift fully shut. "I helped *you*. You're my brother."

Syl Vor smiled, and turned his head to snuggle his cheek against the pillow.

· · · ☼ · · ·

"*Luthia*, will you witness?"

Silain turned from her inventory of the death chest, and considered the shadow at the entrance to her hearth-room.

"On whose account?" she asked quietly, which was the ritual answer. Droi knew the rituals—all of the rituals, for she had a receptive and tenacious mind—and she had asked in full form.

"On my account," she said now, and Silain felt her spirit waver. To witness on Droi's account might mean anything from a murder to a badly seasoned dish.

"We have a death upon us," she said, giving warning that, if the witnessing would be long, it would need to wait.

Droi bowed her head.

"Well I know it," she said, abandoning the ritual, as Silain had hoped she would. "I would dance Dmitri through the door with a light heart, Grandmother. I merely wish to know if I carry the balancing number."

Silain put the memory stick carefully back in the chest. So, the child had taken matters into her own hand—not surprising, really, and perhaps even a good and wise thing, for Droi's Sight, while often terrifying, was rarely wrong.

"Did you have Rafin?"

Droi shook her head. "I didn't think of Rafin, and when he proposed himself, I didn't want him."

This was encouraging; the child of two such fierce souls might have been more than the Bedel in their present state could support. However . . .

"Did you go Outside?"

"No," she said sharply, and then laughed with genuine humor. "Or yes. Rys gave the seed."

Rys, who looked to be Bedel, for all his slightness, who claimed true kinship with several of the *kompani*, and who found acceptance with others. Rys himself might well have been the balancing number, except—

"He has only half a soul," Silain pointed out.

Droi laughed again, not so humorous this time.

"It wasn't his soul I wanted."

Of course not.

"The seed was willingly given?"

"It was." A close and pleased cat-smile appeared. "And with vigor."

"You told him that the child was for the *kompani*?"

"*Luthia*, I did so."

"Then come forward and let us see if you've caught a Bedel soul, Daughter. Did you use the draught?"

"Yes. I dreamed it first; I wanted no error."

Droi would not let such a detail escape her—and dreaming the formula first, so that there would be no error? Of course. That was her way: careful and thorough. Had her Sight not been so dark and so heavy, Droi would have been the *luthia*'s second apprentice.

"Come here, Daughter, and quickly. Dmitri fades into that other world even as we speak. His children pray with him now, but I must return."

"Yes," Droi said and stepped forward.

Silain unshipped the healing unit, and tapped in a code while Droi slipped her hand into the sampling glove.

Silain counted to ten, the machine beeped, and the codes marched down the readout.

Droi, who had learned to read the codes before the *luthia* had found it necessary to end her 'prenticeship, sighed.

"A catch for the Bedel," she said.

Silain sighed as well.

"A catch," she acknowledged, considering the numbers, "but not a strong one. I recommend a dram of the holding tonic."

"Yes," said Droi, her eyes very nearly wholly green.

"Jin will mix it; I must go to Dmitri. Drink it fresh, with no other food or drink, then rest on your bed. You will likely sleep; that is well. When you wake, you may rise, and dance Dmitri across the threshold."

· · · ⁕ · · ·

Adjustments were made, and again; the push-back ratio adjusted.

Rys found his balance and, for the first time in . . . a very long time, walked without support; first, at the center of a smiling triangle of his brothers, and then again, in lonely state, about the forge, his steps quiet and properly timed.

Rafin showed him how he might call for more energy from the brace, by pumping his foot up and down and engaging the hydraulics to do more.

"But use it with care! You will spin in circles if you give one side more power than the other."

Rys laughed, and suddenly dodged 'round Pulka, executing a quick and intricate piece of footwork before leaping into the air and bolting for the ramp.

"Catch me!" he cried, as if the new leg had not only made him whole, but dropped him into boyhood.

Pulka, of course, did not run, but Udari did, and Rafin, pelting after him out of the forge and up the ramp, their laughter bouncing around them from ceiling and walls. At the top of the ramp, Rafin spun, as if to grab him. Rys twisted, danced around, behind—and fled back toward the forge, the others scrambling in his wake.

He threw himself into the rocker under Pulka's astonished eye, grinning as first Udari and then Rafin dropped to the floor nearby, fair quivering with high spirits.

"One thing," Rafin said, shaking his head as if he would dash water from his hair. "One thing, little one. That brace will not tire as a human leg will tire. Listen to your flesh and blood and do not allow the machine to push you beyond what you can bear."

Rys, leaning back in the rocker, nodded.

"It is like the glove," he said, "both a great gift and a great peril."

"As life itself," said Udari and rose of a sudden, his lips still bent in a residual smile. "Brothers, I am sent forth by the *luthia*'s word to fetch the youngest of our sisters from the City Above."

Rys rose from the rocker immediately, and stretched out his ungloved hand.

"I will walk with you to the gate," he said, "Brother."

· · · ⁕ · · · ·

She would have had him rest, but Syl Vor insisted that he walk with Kezzi and Gavit to meet her brother and Malda.

"Tomorrow morning, let's meet as we did this morning," he said, as they walked, "and go into school together."

She thought about that. It would be best not to meet Pete or Luce—or worse, Pete *and* Luce—alone. In fact, if she never saw either of them again, she would be well pleased with the bargain.

"Pitched them two out onnere ears, ain't they?" Gavit asked from behind them. "Fightin' in school?"

"Mother said that Ms. Taylor wished to give Luce and Peter a second chance," Syl Vor said. "She said that she thought they'd learned their lesson."

Gavit snorted. "Your ma, she agreed to that, did she?"

"Yes," said Kezzi. "She said that the teacher knew her classroom best, and that we—Syl Vor and me—could take care of ourselves, and..."

"...and if they fail to use their second chance to advantage, they will have to face the Patrol," Syl Vor finished.

"Oughta had to face the Patrol years ago, the both of 'em," Gavit said. "Might be I'll have a talk with your ma, Silver. Meanwhile, here's your brother, Anna. Make sure you tell him what happened today, hear me?"

"I will. Syl Vor, rest your arm."

"It's all right now," he said. "Good evening, Nathan and Rascal."

"Good evening, small dragon and Streetman Gavit."

"Hey," Gavit said.

"Remember, Anna," Syl Vor said, "I'll meet you tomorrow where we met today."

"Yes," she said impatiently. "I'll remember. Go home and rest your arm!"

"What was it you were to tell your brother?" Udari asked as they walked among the *gadje*.

"When we went into school this morning, there were two boys beating a third, and Syl Vor put himself in front of the third. He broke one boy's arm."

"Well done," said Udari mildly. "And the other?"

Kezzi sighed. "I cut him behind the knee. And I am to tell you, Brother, that I am not to bring this knife that I have to school anymore."

"The teacher says this?"

"Yes."

"Then we will this evening provide you with another knife. What else about the fight? You, I see, were not hurt. Was Syl Vor?"

"His arm was dislocated, but..." she paused.

"But?"

"But he stood there, with his arm dislocated, and his, his *soul*—I could see it, bright as an Affirmation, that he would fight more, if he had to, and they wouldn't—he was determined that they would not prevail." She took a hard breath. "It was why I cut Luce behind the knee, so Syl Vor wouldn't have to fight anymore."

"Well," Udari said, and walked a hand of steps in silence, "do you know what I think, young sister?"

"That I should have gone for Luce's eye?"

"No, that would have been too much. What I think is that you are as fortunate in your brother as I am in mine."

CHAPTER THIRTY-ONE

THE BEDEL CAME NOISILY TOGETHER AT THE CENTER OF THE COMmon space, and sat in the exuberance of light produced by more than a dozen hearthstones.

Rys sat between Jin and Memit, with Udari on Jin's left, all of them in brilliant finery, seeming like so many bright birds flocking. He himself had no cause to be ashamed in this splendid company, as he wore a scarlet shirt and a deeply embroidered indigo vest that had come from out of the depths of Udari's chest. Rys thought they must have belonged to his brother when he was a boy. That same brother was this evening handsomely turned out in a yellow shirt and a plum-colored vest lavishly embroidered with red flowers.

A shadow moved between the hearth and those gathered—Silain, dressed all in white, crimson tassels on her shawl, and a broad band of yellow embroidery around the hems of her long tunic and skirt.

She held a baton as long as his forearm high over her head, and paced 'round the hearth until everyone there had seen it. The chattering laughter stilled, replaced by expectant silence.

Slowly, Silain lowered her arms.

A smaller shadow detached itself from the inner edge of the circle—Kezzi, Rys saw, wearing a red blouse over a long dark skirt as thick with embroidery as his vest, and a gay yellow sash 'round her waist.

She took the baton from Silain-*luthia*'s hand, holding it reverently between both of hers. It seemed, at first, an odd office for a child— and then not so odd at all. After all, Kezzi was the *luthia*'s apprentice.

259

The *luthia*'s apprentice, then, brought the baton to Alosha the headman. Like the *luthia*, the headman was all in white, and he sat cross-legged and calm just a hand's span inside the circle.

He received the baton and began to speak.

"The *kompani* gathers to celebrate Dmitri, who has stepped from this world into that kinder place, the World Beyond. When the memory stick comes to your hand, speak as your heart prompts you, sisters and brothers. Let us remember Dmitri, our brother. Let us remember him well, and with laughter!"

He passed the baton to the woman sitting just behind and on his right.

Dmitri had been well-loved by the Bedel, if even half the stories told of him were true, and laughter frequently attended the baton as it made its way 'round the circle.

When it came to his hand, Rys made to pass it on, thinking it could only be an insult, that one who was not of the *kompani* and who had no story to tell, should speak.

Memit, however, thrust it back on him, so it seemed that he must either speak or enter into a brawl. He took a breath, fingering the baton, feeling slides and nubs beneath his fingers—*controls*, as if it were a recording device, in truth. His thoughts grew, not cold, but cool, and he bowed his head.

"I meet Dmitri as he leaves us, a shadow in the doorway between worlds," he said slowly. "A man of heart, and of skill, whose eagerness to attain that kinder place speaks of a soul unburdened by care. Yet, even as he goes, he pauses to teach a young brother, through the memories of his brothers and his sisters, what it is, to be of the Bedel."

Despite the coolness of mind that had produced this, he swallowed with difficulty around the sudden lump in his throat and thrust the baton blindly in Memit's direction. He felt it slip through his fingers at the same time an arm came 'round his shoulders in a hug and Jin murmured in his ear, "Well said, Rys. Your heart does you credit."

The baton continued its circuit, producing yet more tales, with now and again a cry of, "Yes!" or "That was like him!" from others in circle, at last coming back to the hand of Silain-*luthia*.

Once again she raised it over her head and, smiling upon the wholeness of them, called for song and dancing—

"So that Dmitri will hear in the World Beyond and smile to

know that his sisters and his brothers share his joy and look forward to that time when they are reunited with him, in that *kompani* camped just out of sight."

Rys stood in the shadows of the common hearth, watching the Bedel dance, joyous and bright as birds. The music was unfamiliar, and to his ear chaotic, woven by the dancers into something delightful and strange.

It seemed that all the Bedel were dancing—Silain and Jin made a pair of it, while Droi danced by herself, fueled by the same cruel energy that had characterized her love-making. Further afield, Udari was paired with Vylet, the length of a man's arm separating them, her hips girdled with a rope of tiny bells that she kept a-ringing merrily.

Someone pressed a mug into his hand. He tasted the contents cautiously—beer. Having learnt his lesson regarding Bedel beer, he clung to the mug, but did not drink any more.

"Rys!" Kezzi was before him, her hair half escaped from the braid, her face lit with a joy so pure that he had to look away.

"Udari said your leg is repaired, that you can walk, and run!"

"Why so I can," he said, smiling. He turned in place, to demonstrate his new agility, and caught his breath when she snatched his gloved hand.

"But you're not dancing!"

"I don't know how."

She laughed.

"You just—*dance*," she said, tugging on his hand. "Here, I'll show you!"

There came another tug, which he understood to mean that he was to accompany her. He bent to put the mug down where it might not be kicked, offered his ungloved hand to her clasp, and allowed himself to be escorted out onto the floor.

"Listen," Kezzi commanded. "Just listen. Don't think. Let the music fill you up." She closed her eyes, perhaps to better facilitate listening. Rys did not close his, but watched her, seeing her muscles relax into the sound. Her foot tapped, her leg twitched, the hand in his flexed, and relaxed.

Kezzi began to move.

It was a distinctive dance, and, watching her, he could identify the particular thread of musical chaos that informed her: the stringed instrument, with its sharp, articulated highs and lows.

He moved with her, since it would be graceless to act the part of a stump. At first, he imperfectly aped her movements, but as his ear became more comfortable with the thread and, indeed, he became more comfortable with the reality of *being able* to dance, he began to move more freely.

Kezzi swooped and leapt, and he did. She lunged, and he did. She flung her hands in the air and spun—and he did, coming to rest nose to chest with Rafin.

"He dances! Eh? Eh?" Rafin slapped him on the shoulder with a force that made him stagger, and strode away into Droi's orbit. Captured, he began to stamp and clap his hands, spinning about her like a demented planet around its star.

Rys turned back to his own partner, finding her swaying still, but somewhat heavy of eye.

"Do you dance the night away, little sister? Or is the *luthia's* apprentice permitted to rest?"

Kezzi sighed. "The *luthia* said that I had to sleep tonight, because I have school tomorrow." She put up a hand to cover a sudden yawn, and shook her head.

"Allow me to see you safely to rest, then," he said. "Where do you go?"

"Malda waits for me at Silain's hearth," Kezzi said. "Vylet and Droi will dance late, and I wouldn't want to wake them early..."

"No, that would be too bad, for everyone concerned. To Silain's hearth it is."

He walked with her, and she tucked her hand once again into his ungloved one.

"Did Udari tell you, that I have a brother who is a dragon?"

"He did," Rys said, managing to keep his voice easy. "I am thinking what I must do about that."

"Well, I hope you won't have to do anything about it," Kezzi said, around another yawn. "I wouldn't like to have two of my brothers at outs."

"That would be awkward," he agreed. "I will do my best not to be at outs with your dragon brother, Sister."

A sharp yip sounded, and Kezzi laughed, slipping her hand away and bending down.

"Malda! Come."

The dog arrived, wriggling at her feet. She pulled his ears, and rubbed his tummy then straightened.

"We'll sleep in the hearth-room," she said.

"And I, if it will not disturb you, will sit by the hearth. I . . . must pray."

She smiled. "I'll sleep better, for your prayers," she said, which had the sound of set piece, and then, before he could divine her intent, she leaned close and kissed his cheek.

"Who guards the hearth?"

Rys raised his head, and rolled to his feet.

"Grandmother, it is I."

"So I see, on two strong legs. Is this Rafin's genius, too?"

"A team effort. Udari was the impetus, Pulka envisioned the design, and Rafin . . . brought it into the world."

He stepped forward, offering his natural hand. She placed her unburdened hand into his with a smile. Her skin was as soft as old paper, her bones as light as a bird's.

"Will I make tea" he asked, "or wish you sweet dreams?"

"Tea, if you please, grandson. I will return the memory stick to its place, and come out to you in a moment."

"Yes," he said, and went to find the kettle.

The tea was ready by the time Silain rejoined him, once again dressed in her comfortable motley of scarves and shawls.

"Grandson," she said, accepting the mug. "Sit with me, if you are not tired."

"I dozed by the hearth, while I waited," he said, sitting on the blanket by her right hand.

"It was good of you to keep watch over the child."

He smiled. "Surely, she was at no risk, here in the heart of the *kompani*, and with Malda at her side."

"Surely she was not," Silain said composedly. "But rest comes easier when a brother is by."

He sipped his tea, feeling warmed, despite that the child *had* been perfectly safe, and himself scarcely a deterrent, had danger come to call.

"You will have heard, I think," said Silain, "that your sister's brother, who lives in the house of his mother in the City Above, is a dragon."

Rys drew a careful breath. "Udari brought me this news."

"What will you do?"

"Grandmother, I do not know. I cannot recall the reason for

my fear, though I *do* recall that one who has made an enemy of the dragon would do well to fear."

"So, even if you have forgotten your argument, the dragon will very likely remember."

Rys laughed around the stutter of panic in his breast.

"Oh, yes, and that is enough cause for fear. If I *knew*, then I feel I might draw up my courage to face—to face Korval. But to put myself forward, ignorant of both my fault and its proper answer..."

"You're afraid that the dragon will eat you."

He looked into her face and old eyes, forgiving of his fear.

"Grandmother, I can think of no reason to fear a settling of accounts with Korval, *except* that death must be my Balance." He smiled, though he little felt like it.

"To lay waste to all that you and Udari have fashioned..."

Silain did not smile. She sipped her tea. He did the same.

"The mother of your sister's brother and I will speak together, soon. With your permission, I'll put your name before her and ask how you have wronged her."

Light coruscated inside his head. He held his breath, but no flare or thunder of pain followed.

"Grandmother, I ask that you do not. Not yet. I...I want to think."

Silence.

A sigh.

"Three days, grandson. At the end of three days you'll come here to me, and together we'll go to the dragon Korval."

He swallowed a protest. It was just. Indeed, she was lenient. She could have required him to accompany her to this imminent meeting, and given him to Korval. *He* was not Bedel. The *kompani* bore with him for love of Udari, and in obedience of the *luthia*'s word.

"Grandmother, it will be so," he whispered, bowing his head.

"You're a brave man, and the *kompani* has taken you to its heart. You're not alone, Rys, whatever happens."

It was foolish, but it eased him to hear her say so. He had been alone...clanless... There had been Jasin, and *Momma*—a place, and companionship, but no true belonging. To be among the *kompani*, in the heart of the Bedel, that had approached clan...

"What are you thinking?" Silain murmured.

"That having cheated death twice makes it no easier to face thrice."

"Rys." She gripped his wrist, tightly, her fingers stronger than he would have supposed. "I'll take this woman's measure. Kezzi tells me that she is a *luthia*, or like—a sister in dreaming. If this is so, she'll measure with an even hand."

He laughed.

"That is what frightens me, more than all the rest. But enough." He raised his mug. "More tea?"

"Of your kindness."

He refreshed both mugs, and settled himself again.

"There is a reason I waited for you," he said. "A matter of custom and, in light of our previous discussion, of some urgency."

"Speak."

"Last night, Droi came to me, and we . . . coupled. She said that between us we made a child. A child for the *kompani*. I ask if that is so."

"It is. The *kompani*'s numbers are fixed. Misfortune follows if the numbers go too low, or too high. With Dmitri on the threshold . . ."

"I understand," he said. "I had merely . . ." He sighed and looked up into her face. "In my . . . world. The numbers of the clan are fixed insofar as each adult must provide the clan with a child who will be one's heir, to learn one's lifework, and to succeed to one's honors. I had no child, and even if I had, she would have been in the house, and died, with everyone else."

Silain moved her hand, signaling a question.

"You spoke somewhat of this before, but I wonder—what killed your clan?"

"Yxtrang," he said, and cleared his throat. "It was an Yxtrang raid. I was up early in the vineyards; the rest of the House was asleep. They glided in over the mountain, and—"

The shadow of wings, flickering over trellis and rock; the mountain heaving; the noise, and he rolled to his feet, staring down at the smoke and the crater . . .

He swallowed and bent his head.

"Yxtrang target Liaden worlds. There is nothing new in that."

"I understand. Continue, grandson."

Continue? For a moment he was at a loss, then recalled the reason he had waited to meet Silain.

"The child, yes. I would explain the custom I know. We write contracts, before the proposed couple are joined, and between clans. This insures that there is no mistaking to whom the child belongs, and guarantees that all is properly made ready.

"As I am clanless, there is no one but me to . . . make arrangements

for this child. She will belong to the *kompani*. That is well. However, the way of the *kompani* is not the way of the clan. What is...
expected of me? I have little, and may soon have nothing, but I
would honor the child properly, and put no hardship on Droi, or
on the Bedel."

There was a silence, and a small sound, as if Silain cleared her
throat.

"The child will have brothers, and sisters, and the *kompani* to
keep him and teach him. Maybe you think that Droi would be a
chancy mother. She would be, and she knows this as well as any.
Already, she has asked that Luma bring the child to her hearth."

He thought for a moment.

"Dmitri's daughter?"

"Yes."

"Balance is preserved," he said. "I approve."

Silain nodded.

"How long," she asked softly, "since your clan died in this
Yxtrang raid?"

He turned his hands up and looked down at them—one flesh,
one gleaming mesh—before looking back to her.

"In the first relumma... in Standard Year 1387."

"And have you," she asked softly, "been alone since your clan died?"

He shook his head.

"I was hired as crew on a trade ship—a family ship. The eldest
daughter—the first mate—I became her lover. But it was not clan.
Her brother disliked me and..."

*...and, at Moleria, it was. He was called dockside, to the trader's
room, and there had been, had been...*

Green and violet light flared, igniting the inside of his head.
"Rys!"

"Hold me, don't loose...I can see it...I *can* know it..."

*There had been a man—a pilot. Liaden. And Jasin's brother, stand-
ing there, looking both terrified and delighted: "This is the man, sir."*

"Rys!"

"He sold me...sold me off the ship." His lungs were on fire,
and his head..."Jasin, she didn't know..."

Cold eyes looked him up and down.

"*Rys Lin pen'Chala, come with me,*" the pilot said, in the mode
of greater to lesser. "Your contract has been purchased by the
Department of the Interior."

CHAPTER THIRTY-TWO

. . . .

"WELL, THERE, YOU TWO JUST WON ME A PLATE OF REDITH'S cookies!" Sheyn said with a grin. He stepped back, pulling the door wide.

Instead of grinning and walking through, Syl Vor kept his place on the top step. Kezzi waited beside him, feeling the presence of Udari and Gavit on the street below.

"Why?" Syl Vor asked.

"'Cause I bet her you two'd be early again. How's your arm, Syl Vor?"

"It's okay. You knew Pete and Luce and Rudy were here yesterday before us."

"I did," Sheyn said, suddenly serious. "An' if you'll remember, I told you so—not by name, I admit, and maybe I should've done that. Your mama and Ms. Audrey and Jansy took some time with me yesterday, trying to figure how it all could've been gone about better."

He tipped his head to one side, his expression serious.

"You think I set you up, honey?"

There was a pause before Syl Vor shook his head.

"No. You *did* tell us we weren't the first in." He took a deep breath. "I don't want it to happen again, that's all."

"Couldn't agree with you more. So, I'm telling you that Rudy's ahead of you this morning, and he's in the lunchroom with Patsy, having some 'toot and cookies."

"Who," asked Kezzi, "is Patsy?"

Sheyn smiled at her. "She's one of our bouncers, sweetie. If there looks to be any trouble, you dodge behind a big ol' piece of furniture and let Patsy handle it." His smile widened. "Make sure you take Syl Vor with you."

"I will," she assured him seriously, as a voice rose from behind them.

"Problem up there, Silver?"

"No, Gavit, thank you. We were only talking to Sheyn."

"Well, talk inside. It might be spring, but that don't mean Ms. Audrey wants to be heatin' the whole street."

"Yes," he said softly, and then, louder, looking up into Sheyn's face with a smile that was almost like Vylet's. "Yes."

A *gadje* woman with sleepy green eyes and long black hair leaned against the side wall, her arms crossed over her chest.

Rudy was sitting at the table, his hands wrapped around the mug on the cloth in front of him. In the middle of the table was a plate of cookies. Kezzi sniffed appreciatively: spice cookies.

"Are you Patsy?" Syl Vor asked.

"That's right," the woman said, sternly. "You'll be Syl Vor and Anna?"

"Yes."

"Well, the both of you can stand down. I'll do any heavy liftin' needs doin'. Have a snack."

"Thank you," Syl Vor said, and walked toward the buffet, unsealing his jacket.

Kezzi picked up a mug and poured 'toot from the pot sitting to hand. The brew smelled acrid and strong, much like Bedel tea.

"Take that mug and get another one for me," she told Syl Vor.

This he did without comment, and the two of them took seats side by side across from Rudy, who stared into his cup like he was trying to read his fortune in the swirls of surface oil.

Kezzi stood up so she could reach the plate, and grabbed a handful of cookies. She dropped all but one between her mug and Syl Vor's and began to munch contentedly.

Syl Vor looked across the table.

"Good morning, Rudy," he said, sounding as cool as his mother.

Rudy stiffened, and looked up. There was a bruise along his right cheek, and his eyes were slitted, as if the light bothered them.

"How's your head?" she asked, before he answered Syl Vor.

"My head hurts," he snapped. "What's it to you?"

"Nothing, except Syl Vor thought you were worth fighting for. Did a medic look at you? If your skull's cracked, you shouldn't be here."

Rudy stared at her, his face red.

Patsy laughed.

"The doc down the clinic give 'im a pass to be here. You takin' medic training, Anna?"

"Yes," Kezzi told her, smiling sunnily, and washed the last of her cookie down with a swallow of 'toot.

"Which is why you got brought in for kid-onna-street," Rudy snapped.

She ignored him, and helped herself to another cookie.

Rudy took a hard breath, picked up his mug, and put it down again without drinking.

"Syl Vor."

"Yes?"

"Look, it was—I'm s'posed to thank you, for getting 'tween me and Pete, so—thank you. Now . . ." He did drink this time, like the 'toot was water, then thumped the mug to the table.

"Now, see, you shouldna done it. Wasn't your fight. *Ain't* your fight."

"Sometimes," Patsy said, from her lean against the wall, "you gotta get involved, whether it's your fight or not. Two on one—that's bad. I'd've waded into that, myself, no matter what I thought about the one." She shifted, recrossing her arms; her eyes suddenly not so sleepy looking.

"'Course, I got off-world notions. Couple years in the merc'll do it, maybe."

She might have said more. Kezzi thought she was *going* to say more, but there were voices in the hall. Then Tansy, Kaleb and Rodale noisily arrived, with Kaleb loudly demanding to know what *kind* of cookies.

Rudy sank back into his chair, and Patsy smiled, her eyes sleepy again.

Syl Vor picked up his mug and sipped the 'toot, wrinkling his nose.

· · · ✦ · · ·

Udari brought the *luthia* into Joan's Bakery and seated her, by her command, at a table in the center of the room. Had it been his to choose, he would have taken a table nearer the door, though the best of those was already occupied by a *gadje* slumped over a newssheet spread across the tabletop, one hand in a ragged, fingerless glove curled 'round a steaming cup, and a half-eaten muffin on a plate by the other hand.

Well, it was Silain's meeting, and as she would have him to understand, between sister-*luthia*. The table at the center, which might be so easily surrounded, was an eloquent statement of Silain-*luthia*'s trust in her sister, Nova yos'Galan, mother to Syl Vor, the very small dragon, brother to Kezzi of the Bedel.

"Bespeak tea, and a plate of mixed sweets, for two," the *luthia* said to him in their own tongue. "Ask to have it brought to this table when I am joined by my guest, and no sooner than that. Pay fairly, in local coin. When you have done this, return and stand behind my chair. Listen, watch, but do not speak. Should danger come, I know that you will act in the best interest of the *kompani*."

"Yes, *luthia*," he made answer, and strode to the back of the room, where a *gadje* woman with tired brown eyes waited, her worn face registering interest.

He bespoke the tea and sweets, and paid a little more than she asked—"For use of the table," he said, and she awarded him a faint smile.

Udari returned to the middle table and stood behind the *luthia*'s chair.

Aside from the *gadje* reading her paper at the table most convenient to the door, there were two other customers in the room. A round-faced *gadje* sat at a table rather deeper into the room, his coat flung over the chair next him, all of his attention seemingly on a large slice of cake, which he addressed with gusto. In the back, near the ovens, an old man sat with his chair wedged into the corner, nursing a cup and a plate of broken breads.

Udari sighed quietly. He regretted the absence of another brother, who would have lent strength to his arm, were it needed. That it should *not* be needed in what was styled as a meeting of kin, imparted . . . only a little comfort.

Syl Vor seemed a likely boy, and Kezzi had quickly come to accept his place in her life. Udari himself liked what he had seen of the lad.

Yet, there was Rys, who was no fool, no, nor fainthearted, shivering at the mention of dragons, betrayed by fear into wishing for what no man wanted—that he continue down this life as a stranger to his own soul.

A shadow disturbed the symmetry of light through the front window; the door was opened; the bell above it jangling on its string.

Of the three *gadje* in the room, only the old man at the back turned his head to see who had come in.

This, as it happened, was a broad brown man well-known to Udari. He glanced around the room, seemingly incurious, nodded, and pushed the door open wider to admit a woman who was already pulling off her hat, loosing a quantity of golden hair.

Even across the room, Udari could see that she was Syl Vor's mother—the pointed chin and willful mouth, the improbable color of her eyes, which were not so much blue as violet, made her unmistakable.

She came quietly to the table where the *luthia* sat, leaving Mike Golden to deal with the door and whatever else might be required.

Silain remained where she sat, her hands flat on the table before her. It lacked only a deck of cards, thought Udari, to make it seem as if she were welcoming an unwary *gadje* into the *fleez*.

The woman who so looked like Syl Vor bent her bright head.

"I come as the mother of a girl," she said softly, "to speak to the grandmother of a girl."

"You have found the right hearth," Silain said composedly. "Please sit down. Tea will come directly."

"Thank you," the woman said. She was not, he thought, ignorant of Udari's presence; rather, she had understood that it was not Udari with whom she was to deal.

She unfastened her coat and disposed it along the back of her chair before sitting down and giving Silain her attention. Her expression was austere; he remembered that Kezzi had said she was like a star, cold and distant, and seeing her for himself, he could not say that the child was wrong.

Mike Golden stepped up behind her chair, gave Udari an affable nod, such as a man might afford a man, but said nothing. Udari returned the courtesy, preserving his own silence. It was well, he thought; they were both brought to duty by their own *luthia*, as an extra pair of eyes and ears, as well as backup, should danger arise.

The tea and cakes arrived, and the *luthia* poured two cups, allowing the other to choose which would be hers. In this, Udari saw that Silain seized the high ground, establishing herself as the host.

The golden-haired woman, who was, Udari reminded himself forcefully, a dragon grown, took the cup nearest her hand, and tasted the contents without hesitation, showing herself mannerly as well as beautiful. Silain took the remaining cup and did likewise.

The golden-haired woman set her cup aside and folded her hands upon the table, sitting straight in the uneven chair, slim shoulders level under a sweater made of some napped fabric, its purple sheen reflecting in the depths of her eyes, her hair feathered across it in careless golden threads.

"My name is Nova yos'Galan," she said, her voice cool without being chill, strong, but with no hint of cruelty. "In my own culture, I would say, my name is Nova yos'Galan Clan Korval."

The *luthia* inclined her aged head. She had put her hair into a knot, and had 'round her shoulders many layers of scarves in ruby, citrine, gold, emerald, sapphire, lapis, and amethyst. The long black cape she had cast behind her on the chair.

"My name is Silain," she said, her voice, known to him all his life, reverberated with power as she gave her true-name to a *gadje*.

"Here Above, it might be rendered as Silain Bedel. My office is *luthia*. The child told you that I was her grandmother, and in that she spoke true, for I stand as grandmother to all the Bedel."

"The information is well come," said Nova yos'Galan gravely. "I ask, for I am ignorant, if you may decide for the child in such a matter of kinship as I bring."

"Matters of kinship fall within my office," Silain said. "However, the judgment of how that kinship affects the Bedel, that falls to the headman."

Syl Vor's mother smiled, and very nearly Udari was blinded.

"It would seem that we labor under similar circumstances. In the matter of the child's kinship with my child, and with myself, I have jurisdiction. Where, or if, such a kinship touches Korval—that is for the *delm* to say. For my part, I am willing for the kinship to stand. Already, learning and bonding has taken place. I find this good."

"I find it good, also," Silain said. "You should know that the child is the youngest of us. Her older kin indulge her as if her

years are less, even, than they are, or scold her for not knowing those things that life has not yet brought to her. To have a
brother more near her own years is a gift."

"My child is similarly situated. He is appreciably younger than
his next elder cousins, and those next junior to him in age are
not yet steady on their feet."

"So, then, for the children and for ourselves, we are content
in this situation they have found," Silain said, and lifted her cup
to drink.

"Yes," said Nova yos'Galan, and also raised her cup.

· · · ❖ · · ·

Thus far, Nova thought, placing her cup gently onto the table,
the meeting had been positive. The old lady across from her bore
her years and her authority with ease. If there was a reserve—
well, how could there not be a reserve, when two strangers met
to speak of the future of children?

Or of other things.

"We come now," said Silain the *luthia*, "to those matters which
concern the headman." She smiled as if gently amused by the
headman's necessities, but not in any way as if she found him
improper in his care of duty.

"You must understand that he *is* the headman; he sees and
plans and worries for the future of the Bedel. Children and the
brothers of children are of little interest to him, except as they
might improve the condition of the Bedel, or endanger the future."

Nova returned the smile. "I understand perfectly."

"It is well. The headman, on learning of the child's kinship,
came to my hearth and said, '*Luthia*, the child's new brother. It
is said on the street that he is kin to the Boss Conrad.'" Silain
paused and surveyed Nova from grave black eyes.

"First, I ask if this is so."

Ah, thought Nova, and drew a careful breath.

"It is so," she told the *luthia*. "As we reckon the kinship lines,
Boss Conrad is my son's cousin. Because he is much the elder,
and our families have a habit of easy intercourse, he stands
somewhat closer to uncle in authority."

"Yes. And in addition to this kinship, you are yourself a Boss,
working with the Boss Conrad to achieve his dream for this place."

"That is correct."

"Good. The headman's information is fair. He would therefore ask the Boss Conrad, through the boy or yourself, that the Bedel be left in peace, in that place we have found for ourselves."

Nova inclined her head, her heartbeat a little increased. Here was what Pat Rin had wanted, or at least part of it.

"I can no more speak for Boss Conrad than you may guarantee the headman's word," she said carefully. "It would be best, if headman and Boss would speak together, as we are speaking together now. If that cannot be done..." She let her voice drift off.

"I agree that it would be best, for Bedel and for those Here Above, for the headman and the Boss Conrad to dream together," the elder lady said calmly. "The headman will send a letter with the child, to the Boss Conrad."

"I will be very glad to give such a letter into the Boss's hand," said Nova. She picked up her cup and sipped tea to buy time for thought.

"Another thing," she murmured. "If the headman should have a desire to find a ship..."

Black eyes sharpened, and for a heartbeat Nova thought she had offended the *luthia* strongly enough to lose Syl Vor a sister.

Then, Silain laughed, ruefully, and shook her grey head. "Well, sisters and brothers, they will talk together, will they not?"

"They will. And a brother who cares for his sister will bring her problem to an elder who may be able to solve on her behalf," Nova said.

Silain nodded. "This question also properly sits on the headman's knee. Well," she said again, "when sisters speak, mountains move. Now, the boy. I would have him come to us some day soon, to meet the others of his sister's kin." She raised her hand perpendicular to the table, and rocked it slightly. "It is true that a brother may come to a sister..."

"But there are things that a brother might see, while visiting his sister, that fall into the headman's honor," Nova said.

"You understand. For the meanwhile, then, the child will continue to go to school and to come to you, after. Has she been a good daughter and done all her mother has asked of her?"

"She has been exemplary," Nova said, failing, for the sake of diplomacy, to mention that she had thus far asked Kezzi to do very little. "It would be good if she could come to us for several days together, when there is no school."

"I will dream on it," replied the elder lady.

Silain obviously felt that their meeting was nearing a close. Nova took a breath and reminded herself that she had not hoped to learn so much. And that she had a promise of future contact.

"I should tell you," Nova said. "The school will be moving to another location within the next few days. There is a new Consolidated School, and it will require a trip in a taxi to reach it."

Silain tilted her head to one side, and then nodded.

"I hear this," she said, and rose.

· · · ✳ · · ·

Udari dropped back to the door, in order to give Nova yos'Galan and Mike Golden room to exit.

This they did in proper order, while the *luthia* still gathered her cloak about her. Udari watched, and started, feeling a hand on his sleeve.

It was the *gadje* who had been so absorbed in her newssheet, now looking up at him. Her face was all sharp angles, and her eyes were blue as snow.

"You are," she said softly, with an eye also on the *luthia*, "brother to the one called Rys?"

He frowned, and she held up a hand, as if she would ward off his displeasure.

"I ask nothing for myself! It is only that I found his knife, and I wonder if you will take it to him."

He considered her more closely, and decided that it could do no harm.

"I will gladly take my brother's knife to him."

"Good," she said, softly, and slipped it into his hand, where it rested, cold as the ice in her eyes.

CHAPTER THIRTY-THREE

"ALL RIGHT!" MS. TAYLOR CLAPPED HER HANDS TOGETHER AND looked across the class, meeting each of their eyes in turn.

"All right!" she said again, fingering the pointer out of her pocket while still staring searchingly around the room. "Who can show me the shortest route to the Consolidated School?"

Not one hand went up. Tansy actually turned in her seat, the better to see if anyone volunteered.

"Nobody?" asked Ms. Taylor. "Delia?"

"No, ma'am."

"Pete?"

The big boy shook his head, adding, as if he had just remembered his manners, "No, ma'am."

"Tansy? Rodale? Luce?"

"No, ma'am," came the separate but identical answers.

Ms. Taylor shook her head, her face reflecting disappointment as she continued to scan the room.

"Syl Vor?" she said.

His mother had told him last night that the transfer to the Consolidated School would happen in a matter of days, and that none of his schoolmates knew this, yet. As soon as Ms. Taylor had asked her question, he had expected, grumpily, that he would be called on to explain the new school. Knowing where and what it was, when nobody else did would only mark him out again, and make him odd, and not like them. Rudy would call him a Boss's brat again, and—

"Syl Vor?"

On the other hand, he didn't seem to have any choice.

"Yes, ma'am."

He got to his feet. Ms. Taylor gently threw the pointer to him underhanded. He caught it, and he stared up at the map.

"The Consolidated School is at the corner of four turfs," he said slowly, keeping his eyes on the map. "Boss Conrad, Boss Kalhoon, Boss Schroeder, and Boss Engle. The shortest route from *this* school is to go down Rendan Road four blocks, to where the tollbooths used to be. Turn right for three blocks on Tyson Street, then left for two blocks on Kantico Road..."

As he spoke, he traced the route on the map, slowly and carefully.

"This," he said, making a loopy circle with the pointer around what was marked on the map as a vacant lot, "is the Consolidated School."

"Thank you, Syl Vor," said Ms. Taylor, matching his gravity. She raised her hand. "Please return the pointer."

He threw it back, gently, and sat down.

"Starting the day after tomorrow," Ms. Taylor said, slowly retracing the route to the new school, "we'll be meeting for class in the new Consolidated School, here. Please memorize the route, everyone."

"But," Rudy said, into the stunned silence that had overtaken the classroom. "That's way away from my street, ma'am. Take me all day to walk there."

"No walkin' to it," Rodale said scornfully. "Just take a taxi's all."

Rudy's face colored. "Taxi's spendy."

"Not the school taxi," Tansy said. "My ma don't got nothing extra for taxi fare, neither, but the school gives a chit and the taxi brings me back and forth to home—ain't that so, Delia?"

"That's how it works now," Delia answered slowly. "Might not be how it'll work with this new school, though."

"That's exactly how it'll work with the new school," Ms. Taylor said from the front of the room. She lifted the pointer and again traced the route from the present school to the new one.

"The Bosses will subsidize transportation," she said, "just like they do now, with the taxi chits. You'll get your chits from your teacher at the beginning of each week. If you lose a chit, or sell it, or trade it, you'll have to either pay for the taxi ride out of your own pocket cash, or miss school for the day you don't have a chit."

"But," said Kaleb, "why do we have to go to school so *far away*?"

"That's a good question, Kaleb," said Ms. Taylor. She snapped off the pointer and slipped it away into her pocket. "The Consolidated School is something all the Bosses have been working on for a long time, now. You would've been attending that school already, except there were some problems with people stealing materials from the site, and breaking things.

"Now those problems are taken care of, the school's ready, and all the students from all the street-level schools, like ours, are being shifted to the new one."

"But *you'll* still be our teacher, won't you, Ms. Taylor?" Tansy demanded.

"I'll be your Home Teacher, but you'll have other teachers, too, for other subjects." She grinned. "Subjects I never heard of, some of them. You'll mix in with the students from the other schools, and form up classes. Then, after you get settled, there'll be an open enrollment, so anybody who wants to go to school can. The students who're already in place—and who know how things work—will be expected to help the new students find their feet."

"But—*why*?" demanded Kaleb.

Ms. Taylor nodded. "Another good question, Kaleb, thank you."

"Does everybody remember when we talked about how the Bosses came into the empty space in the power structure that was made when the Gilmour Agency pulled off Surebleak?"

Heads nodded throughout the classroom. Kezzi, noted Syl Vor, who had a very good view of the back of her head, did *not* nod.

"The Bosses come up and divvied the streets 'tween 'em, each one takin' what they could hold," said Anders. "That meant all the different streets and Bosses were workin' against each other, instead of with each other. 'Til Boss Conrad."

"Very good, Anders. The Council of Bosses has made it a mandate to close the gap between the streets, and bring Surebleak people to work together with each other, for the good of ourselves and our world. The Consolidated School is an important step in that direction."

She paused, her head to one side, like she did when she was waiting for questions. None came, though, and after a moment, she nodded.

"We'll talk about this some more during the day, and at lunch. *After* lunch, we'll make a list of who gets taxi chits. Tomorrow, we'll pack up all our things, answer any last-minute questions or concerns and get ready for the move. The day after that, we'll meet for class at the new school." She smiled. "I'm excited. I think you'll be excited, too, when you see the new school—the new possibilities—and meet the other students like you, from lots of different turfs, who've been going to schools like this one."

She took a breath, and let her smile dim somewhat.

"We'd usually do arithmetic about now, but today, we're going to do history, instead." She looked around the room deliberately, and Syl Vor thought her eyes rested just a little longer on Peter and on Luce.

"All right," she said, her tone much sterner than usual. "Who wants to tell us about the insurance business?"

Memit had called upon him to work in the garden, and this he had done with honest joy, turning and trimming until his muscles ached, and blisters rose on his ungloved hand. The blisters earned him a scold from Memit, who smeared a salve on his palm and bound it with gauze.

"Fool. You've been unable to work this while; your muscles are weak and your flesh is tender."

"How better to strengthen both than to work?" he asked, which earned him a box on the ear—gentler than it might have been—and a command to come and give his opinion of her newest project.

"Where did you get these?" he asked, kneeling among the thin green vines.

"I found a stasis packet," she said, hunkering down beside him. "The label said *table grapes and ordinary.* I remembered that you had cared for such, so I brought them, thinking you might teach me. But you had gone to the men's camp, so I heard, and our ways were separate for some while."

The vines were a *gift,* he understood, taking care not to look too closely into her face and perhaps dismay her.

"Do you have the wrappings—or the label?" he murmured, reaching out and testing the new wood with naked fingertips.

Memit stood, unbuttoned the large side pocket on her utility pants and pulled out a closely folded piece of cardboard.

Rys unfolded it, pleased that she had kept all of the packaging.

"It would appear," he said, scanning the printed matter, "that these vines have been engineered for quick growth in less-than-optimal conditions. I have been accustomed to vines that came slowly to fruit, and with a certain rigor in regard to the soil. However..." He looked up into Memit's face with a smile. "However, I think that between us we ought to be able to find how best to please these. Is it your wish to make wine?"

Memit shrugged.

"First," she said, "let us make grapes."

· · · ❄ · · ·

Pat Rin shook his head as he handed her a teacup.

"I must say that I hadn't expected such rapid results," he said. "It's to be hoped that the headman is a person of sense."

"I gather from Silain that the headman's duty is to the best good of the company at large," Nova murmured.

"Yes, and I wish I knew whether that would serve us or hinder us." He sighed and sipped his tea. "Well. I suppose all will be revealed, soon or late."

"I am," he commented, after a few moments of companionable silence, "interested in this *lost ship*."

"Spoken like the son of a piloting House. Unfortunately, I know only that Kezzi asked Syl Vor if he might find a ship that was lost. This, you understand, having been brought up in the wake of a brisk review of ship silhouettes."

"And he said?"

"Being also the son of a piloting House, he said that it was possible to find lost ships, but there were facts to gather, and an adult pilot to enlist on the project."

"Whereupon he brought the matter to you." Pat Rin nodded. "That is well."

"We might," Nova commented, "*give* them a ship, if it will remove them willingly from the warehouses."

"We might, I suppose. Do you think there is a pilot among them?"

"I have no notion."

"Nor do I. And thus we wait upon the headman." He smiled at her. "In the meantime, Mr. McFarland has done his inspection, along with the contract team and a brace of Scout specialists. They pronounce the school ready for occupancy. The teachers are already on-site and preparing to meet their students."

Nova sighed, and shook her hair back from her face.

"I hope," she said, and stopped.

"That it works?" he finished for her. "As I do. And the devil's in it, that we won't begin to know, for years. Though we will make a beginning and show solidarity."

Nova considered him.

"We will?"

"Indeed. It has been decided by the Council of Bosses that the school shall be seen to have the approval of all. The incoming students will be welcomed by a committee of Bosses."

Nova frowned.

"Will they? And will Boss Conrad be among them?"

He raised his cup, but did not sip from it, rather looking at her over the rim.

"Do you know?" he said. "Natesa doesn't approve, either."

"And Mr. McFarland?"

"Mr. McFarland is of the opinion that I am a target wherever I go, and in the instance, he will at least have backup from the other 'hands attending their Bosses."

"There is that." Nova sighed. "Mr. Golden and I will be there, of course."

Pat Rin raised an eyebrow.

"There's no need—"

"There is every need," she interrupted. "Syl Vor and his sister will be among the core students arriving, recall! Not only will Mr. Golden consider it a rare treat to be on hand, but I believe the entire household may wish to be present."

Pat Rin grinned.

After a moment in which she stared with dark intent at nothing, Nova shook her head and drank off what was left of her tea.

· · · ✳ · · ·

The knife was a good one, well-kept, well-edged, and made for a hand smaller than his own. A subtle flick of the wrist brought the blade out, locked and ready for business; the barest pressure on a certain spot in the leather-wrapped handle put it safely away again.

In fact, Udari thought, eying the thing with unease, it was just a bit too apt, this knife, so smooth and so sweet that a man might forget he held a weapon.

And *this* knife—this sleek instrument, not so much contemptuous of life, as dismissive of it . . . *this* knife belonged to Rys?

True, he had seen his brother, small and broken as he had been, use his crutch as a weapon to win Rafin's respect, but that had been done with...thoughtfulness and, as he had thought at the time, calculated intent.

And anyway, Udari thought, snapping the knife closed and holding it in his hand, who had said the knife belonged to Rys?

A *gadje* woman he had never seen before...

...and who had known him for the brother of the one called Rys.

Udari's mouth thinned. He stood up from his hearth, slipped the knife away into a pocket, and went to find his brother.

· · · ⁂ · · ·

"Does anybody have questions about the new school?" Ms. Taylor asked, looking around the table.

"How will we *mix in* with the other students?" Delia asked.

"I expect that you'll mix in fine, and that there won't be as much difference as you think between turfs—just like we've been finding out here," Ms. Taylor said, and smiled. "For the mechanics of it...at first—and for as long as everyone feels it's useful—we'll meet together first thing, and last. That way we'll be able to keep in touch with each other, and talk about things. From our first core class, you'll go to another class that's been assigned—say, spelling, or arithmetic, or history. After that class, you'll go on to another. Classes will last about an hour, and everybody will have a list of classes, and where they are and a map. You know? After lunch, let's do routes! I've got a map of the new school. We can learn where things are together—that'll be fun, won't it?"

As far as Syl Vor could read from his classmates' faces, they weren't necessarily convinced that it *would* be fun. He remembered Veeno telling him that people didn't like change. That certainly seemed to be the case, here.

"Them other kids," Rodale spoke up, from his seat next to Rudy. "They know about not bringing blades and shooters t'school, don't they?"

"Yes, they do. The safety rules have been exactly the same for all the core schools," Ms. Taylor said firmly. "No weapons allowed in school, and no fighting. There will be a self-defense class, required for everybody." She shook her head. "After routes, we'll look at the list of required classes, okay? If there's a question about what something is, or how it'll be taught, I'll make a note and ask after it at the meeting tonight."

"Meeting?" Rudy repeated. "Do you... *know* these other teachers?"

Ms. Taylor laughed. "Well, of course, I do! Not *all* of them, because some have just arrived, but most, I think. We've been working on this curriculum for a long time, and in spite of all these glum faces I'm seeing, I really think you'll be pleased. I know you'll do *me* proud. And I'll be right there, remember! If you need to talk to me, you just come right on and do that!"

"But *where*?" Tansy demanded, fretfully.

"I'll have my own classroom, just like I do here," Ms. Taylor said. "We'll find that on the map, first thing, all right?"

Tansy snuffled, and nodded.

Ms. Taylor looked around the table, and Syl Vor did, too. He had eaten all his lunch, and Kezzi had eaten hers. No one else had seemed to be hungry.

"Okay, here's what. I'm going to go into the other room, and count to fifty. When I'm finished, I'll expect to see everyone back in their seats."

She got up, took her dishes over to the bin, and passed into the schoolroom.

"One!" she called out. "Two..."

"Like hide 'n' seek, only backwards!" said Vanette, and picked up her spoon, attacking her soup with a will.

Anders frowned, then followed suit, and pretty soon everybody but Rudy was eating.

"Better not waste that," Rodale said, nodding at Rudy's plate. "Long time 'til supper."

"Yeah..." Rudy picked up his spoon, and then put it down. "Not sure I'm gonna make the new school," he said. "M'father din't like me comin'—the boss at the machine shop had late hours he could gimme, so that made it okay. This extra travel—even with a taxi...I ain't gonna be able to make m'hours."

"Ask the boss for less hours," Syl Vor suggested.

Rudy glared at him. "Less hours is less pay, stupid. You think I can take less pay?"

Syl Vor raised his hands, palm out.

"I'm sorry," he said, which was proper, in Terran. "I didn't think of that."

"Guess you din't, Boss's brat. You don't gotta think o'hours or money, or nothin' 'cept pleasin' your—"

"*He said*," Kezzi raised her voice to be heard over his, "that he was sorry."

"That's right, Rudy, leave it," Vanette said. "Kid just din't think, is all."

Rudy took a breath, closed his eyes, and opened them on a hard exhalation.

"Oh, all right," he said. "Whatever."

· · · ❋ · · ·

From the garden, Rys went to the men's camp. Pulka's hearth was unoccupied, but there was a pot of tea on the stones, so he poured himself a mug and stood, sipping and staring into the hearth glow.

Physical labor had helped keep memory at bay, but now that he was quiet again—and alone—the moment returned. The moment of his betrayal, when Jasin's brother had accomplished his greatest piece of mischief. The pilot who had purchased his contract had been called . . . lar'Adrin. He had insisted that Rys accompany him immediately, saying that they would send for his belongings.

He had turned to Jasin's brother, and found that one grinning at him.

"First Mate Bell's off-ship with station security," he said. "I'll let her know she needs to hire another crewman, when she gets back."

He remembered that.

He remembered his anger, and his anguish.

He remembered that lar'Adrin had not, after all, sent for his kit.

He feared—he very much feared—that he would be able to remember what had befallen him, in lar'Adrin's care, if he pushed, only a very little bit . . .

"There you are, Brother! I have been searching the camp over for you!"

Relief flooded him. He turned to smile up into Udari's face.

"And here I am found. How may I serve you, Brother?"

"It might be that I can serve you," Udari said, an unaccustomed frown upon his brow. "I wonder, Brother—your lover. What does she look like?"

For a moment, he couldn't speak, the question like a blade to his heart. He took a breath then, shakily; his heart caught its rhythm, and he sighed.

"Perhaps your height, with golden brown hair, cut very short. Three rings in the right ear"—he raised his hand to his own ear, touching the places—"copper, silver, gold. Blue-grey eyes..." Long, sensuous hands, and strong shapely legs; small breasts, and a firm waist...

But Udari was shaking his head.

"Why," Rys murmured, "do you ask?"

"Well," his brother sighed, "I went out and Above with the *luthia* today. A woman stopped me there, and asked if I was brother to the one called Rys."

For the second time in a very few moments, he felt his heart stagger. Silain was to have met with...one of Korval today...

"Was it..." he began, but Udari was speaking again.

"She was your height, this woman, and your hue. Her eyes were blue, but more ice than fog, and her hair was yellow."

He could call to mind no one to fit such a description. A woman—any woman, it might be.

Rys swallowed. "What did she want?"

"Why, she said she had found your knife, Brother, and asked that I take it to you."

He brought his hand from his pocket and held it out, showing a leather-wrapped shape across his palm.

Without thinking, Rys took it up in his gloved hand. He dropped back a step and flicked his wrist...

Silently, the blade snapped out and locked.

Absently, he tried its balance, finding it good, and the handle well-suited to his grip. His thumb found the release, and the blade snapped home.

"It *is* your knife," Udari said, sounding as if he had hoped otherwise.

"At least my hand seems to know it," Rys answered, looking down at it. "Did she give a name, this woman? A reason—"

"Nothing else," Udari interrupted. "You do not, then, know her?"

He shook his head.

"However, it is a good knife, and well-kept. There's no reason not to keep it."

It seemed for a moment that Udari would argue this point, but in the end he only shrugged, and turned the subject.

"What do you, Brother?"

"I had done some work in the garden, and it comes to me"—he raised his mug—"that I ought to find Jin a mug."

Udari grinned. "Does it? Do you have the way of it, or will a brother's teaching be of use?"

"I would expect that a brother's teaching will be of very much use. Are you able to accompany me?"

"I am—and willing, too!"

"That is well, then. Let us go now, before my determination wanes. In fact, you might bear me company to another hearth, before we find the gate."

"Lead," Udari said, gaily, "and I will follow!"

Droi was sitting by the hearth, mending a tear in Vylet's shawl. A shadow flickered, obscuring her light, and she looked up in annoyance—

Into the face of Rys Dragonwing.

"Sister," he said, as soft and mannerly as one might want, "do you need anything?"

Anger leapt to meet the question—anger that was more than half *vey*, and which she made no attempt to soften.

"From *you*?"

It was not well-done to speak to a brother so, but Droi did not apologize. Let him think she despised him. He should certainly *not* think that he owned her, or owed her, or any other such mad, *gadje* thing as might enter his head. *That*, she would not have.

Seemingly, the blade went home; she heard him draw a sharp breath, and was glad. She put her gaze on her mending, thinking next to hear his footsteps, departing. But—

"I am going to the City Above to find a mug for Jin," Rys said, in his quiet, patient voice. "May I find something for you?"

Well, that . . . that was only what a brother might ask a sister, after all. She could—and ought to—answer such a question more gently.

She took a breath of her own and forced herself to raise her head to meet his eyes.

"A spool of red thread would be welcome," she said, coolly.

Rys nodded, once, and went away.

CHAPTER THIRTY-FOUR

· ·

"AND HAVE YOU THE PROOF OF THIS RATHER ASTONISHING assertion, Student Syl Vor?"

Ms. ker'Eklis was pushing again; pushing hard. Syl Vor would have thought that she was trying to make him lose his temper, only that made no sense. She was his math tutor, not his deportment teacher. Grandaunt Kareen was *quite* capable in *that* regard! If she thought his answer was invalid, why didn't she just—

He took a hard breath, and quickly reviewed Pilot's Peace.

"I am waiting, Student Syl Vor."

"Yes, ma'am," he said, minding his mode closely. Student to instructor, nothing more nor less. "You have been waiting for less than a minute."

Her eyebrows rose.

"Oh, indeed. And what is the proper length of time for an instructor to wait for a student's answer?"

"Long enough to allow the student to gather his thought and produce the proof," he answered, still keeping strictly to his mode. "Ma'am."

"Ah, I see! Allow me just a moment of whimsy. In thirty seconds, a navcomp may fail. In thirty seconds, a lifepod may be launched. In thirty seconds an earthquake can destroy a city. But thirty seconds is too short a time for a student to produce the proof for an answer that he asserts to be accurate."

He would *not* efface himself. She was wrong; she was push-ing; and he...

Ms. ker'Eklis rose, bringing her comp with her.

"You may proceed with the lesson by yourself," she said calmly. "Please, take as much time as you wish."

He rose, his legs not entirely steady; after all, she *had* succeeded in making him angry. What he wanted, right now, was to go downstairs and engage in a brisk session with the shadow-spar.

"I will of course report to your mother," Ms. ker'Eklis mur-mured. "It will be for her to decide whether we will continue, or whether you will find someone of your preferred speed to stand as your tutor. Good-day, Student Syl Vor."

"Good-day, Ms. ker'Eklis," he said bowing from student to instructor. He kept the bow until he heard the door shut, then straightened, throwing his arms toward the ceiling.

"Aaagh!"

Kezzi, who was sitting on the floor with her back against the bedstead, and a knee desk across her lap, looked up at him. A box of color sticks sat on the floor by her side, and several sticks in various shades of brown, red, blue, green yellow, and orange littered the surface of the lap desk. She was holding a carmine stick in one hand, and with the other was bracing a cardboard rectangle against the desk.

"Did you misremember a..." Heavy black eyebrows pulled together into a frown. "If it was me, I would say I'd misremem-bered a recipe, because I wasn't very good at tinctures and oint-ments and draughts for a long, long time. I could say out the ingredients; it was the measurements for each that I couldn't keep straight. Better I didn't know the ingredients, Jin said, because if I measured wrong, I could kill someone when all they wanted was relief from the toothache."

Syl Vor stared at her. "Didn't you—?" he began, then recalled that the conversation had been in Liaden.

He collapsed to the floor, facing her.

"I misremembered—well, but I *didn't* misremember! I gave her the answer, and mark you it was correct, or she would have said otherwise! But, no, what she wanted was the *proof*, and immediately."

"And you couldn't give it to her?"

"Well, I *could have*, if she had given me a moment to order myself! She wanted it too quickly, and..." He sighed.

"And I lost my temper," he said. "Grandaunt says that a person of *melant'i* never loses one's temper."

Kezzi looked down at her drawing and back to his face.

"My grandmother says that high temper proves a high heart."

"Is that a good thing—a high heart?"

"It is for the Bedel," Kezzi said, her brows still drawn. "What does your grandaunt say that you should do, when pushed, if not push back, and harder?"

"Write the name of the person who has provoked me, and all the particulars of the incident in my Debt Book, so that the matter may be Balanced, in due time. Which might," he added bitterly, "take *years.*"

She nodded, her eyes drawn again to her artwork.

"What are you doing?" he asked.

"I am making my deck, so that I may tell the futures of the *gadje* on the street."

This was much more interesting than Ms. ker'Eklis, only...

"How old are you?" he asked.

Kezzi lifted her chin and glared at him.

"I am a younger," she said haughtily, which was no answer at all. But, Syl Vor thought, the last thing he wanted was to have *Kezzi* mad at him, too.

"All right," he said peaceably. "In our House, it's not known if someone will be a..." He paused, startled. Usually, when he was speaking in Terran, he knew only Terran words, but the only word he could think of now was Liaden. "...a *dramliz* until they become halfling."

"What's that?"

He sighed, and spread his hand. "Someone who can...see the future, or the past, or-or lift a thing by thinking at it, or—there are many gifts. Aunt Anthora can—" But this was getting into complex territory "—can heal someone who is feeling sad. And Uncle Ren Zel can—he can See far and away into the future. I think." He looked down at her card, raised a hand, but deliberately did not touch it.

"I never knew him to use cards to See ahead."

"Well, of course he doesn't," Kezzi said acidly.

Syl Vor blinked at her. "But you just said—"

"I said that I'm making a deck so I can tell the futures of the *gadje* on the street. The cards are for the *gadje*; they're—they're part of the *fleez*. Your uncle is *vey*, and truly Sees ahead. *He* needs no cards."

Syl Vor frowned.

"So the cards are a ... cheat?" he asked slowly. "They don't tell ... true futures?"

Kezzi shrugged.

"They are *cards*," she said. "They know nothing. Just like *gadje* know nothing." Perhaps she saw his frown deepen, or perhaps she realized she had not explained herself plainly.

"Everyone who learns the *fleez* makes their own deck, but the pictures are the same in every deck, you see?"

He nodded.

"Good. Every picture has a little story attached to it—the same story for the same card, every time, no matter who offers the cards, no matter who draws it—yes?"

"Yes."

"It satisfies the *gadje*; they pay a coin, sometimes two, to hear the story that goes with the card they draw. It's a simple thing, no harm done, and the Bedel gain a coin." She sighed. "But only *gadje* would believe that *cards* are *vey*."

Syl Vor put the tip of his finger on the desk next to the card she had been coloring.

"What does *that* card mean?"

Kezzi sighed sharply. "Have you been listening? It means nothing!"

"You said each picture had a story attached to it."

Her sigh this time was slightly less sharp. "Yes, I did say that," she admitted, and held up the card, which showed a tall house standing in a garden, flowers 'round its base—and a jagged yellow bolt that had quite blown off the roof and started a little dance of flame.

"This is the Burning House," Kezzi said, her voice taking on an odd husky tone. "It foretells change, and good fortune."

"How can it be good fortune for your house to be burning?" Syl Vor demanded.

For a moment, he thought she would throw the card at him, then she shook her head.

"I don't know," she admitted, "but that's the story the card tells."

She frowned at the image, and said slowly. "Maybe there was something ... bad in the house. The people who live there will be driven out by the fire, but the bad thing—it might be burned up." She looked at him. "That would be fortunate, wouldn't it?"

Syl Vor chewed his lip, thinking.

"Maybe it would," he said eventually. "Quin would say—Luck is a double-edged knife."

"The Bedel say that Fortune and Misfortune are sisters, and each must have their share. Oh!"

She put the card down and reached into one of her many pockets, pulling out—his pen.

"Here," she said, holding it out.

"Don't you need it anymore?"

"No," she said, smiling. "U—Nathan found me these colors, for my cards."

She extended her hand a little further, as if urging him to take the pen. "The *luthia* said it had served its purpose, which was to bring us together."

He took the pen, which was still warm from having been in her pocket.

"Is the luthia *vey*?" he asked.

Kezzi snorted and picked up a blue stick.

"Sometimes," she said, bending to her drawing, "you are a very stupid boy."

"I don't think—"

"That's true," she replied, shaking her head without looking at him. "Will that *gadje* tell Mother you pushed her back?"

Syl Vor sighed, surprised to find that he wasn't angry, anymore.

"She said so. She also said I should finish the lesson without her."

"Then you should do it—and do it very well, so she's shown to be rude *and* stupid."

Syl Vor laughed, and Kezzi looked up at him.

"Was that funny?"

"No," he told her, rising into a long stretch. "It was Liaden."

· · · ✳ · · ·

"Your eye is quick and your hand is steady," Udari praised him, as they strolled together down the street, unhurriedly leaving the premises of Al's Hardware Store, Udari somewhat the richer for a box of nails and Rys by two tin mugs.

"I feel that I may have performed similar actions in the past," he said, smiling.

"Do you?" Udari looked at him with interest. "Can you say more?"

Rys moved his shoulders, wishing he could say more, but—

"A feeling only," he said to Udari. "Perhaps it will become clearer, in time. In *this* time, however, I feel I should now find some thread, or Droi will surely eat me."

Udari cleared his throat.

"It was brother-like, to ask her what she might want," he said carefully. "But Droi—"

"Droi is dangerous," Rys interrupted, and laughed slightly. "I know, Brother. And yet... it was me she came to, when the *kompani*'s numbers wanted repair."

He stopped, having heard the sharp intake of Udari's breath.

"Did she so? Brother, this is—have you brought this to the *luthia*?"

"I did, for being so ignorant, I did not wish to offend, or fall behind any obligation..."

"And what said the *luthia* to this?" Udari demanded. "Does she speak to the headman on your behalf? Did she say she would call your brothers to stand before the fire with you when we make you fully Bedel?"

Rys bowed his head, but of course Silain could do none of those things, no matter the tradition of the *kompani*. He was half a man, fear-ridden, with a debt hanging above him and his crime a mystery.

"Silain said that, in three days, she would take me to the mother of the small dragon Syl Vor, so that we might all learn how I have transgressed, and what Balance must be made."

Silence from Udari, followed by a heavy sigh.

"The *luthia* is wise," he said, his voice subdued. "These matters have precedence. A man's soul is his only possession, and that business must be settled before all else."

He put his hand on Rys' shoulder. "When the time comes for you to stand before the fire, I will be there, Brother. Believe me."

Rys blinked his eyes, clearing sudden, foolish tears.

"I do believe you," he said softly, and reached up to put his gloved hand, very gently, atop his brother's hand.

"Yes," said Udari, and raised his head, looking at the sky. "I must fetch the child," he said. "Will you come, or no?"

"The thread," Rys said. "I'll tend to that, and meet you in *kompani*, later." He reached into his deep inner pocket and pulled out the mugs. "Do you take these to Jin for me."

Udari took the mugs.

"I will take them to my hearth. You found them; it is yours to give them."

"All right," Rys said, smiling. "Until soon, Brother."

"Until soon."

· · · ✦ · · ·

"Ms. Taylor said taxi chits would be given to those who lived a distance away from the new school," Syl Vor was telling their mother.

Tonight's meal was a spicy vegetable soup, hot bread and cheese. Kezzi was already on her second bowl of soup and third piece of bread. However, this brought her attention up from her trencher with a jerk. She put the spoon down on the saucer, as she had seen Syl Vor do with his, and leaned forward slightly, watching the lovely, controlled face.

"That is correct," Mother said. "You and Kezzi will both qualify for chits."

She had, Kezzi thought, been afraid that would be the case.

"If we can work out the timing with Mike Golden's watch," she said now, and stopped as Mother's eyes found her face, slim brows raised.

"Yes, daughter? Please continue."

"Yes, ma'am. I don't think it would be . . . I don't think my grandmother would want a taxi to come to me. If Syl Vor's going to take a taxi, I'll walk here, with Nathan, or another of my brothers, and take the taxi with him."

"I agree with your assessment, on the basis of the talk I had with your grandmother today," Mother said calmly. "You may, however, ask the taxi to take you to the location of your choice. You need not go with Syl Vor, unless you wish to do so."

Kezzi chewed her lip, and looked to Syl Vor.

"I don't mind going to school with you," she said. "In fact, it's prolly better that I do, and keep you out of a fight. But if you'd rather not, or Gavit doesn't want me, then I'll tell the taxi another corner."

Mike Golden was heard to make . . . an odd sound. Kezzi looked up at him, suspiciously, but he was paying close attention to his soup.

"I'd like company on the ride," Syl Vor said. "I don't think Gavit will be coming—will he?" he asked Mother.

"That has not yet been decided," she said serenely. "Certainly, he will be with you on the first day, for there will be a great many people present."

Kezzi looked at Syl Vor and Syl Vor looked at Kezzi.

"Ms. Taylor said that our school would...merge with the other schools, but"—Syl Vor looked at Kezzi again, his brows drawn—"I did not realize there would be so many," he said.

"I didn't think so either—a few schools with a few students, like ours." Kezzi nodded.

"In fact, the lesser part of the first-day crowd will be students," said Mother. "The Bosses have decided to...celebrate their achievement, for the school is something they have worked toward for a very long time, and pushed through to reality despite those who did not want a school and who stopped at very little to destroy it."

"So that means," said Mike Golden, leaning back in his chair, "that all the Bosses, and all their 'hands'll be there to welcome all the students. Prolly be some speechifyin', an' maybe a tour." He rolled his eyes and Kezzi laughed.

"You got no respect for the Bosses?" he asked her sternly.

"Why should I?" she answered. "They're not *my* bosses!"

"That's a point, I guess," he said, looking thoughtful. "Still an' all, it's the Bosses who're puttin' things in order and built the school, so I'm guessin' a little bit o' politeness won't go amiss. What d'you say to that?"

"Is it polite to force people who are busy to stop what they're doing and go to *school*?"

"Touché, Mr. Golden," Mother murmured.

"No law says the law's gotta be polite," he objected, and she laughed.

"I think neither side has a compelling argument," she said, "and so rule the debate suspended until more facts are garnered. Now, I see that it is time for Kezzi to leave us—I sought your grandmother's approval that you stay with us for a few days together, child. She said that she would dream upon it, so it might be that she will yet approve. In the meanwhile, we have let the meal go late, and it is time for you to find your brother. My son, have you completed the work your tutor left you?"

Syl Vor drew a breath.

"Yes, ma'am."

"Excellent, you may with Gavit escort Kezzi to her brother. When you are returned, come see me in my office."

"Yes, ma'am," Syl Vor said again, but he sounded subdued, and Kezzi wondered if he were going to be punished.

"His teacher was not kind today," she commented, to no one in particular. Out of the corner of her eye, she saw Mother incline her head slightly, while Syl Vor threw her a wide-eyed look that might have meant she should have said nothing.

"Thank you. Now, I regret, but time presses. Please give my greatest respect to your grandmother."

"Yes, ma'am," Kezzi said, and got up, Syl Vor rising quickly beside her. "I'll be happy to see you tomorrow, ma'am."

Mother smiled. "Thank you, my child. I shall be happy to see you, as well."

· · · ✵ · · ·

Acquiring the thread had required somewhat more guile than that required to liberate the two mugs, the proprietor of the dry goods establishment being rather more tender of her wares. Still, Rys managed the thing without difficulty, and hoped very much that Droi would be pleased, rather than insulted, to receive one spool each of red, blue, and black thread.

Perhaps best to give the blue and the black to Silain, he thought, than put Droi's temper to the test.

He wondered, as he walked along, what might his role be among the Bedel, had he no Balance to make with Korval. Udari had seemed to think that he might become a child of the *kompani*, indeed, though it was hardly clear if that honor came through Droi's choice, or through his own endeavors.

Indeed, he tried to think of anything that he might have brought to the Bedel, save an amount of botheration that would have escaped them, had he merely been found dead on their doorstep. But Udari, having once saved his life, then felt compelled to repair that which had been damaged . . .

And had done so with wonderful thoroughness.

He strode along quite easily, unaware of the embrace of metal unless he brought his concentration to bear. In point of fact, he felt energized, and quite amazingly well. He could, he thought, walk all—

Rys blinked at the sign over Al's Hardware, and shook his head at his own stupidity. Clearly, his brothers had mended what could be mended, but there was no helping a man who could became so lost in his thoughts that he lost himself in truth.

So thinking, he adjusted his course, striking obliquely up the hill. He had hoped to be back underground before Udari returned with the child. Now, he would be fortunate to overtake them.

He quickened his pace, liking the bounce in his step, and the way his body responded to his need. The sensation of movement, of ease, of being whole and under his own command—but wait!

On his right hand was the place where the Blair Road toll-booths had been, in the not-so-distant past.

He had lost his direction again.

Rys stopped, there in the wide place in the road—stopped and deliberately took his bearings. His goal was uphill. From where he stood, he could see the sun's sullen glow off the top of the tallest warehouse building.

He took a deep breath, and centered himself, noticing how well-balanced he stood on two firm legs. He tucked his hands into the pockets of his coat. The fingers of his gloved hand met something hard, and slipped 'round it in a firm and loving grip. The knife Udari had brought him—*his* knife, according to some unknown woman.

Well, that was no matter now.

Now, he needed to get back—to *go home*—before he was missed, and his brothers disturbed themselves to come out and find him.

What a stupid thing, to become thus turned about, not once, but twice...

He began to walk, his eyes fixed on that sullen metal roof...

Lightning stitched through his head, leaving a glowing image of agony on the inside of his eyes. His stomach heaved, and he stopped, gasping, his ungloved hand braced against a kindly, nearby wall.

His gloved hand, still in its pocket, gripped the folded knife tighter still, and Rys swallowed, suddenly and entirely terrified.

And then, as if he were only a passenger in this body his brothers had repaired for him, he felt himself turn, downhill, away from the warehouses, away from...home, and begin, once more, to walk.

CHAPTER THIRTY-FIVE

. . . .

"WHERE'S MALDA?" KEZZI DEMANDED OF UDARI AS THEY TURNED the corner, leaving Syl Vor and Gavit behind.

"With the *luthia*. I regret that I could not bring him to you this evening, and I predict that his joy will be great when you are at last reunited."

She smiled, but said sternly.

"Why couldn't you bring him? He's not . . . sick? Or"—the old fear gripped her—"not *hurt*?"

"Put your heart at rest, little sister. Your faithful friend is well, though, as I say, mournful in your absence. I couldn't bring him because I brought Rys, who had some things to find in the city."

"All right," Kezzi said reasonably. "Then where's Rys?"

"Searching for the spool of thread which belongs to Droi."

She looked up at him, suspecting that he was teasing, which even Udari did from time to time. He met her eyes seriously, and she chewed her lip.

"Droi is too strong for Rys," she said.

Now laughter lit Udari's eyes.

"Oh? And what do you know of a man's strengths, little wanderer?"

"I *nursed* Rys," she said with dignity. "He is very small."

Udari laughed aloud.

"Never say it to him! No, never say it to any of your brothers, be it ever so true!"

Kezzi felt her cheeks warm. This was behavior more common in Pulka than in Udari. And besides, she hadn't meant *that*.

"You are," she said severely, "very stupid."

"I admit it, or such a judgment would never wound me. And before you say that it was Rys so judged, remember that what is brightest in a man is the reflection of his brother."

"If that's the case," said Kezzi, restored mostly to good humor, "then I'll tell you that Rys is a brave man, and kind, who *never* teases his sister. I wish all of my brothers were like him."

"Rys is the ideal to which we strive," Udari said solemnly, his eyes still dancing.

Kezzi snorted and then said briskly, "Brother, the school is moving! On the morning after tomorrow, our students will go by taxi to the Consolidated School, to meet the students like us, from other classes 'round the City Above."

"This is a change."

"Yes. The Ms. Taylor says it will be exciting, and that we'll learn even more and . . . and put ahead the plan of the Boss Conrad, that Surebleak should work for itself, like a *kompani*, instead of like gaggles of *gadje*."

"All of that?"

"All of that—and more. She says," Kezzi added, reserving judgment.

"And how will you travel to this new school? Or will you?"

"I will," she said, faintly surprised to find that she had never really questioned that. "I'll take the taxi with Syl Vor, from our mother's house, so that none need come up the hill. I spoke to Mother about it, and she agrees. She said that . . . grandmother would wish it so."

"So she would," Udari agreed. "You've done well."

Kezzi smiled, pleased.

· · · ✺ · · ·

"Your sister asserts on your behalf that your tutor was not kind. I wonder why she said it."

Syl Vor sighed.

"Because I told her so," he said slowly, and then, because it was true, "and because she was in the same room and saw us speaking."

Mother nodded.

"She is an apt reader of faces and stance, is she not?"

"Yes, ma'am." He paused, considering her face, but saw nothing but her usual cool and calm expression. "Ms. ker'Eklis said she was going to speak with you, ma'am."

"And so she did. Tell me, my child, do you willfully withhold proofs from your tutor?"

"Willfully? No, of course not! I—" He bit his lip, remembering Grandaunt Kareen's lessons. A person of *melant'i* did not make excuses, but it was permissible to explain one's actions. In the present case, however...

"Is there a difficulty, my son?"

"I am not certain if I am about to give a reason or an excuse," he confessed.

"Ah. This can sometimes be knotty, until one has achieved a certain level of experience. Pray allow me to sort it out for you."

"Yes, ma'am. Of course, I shouldn't withhold proofs, but in this case, I hadn't prepared a proof. Ms. ker'Eklis asked me the answer to a velocity problem, and I answered her. Then, she said—she asked if I had the proof for, for that 'rather astonishing assertion,' and I didn't, having only just answered her, you see. I was beginning to frame it—the proof—and she said she was waiting, and I—"

He met his mother's eyes firmly.

"I said to her that she had been waiting for less than a minute, and she...quite properly reminded me that...many unlooked circumstances may occur in thirty seconds. A pilot must be quicker than disaster. I know that."

One golden brow rose. "Do you, indeed?"

"Yes, ma'am," he said. "We—at the Rock—it is what we practiced, all the time, even when lessons were done. We practiced being quick—Quin and Padi and I—so that we could prevent..."
He stopped, thinking of Shindi and Mik, and Grandfather, and Grandaunt, too, who had all of them depended on their quickness, and their skill. He blinked and cleared his throat. "So we could prevent our enemies from prevailing."

There was a small silence, and then Mother said, matter-of-factly. "I see that I have not spoken as closely as an aunt should, with Quin."

Syl Vor looked up at her, startled.

"Mother, Quin did nothing but what he ought! He was the

eldest, and our, our pilot, should we have needed one. It was difficult, for you know Quin does not at all like to put himself forward, but he made sure that we were prepared!" He took a hard breath. "And he certainly never said that I should be pert with my math tutor! He would've rung down a terrible scold on me for losing my temper and set me to do all the proofs in the chapter by hand!"

"I . . . see. And Ms. ker'Eklis, what did she do?"

Syl Vor half-smiled. "She set me to do all the proofs in the chapter. Taking as much time as I cared to," he added, not quite able to entirely suppress his bitterness.

"Have you finished them?"

"Yes, ma'am. But . . ."

"Yes? Is there more?"

"I don't know that Ms. ker'Eklis will wish to teach me anymore," he said, utterly miserable. "I was not . . . convenable."

"Perhaps you were not," his mother said briskly. "However, Ms. ker'Eklis was, as your sister said—and as I agree—not kind. She has been dismissed."

"Dis—" He stared at her. "But, math—Mother, the math we have at—at the day-school is very basic. I—"

"Peace, my child. Eventually, you will have another tutor. In the meanwhile, you and I will continue along in the module together. Pray have the goodness to send your work to my screen before you retire this evening."

"*You* will teach me?" He didn't know whether to be horrified or gratified, though naturally more time with his mother must be grati— But he had been maladroit; his mother's eyebrows were well up.

"I do assure you that I have the required concepts."

"Yes, ma'am, I—thank you, Mother. I will be very glad to learn from you."

"And I will look forward to learning from you, my son."

· · · ✵ · · ·

Rys had not returned to the *kompani*.

Udari had made the rounds, several times—checking at Jin's hearth, in the garden, at the hearth Droi shared with Vylet and Kezzi, at the workroom, where Pulka toiled alone over a broken heat sensor.

He went to the forge, and there unwisely put the question to Rafin, who, upon hearing of the woman and the knife, laughed uproariously and slapped his thigh.

"So the cock has a woman in the City Above! What would you? Surely, he must demonstrate his renewed energies to an appreciative audience!"

"He said that he didn't know her," Udari said.

"But he knew the knife, eh?"

"The knife fit his hand, so he kept it. Wouldn't *you*? It was a good knife."

"Any knife that fits my hand is a knife unto my hand," Rafin said, and gripped Udari's shoulders, not ungently. "Come, Brother. Rys is a man, not a child. A man newly able to walk, and to run. It might be that a walk to the spaceport seemed good, if only to prove to himself that the leg won't fail. Eh?" He gave the shoulders a shake.

Udari stepped back.

"Ah, you don't believe me! Your care for your brother speaks well of you, but I think—I *do* think, Brother—that you worry in vain. Rys will be back tomorrow, or at the most the day after, pockets bulging with thread of every color, and a story or two to tell us."

"There is wisdom in what you say," Udari said, which was courtesy from a brother to a brother, and left the forge soon after.

At last, having checked the gates, and the record of those who had entered them, and stopped for a cup of tea and a song at Jin's hearth, in company with Memit, Isart, and Gahn, he returned to his own place, and sat himself down on his blanket.

It was in his heart to go to the *luthia*, and put his trouble before her. Yet, Rafin had the right of it. Rys was no child, to be curtailed by an adult's hand on his shoulder. Very likely, he had become drunk on his own powers—a man who had thought never to walk again might count a hike down the whole length of the planet as a prayer worth making.

As for the woman...

She had known more of Bedel business than a *gadje* had right or reason to know. It might be that she was a matter for the headman. He thought to seek her out, then thought that Rys might, after all, have gone on that errand.

Best, thought Udari, to wait for Rys to return. They would

smoke and speak together as brothers, finding between them what was best to do.

Having taken this decision, he felt somewhat less distressed, and after a few minutes' commune with the hearth and with his soul, he rolled himself into his blanket and speedily went to sleep.

· · · ❄ · · ·

It had grown cold and dark during the time that he walked. He shivered and pulled the hood out of the collar of his coat and up around his face. This, he could do with ease. He could even pause in his purposeful striding—but not for long.

What he could not do—he could not turn and walk in a direction of his own choosing, nor could he call out to any of those he passed on the street.

The rules under which he labored thus established, and after an initial period of disorientation, he walked calmly and with purpose, as if he were quite aware of his destination. The fact that he *didn't* know where he was bound seemed of...little importance. He would arrive, and all would be, for the first time in a very long time, well.

This refrain did more than once waft through his head, like a misplaced lyric to a half-remembered song. He, foolishly, found it comforting.

And so he continued, walking briskly but without overt haste, until he turned into a street terrible by the standards of even this terrible city; a street that had been uncleanly razed, with broken walls standing solitary amid ankle deep rubble, wires like demented vines snaking along the riven pavement.

Midway down the street, on the side opposite, stood three houses, side by side, the rest of the row having collapsed in whatever cataclysm had taken the street to ground. The first house had no outside wall; it would, Rys thought, have lost that when the house next to it had fallen. He supposed that the third house would be in like state, though was not granted the opportunity to see if he was correct.

His brisk stride took him at an angle across the street and up the steps of the middle house.

The door opened under his hand and he crossed the threshold into a dim hallway. He barely had time to push the door closed before his determined legs took him off again, down the hall, three, six, nine, twelve steps, to another, very tightly closed, door.

This time he did not try the knob. Rather, he raised his off-hand and knocked three times.

He heard nothing, and wondered, briefly and distantly, what would happen if no one opened to him. Would he be released from the... compulsion that had brought him here? Would he be able to return—to return...

A rill of discomfort ran inside his head. He took a breath, and deliberately recalled Silain's hearth, the blanket spread, the metal teapot with its various small dings, and the bottom darkened by heat.

Silain also he saw, her hair swept back from a broad forehead to lie on her shoulders like fog on the mountain; the wrinkles softening her face; the black eyes, and noble nose...

The door before him opened.

So well had he fixed Silain in his mind's eye that for a moment the person before him made no sense. She might have been said to have been Silain's antithesis—her face gold-toned, the features drawn with a timid hand, excepting the hard lines around her mouth, her short hair dry as old grass, her eyes a pale and frigid blue.

She smiled, which etched the lines deeper, and extended a hand to cup his cheek. He tried to recoil; he wanted no touch and no notice from this woman, whoever she was, but his body merely stood there, as if it were an automaton whose gearing had run down.

"Rys Lin pen'Chala," she murmured, and he was distantly horrified, that she knew his name. "And in so much better case than when last we met. Truly," she said, looking him up and down with an air of proprietary pride, "this is *much* better than I had dared to hope for. I must think of a way to thank your brother for his care of you."

That this woman might come near Udari—*that* woke a shiver from his stupid body, and the woman laughed.

"You flatter me," she murmured, cold fingers caressing his cheek.

He tried to find his voice.

He tried to find his *will*, struggling with the inertia that trapped him in this place, with this... person. Pain flashed and flared inside his skull; he welcomed it as something immediate, something *true*. He pushed, as he had often done, seeking now not an errant memory, but his freedom.

His life...

"Peace, peace, little bird, you will harm yourself beforetime," the woman said, raising her other hand to his face. She held him between her two palms, not gently, and said, very clearly...

"*Vaslet kyr novin Rys Lin pen'Chala.*"

It was nonsense, neither Liaden nor Terran nor any other language in his ken. He ignored it... tried to ignore it, yet the words had a peculiar, poisonous resonance. He struggled—struggled against the poison, for his liberty—

And all at once he ceased to struggle, his muscles turned to water, and his thoughts to misty dreaming.

"Excellent," the woman said, releasing him. She turned her back and walked into the room.

"Come here," she snapped.

He had no sense of having moved; he merely arrived within the bright-lit room. The source of that light was a lantern of Liaden Scout issue, which sat on a scarred round plastic table. Beside the table were two chairs: one full in the light; one in comfortable dimness.

"Sit down."

The chair sagged under his weight; the glaring lamplight hurt his head. He lowered his eyes...

"Look at me!"

He stared at her across the searing pool of brilliance, saw the icy glitter of her eyes.

"What is your name and condition?"

"Rys Lin pen'Chala, Field Agent."

"I am Agent of Change Isphet bar'Obin. You are under my command, Field Agent pen'Chala. I apprehend that you are presently experiencing symptoms consistent with a field agent who is not on-mission. Be of good cheer; you will very soon be relieved of your distress, and will no longer be disturbed by doubt, or by any division of loyalty. Before you are granted that happy state, I regret that I must perform some rough and ready repair. I cannot risk failure." She moved forward until he had to lean back in the rickety chair in order to keep his eyes on hers.

"I fear," she said, "that you will find this uncomfortable."

She smiled and bent to him, the words flowing warmly into his ear on the soft exhalation of her breath.

"*Son eber donz, Rys Lin pen'Chala.*"

CHAPTER THIRTY-SIX

· ·

"MY MOTHER WANTS TO COME TO THE FIRST DAY OF SCHOOL," said Delia. "Ms. Taylor, can she?"

"My gran wantsa come, too!" Jeff said excitedly.

"My ma and my little sister wanna see me get settled in," Tansy added.

"My gran'd like to come, but it's a far bit from Gough Street," Rodale offered. "'Less she can ride the taxi on my chit?"

Ms. Taylor clapped her hands.

"Okay, everybody, sit down and let's talk about it!"

They obeyed, chairs clattering as young bodies flung into the seats, then silence of a sort.

"Now, there's going to be a welcoming committee at the school," Ms. Taylor said. She paused and looked hard, first at Luce, then at Peter.

"*Not* the old-style welcoming committee. The Bosses'll be there, some of them, and their 'hands, but there won't be any retiring *or* promoting." She gave them both another hard stare, then smiled out over the rest of the class.

"The first plan was to have all the students from each school go to the new school in their group on the first day. But, this morning I heard from Mr. Sanamayer, who's the principal—call him the Boss Teacher. He's already heard from other core teachers about parents and sibs and friends coming along to see every-body settled, maybe take a tour, have some cake and coffee—like a party! I should get a call a little later today to find out how we're going to deal with that. What Mr. Sanamayer suggested was that we all go to the school with our families, then join up with our class when we get there."

She smiled. "I'm thinking that's what will likely happen, but we have to wait for confirmation from Boss Conrad's office, and from the Consolidated School's security."

She looked around the room.

"Any other questions?"

There were none.

"Good! Now, I've got some boxes here. What we're going to do is count off by fours, then quarter the room. Each quarter-team will be responsible for packing what's in their section of the classroom into boxes. All right! Vanette, you start!"

· · · ✳ · · ·

Rys Lin pen'Chala was content.

More, he was at peace, fully engaged in the mission; entirely cognizant of his past actions and his place in future action, with neither doubt nor uncertainty disrupting the process of his thought. How fortunate it was, he thought, reviewing the steps of the plan and the map for the third and final time, that Agent bar'Obin had found him, and restored him to himself.

He had been called into service to assist the Agent of Change in an oblique strike at Korval. It must, of course, be an oblique strike, as the failed attempt by Otts Clark had the expected result of the Dragon guarding itself even more closely—but it was worthy for all of that.

It was imperative that Korval be prevented from sinking its roots into Surebleak, as it had into Liad. The more unstable the Dragon's situation, the better for the Department. If the population of the planet were to rise against Korval, so very much the better.

The plan in hand, which targeted the work of Korval and of Boss Conrad, Korval-kin and the *delm's* hand puppet—*this* plan would explode across the world, rendering the political base *and* Korval anathema. Given the local tradition of retiring with extreme prejudice those leaders who failed to please, it was not too much to hope, said Agent bar'Obin, that Surebleak would do most of the Department's work for it.

After all, even Terrans valued their children.

"Korval has taken up eight field agents—so much is certain," Agent bar'Obin said now. "We must assume that all the supply caches, the locations of which were common field knowledge, are being watched. This means that we must depend upon local materials, which will make the operation more arduous. However, with two of us, it should go well."

She looked at him, bowed slightly.

"The last part of the plan will be yours, Field Agent. You are something of a marksman, I believe, and will enjoy the opportunity to practice your skill."

He did not recall that he was a marksman of any note. However, it was the Agent's business to know such things, and as she had made that skill a cornerstone of the plan, it must be true.

What he did recall at this very moment, in a soft overlay of the room in which he sat, listening to Agent bar'Obin speak, was Silain's hearth, with the child sitting just behind the old woman, her dog asleep with his head on her knee. He had been part of that hearth-gather on many occasions, and he found himself wondering how they went on, and if anyone had missed him yet.

"Have you any questions, Field Agent?"

He blinked, and brought the room into sharper relief. *This* was what he had been fashioned for. Only in the successful execution of the mission could he find fulfillment. He had nothing else. He *was* nothing else. The mission was his all and everything.

"Field Agent. Have you questions?"

"No, Agent," he said respectfully, and then, surprising himself, said, "Yes. If you please."

She inclined her head.

"Ask."

"I wonder," he heard himself say, "what became of the *Momma Liberty*? I cannot completely recall..."

Agent bar'Obin inclined her head.

"Ah. I had told you that what repairs I might make for you here would necessarily be incomplete. It is what we must accept, though I am dismayed that this memory of all has escaped you. It was of course the defining action of your life, in which you sealed your loyalty to the Department.

"To say it quickly: When you had completed your training, your mentor gave you leave to bring your skill against those who had sullied your honor and used you against your will. It is not uncommon that such actions are approved, if the trainee has made the request."

She paused and bowed in full honor

"You made the request. You made the attempt. That ship no longer exists."

CHAPTER THIRTY-SEVEN

"I WILL GO WITH MY YOUNG SISTER TO THE NEW SCHOOL," THE *luthia* said calmly, continuing to drape the seven shawls of her office about herself.

Udari looked to Kezzi, who had suffered to have her hair braided and tied with a purple ribbon. She wore a purple sweater that Udari remembered Droi had found in the City Above, and a pair of black pants, rather than her usual utility pants. Her expression was one of mild amazement, but he saw no reflection of his own horror.

"Many of the other students are bringing their mothers and grandmothers today," Kezzi explained. "There'll be a party, the Ms. Taylor said. The Bosses will also be there, and their 'hands."

"Yes," Udari said carefully, "but for the *luthia* to go into such a thing..."

Silain laughed. "As if I hadn't gone among *gadje* just as Droi does, and told out the cards for coin!" She shook the last shawl into place, and touched the knot of her hair. "But I will not go unprotected. Rys will accompany us."

Udari shook his head, his voice gone to dust in his throat.

"Does Udari speak for Rys?" Silain asked, rather tartly. "A brother's care may go too far, my son."

"*Luthia*, well I know it, and with all my heart I wish that my brother were by, that he might speak for himself. But—he is gone, *luthia*."

"Gone?" cried Kezzi. "He has...left the *kompani*?"

311

"Little sister, I only know that he hasn't returned."

"Which is not the same as left," said Silain. "Is there more to this tale of your brother, Udari of the Bedel?"

"*Luthia*. Rys came with me into the City Above the day before yesterday. Fool that I am, I left him behind while I went on to meet my sister. He promised that he would return that evening, but as of this rising his promise is unredeemed."

He cleared his throat. "I had meant to bring this to you yesterday, *luthia*. Rafin's counsel was that he was safe enough and... celebrating his strength regained. It seemed not... unlikely, and so I left it."

He bowed his head, ready to accept her censure, but what he heard was a sigh.

"I hear this," Silain said heavily. "It may be found, my son, that you are not so much a fool as I am, and that, indeed, your brother may have left us. I thought his heart was bolder."

Udari raised his head. "He said that you would take him to the dragon."

"So I would have, and stood at his side through whatever came, as I promised I would do. The thought in my mind today was that he would be invisible at my side, in the press of this *party*, and might study those dragons present. I had hoped proximity might revive his memory of the trouble that lies between them." She sighed again.

"Well! All and everything now lies with Rys. Udari, you will accompany us."

"*Luthia*," he murmured, accepting this.

Silain reached for her cloak.

"Grandmother," Kezzi said, "I agreed to meet my brother outside our mother's house and ride the taxi with him."

"Then he must be told that your grandmother has called you to escort her, and that he'll find you at the school." She raised her head, looking past the hearth to a shape that moved down the common way.

"Is that Isart?"

"Yes, *luthia*!"

"Come here, my son. Your sister would ask you to bear a message to another of her brothers."

Silain nodded to Kezzi, who went forward to meet him, and looked again to Udari.

"I think you will see your brother again, Udari."

"Is that a Seeing, *luthia*?"

She shook her head.

"It is a grandmother's wish."

There came a pounding of feet, which was Isart, bounding off. Kezzi returned to them.

"Can Malda come to the party?" she asked.

Silain blinked, looking for just that moment, so Udari thought, as if she had seen through the door between the World That Was, and the World That Might Be.

She blinked again, and looked down at the small creature standing by Kezzi's knee.

"Yes," said the *luthia*. "Malda must come with us."

· · · ✳ · · ·

The work was almost done.

Using local materials, this part of the mission had taken longer even than the agent had anticipated, and in truth, his part had been made more difficult by ... memories.

Random action triggered them, ambushing his real-world senses, oversetting his concentration on the mission.

Setting the first cap, he remembered in vivid serial flashback a score of thefts, and half-a-dozen fires set. Unfolding his knife triggered a memory of how it had felt, the precise and peculiar pressure exerted against the blade, as he severed a man's finger—so very different from the smooth stroke that parted a woman's throat ...

For fully three minutes, he crouched by a pile of broken bricks and furring strips bristling with staples, images flipping before his eyes like cards—mayhem, death, and misery. He had been efficient. He had been deadly. He had been cruel. His deaths weighed him to the ground; he could not rise. All this, he had done, because ...

... because ...

Because, a voice said coolly, *you have a mission. You must not fail.*

He jerked and stared about him for the owner of the voice, but he was alone beside the mound of discards and trash. Alone and once again able to see, the tide of recall for the moment, at least, stalled.

Rys Lin pen'Chala pulled the cap out of his pocket and set it, his fingers only trembling a little. After all, he had a mission. And he must not fail.

✳   ✳   ✳

He positioned his last explosive cap on the far side of a small shed. He inserted the activation plug, and pressed down, being sure it was seated properly.

Seven small-duty caps had been set among the rocks and debris in this open area to the side of the main building.

Inside the building, Agent bar'Orbin would be setting two larger explosives in the equipment room. She of course held the detonators. Additionally, there were timers on both, in the event that the detonator—or the hand—failed of its duty.

The mission, straightforward as it was, called for the caps he had set to be detonated first. The resulting noise would cause confusion and dismay among those gathered. It was not expected that the initial detonation would produce fatalities, though he would certainly do so, by immediately firing into the crowd, seeking to herd them toward the school building, or in any case to keep them within the boundary of the second, extremely powerful explosion.

There would, he thought, surveying his handiwork, be little chance of surviving that.

He stood away from the shed—and paused, for it seemed he saw his grandmother before him—or . . . not his grandmother, but Silain, and with her the child, and the dog, ranged behind them his brothers and his sisters of the Bedel. Silain extended her hand—but no. That was not for him.

For him, there was the mission.

And an aching sense of relief, painful as a knife between the ribs, that none of the Bedel would be in the crowd of *gadje* soon to gather outside.

Well. He shook himself, deliberately casting off all memories.

There was the long rifle awaiting him. And the mission, to be brought to fruition.

He must not—he would not—fail.

· · · ✴ · · ·

Syl Vor shuffled his feet, stuck his hands in his pockets, took his hands out of his pockets, and stared up the street, squinting.

"Take it easy," Gavit told him for the third time since they'd arrived, early, at the corner. "She'll be along in a minute and we can get goin'."

The *get goin'* part was true enough because they had waved

down the first taxi that had cruised past their spot on the sidewalk, and asked the cabbie to wait for a minute, until the rest of the passengers arrived.

It had been much longer than a minute, and Syl Vor thought that the driver was starting to look bored.

Where *was* Kezzi?

"Now, here comes somebody," Gavit said.

Syl Vor spun, expecting to see Kezzi coming down the street, Malda at her heels and Nathan beside her. What he saw instead was a lanky boy about Quin's age, with untidy black hair in a snarl over one shoulder, and insolent black eyes.

"Are one of you Anna's brother?" he asked, stopping twelve steps away, both hands in his pockets and his feet poised to run away.

"I am," Syl Vor said, going quickly forward.

The boy immediately stepped back.

Syl Vor stopped, feeling a flicker of anger.

"Where is Anna?" he demanded, stuffing his hands in his pockets, and almost added her favorite epithet, *you stupid boy.*

"I'm to tell you: Your sister's grandmother decided to go to the party at the new school. Your sister travels with her. She'll see you soon, at school."

Syl Vor blinked, and glared. The boy returned the glare for a long moment before turning on his heel and walking back the way he had come.

"Guess we'll grab that taxi now, Silver," Gavit said from behind him.

"He was *rude*," Syl Vor said.

"Noticed that," Gavit said, jerking his head meaningfully toward the cab. "Last I heard, that wasn't a killin' offense." He sighed. "Sooner you're in that cab, sooner you'll see your sister, right?"

Syl Vor took a breath, nodded, and headed for the cab.

· · · ※ · · ·

The taxi drew into a long, crescent-shaped drive, and stopped at the apex, discharging them amid a small gathering of children and adults, heads bare and coats open in appreciation of the early morning warmth.

Behind their taxi came another, and another after it.

They moved a little away from the curb, to make room for those who were coming after. Udari went first, opening a path for them to an untenanted piece of sidewalk. There, they stopped, forming a knot like many of the other knotted humans up and down the walkway.

The child crouched down to speak to her dog, murmuring love words and instructions to stay by her into his high-pointed ears. Udari kept a lookout over the crowd, his mouth a little tight.

"Is your brother here?" Silain asked as Kezzi stood up.

"I don't see him," the child answered, rising on her toes and looking about them. She shook her head. "I think we're very early. I don't see anybody from school."

Silain nodded and looked about her. A stout *gadje* woman with her hair hidden under a red kerchief smiled as she walked by, and gave a friendly nod. Silain smiled and nodded in return, striving to seem both calm and collected.

In truth, she felt off-center, troubled by fragments half-seen from the World That Might Be. What she saw distressed her— Rys, a flare of fire, a running dog, a splash of blood. She saw the fine building they stood before expand, then crumple in on itself. She saw Nova yos'Galan Clan Korval with blood on her face, her violet eyes staring blindly.

There was no sense to any of it. Perhaps her Sight was failing her. Perhaps the World That Might Be was melting, overheated by the couplings of opportunity, choice, and luck. Perhaps—but there. She closed all of her eyes, deliberately, and bowed her head.

"Let the road be easy," she murmured, the very first prayer a child of the Bedel is taught. "Let the gleanings be good. Let there be brothers and sisters 'round the hearth at the beginning of the day, and at the end."

"Grandmother?" asked Udari, looking up at her with a frown. "Are you well? There's a wall over there you could sit on, and rest."

She smiled for him, and shook her head.

"I'm fine," she said, "and the sun is pleasant here."

A flash of light caught the edge of her eye; she turned her head to watch a cab enter the crescent, even as Kezzi ran a few steps toward the curb, Malda at heel.

"Syl Vor!"

The taxi stopped, the back door opened and a small boy with very bright yellow hair leapt out, followed more slowly by an elder brother. This one paused to look carefully about him. The boy, however, rushed forward, heedless.

Malda barked, and leapt into the air, then sat down by the child's knee, quivering with joy.

"Hello, Rascal!" the boy said, bending down to ruffle pert ears. The sleeve of his jacket twisted as he did so, and Silain saw a glint of copper 'neath the cuff, which would be the bracelet Kezzi had told her of. He gave the dog's ears one more robust rub, and straightened.

"I'm glad Isart found you," Kezzi said.

"Is that his name? He didn't say."

"Well, I didn't tell him to give you his name, only my message. With Isart, you need to be clear."

"We came as soon as we could. Have you been waiting long?" he asked.

"No. Is Mother coming?"

"Yes, with Cousin—with Boss Conrad and Mike, and Mr. McFarland. They should be here soon. Is the rest of the school here?"

"Not yet."

They had by this time returned to their small knot. The boy raised his head and smiled.

"Good morning, Nathan."

"Good morning, small dragon. Streetman Gavit."

"'Morning," the watchful one said.

There was a pause. The boy looked to Kezzi.

"Will you introduce me to your grandmother? Or should I go away?"

"Are you going to be stupid on our very first day in the new school?" she asked him, grabbing his hand and pulling him forward. "Grandmother, this is my brother Syl Vor. I hope he finds favor with you."

Silain smiled.

He was a slight boy. Had she not had the experience of Rys, she would have said, an undergrown boy. Knowing what she knew, she saw a boy who was slight, but supple, and perhaps even well-grown for his age. His face was thin, his nose was straight, and his mouth was firm. Had she not already known who he was, his eyes would have told her that he belonged to Nova yos'Galan.

"It makes my heart glad, to meet the brother of my grand-daughter," she told him, which was only a little different than what she might have said in their own tongue. She gave him her hand.

He took it, his fingers cold, his grip respectful.

"I'm happy to meet you, ma'am." He hesitated, looking up at her seriously. "May I call you Grandmother?"

"Yes. That will do very well. Now, you must introduce me to *your* brother."

"No, ma'am," that worthy said earnestly. "I'm not Silver's brother. One of Boss Nova's 'hands, that's me, come to keep the boy outta trouble."

"But you still need to be introduced," the boy said. "It's polite."

"Well go 'head then," Boss Nova's 'hand answered. "Might as well get some polite done to wash out the rude."

The boy turned, and inclined his head.

"Grandmother, this is Gavit, of my mother's household. Gavit, this is my grandmother."

"Ma'am," he said, giving her a quaint and grave little bow.

"I'm happy to meet you, Gavit," Silain said. She gave him a smile, but not her hand.

"Here comes Mother," Syl Vor said, turning to point at yet another cab drawing into the crescent.

· · · ✳ · · ·

Udari watched as Mike Golden emerged from the car, followed by a very large man wearing a very large gun on his hip. A much slighter man followed him, and then Nova yos'Galan, looking even more beautiful in the free sunshine.

Udari expected them to pass on, as had so many of the others, but no. All four came directly to them, as if they were Bedel, and not *gadje* at all, to give respect to the *luthia*.

"Good morning, Grandmother," Nova yos'Galan said to the *luthia*. "Please allow me to present my cousin, Boss Conrad. Cousin, here is the grandmother of whom I spoke."

"Grandmother." The man bowed with evident respect. "I am very happy to meet you."

"As I am happy to meet the Boss Conrad," the *luthia* replied with a smile that said his manners pleased. "The headman dreams upon a proper course, and I am hopeful that you and he will soon share a pipe."

"I look forward to that, most eagerly," he said. "We are somewhat ahead of our colleagues, the other Bosses. And it would appear that we are somewhat ahead of our scholars, too. Mr. McFarland, would you mind a walk about the courtyard in my company?"

"'S'what you pay me for," the big man said, giving him a glinting grin.

"Ah, yes, how could I have forgotten?" The Boss Conrad bowed again to the *luthia*.

"Grandmother, I take my leave. I look forward to talking with you much more, when we can both be comfortable."

The *luthia* released him with a gracious nod and he moved off, the big man at his back.

"I expect it will be some minutes before the program begins," Nova yos'Galan said, looking over her shoulder at the line of cabs inching up the crescent.

"Malda needs a run," Kezzi said, "if he's going to have to be still and good while people *talk*."

Mike Golden laughed.

"I don't know as they expect to talk all that much," he said. "But it might be a good thing to be sure he don't get restless."

"My granddaughter is wise," Silain said, and caught Udari's eye. "Will you accompany your sister, my son?"

He met her eyes, saw in them her command.

"Yes, Grandmother."

"May I go, too?" Syl Vor asked, looking to his mother.

She smiled.

"Certainly."

· · · ☀ · · ·

Malda speedily took care of his concerns in the rock-laced grass patch at the side of the building. Kezzi found a thin piece of wood by a garden shed and threw it. Malda ran after the toy and brought it back, laying it at her feet, then backing away, front legs flat on the ground, tail stuck high in the air, tongue lolling; his whole body quivering while he waited for her to throw again.

"Here, you throw it for him," Kezzi said, handing him the stick.

Syl Vor took it uncertainly, then grinned when Malda, seeing that his toy had changed hands, barked and jumped and spun in a circle.

Laughing, Syl Vor threw, sending the stick end over end, down close to the building. Malda rocketed off after it, picked it up—and then dropped it, nose to the ground, tail suddenly gone still.

"Oh, no," Kezzi said. "I hope it isn't a rat."

"Best to call him back, Sister," Udari said.

"Yes. Malda! Come!" she called, snapping her fingers.

But the little dog didn't seem to hear her. He continued sniffing the ground, his tail stiff, gave three high-pitched yips and ran full-speed down the school building.

Kezzi said a word Syl Vor didn't know and leapt into a run.

"Come on!" Syl Vor cried to Udari, and raced after her.

· · · ✳ · · ·

The dog vanished 'round a corner and set up a series of yips; the sound meant he had found what he had been hunting.

A rat, then, though Udari, between annoyance and relief. The dog knew very well how to deal with a rat.

Ahead, Kezzi flashed around the corner, her brother not two steps behind her; Udari only four long strides behind him.

The dog stopped barking.

"Rys!" Kezzi cried.

Udari came round the corner and stopped, staring down at his brother, who had the dog gathered to him, gloved hand holding the pointed muzzle tight.

"Brother?"

"Udari."

The other lifted his face, and Udari near cried out, *Brother, what has happened to you?*

It was Rys, and yet it was not Rys. He looked into eyes that had seen terrible deeds done, bleak and blank in the face of a man who had performed horrors.

"Udari," this apparition said, in his own brother's precious voice. "For love of me, take the children and the dog, and *go*! Soon, there will be an explosion—a small explosion, nothing to worry you. After, unless I can stop it, there will be another—and that one will be very bad. Go now. Please. Take the children. Try, if you can, to move those who have gathered away from the building."

"Let me help you, Brother," Udari said. "Kezzi, Syl Vor—take Malda and go. Do as Rys asks."

"You help me best by going with them. By keeping safe," Rys said, and it seemed to Udari that he saw his brother's soul draining out of his eyes, leaving only a terrible stranger. "Brother, will you go?" he whispered.

"Yes. Kezzi, take the dog."

She leaned down, received a shivering Malda into her arms.

"Rys," she whispered. "Do you remember now? Everything?"

"Too much," he told her, his soft voice harsh.

He rose, holding the door open wide; beyond was a long straight hallway.

"Follow this; it leads to the main entrance. Go now, little sister. Please." He looked past her to the boy. "Child of Korval, mind your duty."

The boy went back a step, as if the words had been a blow, then snatched Kezzi's arm.

"He's right. If there will be an explosion, we have to warn people to move!"

He pushed past Rys, pulling her with him. In a moment, they were running down the wide hallway.

"Brother," Udari said, tears in his eyes. "You have a place at my hearth, always."

He followed the children. When he had nearly overtaken them, he looked back, but the door was closed, and Rys was gone.

· · · ☀ · · ·

Kezzi had put the dog down, and he ran ahead of them, claws scrabbling and sliding. The hall bent; the children slowed, wary of the slick floor, and Udari came into the lead.

The door directly ahead of him was flung open. The dog shot past and was gone, before a small, yellow haired woman came out into the hall.

Udari skidded on the slick surface, went to one knee, and leapt up again, his knife in his hand.

"You!" he cried, and lunged.

There was a sharp crack, a sensation of impossible, encompassing pain . . . and nothing.

· · · ☀ · · ·

Syl Vor saw the door begin to swing open, grabbed Kezzi and pushed her into the alcove of a stairway.

"You!" Udari's voice echoed against the walls.

So did the sound of the shot, a moment later.

Beside him, Kezzi stood silent, scarcely seeming to breathe.

Syl Vor inched to the edge of their hiding place and peered around.

Udari lay on the floor, unmoving, blood on his coat, on the floor under his arm. Over him stood a yellow-haired woman. Syl Vor bit his lip, watching as she slid her gun into her holster, and raised her other hand, in which she held something that looked like a remote.

She pressed a button.

A flash lit the length of the hall. Thunder roared, rolled, and died.

The woman stood, in an attitude of waiting. Then, with an exclamation of annoyance, she began to walk toward them.

"She'll find Rys," Kezzi breathed.

Syl Vor didn't tell her that before she found Rys, the enemy would find them.

Instead, he swung into the hallway, and directly into her path.

A blare of noise came from the mic, followed by Penn Kalhoon's voice, asking rather irritably, and at volume, "Is this thing on?"

Mike Golden grimaced, and exchanged a look with Gavit, who shrugged.

"I think we may be approaching a beginning," Nova said from beside him. "Where are the children, I wonder?"

"Have been gone a bit," Mike said, like he hadn't been worrying this while. He pushed his sleeve up and consulted the tracker strapped there, noting the location of Syl Vor—or at least, of Syl Vor's bracelet. Not too far away, either. He looked down at his boss and jerked his head toward the back of the school.

"They're over that way. I'll go 'round 'em—"

A flare of light erupted from the right, beyond the edge of the school building. Thunder rolled, deafening.

Mike Golden leapt into a run—*toward* the explosion.

Where Syl Vor had been.

He was halfway down the side of the building before he noticed that Nova was keeping pace with him.

He thought about yelling at her, but he didn't have the wind.

Wouldn't've made a bit o' difference, anyhow.

He had to be quick; he knew that. Surprise was his only advantage.

The woman checked. Syl Vor was already moving, launching himself into the air for a mid-chest kick.

She dodged to the right, then spun back, backing the punch with her full weight, connecting so hard that he saw stars, and wasn't sure if the crack he heard was a bone breaking or his head hitting the floor.

It didn't matter. What mattered was that he had to roll, to jump to his feet. He had to raise the gun he had snatched from her holster, holding it firm in two hands, like he'd been taught, aiming directly at the enemy's chest.

She stared at him, but she didn't make the mistake of looking down at her belt. Instead, she held his eyes, and raised the remote.

Unless I can stop it, the second will be very bad…

Syl Vor took a deep breath, kept his eyes open, and pulled the trigger.

Crimson dyed her shirt and she crumpled without a sound.

Syl Vor carefully lowered the gun, staring with bare comprehension at the Liaden words over the toggle. Deliberately, he pushed the action switch from *fragment* to *single* to *null*.

Kezzi slipped out of the alcove, kicked the detonator away from the enemy's hand, came over to him, and asked, very calmly, "Are you hurt?"

"I don't know," he told her, and looked up at the clatter of footsteps down the hall, to see his mother and Mike Golden arrive.

His mother's face—she wasn't angry. He didn't *think* she was angry. He took a breath, to tell her, but he didn't seem to know any words, Liaden or Terran.

"Are you injured?" his mother asked. "Syl Vor? Kezzi?"

"No," said Kezzi.

He shook his head, then looked sharply over his shoulder, tracking the sound of voices and footsteps.

"Right," said Mike Golden. He stepped forward and held out a broad hand. "Gimme the gun, Silver. That's it. You'd best let 'em think I took that shot, right? Boss, you wanna take these two in hand?"

"Yes," Mother said, and opened her arms. "Come here, children, and stand with me."

· · · ✵ · · ·

The first of the Agent's bombs had speedily yielded to his suasions.

The second, attached to the underside of the massive heating unit, was being more difficult.

Quite a bit more difficult.

The matter was made worse by distracting flares and flashes of...light...or of some new sort of pain so intense his nerves were unable to process it. His vision flickered...off and on. That had been more of a handicap during the first disarming. For now, he had his hand on the cap that was hidden from view, but could not trigger the deadman switch.

Worst of all were the voices—railing and screaming at him to honor the mission...

But *this* was the mission, now.

He held on to that with what clarity was left him. The mission was to disarm the bombs, to preserve the lives of those who had gathered. The mission was that...The mission was that he *would not allow this*—these deaths, this destruction. He, Rys Lin pen'Chala had set the mission, and he would, on his brother's honor, he *would* fulfill the mission.

He checked his internal clock, and felt a surge of panic. From the moment the Agent of Change had bestowed the mission upon him, he had known that *he* would not survive it. That was not the issue.

Very well, if he could not trip the deadman, he would have to separate the cap from the base and the activation plug. There was a chance that the cap would flare out if he did so, but it would certainly bring the building down if he did not.

He closed his eyes, which did nothing to block out the savage flaying of the light, and inserted his gloved hand under the broiler.

Gripping the cap, he explored it, the mesh covering his fingertips imparting an exquisite sensitivity to his touch. The seal was...*here*. All he need do was break it.

He gripped the cap firmly, hearing the sigh of the tiny motors, and exerted pressure, twisting as he did.

The seal held.

He exerted more pressure, and it seemed he felt the crushed bones in his hand grind together as the glove emitted a scream.

The seal broke.

He rolled, bringing the cap out from beneath the broiler, hardly believing that—

It flashed out in his hand.

He felt no pain at all.

EPILOGUE

. . . .

IT WAS A KINDLY CELL, AS CELLS WENT—CLEAN AND BRIGHT. HE could dim the lights, to a point, though he did not go so far as to assume that he had privacy.

In all, it had ended—it had ended *well*.

Udari had survived his adventure and rested in the care of the *luthia* and her apprentice. The Dragon was, if not safe, at least safe from any more threats from *his* hand. And he...

He had his soul back.

So said Lady Anthora, the Witch of Korval, to whose examinations he had submitted of his own will, Silain at his side, and her hand holding his.

Silain said that the soul and the heart were inseparable. That a man passed as himself through the door into the World Beyond.

Perhaps he would know this for himself, soon. Such a soul as his was no small burden, but now that it was returned to him, he had no wish to put it aside.

There was a step in the corridor outside his cell.

Rys rose, feeling a minute hitch in the working of the brace. He had told Silain that she was to be sure the brace went back to Rafin. It would be a shame to waste the metals.

He centered himself and faced the door, his arm peaceably at his side, the empty sleeve neatly pinned up and out of the way.

The door opened to admit a tall man near his own age, his brown hair falling into brilliantly green eyes.

He wore the leather jacket of a Jump pilot over a plain sweater and work pants.

Rys took a deep breath.

It came now, his judgment.

His death.

He bowed in the mode of lesser to greater, thereby giving his agreement to what would come after, and said, respectfully, "Korval."

Straightening, he met that brilliant gaze, saw a smile on the firm mouth.

"Brother," came the reply, accompanied by the easy nod one might accord to kin.

Rys stiffened.

"*I* am not your brother," he said.

"Are you not? And yet I have never before now met another who had broken training, and regained a measure of what he had been, before the Department had trained him." He tipped his head to one side, eyes speculative. "Surely, that binds us in some way?"

It was true that Val Con yos'Phelium, he who was now Korval, had been an Agent of Change. He was, perhaps, the Department's greatest failure, for he had broken with the Commander and with the Plan, and actively worked to the Department's despite.

As, Rys thought, he would himself, were he to live.

"Well," said Korval, "you will think on it. Perhaps we will speak of it again, sometime later. In the meanwhile, my sister tells me that you have some anxiety with regard to a ship." He reached inside his jacket and withdrew a folded sheet of paper, which he held out with a smile. "I hope that this will serve to reassure you."

Hope and terror clashed in his heart. Rys fairly snatched the paper from the outstretched hand, unfolded it to find a ship's registry page, his gaze running feverishly down the few lines...

Momma Liberty
Out of Waymart
Captain Jasin Bell
First Mate Kayla Bell
Trader Morgan Fairchance
Status active
Taking cargo and passengers

Tears, sudden and grateful. He had not...he had never...He closed his eyes and bowed his head.

"I am grateful," he said. "Korval, I am in your debt."

It was an idiotic thing to say, given what was the most likely outcome of this encounter, but Val Con yos'Phelium inclined his head gravely.

"Let there be no debt between us," he said in his soft voice, and looked up with a gleam in his eye.

"Where will you go now?" he asked.

Rys stared at him. "Go?"

"Yes, go. My sister assures me that you are no longer a danger to the clan; that, indeed, you may prove an ally. We are not so foolish as to turn allies away, you know. So I ask—where will you go?"

Rys took a breath. He had woken this morning knowing that he would be dead before evening. This sudden leap to life—

He studied the man before him; could detect nothing false in face or eyes.

"If my life is truly mine," he said carefully, "I would return to the Bedel."

"I had guessed as much," Korval said, "and took the liberty of calling your brothers to take you home."

"My—"

"They are waiting for you upstairs," Korval interrupted, stepping back and bowing Rys toward the door. "I have the impression that they are eager to see you. Please, do not keep them waiting on my behalf."

· · · ✳ · · ·

Syl Vor lay with his mother under the Tree, his head on her shoulder, her arm holding him close.

"I like visiting the Tree," he said drowsily, "and I'm happy to make the acquaintance of my new cousin Talizea, but I'll be *very* happy to go home again."

"I will be very happy to have you back again. I make no secret, Syl Vor-son, that Mr. Golden has been cast quite into despair by your absence, and Beck is not to be borne!"

He gave a small gurgle of laughter.

"Your Aunt Anthora tells me that you have progressed well in your lessons with her, though she still holds shy of telling me what those lessons were. May I persuade you, my child, to tell me?"

Syl Vor laughed again, and snuggled his head closer against her shoulder.

"Oh, *she* said she was teaching me to be a boy. I think that was a joke, because of course I *am* only a boy!"

"Of course you are," his mother said. "As fine a child as any might wish for. Barring the occasional adoption of sisters."

He grinned.

"Is Kezzi being very bad?"

"Not," his mother said judiciously, "by Kezzi's lights. But I digress. Did your aunt teach you anything other than to be a boy?"

"No-o-o. But she did tell me that many people get muddled when they've been in very great danger, and that I'll probably never really recall how Mike came just in time to, to stop that woman who was going to blow up the school. Do you think if I ask Mike, he'll tell me?"

"To say true, I think that Mr. Golden's memory of the event is a little muddled, as well. Certainly, Kezzi's is," his mother said slowly. "Best, perhaps, to leave it."

"That's what Uncle Ren Zel says. 'The threads are well-woven,'" he quoted, "'and no need to try the knots.'" He sighed.

A bell rang out over the garden, and his mother sat up, tumbling him over into the leaves.

He laughed, and jumped to his feet. She was up, as well, and brushing the leaves out of her hair. She looked at him from beneath her lashes.

"Race you," she whispered, and took off across the lawn, golden hair flying behind her.

Syl Vor shouted, and ran after her.